Excerpts from TALL IN THE SADDLE...

She pulled at the ribbon that tied back my hair. "I have to say that I have dreamed a long time about an afternoon like this. I never met a woman who . . . would enjoy it."

Her kisses burned down my throat as I knocked her hat to the ground. She made an anticipatory low noise of desire as my fingers dug into her scalp. "Yes," I said against her mouth. "Yes, I enjoy this."

—COWBOYS & KISSES, Karin Kallmaker

• • •

As Aimee melted against her, Cory let her hands travel over Aimee's curves, over the swell of her breasts to her cinched waist and on to her curvaceous hips. Aimee moaned softly, making Cory want to rip her clothing off and ravish her right there on the counter. With great effort, she stopped herself and stepped away.

"We can't do this," she said.

—DESERT SPRING, Barbara Johnson

• • •

It's no secret that when riding a horse, women sometimes feel flickers of pleasure from the motion of the animal and the pressure of the saddle. But compared to the feelings from Connie's mouth, the sensations of the saddle were next to nothing.

"Now," she purred a few moments later, spooning me, "I'll give you a few minutes to rest. And then I'll teach you what I like."

Connie was an excellent teacher.

—THE SWEETHEART AND THE SPITFIRE, Julia Watts

• • •

"Wait a minute!" Billy called to Elise. "Let me walk you home." She took Elise by the elbow in her best gentlemanly behavior.

Elise pulled away from her. "I live near enough that you should just mind to your job."

"I don't think it's really that safe out there. Not late at night. Not with all these gunslingers, and bad guys and . . . well, wild animals."

—THE LIFE AND TIMES OF Ornery Crazy Mean BAD BILL, Therese Szymanski

TALL IN THE SADDLE

BARBARA JOHNSON
KARIN KALLMAKER
THERESE SZYMANSKI
JULIA WATTS

Bella
BOOKS
2007

Bella Books, Inc.
P.O. Box 10543
Tallahassee, FL 32302

Printed in the United States of America on acid-free paper
First Edition

Editors: Karin Kallmaker and Julia Watts
Cover designer: LA Callaghan

ISBN-10: 1-59493-106-2
ISBN-13: 978-1-59493-106-2

CONTENTS

FOREWORD: *Julia Watts and Karin Kallmaker* vii

THE LIFE AND TIMES OF ~~Ornery Crazy Mean~~ BAD BILL: *Therese Szymanski* 1

DESERT SPRING: *Barbara Johnson* 91

COWBOYS & KISSES: *Karin Kallmaker* 179

THE SWEETHEART AND THE SPITFIRE: *Julia Watts* 269

ABOUT THE AUTHORS 317

FOREWORD

The American West promised freedom. "Go west, young man," was the sage advice. That advice was, of course, largely for the young and male, but women ventured west as well, giving rise to open gender warriors and generations of women who found that anything a man could do they had to do better if they wanted to control their own destinies.

Some women wore men's clothes for lack of practical alternatives. Others wore them to assume the identities of men. Still others did men's work but kept their long skirts and ruffled blouses. But they were all exceptions. The vast majority of women in the old west faced narrow lives as wives, schoolteachers or prostitutes. Life expectancy—and economic outlook—of these three basic choices wasn't all that different.

The burgeoning film industry of the 1930s captured the remnants of the Old West with iconic scenes of silent, boot-scrapin' cowboys wooing seductive (and surprisingly clean and well-coiffed) strumpets with hearts of gold. From B westerns to pulp novels, man strong, woman helpless. Picture Marlene Dietrich wiping her painted lips clean before she'll kiss her hero and die. Miss Kitty on occasion defended her virtue, but the brave lawman still arrived in the nick of time. Yet even in their staged weakness as foils for the heroes, western women were forthright, proud and indomitable.

That's why the image that sets our hearts aflutter is Barbara Stanwyck, tall in the saddle, wearing leather and brandishing a riding crop as she huskily defies anyone to cause harm to anyone or anything she loves. In spite of its sometimes brutal restrictions, the American West made strong women who flourished in wide open spaces and exploited every hint of freedom that they could. So what if Hollywood tends to ignore them—we intend to celebrate them.

Saddle up for some wild rides, 'cause there's a new sheriff in our town.

Julia Watts   Karin Kallmaker

June 2007

The Life and Times of

~~Ornery~~ ~~Crazy~~ ~~Mean~~ Bad Bill

Therese Szymanski

CHAPTER ONE

"This is a bank robbery," the first masked man said, stepping into the building and pointing his revolver directly at the elderly guard's temple. "Don't do anything stupid."

Four other masked men charged in even as he spoke and disarmed the guard—grabbing the patrons, diving over the counter, moving as one single, deadly unit so swiftly that not even the dust from their horses had settled yet. In fact, it swirled in the heavy oak doors behind them.

"Open the safe!" another masked man yelled at the manager, holding his gun to the teller's head. His voice was deeper than the first masked man's, but all the bank robbers were equally dirty and hairy.

"All your valuables and guns, into the bag now!" the third yelled from the lobby, where he held a gun on the bank's customers. Sweat and spit soaked the kerchief wrapped around the lower half of his face.

The fourth man worked quickly and efficiently at relieving the drawers and other open areas of any and all cash, gold and silver.

"Quick now—before the sheriff shows up!" the man holding the guard yelled from the door.

"The boy hasn't given the signal, has he?" Number three said.

"No. Not yet. But c'mon now already!"

The man holding the teller, trying to get the manager to open the safe, shot the teller in the foot. "Now open it. Yours is next."

They rushed out, loot bags in hand, leaping onto their horses and *giddyupping* them out of the town of Rusty Spur.

"I think we're safe now," the lead man said. He reached into his pocket, pulled out several coins and tossed them to young Billy, who had watched their horses during the robbery. "We'll let you know if we need you again."

"Hey, this ain't what you promised me!" Billy said, neatly grabbing the coins from midair.

"If'n you know what's good for you, Billy, you'll take it and be happy with it."

"I done this for y'all how many times now? Five? Six? And ain't never breathed a single word to nobody 'bout it—so this is how you treat me?" Billy's horse stomped a bit, as if expressing his own aggravation at the way his master was being treated.

"I ain't killing you yet, am I?"

"Buddy, we need to get going now," the number two man, Louie, said, glancing nervously back at the town. "Give the boy his money, 'fore the sheriff gets together a posse and comes after us."

"I could just kill you right here and now," Buddy said to Billy, pulling out his gun and aiming it directly at Billy's head.

"Yup, I reckon you could. But then the next time you need a lookout 'round these parts that you can trust, you wouldn't have me now, would you?" Billy said, still sitting on Pony, who was always a good horse.

"You got balls, boy, and I like that," Buddy said. He pulled some more coins from the bag and tossed them to Billy.

"So when you gonna let me come with y'all?"

"Don't push it, boy," Louie said. "You're handy, for now."

The gang rode one way, and Billy rode another, constantly trying to make sure Pony's hoof prints weren't trackable. Billy liked to confuse trackers, after all, and had yet to be successfully tracked, followed or traced. The rest of the gang had never been tracked neither, likely because of Billy's ingenuity.

That night, after riding hard till sundown, Billy killed a rabbit for dinner with a single shot from Sam, a Colt .45. Billy camped outside, enjoying the freedom of the open prairie, even if it was a little cold. Or even more than a little cold.

It'd take more than a month of the open lands for Billy to miss the comforts of a bed and roof, or other pleasures of civilization. But it'd take a month for even that much to set in, and Billy'd be home within the next few nights.

And someday, the gang would take Billy along with them.

And some time after that, Billy'd be the biggest, baddest, orneriest outlaw of 'em all. And that was something to dream about under a sky as big as the whole universe.

Two days later, Billy rode back into Climax, Oklahoma, contemplating on the predictability of town names in that region, and took Pony to the stable for fresh hay and water, then walked into the saloon to enjoy a meal as well.

Lucky Henry, the town sheriff, walked up to Billy betwixt the stable and the saloon. "Some day, boy, your luck's gonna run out. I sure hope I'm around for that."

"Aw, Henry, you know I ain't the gambling sort," Billy said.

"But you are, boy, you are. And you're gambling more than the worst river boaters do—you're gambling your life."

"Whatever are you on about now, Henry?" Marnie, the bar matron, slid a couple of shots across the bar to the two.

"We just got word the bank over in Rusty Spur got robbed two days ago," Henry said, downing his shot.

"And what's that got to do with lil' Billy here?" Marnie asked, her voice a touch louder than before.

"Ain't you never noticed how whenever a place near here's been robbed, he's always gone? And always just so long as it'd take to ride to the town, rob the bank, and ride on back here?"

"Nope. I ain't never seen that. But I have seen how hungry for glory you are, you're looking under every rock for a bad guy that just ain't there." Marnie stared across the bar—her arms crossed just under her enormous breasts—at Henry, then raised her voice even further. "Now, if you want another drink, it ain't on the house. 'Specially not with you accusing the help—Billy—of all sorts of unspeakable things."

"I ain't accusing your lil' houseboy of anything unspeakable. I'm just accusing him of helping some bank robbers is all." He blew out his breath so his ridiculous handlebar mustache puffed out at the ends.

"Oh, hell you say!" Gracie said, running up and sliding her long, slender arms around Billy. "Girls!" she yelled. "The sheriff wants to take our Billy away!"

"The hell you say!" Martha cried, running from her room half-dressed, the silk robe one of her fellers had given her all but falling from her shoulders.

"Billy's back?" Trudy said, coming from her room in only a robe.

"Henry, you ass!" Sarah screamed, her blond hair trailing behind her as she flew down the stairs.

"Oh, hell," Henry said.

Billy slammed back the shot Marnie had served, then turned, picked up Gracie, and said, "I know the future. I'm gonna be somebody someday," and carried Gracie upstairs to her room.

Billy slept in a small room back at the end of the upstairs hall, little more than a closet, really, so he always followed the girls to their sleeping quarters for any trysts.

"Oh, Billy," Gracie said, falling back on the bed. "Come here."

Billy's tongue snaked out between smirking lips, to coil up teasingly. "Oh, Gracie, is there something in particular you're longing for?" Maybe many thought of Billy as quite young, but Billy was really an adult, in all ways, shapes and forms. Billy was by no means what anyone thought Billy was.

"You're the only man around here I know who can truly please a woman," Gracie said, fully disrobing and displaying herself to Billy. "All the others simply take their pleasures from us, then discard us and move on."

Billy indicated Gracie's naked form. "What can I say? You're all so accommodating."

"We are to men who pay, too," Gracie said, naked, and lying back on the bed. "You're the only one who cares, though."

"Oh, Gracie, It's a good thing I'm no man, then, ain't it?" Billy said, sliding onto the bed between Gracie's open and inviting thighs. "Open your legs further for me, spread yourself for me." Billy slowly and carefully caressed the tender flesh between Gracie's legs, first with fingers, then with tongue . . . up and down, in and out . . . slowly . . . carefully . . . gently . . . tongue on clit, fingers on nipples, teasing and tweaking them.

"Billy, please . . . please . . . your tongue . . . there—oh, yes . . . now your fingers, inside me—omifuckinggodtherenowyesplease!" Apparently she hadn't quite heard what Billy had said.

• • •

"Oh my fucking God!" Bunny O'Reilly yelled, sitting upright in the cheap motel room. She'd been away from her girl for two fucking days, and she was already dreaming of having sex with some long-legged redhead in a . . . brothel? Or was it a saloon?

She locked her fingers in her newly shorn, short blond locks and pulled them—hard—to make sure she was actually awake.

She turned on the lights, poured herself a shot of whisky, turned on the tube, and sat back on the bed.

Her girlfriend was a tall brunette, not a short redhead.

Why was she dreaming of the Old West but having folks talk in modern-day speak, Bunny wondered, as she lost herself in the adventures of Xena, Warrior Princess. She'd have preferred Buffy.

That modern-day speak had her thinking that she maybe might be thinking of something, instead of dreaming of what happened. It was all so three-dimensional, surround-sound that it was as if she was actually there. As if she was remembering instead of dreaming.

She watched Xena snarl and was glad there wasn't any Xena in real life, because, after all, Xena'd effortlessly lay down her evildoing ass with a flick of her chakram.

How had she gone so wrong as to take a life of crime, backed up with a full-on familial history of crime, on the lam with her from upstate New York, away from the love of her life, across country so her lame ass was stuck hiding out in buttfuck nowhere Ohio?

CHAPTER TWO

"So what's going on here, I wonder?" Tall Willy said, walking into Gracie's room. "I want some service. No, make that, I *need* some service."

"You got money?" Gracie said, pulling the bedclothes with her to cover herself when she left the bed.

"I'm a regular, baby," Tall Willy said, tossing cash on her dresser.

Billy slipped out, quietly and quickly. She felt eerily detached from it all. Sometimes, like right then, it felt as if she were watching her life from the outside.

It was now high time for the saloon—men were gambling, swearing and drinking; girls were finding their first, second or third customers for the night.

Billy knew better than to leave the saloon tonight. She'd already been gone a few nights already, so she needed to be here to quell any wrongdoings and wrongdoers. Yeah, Lucky Henry might help, but he'd always be a step behind Billy's pistol since he'd have to come from home or the jail. Plus, he wasn't too bright.

But Billy did want to be elsewhere. But you can't always do what you want.

Billy stopped on the staircase, listening to Willy enjoying himself upstairs, and watching what was happening throughout the entire saloon.

She leapt from the staircase, over the railing, to plant a gun next to a Joe's head just as he tried to slip a card loose from his sleeve. Billy saw everything. Noticed everything. And that was why Marnie kept Billy around. Billy's reputation surpassed Billy's being, which appeared to be that of a fifteen-year-old boy.

And it was what Marnie thought that mattered.

Billy's revolver was already cocked. It was ready to go. Billy was the bouncer, the trigger-happy one that kept things honest in this brothel/saloon in the so-very-wild Wild West.

"That's a gun, isn't it?" the cheater said, slowly raising his hands.

"Yes, it is. And it's pointed where it can best kill ya," Billy said. The rest of the saloon was quiet. Dead quiet.

"Stop!" Gracie screeched from upstairs, almost making Billy pull the trigger. But Billy didn't, instead, running up the stairs, taking two at a time, and then kicked down the door to Gracie's room, yanked the fellow from atop Gracie and tossed him across the room, using his own weight and center of gravity against him.

Then Billy used a gun to his head as the final disciplinary measure.

"What happened?" Billy asked Gracie, still with her gun to Tall Willy's temple.

"He wanted . . . wanted more than he was willing to pay for. More than I'm willing to sell," Gracie said, covering herself with blankets, her face drawn and pale.

Billy knew the girls . . . knew *all* the girls. And *knew* them, too. Billy knew what she meant. And so Billy said, "Stand up," to Tall Willy, keeping the revolver's barrel pressed against Willy's head. "Now go. That way."

"But I'm nekkid!"

"Be nekkid or be dead!" When Tall Willy still didn't respond, Billy shot him in the foot. Billy was glad to use that piece of cold-heartedness so recently learned from the gang. Willy screamed and ran naked through the door and fell over the banister, breaking his neck upon landing and dying immediately. The sound was sickening, and it was all almost anticlimactic, but Billy was glad to see that this was yet another good way to deal with troublemakers.

Lucky Henry was right below. He looked down at Tall Willy, then up at Billy. " 'Bout time somebody put an end to that ignorant son of a bitch. I raise you by a full dollar. Accidental death." He enunciated "accidental" syllable by syllable, stretching it out. "Marnie, I don't think none of us ought to be seeing that," he said about the naked corpse. "So why don't you have somebody haul it out like the trash it is."

Marnie and Henry did a brief showdown, as if each were daring the other not to help Billy haul out the body.

"Hey, I'm off duty right now," Henry said. " 'Bout as close to working right now as I'm coming is in judging this here an accidental death."

"Sarah!" Marnie yelled. "Watch the bar—and till—will ya?" Then, to Billy, "I got the feet."

"Yup," Billy said, picking up Tall Willy by his armpits. "What do you reckon? Leave it out to rot, or bury it?"

"Let's just get haul it out back for now. If the animals leave it be tonight, we can take it over to Preacher for a proper burial." Marnie was a big woman. With Billy carrying most of the weight, she wasn't having any problems carrying her share of the big man. Once outside, she said, "I know them girls like you, Billy, and I know you like 'em, but I think you got too much potential for 'em. I mean, you're a strapping young man—you can do a heck of a lot better than them. Even Gracie. Even Sarah."

"Marnie, I just . . . Heck." The two of them tossed Willy against the wall and Billy toed the dirt with a boot. "I just reckon I'm mighty lucky that these fine girls a yours let me do all that I do to them."

"From what I hear, they're the lucky ones."

"I only treat 'em the way they ought to be treated. And worshipped." Billy'd never liked how Tall Willy treated the girls. And Billy'd been practically raised by bad guys, so Billy knew bad guys when she saw them. And she knew how women ought to be treated.

Billy and Marnie faced off in the alley, staring at each other.

"You, m'boy," Marnie said, "have potential. You can get up and outta this one-bank town."

"Hey there," a cute, young brunette said, stepping into the back alley.

"And this is exactly what I mean as stepping up," Marnie said. "But I better get my butt back inside before Sarah, or any of the patrons, rob or drink me blind." She left rather quickly, leaving Billy and the girl alone in the dark with the body.

"I . . ." Elise—the brunette—said, not looking at Billy, "I heard you were back in town. And all."

"I was barely gone at all," Billy said. "Just a few days."

"What is that?" Elise asked, looking past Billy. "Were you two dragging a body out here?"

"No, no, not at all," Billy said, trying to block Elise from seeing the body.

"So what is it you're doing back here, William? Alone, in an alley, after dark?"

"Um, nothing. Let's walk along together, to the *front* of the building, and enter the building through the *front* doors of the saloon." Billy took Elise by the arm and led her, all gentleman-like, to the front doors.

"Billy? What is it you're hiding from me?" Elise asked.

"Dead body. See, I lied. Marnie and I just threw him in the back alley. We'll bury him later."

Elise laughed. "You have such a sense of humor, William!" She playfully thwapped Billy's shoulder.

It was the tinkling of Elise's laughter that made Billy almost lose herself. She wanted to go wild, push Elise against the wall of the saloon and hold her by her wrists. "Not really," Billy said instead, stopping and looking deep into Elise's big, brown eyes.

Elise reached over to fix the collar on Billy's red plaid shirt. "I don't like where you work. I don't like when you're gone. I don't like even thinking about what you're doing when you're gone. And I definitely don't like thinking about what you do with all those girls you work with. Because I know what you're capable of, and what you can make of your life if you really try."

Billy reached up to cup Elise's hands in her own, stopping them on her collar. She caressed them. "I know these girls in the saloon, and we talk and all, but nobody else understands me the way you do. You get that I can be so much more than I am now—that someday, I'm gonna be somebody!" Elise was about as tall as Billy, maybe just a mite shorter, and a warmth trickled through Billy whenever Elise touched her.

Elise looked up into Billy's eyes. "Yeah, you sure are. Just not the somebody you think you are." She smiled sadly and ran her thumbs over Billy's eyebrows. "You might dream of buildings that touch the sky. Of things that carry people and travel faster than anything we can imagine. Or of bombs that destroy entire countries. But we both know these are just dreams."

"They're not," Billy said, grasping tightly to Elise's waist. "I see them so clearly, all of these incredible things, and . . . and . . . they're more than anything even my father could ever build . . .

make . . . create."

"Your father? What does he do?" Elise's hands lay warmly on Billy's shoulders. "I thought you said he was dead?"

"He—he—it doesn't matter. Don't matter none at all." Billy started to look away, but she really didn't want to move from her comfortable proximity to Elise's warmth. It wasn't that the night was especially cold—though it was a bit chilly—it was just that she liked touching Elise and liked when Elise touched her.

"You always do that—as soon as it looks like you might have to admit something about you, or your past, you suddenly stop. And that's it."

"That's 'cause there ain't nothing to tell. Now, teach, I'm back, so when's we gonna start with the learning again?"

Elise pulled away. "Why do you always do that?"

"What?" Billy's arms felt suddenly empty, but she didn't know what to do to regain Elise's warmth against her. Elise was always much warmer and more filling to her arms than any other gal Billy'd ever been with, or touched, or kissed or . . .

"One moment, you seem well-educated and quite clever and smart. Then, suddenly, you're talking like some sort of stable-hand."

"I *am* just a . . . a . . . stablehand. A wrangler. A cowboy. A bandit. A whorehouse boy. That's who I *am*."

"No, you're not. Sometimes, I'm teaching you things, and it's as if you already know them. For instance, I think you know how to read. You've known how to read since before we met."

"Yeah, right, then why am I hanging out with the school-marm all the time, then?"

"I don't know why you're always coming to me for lessons I'm not sure you need." Elise gazed down at the ground, then back up at Billy.

"But I do need them, Miz Elise. Just like I learned manners and how to treat a real lady from you." Billy toed the ground with her boot. She looked up through her lashes at Elise. "You heard what Marnie said when you got to us—that you were a step in the right direction for me."

"So is that what I am? A step up? Well, Billy, Marnie—and you—seem to be forgetting that I'm the schoolmarm, not one of her employees. I know all about you, and your reputation, and I'm not about to be so easily taken in."

"Wait a minute!" Billy suddenly called out to Elise, who was leaving the property. "Let me walk you home." She took Elise by the elbow in her best gentlemanly behavior.

Elise pulled away from her. "I live near enough that you should just mind to your job."

"I don't think it's really that safe out there. Not late at night. Not with all these gunslingers, and bad guys and . . . well, wild animals."

"Opossums? Raccoons?"

"Wolves, buffalo!"

"Buffalo are vegetarian. I've never heard of them attacking anybody."

"Just . . . just because I cain't read ain't no reason for you to keep throwing all these facts and knowledgabilities in my face." Billy lowered her voice. "That's why I come to you, so you can make me smarter. Teach me to read and all that . . . well, smart stuff. And all." She wanted to make amends for earlier.

"You're smart. You're grasping everything I'm teaching you faster than anyone else I've ever taught. You're picking it up faster than I did. So fast, in fact, I wouldn't be surprised to learn you knew how to read even before I started teaching you." Elise was quite earnest, and Billy was glad to see she'd gotten Elise back on her side.

"I always been a quick learner. Out here, it's the only way to make it, 'specially at my age and all."

"And just how old is that?" Elise said, walking in front of her in the cool night.

"Does it really matter?"

"Are you evading the question?"

"No, it's just . . . I don't know." A downright lie, since Billy knew right well she was twenty-four, but she really didn't know what to say—she didn't know actually what age she should claim, and this was easier, 'cause she wouldn't even have to keep track of it. She could keep saying the exact same thing, always and forever.

"Oh my goodness," Elise said, stopping and facing Billy, who in turn stopped herself. Elise took Billy's face in her hands. "I'm so sorry—I didn't think. You're . . . you're an orphan, of course you don't know when your birthday is." She pulled Billy's head to her shoulder so she could hold her, supposedly comforting Billy from a traumatic upbringing.

Billy was ready to push away, assert her independence, act like the juvenile boy she supposedly was, but Elise smelled nice, and her arms were comforting. It felt . . . nice . . . to be so close to her. Billy'd been posing as male for a while now, and she didn't really hate that, in order to help pass in her role, she sometimes had to be intimate with women. That'd been a fun thing to discover.

And Billy'd always thought of the marm as a prop in the charade she was perpetuating, but the girls at the house—and Marnie—occasionally teased her about a crush. She'd always thought of the marm as a means to an end, but suddenly, she was seeing something else: the softer side of Elise.

She wondered if maybe the girls had been right all along.

"I'm gonna grow up to be a big, bad bank robber," Billy said into Elise's shoulder. "And I wanna be able to read all about it. Me and my gang are gonna do some great stuff, then maybe I'll go to Australia, or South America, and maybe jump off some cliffs along the way." She'd dreamed about such stuff, just like she'd dreamed about the really tall buildings and other impossibilities. She wasn't sure what it all meant, but it always felt real—like she was looking into the real future. A world that was yet to come.

"Billy," Elise said, rubbing her back. "You can do so much, yet you're so convinced of a path that will get you killed young. I don't want to read about your death. Ever."

• • •

There was a persistent tat-tap-tapping at her door, then a shushed, "Bunny. Bunny. Bunny! Are you in there?"

Bunny sat upright in bed. Even with the Bible leaning against the cheap motel drapes, trying to keep them closed, she could tell the sun was rising in the east.

She thought she recognized the voice. She leapt to her feet and ran to the door, peering out the peephole before much more tat-tap-tapping could wake the neighbors.

"Nina!" she whispered loudly, opening the door to her girl-friend. "What are you doing here?"

"Finding you, silly." Nina closed the door behind her, leaned back against it, and pulled Bunny into her arms.

It didn't take long for Bunny to take control of the situation, sliding her thigh between her tall, brunette girlfriend's thighs, pinning her against the door as they kissed, deeply, madly, pas-sionately. She loved the feeling of Nina's long hair cascading around them as they kissed, like a curtain of pure silk.

When Nina moaned into her mouth, Bunny pulled away just enough to say, "You shouldn't have come." Of course, she didn't remove her thigh from between Nina's thighs. All the hot dreams she'd been having had her really worked up.

"I didn't have a choice," Nina said. "I love you. *Whither you goest, so shall I.*" She was breathing heavily as she said it, pushing her cunt against Bunny's leg, writhing against her.

"Oh, fuck this noise," Bunny said, double-locking the door and putting the chain on. She picked up Nina and carried her to the bed, knowing full well how much her girlfriend enjoyed such displays of brutal domination.

That Nina let herself get so turned on by Bunny this easily

and completely was a sign of how much she trusted Bunny. And that found an echo in Bunny—Nina trusting her so completely, even while knowing her totally, turned her on more than any number of women buying her drinks or throwing themselves at her. She couldn't believe Nina'd learned so much bad about her and still chased her and wanted her.

She didn't feel worthy.

Bunny, in just her boxer shorts and T-shirt, laid the fully clothed Nina on the bed and kissed her, long and deep and hard. Then she undid Nina's tight jeans and slid them down her long and shapely legs, pausing just long enough to strip her of her boots and socks as well.

She kissed her way back up Nina's inner thighs, sliding her hands along before her mouth. By the time she got to Nina's cunt, which was still covered by a wispy bit of nothing underwear, her hands were under Nina's top. She pulled Nina up to sitting, slid her hand up to pop her bra undone, then pulled off her top and bra, throwing them haphazardly aside in order to worship her breasts, cupping them and licking the hardening nipples before sucking them, then biting and tugging on them.

"Oh, God, Bunny," Nina said, leaning back on her arms, remaining partially upright as she arched, offering herself completely to Bunny.

As Bunny teased Nina into a frenzy, she remembered standing with the marm in the dream and how that felt, and how fucking the whore felt.

Nina reminded her of all of it, like Nina was all women to her. Now that Nina had found her in the middle of nowhere, Bunny was sure they would always find each other—at any time, at any place. After all, theirs was a deep and abiding love. It didn't matter how many crimes, years or miles separated them, they would find each other.

Bunny leaned up to kiss Nina, slowly pushing her down to lie on the pillow. The lights were still on. She could see everything, and she liked that.

"I love you," she whispered into Nina's ear before she nibbled and licked her way down to her breasts, then down, further, pulling her panties off, so she could kneel before her lover and make her call out her name.

Repeatedly.

It was only later in the night, when she was smoking and drinking, that she thought back on how it was during one of her misadventures that she'd first met Nina.

After all, one couldn't find one's best place in any world, 'specially not the criminal world, without some exploring as to the various options available to one.

Bunny'd briefly run into some old family associates during a really interesting card game wherein she caught one fellow trying to cheat another fellow. Turned out the fellow she'd helped was an old family friend, and somehow she went from that into joining with him on a bank robbery.

"We got us a driver, one with a real smooth ride," Slick Freddie'd said. "I go in and present the note, see?"

"Uh, yeah," Bunny'd said.

"And we got one guy who comes in just as I get to the front of the line, and he grabs the guard at the door, right?"

"Uh, yeah." Why did this seem so familiar? So déjà vu? Well, besides that he was repeating himself practically?

"Well, so right now we got one guy on crowd control in the lobby, which'd leave me to go over the counter and empty the vault and all that stuff, but see, darlin', my old knees ain't what they used to be." He demonstrated by stiffly crouching and coming up even more stiffly. "So it'd be nice if I could watch the lobby and have you two young 'uns go up and over and back and do the emptying."

Little did she know that she'd find someone taking on a second job during the summer to help keep her from jail . . . or worse.

CHAPTER THREE

"How do you spell *ransom*?" Carl, one of the murdering, thieving thugs who had kidnapped her, had said to another while he leaned over a table, holding a pencil in his fist.

"P-A-Y U-S," another, Frank, had responded, spelling it out. He was holstering his pistol and drawing it repeatedly, practicing his quick draw.

"Who the fuck cares if anything's spelled right or wrong!" a third member of the gang, George, said. "Just write the note so we can get the money and get rid of the brat."

"He's not gonna care, you know," Billy said. Though back then, her name was something else. She'd tried since then to dis-remember it, but occasionally she remembered, much to her dismay.

"Oh, poor little rich girl don't think Daddy cares about her," Frank said, taunting her. "You don't know what it's like to come from where nobody cares."

"Fuck, I wish nobody cared about me when I was growing up," George said. "Woulda been good, compared with the abuse I put up with." He rolled up his sleeve and showed his marred forearm to Billy. It was tattooed with ugly scars and markings. "My entire body's covered with this shit. Papa loved to put out his cigars. All over my body."

"It's not like he beats on me or anything," Billy said. "It's just that since Mommy died, he doesn't really ever notice me."

"Oh, yeah, life's so rough," George said. "Finish the note so Nicky and I can deliver it. Sooner we do this, sooner we get our cash, sooner we're on our way."

After Nicky and George were gone, Carl untied her so she could eat. Frank was out back, at the outhouse. The bad guys figured two men could handle one not particularly large young girl.

"Listen, I know you're probably scared and all, but we really don't want to hurt you. If the others start going that way, Frank and I will protect you. Or at least, I will." He put the plate of bread, cheese and water in front of her.

She eagerly dug in, kinda enjoying eating with her bare hands for a change.

"None of us wanted to do this—we're all thieves and criminals, sure, but we rob banks and trains and—"

"Da always talked about the train robbers. *Always*," she said.

"We don't hurt little girls."

"So when he don't pay up, what're you gonna do with me?" Billy asked, eating and drinking.

"Oh, c'mon, he's gonna pay up. He's rolling in it!"

"But Mother died in childbirth, and I think he blames me for it."

"C'mon, you're fed, clothed, schooled . . . that's better'n any of us had it. You heard what some of the boys went through!"

"Sure, yeah, I have nannies, but I always have to wear dresses and bustles and . . . what they teach me isn't what I want to learn.

I barely get to read, and what I really want to know is how to make buildings that touch the sky!"

"He didn't beat you, did he?"

"No, but—"

"Daddy didn't beat me, either, but we was dirt poor, so I had to start looking out for myself when I was still just a young 'un."

"We got money, but it's all Da's. Everybody belongs to him, including me. And we all just do what he wants."

"Hold on, you ain't saying he paid no special attention to you or nothing, are you?" Carl upended a crate and sat on it, facing her.

"What do you mean?" Billy looked up from her simple meal.

"Well, he never forced you to do nothing that didn't seem quite right, now, did he?"

"He barely wanted to see me or even speak to me." Again she focused on her food, picking it apart so as to make it last longer. She rather liked Carl—in fact, none of her kidnappers had been particularly bad or evil to her—so she was enjoying the conversation and, well, not having her hands tied, at the moment. "He's gonna try to figure a way to save money getting me back, 'cause his money's all he cares about these days."

"No. He's gonna pay up for you. He has to."

"What happens if he doesn't?"

"He's gonna."

"Carl, he's not. Really, he won't." She'd actually rather liked hanging with these bad guys. Well, except for being tied up and all. But her normal life was pretty much all about being tied up in rules and what she should, and should not, do.

Suddenly, there was a banging at the front door. "This is the sheriff! Open up!"

"Oh, fuck," Carl said, leaping to his feet. "Nobody's home!" he yelled. "Fuck!" he said, thwumping himself upside the head with the heel of his hand. "Could I be any more stupid?"

"Come in!" Billy called.

The sheriff and his deputy broke down the door and came in.

"We got a tip that a kidnapped girl was being held here against her will," the first man said.

"Really? I hadn't noticed anybody who fits that description," Billy said. "But go ahead and have a look-see." She went back to her food.

Carl was pushed up against the wall, looking most guilty.

Billy was sure Frank had already headed for the hills. But that didn't matter so much. Right then, during those few moments, she realized she could turn the boys in and go back home right away, or she could *not* turn them in and find out if she was right in that her father wouldn't go out of his way to save her.

But what if she stuck around here to find out if he would, and he didn't? What then? What would she do then?

Well, one thing was for sure. She'd sure as shit never wear another dress again. She could really get behind that notion.

How would she survive, though? Eat? Keep a roof over her head? How could a woman in her teens survive in this world all on her lonesome?

The sheriff and his deputy went through the shack room by room—they even investigated the crawl space under the shack. If she wanted to be saved, it was now or never, 'cause it looked like they were almost done with their search. Once they left, she'd be captive again.

Carl was looking at her nervously, waiting for her to say something, turn him in, 'fess it all up to the sheriff—anything but sit there and eat her dinner.

Did she need a roof over her head? Or could she . . . just sleep outside? Be like the cowboys she read about in the pilfered books her father, nannies, tutors and all would be horrified if they knew she'd read?

Her father owned trains, buildings, properties—so much, but she'd never seen any of it, except for her own home. This could be her one chance to do so, her only shot at breaking free, at having her own life, the sort of life she'd always dreamed of, not the sort of life wealthy, properly brought up girls could ever experience.

"You don't look like you belong here." It was the sheriff.

She looked up at him but said nothing, simply shrugged.

"Who exactly are you?" he asked.

She figured they'd finished the search and were just doing one final check. "I'm Carl's niece, Denise. Denise from Ohio." She didn't know where she came up with such a strange name—it was almost as if it came to her from someplace else. It also seemed kinda funny to her for more than one reason, including that sometimes things did come to her as if from someplace other. She put her empty plate to the side, stood and reached out with her hand to shake his.

He ignored that last part, instead saying, "You don't dress like you belong here."

"My parents dressed me up in my best church clothes for my travel out here," she said. Now the sheriff, his deputy and Carl were all staring at her.

With one hand on his gun, the sheriff pointed with the other to the ropes on the floor near her feet. "Those don't look like they belong at no family reunion to me."

"Uncle Carl was just teaching me some knot tying. I told him about some books I've been reading, all about the West and such, and he was showing me what I'd only imagined, 'cause he used to work on some ships so knows all about knots."

"Listen, ma'am," the sheriff said, hand still on his gun, "if you're afraid of this fellow here, there's no need to be. We can take care of him. Just go on and tell us the truth."

"I am. I'm Denise, his niece from Ohio."

After the sheriff and his deputy left, Carl looked at Billy. "Why'd you do that?"

"What? Lie to them?"

"Yeah."

She shrugged. "It's no skin off my feet if you all get some money from Da—but say I'm right, and he doesn't cough up the cash?"

"Well, then, you should have let the sheriff take off with you now."

"But I didn't. See, if I'm right, and he doesn't pay up, I want to go with you."

"What do you mean?"

"Just what I said. I want to go with you if Da doesn't pay up. I can help you, you know."

"Really?" Frank said, coming in from behind the shack. "Just whaddya think a little girl like you can offer us?"

"My father owns a lot. And I mean a lot. I can help you rob him. And his trains."

Her father hadn't paid up, he'd tried negotiating the ransom down, et cetera, so Billy helped them, just as she'd said she would.

She'd always felt safe with the boys, 'cause Carl would never, ever, let any one of them try or do anything. He might not be the lead dog, but he knew where to draw the line. Even if it might be a little crooked due to the shakiness of his hand resulting from the utter fear he felt while drawing said line, she knew he'd make sure none of the rest ever took advantage of her.

And during her six years with them, she'd gotten her Colt, Sam, and learned to use it. She'd learned how to fight and do everything else a young man ought to know how to do. She'd become a criminal, albeit just a member of a low-level gang, but she'd gotten real skills and earned real adventures.

By the time they got to Climax, Oklahoma, where Billy'd hung her hat now for going on two years, she'd gotten a little weary of life on the road, especially with these klutzes, who weren't the greatest planners and were bound for an early grave, no matter what she'd do to protect them.

She kinda liked Climax, and immediately was accepted as a

young man there, one of about thirteen, once she stayed for more than a few days. Didn't matter how old she really was, since as a boy she seemed quite a bit younger than her twenty-two years.

Then, after a few months there, she'd met Elise and wanted to get to know the woman better, get close to her, like maybe she might have if she'd actually had a mother. She had enough money to last her awhile (the boys did have a bad habit of blowing cash soon as they got it, which gave her yet another reason to part from them), so she reckoned she could just settle for a while, till she figured out another, better plan.

So since moving to Climax she'd found a real job—as a he—hooked up with a gang to help out sometimes (but this time a real gang, with real brains and real successes), devised a plan to start moving up in the world and really enjoyed living on her own as she wanted.

But she was beginning to realize that everything she accepted wasn't so acceptable, and was, at times, rather unusual.

She'd taken up at the saloon as peacekeeper and bar backup for just room and board. But she'd been nice and polite to all the girls and always watched out for them as if she were a true gentleman and they were true ladies, until one night, after a real busy night, what with the cowboys coming through after some cowboy or other thing they did, she saw one of the girls naked and . . . well, she musta blushed or something, 'cause Gracie turned around and looked at her, then came right up to her, all barenaked and soft, and said, "Why, Billy, are you still a virgin?"

She'd almost set herself afire blushing so hard, and Gracie'd seemed to enjoy it, but it'd been a right busy night and all, so nothing came of it.

That night.

A bit later, though, on a night made slow due to thunderstorms, the girls and Billy and Marnie were taking it easy and drinking and the girls were teaching Billy how to dance and

Gracie looked at Billy and said, "I'd reckon you ain't never even kissed a girl proper, have you?"

And so Billy learned how to kiss a girl. And she liked it.

And when Gracie finally took her to bed, she liked that, too. She liked all the girls, turned out, like that.

But it was Elise who made her knees tremble and her hands shake—even before she kissed Gracie and sexed with all the girls.

But all the while, once she had settled in Climax, she'd had a plan. She would become a big, bad bank robber and make a fortune, then show her Da how well she'd done by herself. Oh, and yeah, she'd have Elise on her arm by then, too.

And maybe there'd be some cliff jumpin' and world travelin' in there, too. She didn't quite know why, 'ceptin' she rather liked the sounds of such.

• • •

Bunny sat Indian-style on the room's table, drink in hand, staring out at the sunrise.

If Nina had been able to find her so would the cops, even if they simply followed Nina to her. She needed to go farther, hide deeper.

She loved Nina and didn't want to leave her, but she also wanted to keep her girl safe, at least until the heat was off, which, realistically, might be never, but apparently Nina would keep after her no matter what happened. Apparently, the girl really loved her, too.

Bunny looked at the tall brunette lying in her bed now and knew whatever they did, they had to do it together. Nina'd just made that abundantly clear. She'd just keep making her trail clearer to the cops, sending out a virtual trail of breadcrumbs, since she really wasn't the devious criminal sort at all.

Bunny wouldn't have had to do all she'd done if her father, and grandfather, hadn't splurged the family fortune (apparently gained from trains and railroads more than a century before), on booze, broads and gambling.

Yes, maybe she should have gone after a degree and a legitimate career and life, but her familial history seemed to preclude that in too many ways.

'Course, her Da and all other relatives wouldn't have a clue how to perpetrate identity theft. They wouldn't know how to be as sneaky as she was, as conniving and thoughtful and planning. They were just all with the splurging of money, and quick and easy ways to get more, like bad bank robberies (her granddad) with her father moving on down to simple convenience store heists and the like. Bunny did try the full menu of options, or at least, quite a few, before deciding on the safe and simple with identity theft.

Or at least, it'd seemed safe and simple till things went kinda wrong.

But it wasn't as if her Da'd waited around long enough to make much difference in her life or to enable her to really have options, like college, to consider. While her mother died in childbirth, her father lasted until she was thirteen before he was killed by a mark gone bad in an alley one night. He and his partner, Old Tom, were just perpetrating a simple mugging when it all went south and the mark pulled a gun of his own.

If her Da had been half as smart as Bunny, he'd likely have realized he was trying to mug a mafia hitman and his girl of the night.

Bunny was only thirteen at the time and entirely unwilling to submit herself to further authority, especially not more of the same fucked-up sort as she'd already experienced under the unworthy tutelage of her Da, so she carefully slipped off the grid, deciding not to undergo the horrors of the foster system or any other sort of state-run program.

Even at that young age, she knew she'd be better off on her own. At least then she'd be able to lay claim to any and all decisions she made, and take responsibility for where her life went.

But as a rather uneducated thirteen-year-old, she knew she had limited options, and knew in order to survive she had to leverage her strengths by using her quick wits and hands to explore lucrative careers in pick-pocketry, petty thievery, shoplifting and purse snatching. During this time she also became adept at escaping juvy facilities and furthered her skills in lying, cheating, deceiving and pretending to be other than who she was, all of which became the building stones for her future career in identity theft.

She seemed to have an inborn knack for being other than who she really was.

She looked back to the bed and realized the only part of any of it she actually regretted was that it all might cost her a future with Nina.

Nina.

Bunny'd jumped over that counter that day. It was just a small credit union, so the security wasn't too good, and she'd jumped over the counter only to meet a schoolteacher who was working a second job as a teller during the summer.

'Course, she didn't know that then.

She and the other'd gone over the counter, and at the last teller that was hers to hit, Bunny'd been told, "Come with me to the back," and the woman she was robbing led her away.

"They hit the silent alarm," the woman said, not taking her to the vault. Instead, they ran through a door that was propped open with a trash can. "Keep your gun on me. Go out through the doors over there and jump over the fences. You seem athletic enough to do it."

"What the fuck're you doing, woman?" Bunny'd said. It didn't make sense to her, since it was all going like clockwork, like the perfect crime, like something she'd done hundreds of times before, like—

"Saving your ass. Run quick and you can make it. Everyone

else here's gone. Keep your gun on me, like you're making me do this." They ran past a few offices and out the back door.

"Why?" Bunny asked.

The woman looked around. "My name's Nina Nicolas. I teach at Shepherd Elementary. Call me there once the school year begins. And I like your eyes." She put her hand on Bunny's wrist, which lie on her own arm. "And the way you touched me."

That moment burned into Bunny's mind. It was like it'd happened before and would happen again. If not exactly, then enough like to mean—

And then she heard the sirens and had to run off, leaping over the concrete walls separating the credit union's parking lot from the residential neighbors on other sides.

CHAPTER FOUR

It began the same way it always began, with Buddy and Louie coming into the bar. They nodded to her before going up to the bar and slamming back a few shots. Buddy joined a poker game and Louie went upstairs with Veronica, who appeared to be his favorite, from everything Billy'd seen.

Then, about fifteen minutes later, Louie came back down, buttoning his trousers, and went to the bar while Buddy went to Veronica's room.

Billy glanced over at Louie at the bar, then upstairs, and then went up the stairs, her hand on her gun, trying to look as if she suspected some sort of wrongdoing was occurring just overhead. Instead, she waited outside of Veronica's room, listening to her fake cries and moans until Buddy was done, dressed and leaving.

"Train yard, Okee, sunrise tomorrow," Buddy said, stepping past Billy in the hall.

Yippee. Another job. And those jobs sure as heck paid a lot better than her day-to-day. It was just gonna be hard explaining to Gracie and Marnie that she'd have to be gone again so soon.

But the train yard? That didn't sound like the sort of job that'd just have her watching the horses. She wondered if she should ride there or . . . Well. Duh. Of course she had to ride there—it was too far to walk. But what should she do about Pony? How long would they be gone? Did she need to worry about someone watching over him—feeding him—while she was gone on some train?

Well, Buddy and his gang might not be the most organized and powerful outlaws working the West at the moment, but they'd be on top of it enough to plan for the horses if they'd be going somewhere on a train.

But that led to wondering about . . . well . . . if there were no horses, what would her job be?

Maybe she was getting a promotion? That would be really good. After all, becoming a world-famous criminal was part of her entire scheme.

And, also, hey, if she had to go to the train depot, it was likely she'd be part of something that would harm her father in some way financially, and that made it an even better proposition for her.

She waited a few beats after Buddy left, then headed downstairs herself, still thinking on what this job might be, what her role would be, how much fun it was gonna be, and how much dinero it'd land her.

But as soon as she stepped onto the main floor, she saw it: Louie cornering Elise. The sight did not please her.

She met Elise's panicked gaze across the crowded bar and went to her.

"Stranger," she said to Louie. "I'm not reckoning our lil' lady schoolmarm here is much wanting to have anything to do with you."

"And I'm thinking you just might be wrong about that," Louie said, not moving an inch from Elise.

"No, no, he's not," Elise said, trying to sidle away from him. She was obviously uncomfortable in the saloon, which wasn't surprising—she could lose her job and be ostracized by the entire town just for being in such an establishment.

"Nice women don't hang out in places like this," Louie said, making another move for her.

"I was just here to drop some books off for Billy, and to schedule our next tutoring session."

"You reading books now?" Louie said in amazement as he faced off with Billy.

"Louie," Buddy said, grabbing him by his wrist. "Seems to me Sheriff's right over there, so we don't want to be causing any problems here tonight. We got big plans for tomorrow and all."

Louie gave Elise a last look before turning to Billy. "You just protecting her virtue or—"

"Yes," Billy said.

Many of the folks nearby now had their attention pinned to the small gathering at the bar.

"Maybe later you can tell me all about it," Louie said, letting Buddy guide him out the doors.

"Do you want to tell me just how you know those fellows?" Elise said.

"No, not really," Billy replied, trying to lead Elise out of the bar.

"Was that some sort of problem I saw happening here?" Lucky Henry said, moseying on up to the bar.

"Nope, none whatsoever," Billy said.

"Looked like maybe you knew those troublemakers," Henry said, pressing on, even as he slapped his hand against the bar, signaling for a shot.

Billy glanced around, quickly assessing the situation and making sure that no one but Elise had heard the familiarity with which Louie and Buddy had spoken to her. She hoped Elise would back her up on this. "Then I reckon you saw something that weren't actually there. Now, 'scuse me, I gotta go upstairs and check on the girls."

It was only at the bottom of the staircase that Elise caught up with her. "Here. I really did bring some books for you." She pressed them into Billy's hands. "Should I ask who those men were, what you have to do with them, how you know them, or anything else?"

"No," Billy said, taking the books and heading upstairs.

Elise hooked a finger into the back of Billy's trousers and ran up to whisper in her ear, "But I *can* tell Henry what I heard, right?"

Billy stopped, dead in her boots. "I'd rather you not."

Elise pressed up close behind her. "Then I'm going to want to have a chat about it tomorrow."

"Not tomorrow. I'm busy tomorrow."

"Since when?"

"Since now."

"Since them."

"Yes." Billy glanced around. Lucky Henry surely was paying a lot of attention to them right now. He might even be suspecting what they were talking about. "You should go home. Now." Then, "Please."

"You'll owe me when you get back," Elise said. She reached up to squeeze Billy's forearm before she walked away.

Billy could only wonder whether Elise meant for anyone else to see that last gesture, which was amazingly intimate for a schoolmarm in such a place.

Billy was at the train depot in Okee at sunrise, just as she'd been told to be. She rode Pony, since there wasn't any other way to make it on time. She just hoped Buddy'd figured out how to take care of the horses while they were off and about.

Unless, of course, she was supposed to care for the horses while the rest of the gang was off having a grand and fun adventure. That wouldn't be fun for her at all.

As soon as she got there, however, she began to see a greater design behind it all. There was a corral right next to the depot. She reckoned it was for travelers to store their horses, but she also reckoned, since she saw Buddy's and Louie's and several other gang members' horses there, that she should just put Pony there as well.

So she did.

Then she walked over to the train depot, where the rest of the gang waited: Snake and Laredo together, Jethro and Louie together, Buddy all by his lonesome.

They were the only ones at the depot this early morning, so she wondered why they were putting up such a grand façade, but she also knew that one of the reasons she ran with them was because of Buddy's caution on matters like this.

"Do you have any tobacco?" Billy asked Buddy, pulling a cigarette paper from her pocket.

"This is one of them Fairchild trains," Buddy said, looking forward. "We don't have an exact-type plan, but we do know that besides the usual safe, this train also contains the big man himself: Woodward Fairchild. We plan on grabbing him and whatever's in the safe, too. Then we'll hold him for ransom. And we'll get the cash as well."

"And just what is my part in all of this?" Billy asked in a very uncharacteristically verbose fashion. She was so stunned they were planning on kidnapping her father that she didn't know what to say, how to react or anything else.

Buddy looked at her like she'd just lost her mind, but then apparently focused back on work. "You look young. Innocent. We're hoping you'll get us closer to him. You do got your gun, right?"

Billy pulled out her Colt Single Action Army. She was proud of Sam. She was looking forward to introducing Da to her.

"Put that away!" Buddy ordered. "Hide it! You're part of our bait. We get on the train, and you without Sam will be able to walk up and down the train, check things out, and let us know what's going on."

"Hold on," Billy said. "If you know he's on this train and all this other stuff, how do you not know more?"

"That's none of your business. What is your business is that you're lucky to get this promotion—you pull this off right, and stick with it, and you'll get a fair share of the take. What more could you want?"

"All right, then. I'm in," Billy said, accepting the ticket Buddy proffered.

As she walked off, Louie came up to her. "Buddy overheard someone from the trains talking in Bootstrap, but the guy was also cheating at cards. Buddy got in on the game and learned some more, but guy got shot before he could say too much. If there's anything you want to let us know, you can write it down and hand it to me. Buddy don't read, but I do. And 'cause of last night, I'm reckoning you can both read and write."

Billy nodded her acceptance, then continued on to find her own lonesome spot of platform.

The train pulled up and a few people got off and the gang got on, each grouping in a different car. Snake and Laredo were in the second passenger car, Jethro and Louie together in the fourth, and Buddy by himself in the fifth.

Billy got onto the first car behind the engine and made her way back through the train, noticing where each of the gang members was, how many men, women and children were in each passenger car, and anything else that was particularly important, like men who looked particularly mean or well armed or who seemed as if they might be wealthy. She was also trying to find her father and his entourage. Plus a safe. A safe would be good.

Then, after walking through all five passenger cars, none of which were full but all of which held people that Billy wondered about—like where they were going, where they were coming from, what they wanted, what they hoped for—Billy crossed into yet another car.

"Oh!" a pretty twentyish woman said as soon as Billy entered the car just beyond the fifth and last passenger car. "Oh, I'm sorry, this is a private car. All the passenger cars are that way." She pointed in the direction Billy had come from.

Billy looked around. The car wasn't posh, but it was nicer than the passenger cars. "So what is this, then?" she asked.

"This is a private car," the woman said. "So you'll need to get off it and go back onto one of the passenger cars."

Billy wandered farther in. After all, the woman wasn't big or armed. "So who is all this for?" she asked, taking note of the position of the safe, and the fact that she and the woman appeared to be alone. She wanted to know everything about this car by the time she left, and she also wanted to know of any bodyguards her Da might have, as well as his location.

That was when she noticed the two big, burly men in suits sitting on either side of the car. She was sure they were loaded to the nuts with guns.

And then, even as the woman said, "Really, I must insist you leave now," Billy's father came out of the water closet.

"Is something wrong, Rebecca?" he asked the woman, coming up to her and taking hold of her elbow, exerting some supremacy over her.

Billy noticed the bodyguards get to their feet and reach for their guns at this point. She was so stunned to again see her Da after all these years, she didn't know what to think, except that he seemed to be the same bastard she remembered him as.

"No, nothing at all. I was just asking this young man," the woman said, with a gesture at Billy, "to find himself a seat in one of the passenger cars ahead of us."

Her father looked at her even as his guards crowded near him. An expression of recognition passed over his face. "Do I know you?"

She pulled the bill of her hat lower over her face. "Nope, not at all. I'm Billy. Who might you be?" She used her gruffest, deepest, outlawiest voice.

Her father stood up straight and looked down his nose at her. "Woodward Fairchild the Third."

"As in Fairchild Railways?"

"Yes."

Billy looked him up and down. "Huh. You don't look like so much."

"Looks can be deceiving, young man. Are you sure I don't know you?"

"I ought to be moseying on back into the passenger cars. Pleasure meetin' y'all. And all that." She nodded to the woman, then to her father, turned on her boot heel and went back the way she had come in.

She sat down a few feet from Buddy. She wrote up a quick note:

Two armed men watching over him in the car just beyond the one Buddy's in. Safe on the right side as you enter. We should go in, grab his mistress Rebecca, who's not being watched. Hold a gun to her head, he'll empty the safe for us. We grab her, and he'll pay to get her back. We grab him, and nobody can get to his money.

She really reckoned that grabbing Rebecca was the best way to profit from the situation. The guards were watching over him and not her. Billy instinctively loathed Rebecca, for her father obviously cared more about her than he'd ever cared for Billy, but that wasn't affecting her judgment: she knew what they ought to do.

She gave Louie the note, dropping it nonchalantly in his lap when she walked by. She waited until he'd had time to read it, then moved to a seat not too far ahead of him. When she glanced back at him, he nodded slightly.

The plan was on.

A few moments later, Jethro got up, heading into the forward cars, apparently to gather the troops from that direction, while Louie went to presumably let Buddy know the results of Billy's mission.

Snake, Laredo and Jethro returned to the car. Snake and Laredo went on, while Jethro sat for a moment. He looked knowingly at Billy. Billy got up and went back. At the end of the last passenger car, Buddy nodded at Billy, signaling her to continue.

When Billy was in the open-air place between cars, waiting, Buddy walked up to her.

"Louie and Snake went up over the car. They'll come in from the opposite end when we come in the front. You go first. They already know you, so you have the best chance of grabbing the girl."

Jethro caught up with them, as did Laredo. Billy again entered her father's private railcar. Rebecca and Billy's father were sitting at a table near the front.

"You again?" her father asked. His bodyguards had been sitting a few feet behind him, but now they stood, hands on their guns.

Billy kneeled next to Rebecca, pulling her gun in a single fluid motion. She aimed Sam at Rebecca's head. "Who'll pull the trigger faster, me or your boys?"

Woodward indicated for his men to step back . . . right into the waiting arms of Louie and Snake, who held their guns against their heads. Once they were disarmed, Louie held his gun on them while Snake tied them up, hogstyle.

Buddy and the others came up behind Billy.

"Okay, Mr. Fairchild, this is how it's gonna happen," Buddy said. "You're gonna go on over to that there safe and open it up. We're gonna take everything in it, and then we're gonna leave.

With this little girl here. And then, sometime later, we'll let you know how you're gonna give us fifty thousand dollars to get your girlfriend back."

"She's not my girlfriend," Woodward said, not moving, but carefully assessing each of his opponents. Buddy had his gun trained on Woodward, while Billy was still responsible for Rebecca.

Billy sat next to Rebecca, transferring Sam to her left hand so she could wrap her right arm around Rebecca, holding her close. She hated the way the woman had so obviously usurped her mother's position in her father's life, just like Billy was so obviously no longer a part of her father's life.

She kept a tight grip on both the woman and her gun.

Snake kept an eye on the two hog-tied goons in the back. Louie and Jethro went through the car, scavenging for anything worth stealing. Laredo stood guard over the entire car, wary eyes watching for anything to go amiss, even as he balanced his shotgun across his arms. Billy'd seen the holes that shotgun could blast in walls, in cattle and in people. She knew *she* didn't want to be in his line of fire.

"Okay, old man," Buddy said to Woodward. "Time to open up that safe for us."

"Are you sure I don't know you?" Woodward asked Billy.

"Positive." She looked right into his eyes, daring him to see who she really was and to acknowledge all his deficiencies and how he hadn't even looked for her, goddammit. "Get a move on, old man. Open the safe and hand over the cash. Or your little girlie-girl's gonna buy it, right now. Then the rest of you, one by one. And then we'll move on to your passengers."

Jethro apparently didn't have enough to do, because he suddenly pounced toward Woodward. "And don't believe we won't do it, 'cause I'm really looking forward to some bloodshed today. Old Sheba ain't seen near enough action lately," he said, caressing his Colt .45 before aiming it right at Woodward. "I'd say this'd be a mighty fine time to get with opening that safe, else there might be some bloodshed happening today."

Her father raised his hands in surrender. "Please, I'll do whatever you want, just don't hurt anyone." He went to the safe, slowly, keeping his hands up the entire time, knelt and immediately opened it.

Billy couldn't believe this man, this man who was giving in so easily, was her father. What happened to the cheap bastard he used to be?

She looked at the woman in her arms. "It's you, isn't it?" she said to her. "You've got him wrapped around your finger. He must really care for you." She couldn't keep the edge out of her voice. She hoped no one could tell just how jealous she was of the redheaded woman she held a gun on.

"Do you have a bag?" Woodward asked Buddy, crouching in front of the now-open safe.

Louie pulled two from his duster and handed them over. "Be sure to get it all, old man."

"I will. I don't want anyone else getting hurt because of me or my money. Enough have paid enough as it is." He stood, handed Louie the now-full bags, pulled out his bill clip and pocket watch and dropped them into the bag as well. "Shall I stop the train so you may all depart safely?"

"No," Buddy said. "We'll be in touch about you getting us the money in exchange for your little mistress here."

"She's not—"

Buddy clipped him across the ear so he fell to the floor, unconscious. Then Buddy walked over to the two musclemen and knocked one of them upside the head while Snake whacked the other one out. Laredo hog-tied Woodward, and they all headed out the back of the car.

"What're we doing now?" Billy asked, pushing Rebecca along. She had to struggle to remember this was all real, because it kept feeling as if she was dreaming. Or remembering it all.

"We're jumping off the train," Louie said, grabbing one of Rebecca's arms.

"What?" Rebecca shrieked. "I can't jump off a train!"

"We're passing by a lake up ahead," Louie said. "It'll be easy. We jump off and in, then swim to shore."

"But I can't swim!" Rebecca said.

Billy wrapped an arm around her. "Then just hold on to me."

"How can I trust you?"

Billy briefly wondered that herself. After all, she'd love to be the cause of real grief to her Da, and it appeared he genuinely cared about Rebecca. "You're worth a lot of money to us, but only if we keep you alive."

"Plus, why'd we want to off you?" Snake said, leering at Rebecca. "We might be able to get some fun outta you while we wait for the old man to cough up the cash. So I'll help you, too."

"I've got her, Snake," Billy said, pulling Rebecca close.

"It's coming up!" Buddy said. "Everybody get ready to jump!"

"Then I'm right behind you," Snake replied.

Each of the gang members jumped off the train and into the lake as soon as they got to it, with Billy holding Rebecca as they jumped. Her heart beat in her throat, but she knew she had to keep Rebecca calm, so she was brave just for the woman in her arms.

"Relax," Billy told Rebecca when they were safe in the cold water, even as she fought to keep the frantic woman from drowning them both. She wrapped both arms tightly around Rebecca, holding them both afloat in the water. "Dammit, woman! Relax or you'll pull us both down!" It was then that Billy remembered Rebecca from her youth.

"Oh no," the young girl had exclaimed, racing forward toward the pond, untying her clothes. "We shall be forced naked into the water!"

"Shall I rescue thee, fair maiden?" Billy'd said.

"Do . . . Do I know you?" Rebecca asked her.

"No. Now let me get us to safety," Billy said, allowing the swift current to carry them along. She was sure that the current was part of the getaway plan, since there would be no way for the local sheriff, once one was found, to be able to determine where they'd landed, not even with the best bloodhounds around.

It was indeed a mighty fine plan, a mighty fine plan indeed.

• • •

"Y'know, it takes a real butch to keep a name like Bunny," Nina said, leaning against the front passenger's door. Hour after hour Bunny drove, stopping only for gas, munchies and to pee. Bunny wished she knew where she was going, what she was going to do. What *they* were going to do.

"I think my Da had a real sense of whimsy," Bunny said, glancing over at her girlfriend, who never seemed worried, scared, or less than totally by her side. "You're amazing, you know that, right?"

Nina shrugged. "I love you. We'll get through this. Even if it means you have to change your name. I respect you for keeping it this long. What should we name you next, though, I wonder?"

Just then Bunny saw flashing lights behind her.

Nina must have noticed her looking all around, speeding up for a moment, getting twitchy. "Pull over," she said. "You're just attracting more attention by even thinking of running."

"But we don't stand a chance if he pulls us over."

"He's likely after you for a burnt-out taillight. If he's not, I'll flash him"—she pulled at the hem of her shirt—"and we run." She grinned and winked at Bunny.

Bunny pulled over.

"License and registration," the cop said, glaring down through the driver's window of the car.

Bunny handed them over. "May I ask what I've done, Officer?"

"Broken taillight," he said before he walked back to his own car.

"Um, do you think maybe now I should run?" Bunny asked Nina.

"No. He's coming back. Let's wait it out."

The police officer was carrying a clipboard. He leaned against Bunny's window, pulled his gun out from behind the clipboard and aimed it directly at Bunny's head. "I saw you back at that last gas station and thought I'd seen you on some flyer or other. Unlike most of my colleagues out here, I pay attention to federally wanted criminals, even fleeing, non-murdering types like you."

"So I'm under arrest, then."

"Unless you convince me you aren't this identity thiever I think you might be."

"What do you mean?"

"Nothing. By the way, I just looked at a partial list of your crimes. With terrorists and all running wild in this country, you're just not seeming that terrible a criminal."

"Oh." Bunny realized what he meant. "I have something in my pocket that might help prove I'm not the woman you're after." She left her left hand on the steering wheel, then gingerly reached inside her jacket, into the inside breast pocket, and pulled out a ring. "Maybe if you inspect this, you might discover some shred of proof of my innocence?"

The officer opened the box to inspect the $5,000 ring. "You might just be right. And I might just be getting engaged tonight. Carry on, then."

He walked back to his car and got in, turning off his lights and pulling back onto the road. He flipped a U-turn and headed back the way he'd come.

Bunny didn't have a clue as to why she knew he'd be needing such a ring right then. She decided to simply count her ongoing blessings and guess her karma was still relatively clean.

CHAPTER FIVE

"I gotta tell you," Snake said that night over the campfire, "there are some mighty fine women in these parts." He gave Rebecca a sideways look that Billy wasn't altogether comfortable with.

Rebecca, who was bound, tried to inch away from him. Billy planted herself down between Snake and Rebecca. "Remember, she's worth a bunch of cash to us."

"Alive," Snake said. "But that don't mean we can't have our fun first. Hell, boy, you ever even had a woman yet?"

"I've had at least as many as you, but I ain't never had to take a woman by force, unlike you."

"Them's fighting words, boy," Snake said, his hand on his gun.

"Stand down," Buddy said, taking over control of the situation. "You two can have a showdown at high noon for all I care—

once this is done. But not before. I don't need any unnecessary bloodshed complicating matters before that, y'hear me now?"

"Aw, hell," Jethro said. "Let 'em shoot it out right now. Then we'll have fewer folks to divvy the take between."

Louie stood, backing up Billy. "I signed on for robbery and kidnapping. Not rape." He looked down at Snake. "You want some of this here lady, you'll have to go through both Billy and me, got that?"

Snake looked up at Louie, then leaned back, spreading his legs and cupping his head with his spread arms behind his head. "I'll give 'em this 'un, but I'm telling you, soon's we get back to Climax, I'm gonna make that there schoolmarm mine."

"No reason we got to keep you so uncomfortable like," Billy said to Rebecca, deliberately trying to ignore Snake. She untied Rebecca's hands from behind her back.

"You letting our hostage go, boy?" Snake said, leaping back to his feet.

"No," Billy said, retying her hands in front of her. "Just making her a little more comfortable is all." She hated that she suddenly was feeling protective toward this woman. Well, hell, she'd saved her life already, but hated herself about it. The woman took her mother from her. She just felt protective toward women as a whole. And she didn't want to ponder too deeply on it at all.

"Just make sure she won't get away tonight," Snake said, stalking toward them.

"Just make sure you're paying attention when you're on watch, and it'll be fine," Louie said, standing and planting one bear-sized paw against Snake's chest. "Not like that last time, when I found you sound asleep."

"Last time it was just the lawmen we were worried about, now we got something that might run away all on its own, 'specially with Billy here being all easy on her. I said we oughtn't use the boy like this."

"So that means you won't be taking no naps on your watch tonight, then?" Buddy said, pissing all over the others so they'd remember who was in charge.

"Yeah, that's what that means," Snake said, backing off.

"Then that means there's no reason we gotta make the little lady quite so uncomfortable. We're bank robbers, not rapists or torturers." Buddy knelt next to Rebecca. "Now, we're gonna be nice to you, mainly 'cause there's all sorts of snakes and bears and stuff out there." He nodded beyond their campsite. "Without a gun, and without us, you really don't stand a chance. You understand?"

"Uh, yes, yes sir," Rebecca said.

Buddy nodded toward Billy. "You'll take care of our guest?"

"Hey, how come you're putting the kid in charge of her?" Laredo asked.

" 'Cause I reckon the kid's the most trustworthy of all you louses," Buddy said. "He works in a brothel, so he's all accustomed to resisting temptation and all that. Ain't that right, little buddy?"

Billy wrapped her jacket around Rebecca's shaking shoulders. "I'm gonna grab us some eats now, 'kay?"

"Yes, yes, thank you. Please don't let them hurt me."

Snake had killed a couple of rabbits for dinner and Louie'd cooked them up right nicely over an open fire. Billy yanked some of the meat off, pulled out her handkerchief, piled it up in that, and carried it over to Rebecca, whom she'd left sitting on a downed log.

"Not quite the fine style you're accustomed to, but—" Billy began.

"It's food," Rebecca said, grabbing a chunk and eating it ravenously. "And I'm not all that used to everything Mr. Fairchild gave me."

"*Mister* Fairchild? Do you refer to all your lovers so formally?"

"He was my employer, not my lover!" she exclaimed, apparently offended by Billy's assumption.

"You were in his private car, and he obviously cares very much for you. What else would I assume?" Billy said, gnawing at a chunk of meat herself.

"Mr. Fairchild might look as if he has everything—money, luxury, power—but really, he doesn't. He lost his wife years ago, and his daughter later on. He's all alone in this world, blames himself for everything that's happened." Rebecca eagerly drank some water.

"So how do you fit into all that?" Billy asked just before she went to get more food for them both. She was surprised at Rebecca's robust appetite. It was easier to be surprised at that than at the idea her father actually missed her.

"My mother was his secretary. When his daughter was kidnapped and killed, he took more of an interest in me."

"His daughter was killed?" Billy'd never heard anything about it. The rutting bastard just never paid her ransom.

"She was kidnapped, and even when he paid the ransom they didn't return her. He's always wished that he'd gone after them himself. She was all he had left of his wife."

They'd lied to her. Carl and Frank and the others had lied to her—her father *had* paid her ransom, but they'd kept the money so she'd help them out!

"I'm sorry," Rebecca said, putting a hand on Billy's arm. "Is something the matter?"

"*We* kidnapped *you*, and *you're* asking *me* if there's something wrong?" Billy couldn't believe this woman was being so kind to her.

"You just don't seem like the others, I guess. You're nicer. And I think I wouldn't be so safe if it wasn't for you." But she still pulled her hand away from Billy.

"Are you sure his daughter was killed?" Billy said.

"We just had to assume it. We never heard from them, or her, again."

Billy suddenly realized how carefully Rebecca was looking at her, and how suspicious she was likely sounding. "So anyway, Fairchild started paying more attention to you. How so?"

"Oh, not what you're thinking. I mean, you must see all manner of things, working in a brothel like you do—that is, if what your friend over there said—"

"It is. I do," Billy said, nodding.

"I thought so. But anyway, Mr. Fairchild just made sure I was educated, well-clothed and fed. Treated and raised well. My own father died in a bank robbery when I was young, so when Mr. Fairchild lost his own daughter, he took me under his wing."

"What did your mother think about that?" Billy asked, finishing off the last of the rabbit she'd brought over on her latest trip to the campfire. "Have you had enough?"

"Yes, I have. Thank you. You know, you're not like the rest of them."

"I know. I'm younger and cuter."

"I wouldn't be surprised to find out none of them have ever attended a day of school, but you, now . . . You've been to school."

"Actually, I just have a thing for the local schoolmarm is all."

Rebecca smiled at her then. Billy reckoned they were about the same age. "I can see why she might be interested in you, too. Especially if you were a few years older," Rebecca said. She looked away then. "There was no way Mama could've afforded the advantages and education Mr. Fairchild made possible for me, so she was grateful."

"So what happened to your mama?"

Rebecca shrugged. "She died a few months ago."

"You gonna take first shift then, Billy?" Buddy yelled over the fire to them.

"Yeah, yeah, I will," Billy replied. She looked at Rebecca. "I hate to do this," she said, holding up the rope.

"I understand," Rebecca said.

"Listen," Billy said, retying Rebecca's outstretched hands, "it's gonna get wicked cold out here, and we didn't really pack for this sort of thing. I don't want to appear forward or anything, but I'm thinking it might be good if we lay down together."

"You're cold, aren't you?"

Billy shivered. "Yes." She wished the boys had planned this escapade a bit better, as it was they were walking back to where the horses were with minimal provisions and supplies.

Rebecca glanced at Billy. "Can I trust you?"

"Yes."

"How are we going to do this, then?"

Billy lay down on the dirt, gently pulling Rebecca down with her, into her arms.

"This might work better if we use your coat as a blanket," Rebecca said. Billy helped her pull it off and covered them with it, wrapping her arms lightly around Rebecca as she did so—one arm under Rebecca's head, so the woman could use it as a pillow, the other over her waist.

Rebecca settled in further, apparently realizing Billy wasn't going to try anything, and she said, "I love Mr. Fairchild like the father I never knew, but I also agreed to go on this trip with him because I found a map in my mother's possessions."

"A map? To what?" Billy was glad everyone else appeared to be asleep. She was sure she didn't want the others paying attention to all they were talking about, even without thinking about the harassment she'd take over their apparent snuggling.

"Okay, here's the thing. I think my real father was a gold-rusher, as well as a criminal of some sort. I think *he* left Mama the map, and so I agreed to this trip because I want to know once and for all what the map leads to." She laid her arms on Billy's stomach. "If you get me out of here, if you help me, I'll split whatever we find with you, sixty/forty."

Billy glanced around, making sure no one was listening. "And I'd get the sixty?"

"No, you'd get the forty."

"Then it's no deal. Lowest I'll settle for is fifty/fifty."

"It's a deal then . . . Billy. That is your name, in't it?" Rebecca snuggled in even closer.

"Even if you get my gun, you still won't stand a chance out here," Billy said, paying close attention to where Rebecca's hands were. "Even if you get your hands untied. Do I need to tie your feet together as well?"

Rebecca pulled away slightly. "I'm just trying to get warmed up."

"Where's the map?"

"You'll have to untie me for that."

"Where's the map?"

"If you work in a brothel, you ought to know where any woman would hide such a thing."

Billy leaned up and over Rebecca. "Please excuse me, then, ma'am, 'cause I mean no disrespect, but I have to know." She reached down and slipped the map from Rebecca's cleavage. In the last of the firelight, she examined it. "This just might be something worth something."

"Fifty/fifty?" Rebecca said.

Billy thought about just grabbing the map and taking off, but she didn't trust the rest of the gang with Rebecca. She resented that Rebecca had the affection her father'd never given her, but she couldn't hate the woman for it. She couldn't believe how much her attitude toward the woman had changed since when she'd first seen her on the train. "Yes," she said, somehow knowing it was important for her to get that map and to use it. Sometime. Someday.

"Let me guess," Elise said when Billy and Rebecca knocked on her door late one night, "she's part of what I'm not supposed to talk about."

"Yup. Marnie and the girls aren't being too friendly-like toward her, and I'm hoping you might be a bit better with the hospitality and all." That morning, it'd been decided Rebecca would be safer with Billy than with anyone else in the gang, and so they—the rest of the gang—would contact Woodward Fairchild and arrange for the ransom and all of that, while Billy ensured Rebecca's safety.

"I won't keep her tied up, though," Elise said.

"I didn't think you would." Billy untied Rebecca. "This here's Elise. She's the one who's making sure I can talk all fancy-like and shit."

"And why should I allow this?" Elise asked. Billy liked the way Elise was looking at Rebecca, like she was competition or something. Elise never looked at any of the girls at the whorehouse like that.

Billy studied the two women, then said to Rebecca, "I suggest an equal three-way split. I don't have any other place to store you where I know you won't come to harm. It's worth a bit of cash money to me to keep you safe until we can follow that there map of yours. What do you reckon?"

Rebecca slowly studied Elise. "I'd rather stay with her than with your friend Snake."

Elise met Rebecca's gaze. "When you say it like that, then yes, Billy, leave her with me."

Billy left Elise and Rebecca alone together, to eat and chat, while she went to the local newspaper office and anywhere else she reckoned she could find information about her father. All to no avail.

And finally, that night, Elise came into the saloon.

"Billy," she said, sitting on a stool. "What's going on?"

"What do you mean?" It always seemed as if Billy had to be explaining things to folks, even when those things ought to be quite obvious to comprehend.

"I know what happened, I now know better who and what

you are—"

"Are you okay with that?" Billy looked up at Elise through her lashes even as she went around the bar and busied herself with cleaning glasses. She did usually try to help Marnie out, after all.

"Yes. But I have to know . . ."

But Billy really didn't want to be having this conversation with Elise right then. After all, she herself still didn't know quite what it all meant. "What?"

"I can't see you killing anybody, and I can't see why you've been so interested in Rebecca's past." Elise grabbed Billy's arm, stilling her and holding her in place.

"What are you saying, Elise?"

"Rebecca told me you were defending even me, like you always do." Her touch seemed familiar, somehow. Like it'd happened before. But it hadn't. Not before . . .

"And that means what?" Billy wanted to run, even as she said the words.

"I'm wondering who you really are."

"What do you mean by that?"

"You've come to me looking for me to teach you, and sometimes I think you know more about some things than even I do. You keep slipping from whatever play-acting you're doing and showing your real self."

"Shh!" Billy hissed. "Don't talk about this here. Now. Shut up."

"How dare you talk to me like that!"

"I'll . . . I'll talk to you later." Billy took Elise's hands in her own. "Please, please give me this. Later. We will talk later."

• • •

It was more than a hundred miles later, when they were in Kentucky, that Bunny and Nina saw even more flashing lights behind them. Bunny didn't feel overly safe in Kentucky no matter the reasons.

Bunny really didn't want her girl showing off her ta-tas to just any storm trooper come calling, and now she lacked even a really good bribe. She'd been unhappy to give Nina's ring, or the ring she'd planned on giving Nina, to some random cop, but it was all she could think to do, and Nina seemed to understand. After all, Nina understood her having to run from the law and . . . well, even running from Nina.

And now Bunny didn't think about it, she just went with her gut instincts and hit the accelerator, zooming up the off-ramp and flying down a side street, then another and another. She didn't know what she was doing, except that so far her guts were paying off.

The cop stayed on her tail, following her every move. Bunny was sure more would soon be on their way. She hated the idea that some folks might die in a high-speed chase. She needed to either lose this guy or give up.

Nina leaned over, placing her hand on Bunny's thigh. "If you can get just a few turns ahead of this guy, you can hide behind a house. Any house. Are we even sure he knows just who you are?"

"With the way I've run, he knows enough to blow my head off if I even blink wrong at him."

"*If* he catches us."

Nina was looking both at Bunny and around them. Bunny knew she, too, was trying to figure a way out of this mess.

"Do you know how to ride a horse?" Nina suddenly asked.

"Um, not sure."

"Well, can you hot-wire a car? Any car? Break in and make it work?"

"Pretty much yes."

"Then turn right *now!*" Nina yanked the steering wheel to emphasize her point.

Bunny found them barreling down a dirt road. She realized the dust behind them might give them away, but might also help to impede anyone who might be following them.

Nina was practically driving from the passenger's seat, like *she* knew what she was doing, yanking the wheel to and fro until they ended up at a . . .

Barn?

"Get out!" Nina yelled, leaping from the vehicle. She ran into the barn and Bunny merely followed, leaping onto the horse Nina saddled for her faster than anyone should've been able to saddle a horse.

They rode out and Bunny suddenly realized she didn't know nearly as much about Nina as she'd thought she did. It was fun learning more about her lover.

And she was learning about herself. She'd never been on a horse before in her life, but she was comfortable on one, like she'd been on one in a previous life or something.

She looked back and saw that Nina was already catching up with her. Nina'd seemed like a settled sort of woman when they'd first met, but all this—the crazy driving and this mad-dash horse race, which was seeming a lot like a wicked team-building/trust exercise, was showing her more than ever why Nina had come with Bunny after she'd robbed the bank where Nina was.

"Don't ask!" Nina yelled as she came up behind Bunny. "I learned it all in a dream!"

CHAPTER SIX

"I remember you," Billy confessed to Rebecca the next day over dinner at Elise's. "I remember your mother, too. My mother worked for the Fairchilds when I was younger. I never knew who my father was, and I thought maybe he was Woodward Fairchild. That's why I wanted to kidnap you. I wanted to know if he was my father and if he was as evil and bad as I remembered him."

"But wouldn't that have worked better if you'd kidnapped him instead of her?" Elise said.

"Who would have authorized the payment, gotten the money together, if we'd had him? I don't think even you could've done that," she said to Rebecca.

"I could've arranged it," Rebecca said. "Mr. Fairchild trusts me implicitly."

"I kinda got that—*now*," Billy said. "I thought maybe you

were his lover, so he'd definitely fork over the cash for *you*. Plus, maybe you'd tell me the truth about him, whereas there wouldn't be a chance in hell that he would."

"Hold up," Elise said. "You were growing up in some ritzy household, and you left because . . . ?"

"My mother died and I had to make it on my own."

Rebecca shook her head. "This isn't making any sense. How come you remember me and I don't remember you? I'm probably a few years older than you. I mean, you're what, fifteen or sixteen at the most?"

Billy stood up, went to the counter, poured herself a shot of whisky, downed it, rolled a smoke, lit it and faced the other two. "I'm twenty-four. I went into that rail car to check out the situation. I saw Woodward and how he immediately came up behind you, real protective like, and I knew I wanted to get you alone to find out the sort of man he really is."

Elise stalked over to Billy and said, "There's no way you're twenty-four. I'm twenty-four!"

Rebecca flew over, yanked the hat from Billy's head, grabbed her shoulders and whipped her around to face her. "Oh my goodness! You're not the *son* of some maid—you're Margaret Fairchild!"

"Oh, hold everything now," Elise said. "You're saying that Billy here *isn't* just some boy, but the *daughter* of some train tycoon?" She ran her hands over Billy's face and back through her hair. "Tell me it isn't true, Billy."

Billy pulled away, downed another shot and smoked some more. "My mother died in childbirth. I never knew her. I never knew my father, either. He was all about his business. Nannies and maids raised me. When I was kidnapped, I saw it as my way out. I made a deal with my captors. If Da didn't pay the ransom, I'd go with them. He didn't pay, and I went with them."

"He paid your ransom!" Rebecca said, her face red as she clenched her fists.

"You told me that, but Carl and Frank and the rest said he didn't, and that's why they took me with them. Why I went with them. The deal was that I'd help them steal from Da if they took me with them."

"Did you ever guess they lied to you, just to get your help?" Elise shook her head. "Do you have any idea what you gave up? The privilege? The education?" Billy couldn't figure out why Elise was practically yelling.

"You don't know what it was like," Billy said. "He wanted me to be a proper young lady—enough so that he was only having me trained in such things. He wasn't being a father to me, and he was keeping people from being close with me or teaching me anything I wanted to know. Letting me do anything."

"Do you have any idea what you could do with that kind of money and power?" Elise said. "You stood to inherit it all!"

Billy whipped about to face off with the two women. "Yeah. If he left any of it to me, he would've done it through some sort of lawyer or other *arrangement*. My entire life was *arranged*. I was just a girl, so I wasn't capable of anything."

Elise stared at her. "So you became a boy."

Billy shrugged. "Not like I could become a man or nothing. Plus, as a boy, women trust me and folks are willing to teach me stuff, stuff I want to know. Stuff I want to learn."

Elise slapped Billy and stalked off.

Billy stared after her in stunned silence.

"She's in love with you, you know," Rebecca said from behind her. Then, after a long pause, "Your father and I were never lovers. And he wasn't my mother's, either. He's a good man. He loved your mother, he loved you and now I'm the nearest thing he has to family, so he will give you the money. Just make sure *you* deal with him, because I wouldn't quite trust your cohorts."

"What do you mean?"

"I mean, your gang turned on you once before, lying to you about your father *not* paying your ransom. Now that you're just in it for the money, if they lie to you again, I'll be dead and you won't have the money either." When Billy finally turned around, she finished, "Please. I don't want to die. Protect me."

"That's not what I meant."

"Then what did you mean?"

"You said . . . you said . . ."

"What did I say?"

"She said you loved that there schoolmarm," Snake said from the doorway, holding a gun on the two of them. "And that alone explains a lot. Now I want both of ya to raise your hands, up over your head, real slow like."

"I said the schoolmarm loved her," Rebecca said, raising her arms over her head.

Billy briefly considered reaching for her gun, but then decided against it. She didn't want to risk her life, or, more importantly, Rebecca's life. She knew Snake was a crazed madman who likely wouldn't think twice before killing the both of them. She wouldn't be surprised if the only thing keeping them alive was that Snake needed Rebecca for the ransom.

So she raised her arms, very slowly.

"Now, don't go misunderestimating me or nothing. I will kill one, the other, or both of you without a problem. All I need to collect the ransom is a finger or two from your little friend here," Snake said, indicating Rebecca. "And I also know all I need to know about what to do to get you to behave, Billy. What I got to do is grab that there schoolmarm upstairs."

"Do you mean to chop off one of my fingers for some reason?" Rebecca said shakily.

"I can't use your corpse to prove I've still got you," Snake said. "So your old man'll cough up some right serious cash for you. I'll just chop off a finger or two, send those and some jewelry to prove I've got ya."

"Killing her was never part of the plan," Billy said.

"No, it wasn't. But then Buddy and Louie got all soft 'bout

you and this 'un. So Jethro and me, well, we figured maybe it was time for us to part ways and all. Start up our own gang." He walked into the house, right up to Rebecca. With his non-gun-holding hand, he felt her up, roughly grabbing at her breasts.

Billy gulped air, hating this, but unable to figure out what to do when he had his gun pointed right at her head.

"So I need you to slap these on Billy's wrists," Snake said, releasing Rebecca's breasts long enough to pull the shackles from his pocket.

Rebecca took them and cuffed Billy's hands together in front of her.

"Tighter," Snake said.

Rebecca complied. "What do you want from me?"

"Take his gun and put it over there, on the kitchen table," Snake said. "But be careful. I see that you might use it against me and you're dead."

"You're dead no matter what you do," Billy said to Rebecca.

Snake slugged Billy over the head with his gun so she dropped to the floor.

With two fingers Rebecca pulled Billy's gun from her holster and placed it on the kitchen table.

"Kill him," Billy said from the floor. Somehow she was sure her story would go on from here.

"Drop it," Snake said.

"No, you drop it," Elise said from the outside door, holding a gun in her shaking hands.

Snake didn't drop it. He turned toward Rebecca and pulled the trigger.

Elise pulled her trigger.

And in those few moments when two people fell over dead, Billy remembered that Snake had mentioned Jethro being in on it with him, so she lunged for the nearest gun—the gun that fell out of Snake's now-dead hand. From her position on the floor she rolled around to figure out where Jethro was, and it only took her a moment to catch him kicking in the front door, gun at the ready.

But she was readier.

He kicked in the door, gun up, and she shot.

He fell to the floor.

Billy rolled over to Rebecca, kneeling beside her and leaning over her. "No! I was supposed to protect you!"

Elise walked over to Snake and kicked him. Then put a bullet through his skull. "I wasn't sure about my aim," she said to Billy. Then, as Billy tried to wish Rebecca back to life, Elise went over to Jethro and put a shot through his forehead as well. "I didn't trust your aim, either." Then she pointed her gun at Billy. "Now tell me why I shouldn't kill you, too."

"I can't. I've lied to you from the first. I'm a criminal, and you've known that for a while. But I'm not like Snake and Jethro. I don't kill people."

"Can you honestly say you've never killed anyone before today?"

"Yes."

"And I'm supposed to take you at your word?"

Billy shrugged. "It's all I've got. I've lied the entire time you've known me, but I'm telling the truth now. So just go ahead and put a bullet through my head." She climbed to her feet. "You know I've lied to you this entire time, so if you want to kill me, just do it now."

Elise stood, gun pointed right at her, hands shaking.

Billy walked up to her, inching closer and closer with each step.

"Stop," Elise said. "Stop or I will shoot you. I will kill you."

"Then do it already. I hate myself for letting Rebecca die, so you'll just save me from myself." Billy reached forward, took the gun by its barrel, pointed it directly at her head and looked right into Elise's eyes. "Now's your chance. One shot and I'm dead."

Elise lowered the gun and turned away. "I hate you, but I

can't do it. And you know it."

"No, I don't. Didn't."

Still not looking at Billy, Elise continued, "You and all the girls at Miz Marnie's, what do you do together?"

"What do you mean?"

"I've heard they like you more than any man they've ever met."

Billy toed the floor bashfully. "Oh, um. Yeah."

"They all think you're a boy. A male."

"Yes, they do."

"So, what I'm trying to ask is . . . what do you do to them to make them so happy while they still think you're male?"

Billy examined the ceiling, the walls, the floor, the growing pools of blood . . . "Men are only after their own pleasure. I get my pleasure from pleasing them, the women."

"But how do you do that?"

"I use my mouth. I use my tongue. I use my fingers and hands. On and in them. I touch and caress and . . . and . . ."

"And what, Billy?"

"And kiss them. Like they've always wanted and needed to be kissed."

Elise took a long, deep breath. "And just . . . just how is that?"

Billy took a deep breath, put her hand on Elise's hip and pulled her to her. She gazed deep into Elise's eyes, glanced down at her full, lush lips, then back up into her eyes. "Like this," she said, slowly leaning down—granting plenty of time for Elise to stop her—to brush her lips over Elise's. She caressed them with her own, feeling them, exploring them, sucking on them.

When Elise didn't stop her, she put both hands on Elise's hips and drew her closer, then slowly slipped her tongue into Elise's mouth, to caress and explore Elise from within, in the first of the many ways she had wanted to for a very long time.

Elise pulled away slightly, gasping for air. "Please, Billy, before I couldn't because you were just a boy."

"I'm just as old as you are."

"But . . . but now . . . you're a woman, and we can't."

"Why not?"

"It's not right."

And for the first time ever in her life, Billy pushed the issue. She ran her hand over Elise's face and back through her hair, then whispered to her, "What about this isn't right?" She kissed Elise's earlobe and down her neck, cupping Elise's waist in her hands. "If you tell me to stop, I will. Just say so, and I'll back off." She picked Elise up, carrying her over-the-threshold style to the back of the house, to Elise's bedroom, where she tenderly laid Elise upon the bed.

When she tried to release Elise, though, Elise held on. Tightly. "We're both women. We shouldn't be doing this."

"Was what Rebecca said true?"

"That I love you?"

"Yes."

"I thought you were male. A boy. A . . ."

"Is it true?"

Elise relaxed and lay back on her bed. She ran her hand through Billy's hair. "It's so soft, and wavy. And yes. I do. Was what that . . . that Snake person said true?"

Billy pulled away and caressed Elise's hair, running her thumb over her lips and her cheek, then down her neck. "Yes. I love you."

"Then how could you be with all those other women?"

"I was living a lie and I didn't think I could ever have you."

Elise smiled wistfully up at her. "I'm more scared now than I've ever been. I'm even more nervous than I was just a little while ago, when I was holding a gun on a bank robber in my own kitchen and dear sweet Jesus, I just killed a man. In my kitchen. And he's still lying there!"

Billy gently pushed her back down onto the bed. "He'll still be there later." She pulled the bedclothes over Elise and snuggled in beside her. "Right now, just rest. Is it okay if I hold you?"

Elise sighed, rolled onto her side and pulled Billy's arm around her waist, gradually bringing Billy's hand up to rest between her breasts. "Yes, it is."

Billy curled into the back of her, spooning her, enjoying the sweet intimacy of their position. For the first time ever, she thought she might actually have a chance with Elise. 'Course, first she'd have to let Elise fall asleep, then haul the three dead bodies back to town and find Lucky Henry, get back here and . . .

"Are we going to be okay?" Elise asked.

"Everything's going to be fine. Just fine, baby."

• • •

Bunny still wasn't sure how it was she knew how to ride a horse, but after she and Nina stole the horses, the cop was no longer able to follow them. They rode through forest, over hill and dale, with Bunny following Nina every gallop of the way until they came out of the forest.

Bunny hadn't killed or kidnapped anyone, so the police had no reason to devote too many resources to her capture.

Being just a minor, non-lethal criminal had its bonuses, after all.

So they left the horses in the wilderness, Bunny hot-wired a car, and they continued along.

As soon as she caught her breath, she'd ask Nina if *she* knew where they were going—if they were both dreaming of the same place.

Bunny wondered just how she'd gotten along for so long without Nina.

But still, it was, and always had been, like she'd known her from another time and place.

Chapter Seven

After a few busy hours of carting three bodies to town (on two horses), and explaining as much as could be explained to Lucky Henry . . . well, about the two dead men she delivered to him, and burying Rebecca under the guidance of the town preacher, who owed Billy a few favors, all of which were used up in this one instance of burying a good Catholic girl in a Catholic cemetery (Billy knew Rebecca was a Catholic from the cross around her neck and from the time they'd spent together when they were younger), Billy came back to bed, cuddling up next to her woman.

She liked the thought of Elise being her woman. And she definitely wanted to make her hers, to claim her and . . . and . . . well, dammit, live happily ever after together. However such a thing was done. She wasn't quite sure, she'd only read about it occasionally, in some of the nonsensical books previously deemed suitable for a young woman of her caliber.

But for right now, she still hadn't even really touched Elise. They hadn't yet been intimate. And she wanted that so very, very much.

"Billy?" Elise asked, rolling over in her arms. It was only then that Billy realized that, while she was gone, Elise had removed many of her layers of clothing.

"Yes. It's me."

"Where were you?"

"Taking care of things. I told Lucky Henry I walked in for my tutoring and those two were trying to rob you. I suggested maybe he might check with other sheriffs aroundabouts, 'cause it seemed as if they might be part of that string of bank robbings he's been trying to blame on me." Billy wanted to feel this woman every day of her life, and beyond.

"What about Rebecca?"

"Father O'Ryan owed me a few. We're flush now, and she's buried in consecrated ground. Best we could do for her, really."

Elise huddled close against Billy, as if trying to bury herself in her arms. "I killed a man today."

"And he deserved to die."

"But it's not up to me to make such decisions!"

"He deserved to die."

"That doesn't matter!"

"He killed Rebecca." And that was when Elise broke out in tears, struggling against Billy's embrace, until she finally submitted and let Billy hold her, and stroke her and then kiss her tears away. "I want to make love to you."

Elise lay still, breathing deeply, for several moments, so long that Billy thought she was about to be denied. "Yes. Please."

Billy knew she had to be careful. She knew she had to be truly loving. She knew it all had to be about Elise. Elise had just watched someone die, and had killed someone else. And found out that the boy she loved but shouldn't was a woman she loved but shouldn't.

So she caressed Elise, holding her tight and loving her more than she'd ever loved anyone in all her life. She kissed her, going inside her with her tongue, moving against her, tenderly exploring her curves, touching her reverently, slowly divesting her of her remaining clothing and making love to her as best she could.

Elise was naked, giving herself to Billy, and Billy knew no one had ever touched her like this before.

Billy cradled Elise's head in an arm, kissing her. "I love you," she said. She ran her fingers lightly down Elise's arms until she took Elise's hand in her own. She slid her leg between Elise's thighs, pushing lightly against Elise's heat until Elise moaned and pushed up against her.

She slowly moved more of her weight onto Elise, situating her entire body between Elise's legs and pushing down against her center.

"Billy, oh, God, Billy," Elise said. "What are you doing to me?"

Billy kissed down her neck and across her collarbone, laying full on her, cupping her breasts and just lightly running her thumbs over her already hardened nipples. She pushed harder against Elise's heat. "I love the feel of you, naked, against me." She put a hand between Elise's leg, to enjoy her heat, to feel her, to explore her wetness. She carefully slid a single finger up into her, but not far enough to devirginate her.

She'd make love to her without hurting her. She'd make this the most wonderful thing Elise had ever experienced.

She slid another finger into Elise and caressed her clit with her thumb, kissing her and moving with her as she gasped and writhed.

Elise pulled her tight against her, holding her. "Billy, please . . ." And then she spread her legs just a little bit further.

And Billy looked down into her eyes, kissed her, and made Elise hers.

The next morning, Billy woke up, still holding Elise tightly to her, but now Elise was the one holding on to her. They were together, but they had been already and were to be yet again.

"Is that what it's all about, then?" Elise asked.

"Was it okay?"

"Now I know why all the girls like you the way they do."

Billy held Elise just a little bit tighter then. "I love you."

"Yeah, like that's a big surprise." Elise rolled over in her arms to face her. "You know I can't let you go back there now."

"I don't want to."

"So what do we do?"

Billy held Elise tight with one arm while her other caressed her hair, then the full length of her back, stopping only to cup her full, shapely ass. "We've got horses. Can you ride?"

"Hell, yes, I can ride."

"So we got us horses, a treasure map, and the rest of our lives. What's say we go for it?"

Elise rolled Billy onto her back, ripped open her shirt, and said, "Start speaking proper English, stop acting stupid, and let me see you as you really are and we might have a deal."

Little did Billy know Elise was practically defining butch/femme relations for the next century with that single move.

They packed up what they needed, and they let everyone who needed to know about their absences know about them without a lot of fanfare. They knew they could always go back to Elise's if need be, but there was also Rebecca's treasure map, holding promise of something worth much, much more.

Of course, that was before the three-day trip during which Billy taught Elise the joys of camping out beneath the stars, of sitting near a campfire, of cooking over an open flame and hunting for dinner. Well, as it turned out, Elise was a reasonable shot, but Billy was responsible for most of the hunting and skinning, since Elise really didn't like the killing parts of living in the Old

West. But camping out was fine, since they had to snuggle for warmth.

That was also before they got to where the map indicated the treasure was. Or was supposed to be.

"Okay, so Rebecca's lucky map appears to be about as lucky as the dead girl herself," Billy said, staring down at the empty trunk they'd just unearthed.

"I don't suppose the map we followed that apparently leads directly here actually points to somewhere else?" Elise said. "Or does this mean I'll be going back to teaching school?"

"Maybe we could hit the trail, become famous bank robbers on our own, then maybe run off to Australia or South America? Jump off a few cliffs along the way maybe?" She said the line again, still thinking that there was more to it than what she was saying.

"Either that or you can duck and we can grab whatever it is those guys are stashing once they're done stashing it," Elise said, pulling Billy down and pointing off into the distance, where two men were burying something with shovels and picks. It was a something in a heavy-looking chest.

Billy pushed her hat back on her head. "Yeah. I guess we could do that, too."

• • •

Unfortunately for Bunny and Nina, the cops were the nicest folks after them.

"Um," Nina said, looking behind their racing Honda Civic. "That dark sedan . . . is that undercover cops?"

Bunny adjusted her rearview mirror. "Oh, shit. Duck. Now. As far down as you can go, get."

Nina leaned down just as the car behind them opened fire. Then she reached inside Bunny's jacket, pulled out Bunny's gun, opened her own window, leaned out and shot just twice.

Bunny saw the car behind them go skidding off the road.

"I shot out their front tires," Nina said. "Now, do you want to tell me who *they* were?"

"Um. I don't think they were cops."

"Um, *no!* So who were they? Firing off at us like that? Bunny, what've you gotten us into?"

"I, um. You might want to leave me now, 'cause if I saw who I saw in my rearview mirror, we've got some real bad guys after us," Bunny said.

"You're driving, like, seventy miles an hour. How the hell am I supposed to leave you now?"

"I can stop and you can get out."

"The hell you say," Nina said before leaning over to kiss Bunny on her cheek. "Now just tell me who all the hell is behind us before I get really upset, and let me tell you this—you never want to see me well and truly angry."

"Okay, fine," Bunny said, still driving fast. "You know the cops are after me."

"Which means you should probably slow down before you get pulled over. It'd be pretty silly to get pulled over for speeding and have that be your undoing."

Bunny eased up on the gas pedal till she was going just nine over the limit. "The police are after me because I, er, rather borrowed some people's identities over the past few years."

" 'Borrowed'?"

"Okay, fine. The police are after me because I perpetrated identity theft multiple times."

"So more than bank robbery."

"That was only that once."

"Answer this question, then. Is your name really even Bunny?"

"I'm butch. There's no way in hell I'd keep a name like Bunny if it weren't mine."

"Okay, fair enough."

"Now these guys, the ones just shooting at us, I worked with them before I went into business for myself."

"And stealing people's identities, thus ruining their lives, was your business." Nina tossed her head, throwing her long, dark hair over her shoulder as she turned to look directly at Bunny, as if daring her to lie to her.

"Yes, yes, it was."

"Why am I afraid to ask what you did before that?"

"Because you should be." Bunny hardened her features, trying to not betray any of her emotions through her face.

"Then maybe I really ought to ask you to pull over so I can get out."

"I can do that, but it might be best if we wait until the next town."

Nina put one hand over one of Bunny's on the steering wheel. "I said *maybe* I ought to. I didn't actually ask." She caressed Bunny's fingers. "See, I've got this problem. I love you."

"You probably shouldn't."

"But I do. And it's been a really long time since I've loved anyone, and I've never loved anyone like I love you. I find that a really hard thing to walk away from."

"I've been having really strange dreams lately," Bunny said. "I keep dreaming that we're in the old West, but kinda talking like we do today, and I'm posing as a boy, and you're the school-marm—"

Nina burst out laughing. "Me? A schoolmarm? You have *got* to be kidding me!"

"So anyway, we run off to be criminals together—"

"That's more like it."

Bunny smiled and glanced at Nina. "You're really something special, y'know?" She entwined her fingers with Nina's. "I think I love you."

Nina thwapped Bunny. "Think?"

CHAPTER EIGHT

"This is a bank robbery," Billy said, stepping into the building with her gun leading the way.

Elise was just behind her, holding her own gun, using it to cover the room. "Nobody move!" she yelled in her best bad-guy voice, which wasn't really all that convincing. Fortunately, she had the gun to help with the convincing.

"Get down and stay down!" Billy said.

"Which is it?" a woman asked.

"What do you mean?" Billy asked.

"Don't move, or get down and stay down?" the woman said.

"Get down and stay down!" Elise yelled.

"You cover them, I'll go get the loot," Billy said to Elise, moving swiftly across the room toward the tellers and safe, pulling any guns she saw from the customers or employees and dropping them into one of her bags.

"Hold on, I've heard about y'all," one of the bank employees said, glancing up when Billy took his gun. "You never shoot nobody. You two, it's just the two of ya, right? You come in, rob the joint and leave, never hurting nobody."

Billy pressed her gun to his head. "Are you so sure about that you're willing to risk your life? And the lives of everyone else here?"

"Uh, no."

"No what?"

"No . . . sir?"

"You got that right." Billy sometimes liked re-establishing her male identity. She reckoned it'd also help them get away if it ever came down to it. "Now stay down like a good little boy while I make a slight withdrawal, y'hear?"

"Yes, sir."

Billy then went about her routine of emptying the safe and all the teller's trays into her second bag. "Let's go," she said to Elise, making sure Elise left first, even before she backed out of the bank.

They had been inside less than two minutes.

They rode quick as lightning from the small town. But one of the critical parts of their gambit was what followed: they would ride from town, hide their loot, change their garb and head back into town. Their horses were innocuous enough to never get any undue attention, except for what they wanted people to notice. So when they changed their disguises from two armed men, they would also wash a few identifying spots off their horses.

Then they'd head back into town—as a woman and her son or a man and his wife—and stay in the town until any possible posses gave up on them. The best hiding place was always right under someone's nose.

"That worries me," Billy said as they rode back into town.

"What does?" Elise said, from her graceful position sitting sidesaddle upon her horse.

"That that teller knew of us and was thinking maybe we wouldn't hurt him because we never hurt nobody."

"Anyone."

"What?"

"Anyone. What you said, 'We never hurt nobody,' is a double negative and, thus, incorrect."

Billy pulled her horse back, just a bit, so as to be able to lean over and kiss Elise. "Always the schoolmarm."

Elise ran her hand through Billy's beard. "I'm so glad we worked out how to do this. I didn't like having to stay quiet when you made love to me at night, just because everyone thought you were my son."

"I much prefer being your husband than your son," Billy said, lightly fondling Elise's breast until Elise gasped.

"Oh, please . . . Billy . . ."

Billy reached into Elise's dress to caress her naked breast. "Please, what, baby?" she whispered.

"God, not here, not now, we can't, but I want you so much . . ."

Billy stopped Elise's horse, then slid from her saddle onto Elise's, just in front of her, so they were quite close together. She unlaced the front of Elise's bodice so she could reach in and hold both of Elise's breasts at once.

"Oh, God, Billy—"

Billy squeezed both her nipples. Hard.

"Billy," Elise whispered, "you're going to make me come here and now."

"And you have a problem with that?"

"It would be most unseemly . . ." Elise gasped when Billy took one of her nipples into her mouth. "And totally out of the roles we're playing"—she yanked Billy by the hair as close as possible to her breast—"to be caught in such a compromising situation at this point," she finally managed to gasp.

Billy pulled back, re-laced Elise, kissed her and switched back to her own horse. "Till tonight, then."

Elise took a deep, deep breath, as if trying to gather herself, then looked up at Billy. "So what did you mean?"

"By what?"

"When you said it worried you. And you have to stop doing things like that to me. Any time you touch me, I melt. I always have. It's really most distracting."

"I'm worried people don't believe we might kill them. I'm worried it makes us less effective as bank robbers, if they think that. And I love distracting you. I love you."

They rode on in silence for a few more minutes, then Elise said, "So let's pick up someone to help us next time. Just for that once. She, or I, can pretend you shoot us. We'll change folks' opinions of us right quick that way."

"But how can I pretend to shoot you?"

"We just play-act. I'll put pig's blood on my shirt, keep my jacket closed over it and open it just in time to make it look like you shot me. That sort of thing?"

"I like that idea. I think it might work, really well." Billy smiled over at Elise. "Every day, you remind me why I love you so."

"Because I'm really good at crime?"

"Well, that's just a bonus. I like that you're beautiful, smart, sexy, funny and really hot in a corset."

"Behave!"

"I am!"

"Are not."

"Are too!"

"Propriety," Elise said. "We're entering town now, my dearest William, so we must behave in the manner in which we are portraying ourselves."

Billy sat up straighter in her saddle, trying on a bit of propriety. "Remember, we can still run off to South America or maybe Australia. Jump off a few cliffs along the way. That sort of thing."

"You're really stuck on that all, aren't you?"

"Sounds like fun is all."

"Do you even know where Australia is?"

"No, not really. But I've never let not knowing something stop me before." Billy was merely nodding, grunting and frowning at folks she saw as they made their way into the heart of town, which was where the hotel always was, if there was one. Billy would've reckoned this even if she hadn't been there earlier in the day, when they robbed the bank. At that point, she'd noticed where the saloon and hotel were, so now she just tried to make it look as if she'd never been there before.

Once they were checking into the hotel, Billy glanced back over her shoulder. "Honey, isn't that the gentleman we saw back in Climax?" she whispered to Elise, indicating a fellow she was sure she'd seen several times recently.

Elise winked at Billy. "I think it rightly might be. Perhaps we should go and introduce ourselves?" With that she wiggled her hips and led the way across the room to where the man in question lounged on a sofa, reading the newspaper.

Billy followed obediently along after.

Elise draped herself over the arm of the sofa, sitting on it while still lounging toward the strange man who really wasn't that much a stranger to them. "Are you following us?" she whispered into his ear.

Only Billy saw that Elise had a gun in her hand already. And Billy covered her move, so that not even the fellow Elise was questioning knew that gun was there yet.

"Excuse me?" the fellow said. "Do I know you?"

"I don't know," Elise said. "My name is Elizabeth, and this is my husband, William. But I believe you already knew this, as you've been at the exact same hotels as us for half of the last two months."

"I . . . I'm sorry," the fellow said. "You must have me mistaken for someone else."

Billy slid onto the sofa next to him, pulling her gun out to dig its barrel into his ribs, but still hiding it from view. "No. Now I'm sure we've not. Come up to our room with us."

"Or what? You'll shoot me right here and now?" he said.

"Yes. I will," Billy said. "I don't know what kind of bounty hunter you are, but you've just admitted to every worse thing I mighta thunk of you. So now you're gonna come upstairs with us, real quiet like, or I might just have to do what you don't think I will. And that might leave a nasty stain on this here nice sofa."

"You might want to listen to what my husband says," Elise said. "He's had a really bad day. You're the second person to challenge him like that. You probably don't want to know what happened the first time. Let's just say there were more than a few graves dug that night." Elise had gotten very good at lying.

The man looked up at the two of them, then, keeping his hands away from his sides but without looking like he was being held up, stood and said, "Let's go. I don't think you'll shoot me, but I do know that we need to talk."

Elise led the way down the hall and up to their room, with Billy walking next to the gentleman. Once in the room, Billy closed the door behind them and indicated that he should sit on the bed. She did this indicating with her gun, which she now held openly.

"Who are you and why are you following us?" Billy asked.

"My name is Edwin Burton, and I'm a Pinkerton's agent."

"I knew it!" Elise said.

"Your father hired me to find you," Edwin said.

"My father died a long time ago," Elise said, deliberately mistaking to whom he was referring.

"Not your father," Edwin said. "Hers."

"My name is William."

"No, it's not," he said. "It's Margaret Elizabeth Fairchild."

"Do I look like a Margaret?" Billy said.

"You're originally from Boston, Massachusetts," Edwin continued doggedly. "Your father's name is Woodward Charles

Fairchild, and your mother was Elizabeth Margaret Fairchild."

"Again," Billy said, right into his face. "Do I look like a Margaret?"

"Your disguise is convincing, I'll give you that," Edwin said. "That's why it took me so long to track you down, and then even longer to approach you."

"You didn't approach us," Elise said. "I approached you."

"I let you see me. I'm a Pinkerton. That wouldn't have happened unless I let it," he said, then to Billy, "You were named after your mother."

"Okay," Billy said, "you said Woodward Fairchild hired you? Why would a railroad tycoon need to hire a Pinkerton's agent to find his daughter?"

"Because you ran away from home nearly two decades ago," Edwin said. "Well, you were kidnapped, and the kidnappers kept you even after your father paid your ransom."

"He did no such thing!" Billy yelled, then realized what she'd just admitted. She turned from both Edwin and Elise. "He never paid, and that's why I went with them."

"He paid," Edwin said.

"Why wouldn't he have paid your ransom?" Elise asked. "I've always said he did!"

"He never loved me," Billy said. "He blamed me for Mother's death, and he never forgave me." She knew the truth of the matter from Rebecca—that Carl and Frank and the others lied about the ransom to use her, and it was just easier to say he didn't pay.

"He paid your ransom," Edwin said.

"No, he didn't."

"Billy," Elise said. "Who are you going to believe, your father or the men who kidnapped you? After all, you *did* tell me you helped them steal from your father's trains, so why would they let you go if you could help them like that?"

Before Billy could say anything, Edwin said, "He wanted you

back then, and he still does. He was convinced the kidnappers had kept you, that you were working with them, but it was only once he realized he was dying that he hired us to find you."

"Hold up," Billy said. "What'd you say?"

"I said," Edwin said, "it was only once he realized he was dying that he hired us to find you."

"He's dying?" Billy asked.

"Yes, he is," Edwin said. "That's why he was traveling to California. He thought that might be where you headed. He couldn't accept that they might've killed you. He couldn't lose you, too."

"What's he dying from?" Elise asked.

"Blood in his lungs. He doesn't have long to live."

"Why does he want to find his daughter?" Elise asked.

Edwin shrugged. "He loves her."

"What's Billy here going to gain from going back to him?"

"Well, she—and you—will get a trip to California," Edwin said. "And, from what he said, Margaret here will also get all his money and everything else when he dies. I'd go with me if even just for that."

"How'd you find me?" Billy asked.

Again Edwin shrugged. "We started with your kidnappers and ended up at a dead end. Then your father telegraphed me to let me know you were one of the 'men' who robbed him and kidnapped Rebecca. That gave me a more recent starting place that I could work from."

"Does he know they killed Rebecca?" Billy asked.

Edwin looked down. "Hey, can I get a drink or something?"

"Honey," Billy said to Elise. "Can you go down to the saloon and get us a bottle? I really don't want to be having this conversation in public."

"I think maybe you might want to be the one going into the saloon," Elise said.

"Okay," Billy said. "You're right about that. You got your

gun?"

Billy did worry about all that Edwin might tell Elise while she was gone, just like she worried about all that Elise might tell Edwin, but what it really came down to for her was that she knew she needed to trust Elise and couldn't keep holding back from the woman she loved and planned on spending the rest of her life with.

When she returned with the whiskey, Elise was sitting in the one chair in the room, looking at Edwin. Billy could tell they'd been talking. She could only guess that Edwin had filled Elise in on any facts she hadn't yet shared with her.

And now she said, "So Da recognized me on the train, and he's all right with me being a boy?"

"I met your father, once," Edwin said. "When he first became a client. I was one of the initial investigators. He said you read a lot. You really liked Westerns and wanted to be an explorer, an adventurer, a bank robber and a lot of other things. Given all he said—can I get that drink now?—I really wasn't surprised when he said you were consorting with train robbers."

Billy poured all of them a drink and said, "So how did you track me down?"

"Good, hard, precise detective work," Edwin said. "I knew where and when the train was robbed, and that nobody ever contacted Mr. Fairchild about the ransom on Rebecca Smythe. I could only suspect that Miss Smythe was no longer alive. So I started investigating areas near where the train was held up, and found evidence of a great many bank robberies, and then . . . a missing schoolmarm. I went from there."

"And you made the leap from me being female to male how exactly?" Billy asked.

"Your father told me that. Once he realized that was you he'd seen on the train. And your male/female identity is a key point of your disguise. I just had to follow the clues from there." He sipped at his drink, looking over the rim at Billy.

"And yet you could just be a bounty hunter," Billy said. "Trying to get me to admit something."

"You've already admitted enough that you've got to either believe me or kill me." Again he sipped, calmly.

"So what do you want us to do?" Elise asked.

"Come with me, to California, so Mr. Fairchild can say good-bye to his only child before he dies."

• • •

It was when they were driving through the remains of Climax, Oklahoma, that Bunny had a serious case of déjà vu. And then she remembered the map that was the bulk of her inheritance from her father.

"What is it?" Nina asked. "Do you recognize something?"

"Yeah, actually, I kinda do," Bunny said, pulling a sheet of paper out of her hip pocket. "Tell me what you see on this."

"Well, I see Climax, and I see that mountain there, and . . . Wait a minute. You *have* been here before!"

"No. I haven't. Da left me this. And I'm suddenly thinking that . . . Well. When I was growing up, he kept saying we just needed to make it to Climax for all our problems to be solved. When I was young, I didn't know what to make of it. Later, when I thought back, well, I thought it was a dirty joke."

"And now you think he meant a place in Oklahoma?"

"Yeah. Because I'm sure I've been here before." Bunny pulled off to the side of the dirt road, parked the car and got out. She turned around in the fading twilight and saw the town as it was in its heyday, which wasn't much. She ran into the saloon, bursting through the swinging doors.

"What is it?" Nina said from right behind her.

"This is it. This was the saloon. The brothel. Marnie, Grace, Lucky Henry . . . they were all here . . . I ran, just like this, before, through all these doors! I dreamt all of this—I saw all of this!" She charged upstairs, kicking in one door after another until she stopped.

Nina grabbed her from behind. "Stop! This is probably some sort of historic landmark or something!"

"Oh, and yeah, with my list of felonies, that's just what I gotta be worried about," Bunny said, pulling out of Nina's arms. "I'll tell you what, if there's not money under . . ." She moved across the room, trying to remember the pacing, seeing back in time to remember just what the then-she was doing until she stopped on a floorboard. "If there's no money, cash, gold, under this floorboard, we'll leave this town."

"Otherwise?"

"Otherwise, we'll follow the map Da left me and see what that turns up for us." Bunny ran across the room to Nina, to grasp her hands in her own. "I love you. I can't believe you're still with me, and I want to do something to make it all right. I want to somehow be worth it all."

"Then you're on."

CHAPTER NINE

His room was dark, with the shades drawn all the way down. He looked pale and thin, not at all the robust and powerful man she remembered from her youth, or even the last time she saw him a bit over a decade before.

"Margaret," he said, though it was barely more than a whisper, "they found you."

Billy, dressed as a man—as Elise's husband William—went to her father's bedside and took his hand, sitting on the side of his bed. "Da?"

"Seeing you like this really doesn't surprise me," he gasped out in halting breaths. He reached up a shaking hand to touch her fake beard. "You never were content to be just a girl. You never wanted to marry—"

"But I did, Da. I have a partner. A mate." Billy stood and opened her arm to indicate Elise. "Her name's Elise, sir."

Elise haltingly stepped forward, took Mr. Fairchild's hand and shook it lightly. "Pleasure to meet you, sir."

Woodward Fairchild smiled. "I wanted a son. I guess now I got one. And a daughter as well. Now, if you two could only give me a grandchild, I could die a happy man."

Elise smiled down at him. "Oh, sir—"

"Please, feel free to call me Woodward."

"Woodward," Elise repeated. "I'm sure things are not as bad as you think they are."

"I'm old, I'm tired, I'm sick, I'm dying." He broke out into a massive coughing fit.

"Oh, balderdash," Elise said, sitting on the bed next to his head and rubbing his back, apparently trying to ease his suffering.

"Young lady, I know what's happening and have no need for useless hope." His face was red from coughing.

Elise ran a hand over his heated forehead, picked up a washcloth from the bedside table, dampened it in the basin of water next to it and used it to cool his overheated head. "Back home in Oklahoma where I come from, I saw people a lot older, sicker and tireder than you are, and they lived for years with far less than you've got, old man."

" 'Tireder'?" Woodward said. "Is that even a word?"

"Hey, she's a schoolmarm, so if she says it, it's got to be right," Billy said.

"A schoolmarm? Leave it to my daughter to find herself a smart woman," Woodward said. "Now, maybe you can just teach this daughter of mine some manners."

Elise wrapped an arm around Billy's waist. "I've been working on it."

"Aw, hey, I'm not that bad!" Billy said.

"Except when you're acting like an adolescent male," Elise said, crossing her arms over her chest and staring at Billy with a raised eyebrow.

"Margaret—" Woodward started.

"Da, it's Billy now. Or William."

"I'm not sure I can get used to that," Woodward said, "but I'll try, because I don't want to lose you again. Especially now that you're all I have left."

"What about all your friends and business partners back home?" Billy asked.

"They don't really matter. They never really did. You and your mother are my family. Especially now that I'm here, so far away from everyone else . . . I came all this way to die just with the hope that I might see you one last time."

When Billy finally stepped out to get dinner, after she and Elise determined they would eat in shifts, at least for a while, Woodward indicated to Elise that she should take his hand. "There's something I want you to do for me."

"What is that?"

"I want you and her to have a child."

"That isn't exactly possible."

"Don't be silly, girl. I know that. I meant that you two should adopt a baby—maybe one of the girls Billy used to work with has one she doesn't exactly want, or maybe you can go to an orphanage or some such and get one that way. I want you two to have a child because I know how much Mar-Billy meant to me when I lost her Ma."

Elise smiled. "And this doesn't have anything to do with preserving the family name or anything like that?"

"No. Though I wouldn't mind if the trains and buildings and everything else I've spent my life building stayed in the family somehow. Even though the name might be lost, I'd like to think that it stays with us. That what I've spent my life doing continues to matter to people loved by those I love. And that it helps them and makes life easier for them."

"With you being so earnest, if you actually had a son, I might lie with him just to try to give you a real grandchild. A real heir."

She held Woodward's hand and laid a hand on her own belly.

Woodward laughed for the first time in Elise's presence. It was a dry, heaving laugh, but a laugh nonetheless. "If my Mar-Billy is anything like me, she'd never allow such!"

"No, I don't reckon that she would, either."

He took Elise's hand in his. "I'm glad she has you to make her happy, though. And it's not all about blood. It's really about love."

"You're not like any man I've ever met before."

"I got everything I ever wished for and lost everything I ever loved. It changes a man's perspective. You start to realize what's really important." He held Elise's hand even tighter. "Take care of my daughter, and try to make her happy. But make sure she makes you happy, too. Keep her on her toes, and don't let her get too distracted by everything else. That was my undoing for a while there. I lost too many years to everything else, and what was important was gone before I knew it."

"Whatever are you talking about, old man?"

"That dresser, over there, across the room . . ."

"What?"

"In the top drawer are two envelopes. Bring them to me, please."

Elise did as instructed, curious, but unwilling to open them to peek inside while he was right there.

He took them both, looked at them, and handed one back to her. "Toss this in the fire, please."

"But—"

"Just do it, Elise. It's just the alternate will I brought with me in case I was unable to locate Margaret."

And it was that easy. Woodward had brought two wills with him, and the one that survived left everything to Margaret Fairchild, aka Billy.

Before he died just over a year later, Woodward Fairchild held his grandchild, the natural daughter of Grace, the adopted daughter of William and Elise. He also turned over all his businesses to Billy and Elise, teaching them as best he could how to run them.

After all, they'd been successful in many different endeavors before, so he was sure they'd be successful no matter what task was put to them. How different was armed robbery from business when all was said and done?

He lasted longer than he ever thought he would.

And he went back home, back to Massachusetts, on one of his own trains, to be buried next to his wife.

What he didn't know was that Billy and Elise took his initial offer with more than a few reservations. They hid their fortune so in case he wasn't sincere, and in case he tried to take over their lives and run them himself, they could leave him. And they hid all that money in a place Billy knew as well as she knew Elise's body . . .

"I just know we got to do this, baby," Billy said, as they left the fortune, the clues, the . . .

Maybe with their own last breaths they'd trust Woodward Fairchild, but until his, Billy still wasn't quite able to.

• • •

Bunny yanked up the floorboard, prying it up with her keys. Underneath lay a satchel full of gold coins. She opened the velvet bag and showed it to Nina, pouring the coins out onto the floor.

"That's . . . That's . . . this is kinda eerie, y'know?" Nina bent down to finger the gold coins. "Unless, of course, this is some sort of elaborate con aimed at me."

"Oh, God no! What would make you think that?"

"Everything you told me was a lie, and the more I learn about you, the worse things get."

"And now I'm telling you the truth because I'm in love with you and I've been trying like hell to get you to leave me but you're not and so now I'm just telling you the truth. I've dreamt about this place. I've dreamt about all sorts of people, and some of them are like . . . you and me in a different life. I think that just maybe you and I buried a treasure centuries ago, and this is the map to it. I think us ending up here, together, with you giving me the strength to keep running, and now to go looking, is just what we needed to find this treasure and change our lives, our futures, once and for all."

"What are you saying, Bunny?"

"I'm saying I think maybe we might just want to go on a treasure hunt, 'cause, just maybe, we might've found the starting point."

"What the heck are you talking about?"

"Da left me a treasure map. It was about all he left me. It starts at a town called Climax—and you just would not believe how many towns are named that in this country—but I think maybe we found the right one. The starting point."

"So this is all based on dreams and a map your broke, drunk father left you?"

"Yes. But I've never been west of Ohio before, yet I knew this would be here," Bunny said, indicating the golden doubloons. "I reckon this means it's worth it to follow the treasure map, because . . . well . . ."

"What?"

"Maybe, just maybe, my dreams are real. And the map is real."

"Your dreams are real?"

"Yes. You and I were bank robbers in the Old West. But my Da was a train mogul and left us a fortune."

"Oh, shit," Nina said.

"What?"

"Um, have you forgotten that when we met you were a bank robber?"

"Well, um, technically I was a credit-union robber—"

"And would-be robber-baron," Nina said. "Now come here and steal a kiss."

DESERT

SPRING

BARBARA JOHNSON

Chapter One

A painted wagon, its once bright colors dulled by the elements, lumbered down the crude desert road. Dust devils swirled around its wheels and the sturdy legs of the big red horse that pulled it. High up in the driver's seat, Corinne coughed and blinked. Sweat ran down her suntanned face, leaving jagged lines through the fine powdery dirt that covered her from head to foot. The day was miserably hot; she could see her horse's exhaustion in its plodding gait and drooping head. Corinne shaded her eyes and squinted into the dazzling sunlight. She knew if she didn't find a town soon, both she and the horse would surely die. Their water supply was dangerously low. Was that an outcropping of rocks ahead, or yet another mirage?

Gently she shook the reins and clucked softly. Stumbling, the horse gallantly quickened its pace, only to drop back to its tired plodding after only a few minutes. Half an hour later, wagon and horse reached the outcrop of rocks whose surfaces glittered with gold flecks. Corinne gratefully pulled into a meager patch of shade. The temperature dropped by a least five degrees. She quickly jumped down from the wagon and immediately released her horse from its harness. From within the cool, dark recesses of the wagon she poured some precious water into a bucket and gave it to the horse to drink before she herself drank from the canteen hanging at her waist.

For a few peaceful moments, woman and horse enjoyed the cool shade and refreshing, though warm, water. When the horse finished drinking, Corinne put the bucket back inside the wagon and then slid down against the rock until she squatted on the ground. She closed her eyes, trying not to let the depression take hold of her. She'd been on the road for months now, traveling she knew not where. Sometimes the hardship and uncertainty kept her from remembering, but most of the time she could still vividly see the empty, burned-out shell of what was once a log cabin. The outlaws had attacked swiftly while Corinne was away hunting, sparing nothing and no one, least of all the woman and her young daughter, who they left raped and murdered not far from the cabin. The animals they'd chosen not to take were also slaughtered, their carcasses left to rot, though wild scavengers had made swift work of them. Corinne had been gone only two days.

Whimpering, Corinne opened her eyes again, staring out into the desert that had become her home. It was dry and barren, so unlike the lush Virginia forest she had left behind. She didn't notice the beauty of delicate spring flowers on the desert cacti. She felt only the heat and the dryness in her throat. With a sigh she glanced at the sky, hoping to see a sign that a thunderstorm might sweep through, but only the shimmering sun filled her vision. A fat lizard scurried across her boot, drawing her attention. It reminded her that she hadn't eaten in two days.

Her remaining rations consisted of some beef jerky, dry biscuits and wrinkled apples. Even her horse's oats and hay were in short supply. The thought of eating made her throat feel more parched. Swallowing painfully, she stood up and brushed the sand off of her denim trousers. The action brought her loosely knotted hair tumbling down to her waist. It felt hot against her blue, cotton work shirt.

"Damnation!" she swore out loud as she hastily scooped her hair onto her head again. "Why don't I just cut this?"

The horse looked up at the sound of her voice, almost as if in surprise. Its long-lashed brown eyes regarded her solemnly. Corinne smiled wanly and walked over to stroke the animal's neck. Her fingers through the coarse hair stirred up a fine dust that made Corinne sneeze. The horse had been her sole companion for months now, and she realized in that moment that it deserved more than the cursory attention she gave. She hadn't even named the poor beast.

Scratching under its tangled mane, she said, "I think you deserve a name, don't you? What should it be?" She contemplated its strawberry roan color. "Maybe I'll just call you Red. Simple. Easy. Yes, that's it. How ya doin', Red?"

Corinne sighed, then led the animal back to the wagon, intending to hitch it up again. But first, another drink for the road. She had a new compassionate respect for Red and intended to make up for her months of shoddy attention. Just as she was about to reach into the wagon, she heard the jingling of reins. Immediately on guard, she pulled out a rifle, having left her Colt revolver still hung in its holster on the back of the driver's seat.

Cautiously, she stepped away from the wagon, looking around it to the front. A strange contraption greeted her eyes— a two-storied wagon with walls decorated in brightly painted murals. In the driver's seat sat a man who wore the biggest darn cowboy hat she had ever seen. She blinked her eyes. Was he really shirtless?

Standing in the road with her legs spread in an aggressive

stance, she held the rifle against her chest, finger on the trigger, ready at a moment's notice to fire. As the other wagon came to a halt, the two regarded each other in silence.

To Corinne's eye, he was not too unpleasing, for a man. He was indeed shirtless, his deep bronze tan showing off finely developed muscles. She couldn't see his hair under the uptilted hat, but she assumed it was as dark as the deep black of his twinkling eyes. He had an aquiline nose and a generous, almost feminine, mouth. He appeared to be tall; his denim-encased legs were long and slender. Black boots elaborately decorated with silver were, in her mind, too fancy for desert wear. Her gaze followed the long line of his smooth arms and registered surprise at his perfectly manicured longish nails. Finally, she realized that he was completely clean shaven; not one hair marred his smooth baby-face cheeks, chest and arms.

Corinne shifted a trifle uneasily as the stranger continued his silent assessment of her. Was he noticing that her hips were a little too wide to be male, and that the rifle didn't really hide a pair of very obvious feminine breasts. She gritted her teeth, feeling the pain of her cracked, dry hands as her grip on her rifle tightened. She glanced down ever so briefly, noticing her sun-browned skin and broken nails. Surely they did not give away her sex? It was important to her that she pass as a man, for her own safety if nothing else, and most times she succeeded.

The man relaxed his shoulders and dropped the reins. He tipped his hat ever so slightly and smiled broadly. "Well, howdy, ma'am," he said with a soft western drawl. "The name's Davy Millwood, travelin' medicine man and tinker by trade, actor by desire."

Corinne didn't move or change her stance, but she loosened her grip on the rifle and lost the seriousness in her eyes. She smiled back at him, instinctively recognizing a kindred spirit. Her virtue would have nothing to fear from this man. "Corinne Adamson," she answered. "No trade, no desire."

"Been travelin' a long time, have you?" His eyes raked over her and her belongings. "Alone?"

Corinne's grip on the rifle tightened once again. Maybe she was wrong in her assessment of him. Wondering if he had an accomplice hiding in his wagon, she glanced nervously behind him. The smile left her lips as she gazed at him without answering. He cocked his eyebrows, perhaps at the smoldering suspicion in her eyes. Unexpectedly, he jumped down from the wagon with a dancer's grace and stood in the road, crossing his arms in front of him and leaning with his weight on his left foot. Corinne stepped backed involuntarily and pointed her rifle at his chest. She didn't like the situation one bit.

"You certainly are a suspicious lass," he drawled, apparently unperturbed by the rifle aimed at his heart. "I don't have dishonorable intentions." For emphasis he opened his arms with a wide theatrical flourish and let them fall to his sides.

"What're you doin' out this way? You alone too?"

Davy sighed. "Yes. My companion left me a couple of towns ago. Said he couldn't handle being unsettled anymore. Left me for a bartender. Can you believe it?"

Corinne laughed in spite of herself. It was a light musical sound. She lowered the rifle and relaxed her stance. They smiled at each other, almost like two old friends meeting after a long time apart.

"Could you take off that darn hat?" she asked suddenly.

Davy swept it off his head to reveal hair as black as coal, thick and wavy. It would be the envy of anyone, man or woman. His dark eyes sparkled with laughter as his wide mouth curved into a smile to reveal surprisingly good teeth. "Does it meet with your approval?"

"Most certainly." Corinne chuckled. "That's the biggest darn hat I've ever seen."

"I keep it to look intimidatin'. Josh told me it didn't work. What does he know anyway? So, where ya headed? Might be we could travel a ways together?"

Travel. Corinne suddenly felt very tired. She looked over at Red, whose ears pricked up with interest at the goings on, especially the fact that another horse was nearby. Maybe it was time for her to find a place to settle. She didn't realize until now how much she missed being around people. Having someone to talk to. It would be pleasant to travel with Davy.

"Do you know where I can get some water and supplies?" she asked. "I'm just about out."

Davy put his hat back on and hooked his thumbs inside the waist of his denims. He tapped a booted toe, its silver toeplate flashing in the sun. "I just passed through a town 'bout twenty miles back. Bisbee I think the name was. I was gonna stay awhile, but it was early mornin' an' I just didn't. Don't really know what's there, but we could check it out."

Corinne shook her head. "I don't want you backtracking, but thanks. I'll just go on by myself. I think my supplies will last another twenty miles."

"Nonsense! Now, you go harness up that old nag o' yours and we'll git goin'. I'm kinda tired of travelin' anyway. Maybe Josh was right." He turned toward his wagon, then spun around again to face her. "If you cut that hair, you'd feel a heck of a lot better."

Corinne reached up and patted her thick hair. Wasn't it supposed to be a woman's pride and glory? Still, being out West had made her think often of cutting it off. And it wasn't like she had anything or anyone back east waiting for her. "Think you could do it, Davy?" she asked with a note of trepidation. Scissors hadn't touched her hair since she was twelve.

Davy had leapt onto his wagon and was rummaging around in the large carpetbag sitting on the seat beside him. With a small shriek he held a pair of scissors high above his head, then jumped to the ground and walked sedately over to where Corinne stood in the shade.

"Voilá!" he said with a smile. He fingered her tresses. "I knew a prostitute once whose hair was just this lovely cinnamon color."

Corinne choked on her laughter, not knowing whether to be insulted or amused. Instead, she retrieved a small three-legged stool from her wagon and sat down. Davy got to work without another word. She could feel her thick hair slithering down her back as he snipped. He made little humming noises as he worked, and she could just visualize his mouth pursing in concentration. His fingers lightly brushed her neck, causing goose bumps to rise up on her scalp. Her head tingled all over. With one last snip, Davy stepped away from Corinne on her stool. He stood looking at her, one hand on his hip and the other holding the scissors at shoulder height. His self-satisfied smile made her nervous. She reached a tentative hand to her hair and gasped. He'd cut it as short as a man's! After almost fifteen years of being weighed down by length, her new short hair felt like a springy mass of unruly curls and feathery spikes. Corinne closed her eyes and asked for a mirror.

She almost shrieked when she opened her eyes and stared into the small mirror Davy handed her. Her gray eyes wide with surprise, Corinne turned her head slowly left and right. Despite its wild appearance, she decided she liked the haircut. With a little time it would settle down, and she wouldn't look as if she'd just come from bed.

"It'll look better after a few days," Davy said, trying to hide a smile behind his hand.

Corinne reached down and picked up the pile of cinnamon-colored hair that circled around her ankles. It felt like silken threads in her hands. She sighed. Anne had loved her hair, but that was all part of the past now. She looked up and smiled at the handsome man standing uncertainly before her.

"I like it just fine, Davy."

He let out an exaggerated sigh of relief. "Well, Cory my girl, let's get a move on. The idea of sleepin' in a real bed tonight sounds mighty good."

Corinne quickly hitched the newly named Red to harness. They'd have to travel quickly if they wanted to reach Bisbee in time to check in at the local hotel. That is, if the town even had a hotel. She didn't really think they could make it. The afternoon in the desert was the most brutal time of day, and their horses would need to rest frequently. Still, she felt more lighthearted than she had in a long time. As Red picked up speed to follow Davy's brightly painted wagon, Corinne liked the exhilarating feel of the wind through her newly shorn hair. She knew she should put on a hat, but decided to wait until the sun became unbearable. For the first time since Anne's and Lisbeth's deaths, Corinne felt the burden of depression lifting. She had a good feeling about this town called Bisbee.

CHAPTER TWO

The glowing yellow sun rose brilliantly above the magnificent Mule Mountains whose deep purple shadows crept over the sleeping copper-mining town of Bisbee, Arizona. Everywhere, desert creatures were scurrying into or out of burrows deep in the grayish-white sand or in the crags of scattered rocks and boulders. It was springtime in the desert, and the sparse vegetation was growing and glowing with new life following a heavy rain. The cacti presented jewel-like flowers that attracted insects and birds alike. Some, like the prickly pears and chollas, would provide Bisbee's residents with succulent fruit, the likes of which they had only a few short weeks every year.

The morning's sounds echoed in the little valley. Domesticated animals began to cry for their morning feedings, and the rumble of horses and carts as they headed for the mine after a day of rest broke the quiet stillness of the desert night.

Like the wives of the miners, Aimee Calhoun was awake and up before dawn. She had already fixed breakfast for her husband, Jim, and left it warming on the coal stove. He would not be up for another hour at least. Aimee loved the early morning, however, and enjoyed the time alone in the general store that was her pride and joy.

Aimee entered the store, which was below their living quarters. In the gray dawn light she could see dust motes playing in the faint sunlight beginning to stream through the sparkling and spotless windows. She gazed around her with satisfaction at the neatly stocked shelves—the colorful bolts of fabric on the big table in the center of the room, the large bags of flour and sugar and other staples that leaned against the walls, and, her favorite thing, the books that lined the low shelves under the front windows. Not many people bought those books, but Aimee loved to read and she felt the books made her store just a bit more special than anyone else's. And on the ledge right under the window, the morning sun caught the glint of pyrite. Fool's gold. The children loved it, and though the rocks could be found easily enough, Aimee sold palm-sized chunks of it for a penny apiece.

Her Siamese cat, which Aimee had taken as payment from one of the Chinese launderers, came over and rubbed itself against her light wool skirt. She bent down to scratch under its chin.

"How are you doing today, Puss," she crooned softly as the cat began to purr loudly. "Did you keep the mice out of my grain last night?"

Aimee straightened up and walked outside to behind the store where a thickly walled building housed their perishable foodstuffs. Inside, a well dug deep into the earth helped keep the building cool even in the hottest months. She poured thick cream into a saucer and came back into the store. Puss jumped up on the counter and began to lap up the cream, purring contentedly. Aimee smiled, then took up her broom to sweep the store's already immaculate floor. Every night she swept and mopped the floor after the store closed, then she restocked the shelves and rearranged and straightened the bolts of fabric. Jim dictated how things were arranged, but she didn't mind. Sometimes she wished no one would come to the store and disturb its perfect order. That was one reason she loved Sundays, because then she got her wish and could come and enjoy the peace and quiet and read a book.

As she swept, she caught a glimpse of herself in the mirror behind the confectionery counter. Her snow-white blouse, immaculately ironed and starched, was tucked perfectly into her pale-blue, wool skirt. A brown leather belt circled her tiny waist. She knew her brown boots were polished to a high gloss. Her thick chestnut hair was plaited and gathered into a bun at the nape of her neck, leaving wispy tendrils to frame her face. From her wide brown eyes radiated fine lines that deepened when she smiled. Her once porcelain skin was permanently tanned a rosy brown. She stopped to gaze at her reflection, seeing for the first time a face grown worn with the hard life of a pioneer woman. It was a life the drawing rooms of her youth had not prepared her for, yet she had survived and could even say she was happy now. This morning, however, she was surprised to feel a strong twinge of discontent, but she dismissed it quickly by thinking it a symptom of her coming monthly cycle.

Propping the broom in its corner, she checked everything in the store one more time before heading back upstairs to wake her husband. When he wasn't working in the store he was traveling to buy and order goods, and today would be a traveling day. He would be gone at least two weeks and, though Aimee would never acknowledge it, she enjoyed the time alone. It just didn't seem decent to be glad that one's husband was away. Jim was a fine man, strong and handsome, and a good provider, but Aimee had felt a dissatisfaction for some time now, a dissatisfaction that she believed she'd overcome years ago.

Having been born and brought up in the east, Aimee's parents had schooled her well. She hadn't really given any thought to marriage because she had ambitions to become a teacher, but then Jim had come into her life and swept her off her feet before she realized what was happening. And although he was almost fifteen years older than she, her parents had consented to the marriage. They were content that first year in New York, until Jim got word of the opportunities out West. Despite Aimee's objections, he'd packed them up and they'd traveled by wagon train to Arizona, an arduous journey that had almost killed them both.

In the beginning it was hard for her not to feel resentment. Her privileged upbringing had not prepared her for such a hard life, one that made her feel at times like a caged bird. She had no say in any of their decisions. Jim thought he'd become rich from gold or silver or copper, but he'd not listened to her misgivings. Like she'd warned, he discovered the life of a miner was just too hard for a college-educated New Englander, so he gave up after only a year. And instead of returning home, for fear of derision from his family and friends for unrealized dreams, he used the small amount of gold he had found to build and stock the general store in the new town of Bisbee, where he and Aimee had lived for five years now. It hadn't been easy trying to make a living from the store at first, but by the second year they'd actually made a small profit. It didn't help that Aimee had been desperately unhappy and very homesick, but she'd come to enjoy her somewhat predictable existence, though she still wished Jim wasn't so controlling. The books made all the difference in the world. She'd read them all several times, but never tired of any of them. It almost made her cry when a customer did buy one.

And though she would never admit it to anyone, there were still times when she wished she'd never married. She chided herself when such thoughts entered her mind, feeling she was being ungrateful for everything Jim had provided.

But this day, she entered the darkened bedroom and pulled on the white window shade. It flapped up loudly as she approached the bed. Jim looked so like a child when he slept that Aimee couldn't help but smile as she brushed his brow softly, pushing aside a golden curl.

"Wake up lazy one," Aimee said as she shook him. "I swear, you'd think you were a schoolboy instead of a married man."

Jim opened one eye and groaned. He never had gotten used to the early hours in the desert town. "You look delectable," he responded as he pulled his wife down on the bed. "How about staying for a while?" He kissed her as she struggled in his arms.

"No use actin' like some rich easterner with time on your hands," she laughed as she extricated herself from his firm grasp. "I got your breakfast ready and your bag all packed. Now, up with you."

He threw the thin linen sheet off of his lean body and stood tall. He didn't have a stitch of clothing on, which is how he'd slept ever since they'd arrived in the hot Arizona town. Aimee averted her eyes from his obvious arousal, instead going to the chest of drawers upon which stood an old and chipped china basin. She poured the water for his wash and shave. He came up behind her and pressed his body into hers, rubbing against her sensually.

"Come on, darlin'," he murmured into her ear. "We have time. Don't be so distant, my love. You know how long it's been?"

She twisted her neck as his tongue shot into her ear. He knew she hated that. His hands had her arms caught in a steel grip. He continued to press his body into hers. With a sigh she turned her face toward his, knowing there was no way to get out of doing her wifely duty that morning. You'd think after seven years of marriage he'd be tired of sex, she thought, as she allowed him to remove her belt, then unbutton her skirt to pull it off. As he tugged impatiently at the laces of her boots, he accidentally ripped the lace edging at the knee of her pantalets. Frowning, she knocked his hands away and finished undressing herself.

The light got brighter through the open window as the sun rose high in the sky. An insect buzzed incessantly, caught in the white, lace curtain moving gently with the desert breeze. Aimee lay on the bed on her back, staring at the cracks in the ceiling. Her fingertips rested lightly on the broad shoulders of her husband as he rutted and groaned above her. A few minutes later he let out a coyote-like yelp and collapsed in a sweaty heap on top of her. The whole act had taken place in less than fifteen minutes. Aimee counted slowly to ten and, as he had done for seven years, Jim rolled off of her and lay breathing like an overworked draft horse.

Silently, she rose off the bed and walked to the chest of drawers. Placing the china basin on the floor, Aimee stood on a braided Indian rug and proceeded to sponge the harsh male scent of him off of her skin. Even after seven years, sex was one aspect of married life that she detested, for she took no pleasure from it. Sometimes she wished Jim would visit Fanny Palmer's brothel just so he would leave her alone. Either that, or take a mistress. She knew he admired Belle Foster, the woman abandoned by a no-good husband.

She finished washing and padded softly to the clothes cupboard, where she took out fresh undergarments. She dressed quickly, catching her husband's eye in the mirror as she tried to fix her hair without having to rebraid it. He watched her dress, a satiated grin on his face.

"You are the best wife in the world," he said as she turned to face the bed.

She smiled, as he expected her to. "Enough dillydallying. It's already late, and you'll be lucky if your breakfast isn't hard as a rock." From the doorway she added, "I have to open the store."

Aimee descended the steep wooden stairs to the store. It was much warmer inside now, but the quiet soothed her jangled nerves. She always needed time to recover after Jim had sex with her. In the beginning it was very frequent. Giving her a few days' respite after the initial shock of her first time, Jim had then demanded her body daily. He hoped for children, but that was not to be. At times, Aimee wished she'd had children because maybe then he would have left her alone. He blamed her for not conceiving, but she was educated enough to know the man could also be at fault. Absently fingering a piece of calico material, she told herself to be grateful her husband's demands had decreased to the point where four or five times a month was enough for him.

Hearing a scratching on the window, Aimee looked up to see the widow Adams peeking in. Nearly every morning the old woman was hovering outside long before the store was due to open. With a shake of her head, Aimee unlocked the doors and stepped back in haste as Mrs. Adams hobbled in, swinging her cane like a weapon.

"You youngsters sleep too long," she croaked. "I've been up since before the cock crowed. Now, where do you have canning supplies?"

Mrs. Adams had to be close to ninety years old. No one in Bisbee knew her first name, or when exactly she'd arrived. Having outlived three husbands, she was regarded with awe by most residents and she terrified the young children.

She rarely bought anything in the store herself, but every morning she asked where the canning supplies were. Mrs. Adams had a young Chinese housekeeper who did all the shopping for her, and who took care of her and the house. Aimee secretly believed Mrs. Adams insisted on riding into town each day on her rickety buckboard with its decrepit, swaybacked nag because doing so kept her alive. She'd seen three husbands take to their beds and never get up again, and was determined not to suffer the same fate. By the time Aimee set the latch so the door would stay open, Mrs. Adams was at the middle table, fingering the colorful bolts of cloth.

"Let me know if I can help you, Mrs. Adams," Aimee said

automatically as she walked behind the apothecary counter. She began an inventory of the herbs and medicines and tinctures stored in darkly tinted bottles. She wished she knew more about them, but learned more each time the town's doctor or the Chinese came in for an order. The stock was low; she'd have to remind Jim to buy some.

Two young children ran into the store just as Jim came down the stairs, and all three collided. Jim caught himself on the nearest countertop, but the youngsters landed with thuds on their bottoms. The boy began to yowl. The girl stood and wiped the dust off her lavender cotton dress, tossing her long blond pigtails in disgust.

"Oh, stop yer yammerin'," she said sharply to the boy and swatted his head, which made him scream louder.

Jim quickly walked to the confectionery counter and scooped a handful of jellybeans out of a large glass canister. He went to the boy and held out his hand. The candies nestled in a colorful bribe in his palm. The boy stopped yelling and scrambled to his feet. He stuffed the jellybeans into his mouth all at once, then stood there scowling and chewing, his cheeks puffed out like a chipmunk's.

Aimee came from around the opposite counter. The whole incident had given her a headache. She glared at Jim. How dare he give away jellybeans to that horrible little boy? Every time Amos came into the store he caused trouble, and if Jim was there he would give the child some kind of sweet. Aimee shook her head in exasperation. Jim might be the one who ordered and purchased all the merchandise for the store, but if not for her their ledgers would show nothing but IOUs. Jim was a sucker for a hard-luck story, especially one from a comely woman. If she owned the store, things would be a lot different. But she didn't own the store, so what could she do?

"Amos. Jezebel. What are you doing here without your mother?" Aimee asked, standing before them with her hands on her hips.

The girl gave a disdainful sniff. "Mama needs some Indian bark fer her monthly pains. An' she said we could have some rock candy too."

Aimee glanced at Mrs. Adams, who was listening intently. Everyone in town knew that the children's mother couldn't pay her bills since her card-cheating husband had fled for his life.

"I'll give you the Indian bark, but no rock candy until your mother has paid her last bill."

Jezebel stamped her foot. "You know Mama can't pay. Why do we have to suffer 'cause she were too stupid to keep Daddy around?"

Jim came over to Aimee and put his arm around her waist as he led her into the back of the store. Aimee knew he felt protective of the children's mother, another eastern transplant and a petite and frail young thing who was more at home in an elegant drawing room than in a dusty mining town. Aimee also knew full well his feelings for Belle Foster were more than just protective, but she let him continue thinking she didn't know. Aimee wondered sometimes though if it wasn't just a matter of time before he approached the mother to suggest a clandestine relationship. If it weren't for the ensuing scandal, Aimee would welcome it.

"Now Aimee darlin'," he whispered, tickling the back of her neck with his breath, "you have to be understandin' of the situation. Let the kids have some candy. They're havin' a hard time, being abandoned by their daddy and all."

Aimee shrugged away from him and hissed, "If you want to be generous, give them medicine or supplies. They need food, not sweets and toys."

"If you had children you'd understand," Jim replied peevishly. "Now, go on and give them what they want. I'll pay for it."

With an exasperated sigh, Aimee walked angrily toward the children. Jezebel had a smug look on her face; her brother a disagreeable one. They snatched the candy Aimee proffered and ran shrieking out the door, forgetting the Indian bark their mother had sent them for. Mrs. Adams shook her head and tut-tutted. She was always commenting that children nowadays just weren't brought up the way they used to be. Aimee grimaced in distaste. Amos and Jezebel were the two most obnoxious children in the whole town. None of the shopkeepers liked them, and even the schoolmarm wished she could keep them away from school. They were mean and selfish, not caring who they hurt, especially if it was their own mother.

It irritated Aimee that Jim didn't want to see them that way. He thought they were as sweet as their mother. He always bought Belle something special during his travels. Aimee scowled at him, not letting his smile soften her mood.

Mrs. Adams intercepted him. "Ye better be careful with them children, Mr. Calhoun. They be as wicked as their pa." She nodded toward Aimee. "Listen to yer wife."

His smile changed into a frown as he brushed past her quickly without acknowledging her words. Aimee's scowl deepened at his lack of manners. She knew he didn't care for the widow Adams, calling her a nosy busybody, yet his rudeness was uncalled for. More than once, Mrs. Adams had asked Aimee how such a nice girl like her could be married to a boor like him. She watched the old woman shuffle out of the store.

"I'm gonna miss you, darlin'," Jim was saying. "You know I'll be back within a fortnight. Need anythin' special?"

Aimee shrugged out of his embrace. She was still angry over the incident with the children. "Medicine," she replied curtly. "We need medicines and herbs."

Picking up his saddle bags, he walked briskly out the front door. Slinging the bags onto his horse, he said, "I think I'll drop by and visit the children's mother before I head out." In the doorway, Aimee stood like a sentinel. It wasn't until Jim was out of sight that she could relax. At that moment, a miner's wife came up the steps, accompanied by her two small children. Aimee smiled and welcomed them into her beloved store.

CHAPTER THREE

The sun was setting in a glorious burst of color—purple and gold and pink. It never ceased to take Aimee's breath away. Back east, the sunsets had never been like this. On the evening of the day Jim left, Aimee sat in a rocking chair on the porch in front of the store, enjoying the last light of day. A clamoring caught her attention—one garishly painted wagon was followed by another, more subdued one. Both were accompanied by a group of laughing children and barking dogs, who ran alongside or behind. Aimee stood and watched the wagons roll into town, their wheels stirring up clouds of dust. Each wagon appeared to be driven by a lone man.

A tall man of slender build jumped off the first wagon. An enormous cowboy hat shaded his face, but Aimee could hear his laugh, deep and genuine. The second man was also of slender build, though much shorter. Like his wagon, he appeared in attire less well-off than the other man. Aimee came down the steps.

"Welcome to Bisbee," she said to the taller man.

With a flourish, he took off his hat to reveal hair as black as a crow's wing, and eyes as dark as obsidian. With a deep bow, he said, "Thank you, ma'am. Davy Millwood's the name." He turned to his smaller companion. "And this is Cory Adamson."

Cory too bowed but did not take off his hat. Aimee thought that a trifle odd, but when Cory lifted his head and looked into her eyes, she realized immediately that Cory was no man, but a woman. Aimee gasped at the scandalous thought, and the scandalous apparel. With a grin, Cory took hold of Aimee's hand and kissed it.

"Pleased to meet ya, Miss . . ."

"Mrs.," Aimee corrected, feeling a blush spread warmly across her throat and cheeks. "Mrs. Aimee Calhoun."

"We're lookin' for a room for the night," Cory said.

The children were still jumping around, pleading with Davy to open up his wagon and reveal its hidden treasures. Distracted, Aimee turned away from Cory, then gasped again when Davy threw open the doors of his wagon to reveal a shiny, hanging array of brand-new pots and pans, yards of colorful ribbons, and shelves of bottles in every shape and size filled with everything from laudanum to mercury-based elixirs to castor oil. From somewhere deep inside, he grabbed a fistful of candies, which he threw into the air for the children to catch. Squealing with delight, they scrambled for the shining pieces, unwrapping the gold foil to find taffy—a delightful and unexpected treat.

By this time, several of the townspeople had come out into the twilight to investigate the goings on. Mothers grabbed their children, and men took up protective stances along the street.

"Why, it's just a couple o' travelin' snake oil salesmen," someone said.

Aimee could barely contain her own excitement after seeing

what was inside Davy's wagon. Jim usually did not bring much in the way of medicines back from his travels, and Davy looked to be well-supplied, though she knew he could very well be nothing but a fraud. She was intrigued by his colorful bottles and mysterious items wrapped in oil paper. She glanced at Cory, wondering if she too had such goods in her wagon. With a slight shake of her head, Cory answered Aimee's unspoken question. It made Cory even more intriguing, as Aimee wondered at her story. Were she and Davy married? Why did Cory dress like a man? And where did they hail from?

Aimee looked back at Davy in time to see him tip his hat to Mrs. Smith, who was pointing out the town's lone hotel, a clean and respectable establishment. Closing the doors of his wagon, Davy hopped aboard. Imitating his every move, Cory did the same, the leap to her driver's seat just as graceful and sure as his had been. Both tipped their hats, then jerked the reins, urging their tired horses on to the local hostelry. No children followed this time, their mothers having called them to order.

Aimee thoughtfully went back up the stairs to her store, checking one final time on the door's sturdy lock. She followed the porch around to the back and took the staircase to her apartment. Normally, she looked forward to quiet evenings without Jim, but for some reason this day, the idea of the long evening stretching into night was not that pleasurable. Perhaps dinner out? The hotel had a decent restaurant, though she'd never gone without Jim. Surely if she went early, there could be no impropriety? Besides, perhaps the two newcomers would welcome a chance to speak to someone they'd already met?

In the bedroom she shared with Jim, Aimee half-filled the tin tub with lukewarm water and stripped off her dusty clothing. Quickly rinsing off the grime, she stepped out of the tub, wishing she could have washed her hair too. Instead, a vigorous brushing would have to do—one hundred strokes, just like her mama had taught her to do. Forgoing the tightly braided bun she usually sported, she put her hair back in a loose chignon, liking the way it made her features appear softer. She stepped from the mirror, examining herself critically. Was her rose-patterned gingham dress too girly, too young? Was it fancy enough for the hotel's restaurant? She smoothed down the pristinely starched white collar and cuffs, then pinned a cameo at her throat. She looked perfectly respectable. She frowned. When had she become so matronly?

Throwing a fringed shawl around her shoulders, she then grabbed her reticule and left the hot apartment. The Copper Queen Hotel was only a short walk from the store. She did not see Davy's and Cory's wagons. Could they have decided not to stay after all? She was surprised to feel a sharp pang of dismay at the thought. Why should she care if two strangers chose to travel on?

She walked into the dim interior of the hotel, nodding an acknowledgment to people she knew. Crossing the ornate lobby, she entered the restaurant, glancing quickly at the tables. She smiled when she saw Davy's unmistakable black hair. The person seated with him had to be Cory, still dressed in male attire. Aimee felt a pleasurable tingle as she remembered the feel of Cory's lips against her hand. She shook her head to rid herself of the thought.

"Miz Calhoun. You dinin' alone tonight?"

Aimee smiled and nodded. "Yes, Jeremy," she said, feeling very independent. She pointed toward the back of the room. "How about that table by the window?"

Just as she'd hoped, when Jeremy led her past Davy and Cory's table, Davy stood. "Mrs. Calhoun," he said, "why don't you join Cory and me for dinner? I'm sure it will be no problem to add one more person to the bill."

Hesitating so she would not appear too eager, Aimee then nodded. "I would love to."

By this time, Cory too had stood, and she now held Aimee's

chair. Aimee smiled at her, then sat. Her companions followed suit. If they were surprised to see her out without her husband, they gave no indication.

The waiter came over. "One more for dinner?" he said, then turned to Aimee. "Can I get you a beverage?"

"Tea, please," she said, then carefully draped her shawl over the back of her chair. She was a lot more nervous than she'd anticipated.

As if sensing her discomfort, Cory smiled. "You look very lovely tonight, Mrs. Calhoun," she said.

"Thank you. But please, call me Aimee," she replied, defying convention. Her mother would never have allowed the use of her Christian name to a total stranger.

"This seems to be a very nice town," Davy said. "Have you lived here long?"

"About five years. My husband, Jim, owns the general store." She laughed. "We came out West so Jim could satisfy his sense of adventure, but he was not cut out for the harsh life of a miner."

"Ah, I thought I detected an eastern accent," Cory said. "Where was home originally?"

"New York."

"I'm from Virginia myself," Cory said.

Aimee glanced at her, detecting a deep sadness in her voice. And despite Cory's appearance, Aimee reminded herself that Cory was indeed female as, in typical female fashion, Cory kept her eyes down and averted, hiding some painful memory. Instinctively, Aimee reached out and placed her hand over Cory's. In response, Cory looked up and Aimee found herself staring into a pair of dove-gray eyes that revealed a hurt so intense it took Aimee's breath away.

Abruptly, Cory pulled her hand away and scowled. "It's nothing," she said.

"How long have you two been traveling together?" Aimee asked.

Cory's face relaxed at the change in subject, but Aimee was determined that she would find out what in Cory's past hurt her so.

"We only met this very afternoon," Davy was saying, "and decided we're both tired of travelin' solo. Actually, we might be interested in settlin' here for a bit."

"Really?" Aimee couldn't help a pleased smile. "Bisbee's a lovely little town, but there's not much here unless you want to work in the copper mine."

"Surely there must be other work? Farm or ranchhand perhaps?"

The waiter brought over large bowls of beans and mashed potatoes, a crock of beef gravy and a platter of brisket and onions. Aimee automatically picked up Davy's plate and loaded it with a large portion of everything. She placed the plate in front of him, then caught herself. "I'm sorry," she said, "I didn't mean to be so presumptuous."

Davy laughed. "Don't bother me none."

Cory grinned as she handed over her plate. "Not so generous a helping for me," she said, laughing.

Once she'd served Cory and herself, Aimee turned to Davy. "In answer to your earlier question, there are a couple of large cattle ranches in the area. But I think you'd find work here as a tinker, both in town and out at the ranches. That is what you do?" She took a forkful of mashed potatoes before continuing. "In addition to the medicines you sell?"

"I do a little bit of everything. And far as the medicines go . . . Well, I'm not claiming to be a doctor or anything like that, but I learned some traditional Chinese medicine from the laborers on the railroad gangs and picked up some natural remedies from the Indians."

"Doc Templeton will be glad to hear you're not interested in taking over his practice," Aimee laughed.

As Davy regaled them with amusing tales about other places in the West and the people he'd encountered, Aimee couldn't help but feel envious of his experiences. When she and Jim had first arrived, she'd yearned to see the places she'd only read or heard about. She'd even wanted to meet up with an honest-to-goodness outlaw. The only real excitement in their lives had been the gunfight four years ago in the nearby town of Tombstone. Aimee sighed, thinking about just how many of her dreams would never come true.

Suddenly realizing the dining room had grown quiet, Aimee looked around to see most of the other patrons had left. The waiter came and took away the leftover food, replacing it with plates of apple brown betty. Aimee marveled at how much time had passed and how little Cory had said about herself. She turned to Cory. "And what do you do, Cory?"

"Survive."

"I think my friend here's been on the road too long alone," Davy said.

"Well then, it's good you're stayin' on for a while." Aimee took another forkful of the delicious dessert. "I could actually use a bit of help right now. Jim's gone for a couple of weeks, and I'm expecting a shipment of flour and grain any day now. I've got some loose roof shingles too."

"We're at your service. Aren't we, Cory?"

"Of course."

Aimee looked at Cory. Her reticence to talk about herself only made her more intriguing. As if reading Aimee's mind, Cory smiled and said, "My life's not all that interesting. Really."

Aimee smiled back, then pulled her shawl from the back of her chair. "I think I'd best get along home now. Do you mind calling over the waiter for the bill?"

Davy and Cory both stood as Aimee rose. "I'll take care of this," Davy said. He nudged Cory. "Why don't you walk Miz Calhoun home?"

"There's really no need—" Aimee began.

"I would be happy to escort you," Cory said.

Pleased, Aimee allowed Cory to take her arm and guide her from the hotel. Outside, Aimee shivered and pulled her shawl more closely around her. In the desert, the intense heat of the day could give way to chilly nights. The two women walked in silence, the sand crunching beneath their booted feet. Light and sound spilled from the saloon on their left. Suddenly, a man came flying through the swinging doors to sprawl with an oomph in the street, his head barely missing a wooden post as he tumbled down the steps. Another man followed, eyes blazing and pistol in hand. Cory grabbed Aimee's arm and hurried her away just as several men crashed from the saloon, fists and curse words flying.

Laughing, Aimee tugged on Cory's hand and ran down the street to the store. Breathing heavily, she hurried up the stairs at the back of store and pushed open the door to her apartment. It felt cold inside. Cory followed her.

"Normally I'd have a fire goin' by now," Aimee said as she hung her shawl and reticule on a peg by the door.

"I can take care of that for you," Cory said, heading for the small fireplace. The mesquite wood was already placed, only awaiting a match. She soon had a good fire crackling.

"Can I offer you a whiskey?" Aimee asked.

"I should be going."

Aimee laid her hand upon Cory's arm. "I'd like you to stay."

"That wouldn't be wise. What will the townspeople think about you having a strange man in your quarters? At night?"

"You're not a man."

If Cory was surprised, she didn't show it. "The others don't know that."

"I doubt anyone noticed you come here. And if they did, once they found out you're really a woman—"

"You can't tell anyone!"

Surprised at Cory's vehement outburst, Aimee didn't answer, instead busying herself with fluffing pillows. She felt Cory's fingers, soft on her arm.

"I'm so sorry. I didn't mean to yell." She turned Aimee to look at her. "Please say you forgive me."

Aimee smiled. "Of course I do. I'll protect your secret."

"Thank you. It's just that I think it's safer for the time being." She let go of Aimee's arm. "I really should be going though."

"Will you come see me tomorrow? I truly could use your help."

"Yes, I'll come by." She opened the door, then turned to look at Aimee. "Good night."

Aimee stared at the closed door for a long time, oblivious even to Puss rubbing up against her. It had been ages since she'd felt this alive. Who was this mystery woman who defied convention, dressing like a man and traveling on her own without fear? What terrible secret from Cory's past haunted her?

Finally, Aimee sat down to pull off her boots. She then quickly unbuttoned her dress. As she tugged on her sleeve to pull it down, her pulse raced at the memory of Cory's hand upon her arm. She felt herself flush warmly. It had been a long time since she'd felt like this—not since she was a mere slip of a girl and Mary Curtis had kissed her. The memory sent tingles down her spine, much like the tingles she'd felt the first time it happened.

Mary's lips had been so soft. Taken by surprise, Aimee had kept her eyes wide open but she'd not pulled away. Eventually, she closed her eyes, yielding to the sensation, gasping only a little when Mary's tongue flicked over her lips and into her mouth. There was no way of knowing how long the kiss had lasted, but Aimee pulled back and stared wide-eyed while Mary laughed and ran her fingers along Aimee's chin.

"You are such a child, Aimee," Mary said.

"No, I'm not. I am fourteen after all. Only two years younger than you."

"Ah, but that's what makes you a child and me a woman." Mary continued her caress, letting her fingers stroke Aimee's cheek. "You are so pretty."

Aimee felt herself blush. She'd always considered herself kind of mousy, but when Mary looked at her that way, she did feel pretty.

"Do you mind that I kissed you?" Mary asked.

Aimee shook her head. She was afraid to speak, afraid that if she opened her mouth she would ask Mary to do it again. Mary must have seen something in Aimee's expression, for she leaned forward and kissed Aimee again. This time, Aimee felt her toes curl and butterflies in her stomach. She sighed and opened her mouth, letting Mary's tongue dart in and tickle her. Tentatively, she let her own tongue enter Mary's mouth, tasting the sweetness of honey.

Each time they got together after that, Mary grew more bold. Her fingers would curl themselves in Aimee's hair, travel down over her throat, and then flutter over Aimee's heaving girlish bosom. Mary's fingers burned hot through Aimee's clothes, sliding down the side of her and over her hips. Sometimes Aimee would feel them under her skirt on her calves and knees, making the goose bumps rise under her stockings as Aimee willed Mary's hand to go higher. At those times, Aimee wished she was naked. Wondered what it would feel like to have Mary's fingers on her bare skin.

Then, when Aimee was fifteen, her world came crashing down. Without warning, her parents packed her off to boarding school without any explanation. Her letters to Mary went unanswered. She would spend hours each day crying in her room. Finally, the head mistress took pity on her.

One day, Miss White came into Aimee's room and sat next to her on the bed. "Aimee," she said, "you cannot spend all your time in your room. I know you must be missing your friend, but this is for the best."

"What do you mean? What do you know?"

Miss White's hand softly brushed Aimee's hair. "Mary is in a special hospital, for girls like her. And you're here so you don't end up there too."

"I don't understand."

Miss White smiled sadly. "Of course you don't. But Mary was not a good influence on you, and your parents thought a new environment would help you heal."

"I didn't know Mary was sick. Is that why she doesn't answer my letters? What's wrong with her? Is it TB?"

"She's not allowed to write letters right now. I'm sure she'd write you if she could." Miss White paused. "Mary has an unnatural affection for girls. It's not too late though to keep that from happening to you. Here, you'll learn to be the proper young lady your parents expect you to be. You'll learn how to make someone a good wife."

Aimee still didn't understand, but she closed her eyes as Miss White kept caressing her hair. Aimee knew it was meant to be soothing, just like how her mother would comfort her when she was ill or sad, but it felt so good. She could imagine it was Mary's fingers in her hair. Then Miss White's fingers were on Aimee's cheeks, wiping away her tears.

Abruptly, Miss White got off the bed. Aimee opened her eyes. Miss White was the color of her name. "Everything will turn out fine," she said. "Give it time."

Aimee watched Miss White leave the room. They were never alone together again during the next two years Aimee spent at the academy. Like Miss White had predicted, Aimee got over her pain and in time, Mary faded from her memory.

Until that is, this day.

When Aimee went to bed, she let the memories wash over her. She felt again Mary's soft lips and gentle caresses. She remembered how their tongues would meet, how Mary always tasted of honey, how Mary's blue eyes would sparkle with happiness, and how the gold crucifix chain she always wore would glitter against her pale skin.

Feeling the tears against her cheeks, Aimee curled into a ball and fell into a troubled sleep.

Chapter Four

Two days later, a loud clattering outside drew Aimee and her customers out into the street. Davy Millwood had driven his painted wagon from the hostelry and now, with great flourish, was opening its doors.

"Come one, come all," he was calling. "I've got medicines for all that ails you, and trivialities to make your heart joyful." He tapped a hanging frying pan, creating a clanging cascade of tin against tin and iron against iron. "Buy a brand-new cooking pot or I'll fix yours."

It didn't take long for a good-sized crowd to gather 'round. Rather than be annoyed that he might take customers from her, Aimee hung back, enjoying the show. Davy cut quite a fine figure in tight-fitting denim trousers tucked into black boots adorned with all manner of silver filigree, embroidered red shirt, and black hat with silver band. His enormous silver belt buckle caught the sunlight, as did the silver medallion on his cravat tie.

Aimee couldn't help but smile at the expressions of some of the women, especially those she knew to be unmarried. Davy was quite the handsome fellow, and charming besides. Yet Aimee instinctively knew that those comely lasses would not interest him. And whose father would allow his daughter to marry a mere tinker and snake oil peddler?

Holding up a brown bottle, Davy uncorked it and offered to rub some of the liquid on a grizzled old miner. "Just a little o' this everyday on your joints, and you'll feel your pain fade away." At the man's skeptical look, Davy said, "I got this from a real Chinese medicine man, came all the way from China."

The miner looked less skeptical. Davy leaned in, eager to cash in. "It's called *shéyóu* in Chinese. How do ya s'pose I'd know that if I was lyin'?"

Aimee almost laughed out loud as the miner pulled some coins from his pocket and handed them over. She'd heard of the supposed healing powers of the oil, but she preferred to sell the more traditional remedies. She just hoped Davy didn't end up run out of town like the last peddler who came through. But he had other things for sale—bright ribbons, silver buttons, tobacco, wooden soldiers, corn husk dolls. By the end of an hour, he'd sold quite a lot and had taken in pots for repair. Watching him had been quite the entertainment.

As he was about to slap his horse on the flank to head back to the hotel's stable, he noticed Aimee standing on her stoop. He removed his hat with a theatrical bow. "Good morning to you, Mrs. Calhoun," he said, grinning.

"Good morning, Mr. Millwood," she said, imitating his formality, yet she too was grinning. "You did a mighty brisk business this day."

He approached her. "I hope you don't think I'm trying to steal your customers."

"Not at all," she said, stepping aside so he stood right next to her. She had to look up at him. "As long as you don't make it a habit."

"Never."

She went into the store, indicating he should follow. "I've got a pot or two that could use tinkering." Once inside the cooler interior of the store, she turned to him. "So, does that snake oil of yours really work?"

He shrugged. "Depends on if you believe it does. To tell the truth though, I never stayed long enough anywhere to find out."

"Probably smart. So, does that mean you and Cory will be leaving us?" She tried to make her tone nonchalant.

"Don't reckon so. Least aways, not yet. My friend Cory's been traveling a mighty long time. He's pretty tuckered out."

"You don't need to pretend with me, Davy."

He arched his eyebrows. "Ma'am?"

"I know Cory is a woman." She waited for his look of surprise, but got none. "You don't seem surprised that I know."

He leaned against the counter, crossing one booted ankle over the other. "Well, you seem a bit more intelligent than most. No disrespect to anyone. Most people see what they expect to see. And I kinda sensed the other night that you might've figured it out."

"What's her story?"

"Don't really know. We only just met ourselves. But I can tell she's had a great tragedy and a hard life. And I ain't talkin' 'bout just recently."

"So, you'll stay for a while?"

"Like I mentioned at dinner, we're both pretty tired of travelin' right now, so I reckon so, as long as we can find work." He winked. "Don't think I could stay long if I was only selling my wares."

She laughed in agreement. "If I hear of anything, I'll let you know."

"That would be mighty generous of you." He pushed away

from the counter. "I'd best be gettin' my horse back to the stable."

She followed him to the door, watching as he untied his horse from the rail and then hopped up on the driver's seat. With a click of his tongue and a toss of the reins, he got his horse moving. With a wave to Aimee, he headed back up the street.

Thoughtfully, she went back into the store, where she settled on the cushioned window seat above the book collection. She'd spent many hours sitting in this very spot, reading, but today books held no interest for her. She couldn't help but think about a red-haired drifter with sad gray eyes.

"New Sears catalogue come in yet?"

Startled out of her reverie, Aimee finally noticed Mrs. Johnson standing before her.

"You all right?" Mrs. Johnson asked.

Aimee stood. "Yes, I was just daydreaming."

Mrs. Johnson laughed. "No use for that here. Ain't nothin' gonna be changin'."

Aimee smiled. "What can I get you?"

"My darn button hook's bent again." She looked askance at her own colorful language. "Pardon my tongue, Miz Calhoun."

Aimee pulled open a drawer and took out a metal button-hook. "This one's on me."

"Oh, there's no need for that," Mrs. Johnson said, but she tucked the implement into her reticule without taking out a coin. "You see them two strangers come to town?"

"Why yes, I met them a couple days ago. They seem quite amiable."

"They be a pair o' fine-looking fellers." She clucked her tongue. "Abigail Smith's already talkin' 'bout matchin' one up with her Rachel."

"I doubt they'll be in town long. The one's a tinker and snake oil salesman."

Mrs. Johnson pursed her mouth in disapproval. "I'll have a

talk with Abigail." She shook her head as she walked out of the store. "What a scandal that would be, her daughter runnin' off with such a feller."

A few minutes later, Cory came into the store. Aimee felt her pulse race. Why did this woman have such an effect on her? To regain her composure, she scurried behind the counter and took a throat lozenge. "Dry throat," she said, feigning a cough.

Cory smiled. "Not surprising." She glanced around the store. "You said you could use some help."

"Yes, I'm expecting a shipment of clothing and boots today. But I've got a few things that need repair too."

"I can help you with that."

"I'll pay you fifty cents an hour, with meals."

"Deal." She shook Aimee's hand.

Taking a deep breath, Aimee answered, "Deal." She withdrew her hand slowly from Cory's. With a twitch of her skirt, she turned from Cory and pointed to a cabinet door sagging on its hinges. "Can you fix that first, please."

For the rest of the day, Aimee avoided straying too close to Cory. She was confused by the feelings that being near her evoked. But that didn't stop Aimee from watching. The physical activity made Cory's skin flush pink under her tan and glow with sweat. Her hair, curling damply on her forehead and around her ears, made Aimee want to run her fingers through it.

As the sun rose higher in the sky, customers stopped coming. There would be a couple of hours when Aimee could close the store, though she never did. She settled onto the cushioned window seat once more and languidly fanned herself, all the while watching Cory work.

"Would you mind if I rearranged these shelves?" Cory asked from atop a ladder. "I think the shirts should all go below the frock coats and vests."

"Do whatever you think best," Aimee said, not caring that Jim would have a fit when he returned. The arrangement of goods in the store was one thing he had final say over.

Lulled by the heat, the buzzing of flies, and the security of having Cory in the store, Aimee felt her eyelids closing. She was more tired than she realized. Or perhaps it was merely feeling more relaxed without Jim home? Guiltily, she opened her eyes. Cory still worked, oblivious to Aimee's unwifely thoughts. Aimee closed her eyes again and leaned back against the wall.

The soft touch of fingers in her hair made her smile. She sighed, willing the fingers to continue their caress. She didn't want to open her eyes and break the spell.

"Aimee? Are you awake?"

"Yes," she said, opening her eyes. Cory stood above her, looking concerned. "Just taking advantage of you being here to rest a bit."

Cory sat beside her. "Will you have more for me today?"

"Don't think so. Thank you. I owe you lunch."

"Let's grab a bite at the hotel."

"I don't think I can close up the store."

"Sure you can." Cory stood and took hold of Aimee's hands to pull her up. "It's too bloody hot for man or beast to be out. No one will venture out now until after two."

Aimee laughed. "If it's too hot for man or beast, what are we doing?" She grabbed her sunbonnet from its hook by the door.

"We're neither," Cory said as she also grabbed Aimee's parasol for her. "Man or beast, I mean."

Aimee closed and locked the door. She didn't like to think someone she knew would steal from her, but she took no chances. She turned the sign to CLOSED, then followed Cory down the steps. She clicked open her parasol for the stroll to the Copper Queen Hotel. "This will be a first for me," she said. "Dining at the hotel twice in one week."

"Doesn't your husband ever take you out for the evening?"

"Jim doesn't believe in that kind of frivolity. Why eat out when he has a wife at home to cook?"

Cory sidestepped a scorpion, watching briefly as it scuttled out of sight. "You must get awfully bored. Work in the store all day, then go upstairs to cook and spend the evening at home. It's the same thing every day?"

"Well, yes." Aimee paused. She'd never thought of her life as boring before. At least, not that she was aware. "I'm content with my life."

"Are you?"

"Why would you question me?"

Cory blushed. "I mean no disrespect. I just . . . I guess I couldn't be content with that, so I assume no one else could either. It's wrong of me."

"Your life back in Virginia . . . it varied day to day? Did you not have a stable home? Have you always lived out of your wagon?"

This time Cory's face blanched. "No. No."

She turned her face from Aimee, but not before Aimee saw the tears in her eyes. Aimee put a hand on Cory's arm. "I'm sorry to bring up a painful subject. If you ever want to tell me about it . . ."

"Here we are," Cory said as they arrived at the hotel.

She seemed to have not heard Aimee's words. Aimee walked through the door Cory held open, feeling slightly miffed at Cory's dismissal of her. But then she scolded herself silently for not being more understanding. If Cory wasn't ready to talk about it, who was Aimee to demand otherwise?

The interior of the hotel was cool. Aimee took off her bonnet, handing it and her parasol to a Chinese servant girl before following Cory to the restaurant. Cory stepped back so Aimee walked in front of her to their table. There weren't many people in the restaurant, but Aimee nodded to the ones she knew. If they thought it odd that she was lunching with a man other than her husband, they gave no sign, though Aimee was certain she would be the subject of gossip later on.

As if reading her thoughts, Cory asked, "Are you sure it's okay for us to be having lunch together? Maybe my idea wasn't a good one after all."

Aimee sat at the table, letting the waiter push in her chair. "Don't worry about it. My husband has eaten here without me, I'm sure," she said, thinking of Belle Foster, though she had never heard talk of such. After the waiter brought over cups of steaming coffee, she continued. "Tell me about yourself, Cory. Is Cory your real name?"

"Actually, it's Corinne. Cory was Davy's idea. He thought it would be easier than sayin' Mr. Adamson all the time for my temporary disguise."

"I like Corinne. Are you originally from Virginia?" She smiled at the waiter as he delivered a small platter of biscuits and gravy with bacon rashers and early corn.

"Yes. My father was a tobacco farmer. He was disappointed to have a daughter. I left home at sixteen. Managed to find work in the kitchen of one of the big plantations down South, but knew I was not cut out for that."

Aimee took a bite of her gravy-covered biscuit. "Is that when you decided to pass as a man?"

"No, not then." Cory lowered her eyes and turned her head slightly, as if she didn't want Aimee to see her face. She took a deep breath. "I lost someone very dear to me, and when I left Virginia it seemed the safest and easiest way to travel. I wanted to get as far away as possible." She looked up. "That's all I can tell you right now."

For the rest of the meal, they exchanged stories of their travels, but Aimee thought Cory's endeavors much more exciting. Again, she admired Cory's bravery in partaking of such an adventure. But her curiosity about what had brought Corrine out West was eating away at her. Still, she knew she had to be patient. Cory would tell her in due time.

CHAPTER FIVE

Someone was licking her face. Smiling, she reached out and encountered . . . fur! Startled, Aimee sat up and saw Puss staring at her with a reproachful look. "Oh, no," she said, flinging the covers off as she noticed the time. She'd overslept! The store was due to open in only fifteen minutes. Scrambling out of bed, she performed a hurried toilette, pinning her hair back in a sloppy bun. There was no time for breakfast, so she grabbed a cold biscuit and some cheese before descending the stairs to the store.

Feeling unusually tired the evening before, she'd not done her usual ritual of cleaning and restocking. She glanced critically around her store, then heard banging. She recognized Rufus Jones, the foreman from the Johnson ranch.

"Mornin', Miz Calhoun," he said as he clumped into the store. "I need some extra ammo. We got word there might be cattle rustlers in the area."

"Really?" she said as she led him to the back of the store.

She let him take the boxes of bullets he needed, then wrote the amount he owed in her ledger. Most of her customers ran tabs. It was not something Jim liked to do, but that was the way it was out here. And sometimes people would pay them back in goods rather than cash. Jim really hated when that happened. He'd just about had a coronary when she'd accepted, of all things, a Siamese cat. But he had reluctantly admitted Puss did keep the vermin in check. The cat had even stared down a gila monster once.

"Do you think you could use a couple of extra hands?" she asked, thinking about Davy and Cory.

"Sure would be good to have another man or two, but the mine can't spare anyone."

"I happen to know the two strangers who came into town five days ago, and they're looking for work. They're staying at the Copper Queen."

As soon as the words were out of her mouth, she regretted them. How could she send Cory to do a man's work? What would happen if they discovered the truth about her? And was Davy really the sort of man who would relish being out on the range? Then she remembered he had inquired about such work.

Rufus' eyes lit up. "No kiddin'? I'd best get over there then and snatch 'em up before one o' the other ranches gets to 'em first."

She took hold of his arm. "I'm sorry, Rufus, but I forgot I got one of them to agree to help me out here at the store." At his disappointed look, she hurriedly added, "But when he's done here, I'll send him out your way."

"You got names fer these fellas?"

"Davy Millwood and Cory Adamson. Davy's the one you can ask for now. He looks strong and capable."

Rufus tipped his hat. "Thanks, Miz Calhoun."

He and Cory almost collided as he went out the door. He

gave Cory a once over, then headed straight for the hotel.

Aimee smiled when she saw Cory. She looked mighty fine this morning, dressed in clean but tight denim trousers, a leather vest over a red shirt, and a red and white bandanna around her throat. She held a black cowboy hat in one hand.

"That was Rufus Jones, foreman of one of the area's biggest cattle ranches. He's lookin' for a couple of extra ranchhands to guard against reported cattle thieves."

"He seemed in an awful hurry to get outta here."

"I told him about two strangers come to town lookin' for work, so he was headed to the hotel."

Cory frowned. "I'd best get over there then."

Aimee quickly grabbed her arm. "No need. I told him I'd hired you first. He can make do with Davy for now."

"I'm sure the pay will be quite good."

Aimee felt her heart jump at Cory's words. "I'll increase your wages to whatever he'd pay you," she said.

Cory smiled at her, the sadness in her gray eyes replaced with good-natured mirth. "You probably couldn't afford it, my dear."

At the endearment, Aimee's pulse quickened. She knew it meant nothing, but she loved hearing it nevertheless. Jim never used that particular endearment. He liked to call her "darling," but even that was less and less.

"Well, I suppose if you really want to go with Rufus, I can't stop you. But I really could use your help for a couple more days."

"Of course. I never go back on my word."

Just then, a group of customers came in. Cory obligingly helped her, loading sacks of flour and barley and sugar onto wagons, clambering up ladders to haul down boxes of trousers and men's shirts, and even measuring out jellybeans and tea and tobacco. At last, they were alone in the store, and Aimee became very aware that she'd not had a decent breakfast. Feeling light-headed, she grabbed hold of the counter. Cory was beside her in seconds.

"Are you all right?"

"Yes," Aimee said. "I just didn't eat much this morning."

"Let me help you."

Cory put her arm around Aimee's waist and led her to the window seat. The feel of Cory's hand on her hip almost made Aimee swoon again. She could feel her skin flush. She took a deep breath in an effort to calm her jangled nerves.

Cory sat her gently down. She swept an errant curl off Aimee's forehead. "Are you sure you're okay? You look all flushed."

"Just a bit warm," Aimee said. She pointed. "Could you grab me a fan?"

Cory brought over a fancy one made of ivory and lace. Aimee snapped it open and fanned herself vigorously. It gave her something to think about other than wanting to kiss Cory. She blushed even more at the very thought of it.

"Let me get you some water," Cory said, then headed outside to the pump.

"Are you all right, Miz Calhoun?"

Aimee looked up to see the widow Adams staring intently at her. Aimee sighed. Was there never a day when the lonely widow didn't just stay home? At that moment, Cory came back with a bucket of water. She scooped some into a ladle and handed it to Aimee.

Mrs. Adams chuckled. "Why, Aimee Calhoun, be you with child?"

Aimee choked on her water. "No, Mrs. Adams, I'm not. Please don't go about tellin' people that. I'm just a bit touched by the heat is all."

"And who is this nice young man?"

Cory bowed her head. "Cory Adamson at your service."

The widow chuckled again. "We got similar last names. You must be the tinker everyone's talkin' about."

"No, that would be my friend Davy Millwood."

Before Mrs. Adams could answer, Belle Foster came in with her two children. As usual, she looked small and vulnerable, but impeccably dressed. She had a fine figure, small waisted with gently curved hips. Her eyes lit up when she spied Cory.

"Mrs. Calhoun," she said, "I came to thank you for the treats you gave Amos and Jezebel last week. It makes a difference in their day."

"You're very welcome."

"Is your husband back?"

"Not yet. I don't expect him home until toward the end of next week."

At the look on Belle's face, Aimee began to wonder if her husband was having an affair with the lonely young mother after all. Although if he were, it would seem he would have told Belle how long he'd be gone. It would be odd that he hadn't, unless Belle was only pretending that she didn't know.

"He promised to fix my roof," Belle said.

"I can do that for you," Cory said.

"Mama! I want licorice!" Amos demanded.

He began to run around the store, circling the tables laden with fabric that stood in the center. Round and round he went, until Aimee felt dizzy from watching him. The commotion was enough to make Mrs. Adams take her leave. Aimee noticed Jezebel surreptitiously slip a bright yellow ribbon into her sleeve.

"I'd be ever so grateful," Belle was saying, managing to make her luminous blue eyes look thankful and forlorn at the same time. It was the way she'd managed to survive in this town after her gambling husband had taken off, leaving her with two young children to feed.

"I'll come around this afternoon, then," Cory said.

"Come along you two," Belle said, pointing with her parasol to the doorway.

"What's her story?" Cory asked when she and Aimee were

alone again. She reached down to pet the cat.

"Husband's a gambler. He left after being accused of cheating in a card game, and the other player threatened to shoot him. He's been gone about four months now. Alive or dead, no one knows."

"How's she getting along?"

"Some o' the other womenfolk give her sewing to do. She raises chickens and sells the eggs." Aimee shrugged. "She's living off credit here. It's the least we can do." Not wanting Cory to think she was uncharitable, she didn't mention it was at Jim's insistence. She led the way out of the store and settled into one of the rocking chairs on the front porch. Cory followed suit. "I like this time alone," Aimee said.

"When the store's empty?"

"No, when Jim is gone."

"You don't get lonely?"

Aimee hesitated. Though Cory had been working at the store for a few days now, she wondered how honest she should be with someone who was still basically a stranger. In a way, it would almost be a relief. It wasn't like she could talk to anyone in town. She took a deep breath. "I've not been happy in my marriage for a while now. Don't misunderstand. Jim's a good husband and provider. He is not an abuser or a drunkard." She paused. "Though he can have a temper."

"Perhaps it's discontent because you have no children?"

Aimee shook her head. "No, I'm happy to be childless." She looked at Cory to see if she was shocked at this confession. Her face was impassive. "I can't really explain it. Perhaps it's being in Bisbee these five years. Nothing changes."

"You said you come from New York. What did you do there?"

"My parents were relatively well-to-do. I had hoped to become a teacher." She smiled ruefully. "Then I met Jim and changed my mind. He was so handsome and so courtly. I truly believed we could be happy."

"But he wanted adventure? I can understand that."

Aimee rocked gently in her chair. "I'm sure your story is a lot more interesting than mine. What makes you pass yourself off as a man?"

"It's safer to travel that way."

"But what brought you out West to begin with? Surely you didn't travel all this way in disguise?"

Cory smiled. "No, not really. It wasn't until I met Davy that I cut my hair, though I did hide it under a hat." Her smile faded. "I had to leave Virginia, so I loaded up my wagon and left for good."

Again, Aimee detected sadness in her voice. "Something bad happened there, didn't it?"

Cory stiffened. Her face flushed, but she looked straight ahead. "I can't talk about it."

Aimee placed her hand over Cory's. Cory made as if to pull it away, but then left her hand under Aimee's. "If you ever need to talk, I'm here," Aimee said. "And anything you tell me will be in confidence."

This time Cory looked over at Aimee, her eyes glistening with unshed tears. She nodded, then abruptly stood. As if on cue, a wagon loaded with sacks of flour pulled up in front of the store. Without a word, Cory walked down the steps and began unloading the heavy bags.

• • •

The physical activity helped Cory dispel the memories that Aimee had disturbed. Lifting sack after sack of flour, she could feel the sweat bead up on her skin and just as quickly evaporate in the heat. The muscles in her arms and shoulders knotted in pain, but she welcomed it. She'd much rather be out on the range with Davy, but she had promised Aimee she'd help out for a bit.

Bringing the last bag of flour into the store, she glanced over at Aimee and couldn't help but smile at the sight of her. She looked so pretty in her blue and white calico dress covered with a snow-white apron. Cory marveled at how it remained so pristine despite the desert dust. Aimee's shiny chestnut hair was tousled, seemingly waiting for someone to run their fingers through it. The heat brought a rosy blush to her cheeks and a sheen to her skin. She looked up just then and caught Cory staring. Her smile made her brown eyes crinkle at the corners. Cory couldn't help but smile back.

It was the first time since she'd left Virginia that Cory had even noticed a woman—not that she'd encountered many of them on her travels. She'd avoided the towns and cities whenever possible, preferring to sleep in her wagon or on the ground with only Red for company. But now she was beginning to realize that she missed having female companionship. And although she'd decided she'd move on with Davy when he was ready to leave, she was beginning to think that would not be so. At the same time, she realized she might be playing a dangerous game here.

Cory watched as Aimee paid for the flour before she walked over to where Cory leaned against the counter. She raised a corner of her apron to wipe the sweat from Cory's brow. Cory caught her breath as she stared into Aimee's expressive eyes. Then, the touch of Aimee's fingers on her cheek made Cory groan. She turned away, but Aimee took her face in both hands and looked directly into her eyes.

It seemed only natural that they should lean together, lips touching lips. The sensation made Cory shudder in a not unpleasant way. She felt the tingles all the way down to her toes.

"Aimee," she said, "do you know what you're doing?"

"Shhhh," Aimee whispered, "don't say anything. Just kiss me."

Despite her better judgment, Cory did as she was bid, letting her tongue play over Aimee's soft lips before darting into her sweet mouth, As Aimee melted against her, Cory let her hands travel over Aimee's curves, over the swell of her breasts to her cinched waist and on to her curvaceous hips. She pulled Aimee to her, kissing her more deeply and with more urgency. Dormant feelings came to life as Cory moved her mouth over Aimee's cheek and down along the smoothness of her throat. Aimee moaned softly, making Cory want to rip her clothing off and ravish her right there on the counter. With great effort, she stopped herself and stepped away.

"We can't do this," she said.

Aimee looked stricken, but whether with remorse or disappointment, Cory knew not. Aimee put her fingers to her mouth. "I don't know what came over me," she said.

"Nothing," Cory said. "It was me. Only me."

"No, it was me too. You're not the first female I've kissed." She laughed. "Don't look so shocked."

Cory was more than shocked. She was speechless. "I'm not?" she finally asked.

Before Aimee could answer, a new customer came into the store. The sight sent a rush of fear through Cory, reminding her that they'd taken a terrible chance earlier. What if someone had walked in on them? She vowed to be more careful next time. Next time? There would be no next time. She wouldn't put Aimee at risk. With a glance and nod at Aimee, she quickly left the store. But as she walked along the street, kicking up dust and sand with every step, she couldn't help but think of beautiful brown eyes and lustrous chestnut hair. The image made her forget her promise to Belle Foster.

CHAPTER SIX

"I tell you," Cory said to Davy hours later in the privacy of his room, "I don't know what came over me. There I was, in public, kissing her."

Davy laughed. "My word, girl, you work faster than a cow-poke coming in off the range after three months with only cows for company."

Cory felt her face grow hot. "I'm not normally like this. In fact, I haven't even been around a woman in goin' on eight months now." She paused, thinking of Anne. Was it really only eight months ago that she'd come home and found her and Lisbeth murdered? Then a terrible guilt descended upon her as she wondered how she could be so disloyal to Anne's memory so soon.

She felt Davy's hand upon her arm. "You all right, Cory?"

She looked at him, seeing the concern in his dark eyes. "Yes, it's just . . ." She caught a sob in her throat. "I . . . you don't know . . ."

"You lost someone, didn't you? Someone you loved very much."

With his words, her tears came. He took her in his arms and let her cry on his shoulder. Finally, with one last hiccup, she leaned away from him. "Thanks, I needed that." She laughed a little. "Wouldn't do to have someone walkin' in on us, seein' as how they all think I'm a man too."

"A lot more dangerous than them findin' you kissin' Miz Calhoun."

"I guess you're right."

"Want to talk about what happened? Back then, I mean."

She shook her head. "No, not yet. But I think Aimee could help me get over it." She played with the rough woolen blanket on his bed. "You probably think I'm silly. After all, we only met just a week ago."

He patted her hand. "There's no rules to fallin' in love."

She looked at him askance. "I'm not in love!"

"If it makes you happy to think not, then so be it." He stood. "How 'bout we go to the saloon and get ourselves some whiskey? Don't know about you, but I'm mighty sore from helpin' Rufus Jones. Can't remember when I worked so damn hard."

Cory stood and flexed her muscles. "Yeah," she said. "Aimee had me haulin' so many darn sacks o' flour, I just about lost the feelings in my hands."

They put on their cowboy hats and walked out of the room together, making sure to clump loudly down the stairs so the spurs on their boots clicked. Outside the hotel the moon overhead was almost full. Cory glanced down the street in the direction of the general store, wondering what Aimee was doing. Wondering if she was lying in bed already. Would she be clothed on a warm night like this? Or would she be naked? The thought sent shivers of desire up Cory's spine. She had a feeling this would be a multiple-whiskey night.

As she and Davy walked up the steps to the saloon, something made Cory look down the street. Lifting her eyes to the window above the store, she glimpsed a pale face and a cascade of shiny hair caught in the light of a street lamp. *Aimee*. Cory smiled, feeling the quickening beat of her heart.

• • •

Aimee peeked out from the curtain of her sitting room, which overlooked the street. Feeling a bit silly, she drew the curtain fully away from the window and sat in a chair so she could enjoy the night. The temperature had already fallen from the heat of the day, though it was still warm. With Jim gone, she'd stripped down to just her cotton chemise and pantalets. When he was home, she had to stay fully clothed until bedtime. His edict.

Her cat sat on the windowsill, and she absently stroked his soft fur. Her thoughts drifted to earlier in the day, when Cory had kissed her. It was so different from Jim's sloppy and some- times harsh kisses. She couldn't remember after all these years if he'd always kissed that way. Surely in the beginning it wasn't so? She ran her fingers along her lips and closed her eyes. She thought about Cory's lips and tongue, felt again her hands as they caressed her body. The familiar tingling began between her legs. How she wished Cory was here with her this night, that Cory's hands and fingers would find her secret place. Shocked at her thoughts, she opened her eyes. Even Jim, her husband, had never touched her there. At least, not with his hands. She groaned. How would she endure his attentions when he returned home?

The noise from the saloon drew her attention. She leaned out of the window so she could look down the street. Even at this distance, she could hear the faint laughter and music. She saw several men go into and out of the place, the swinging doors sending shafts of light darting into the street.

Sometimes she envied men their freedom. It wasn't that she wanted to go to the saloon, but being able to go if she wanted would be such a wonderful thing. She thought then of Cory, envying her courage in passing herself off as a man, envying that she'd traveled all across this great country in a painted wagon. It didn't matter that Aimee too had traveled the same distance, at times fearing for her very life. Cory had done it alone. And survived.

Just then, two figures caught her eye as they approached the saloon. It was Davy's enormous black hat that identified them. Light spilled from the doors, catching the glitter of silver belt buckles and spurs. Just as the two were about to enter, the shorter figure appeared to look up the street in the store's direction. Aimee caught her breath and backed away from the window. If she didn't know better, she would swear Cory had just reached out and touched her.

Grabbing the candle, Aimee left her sitting room and retired to the bedroom. From the window there, Aimee had a glorious view of the great expanse of the desert and the Mule Mountains rising majestically in the distance, their steep slopes covered with conifers. Looking out, she caught glimpses of skulking shadows among the junipers and manzanita brush—a coyote or maybe even a mountain lion. As beautiful as the desert could be, especially now in the spring with the bright red flowers of the ocotillo, there were times when Aimee was homesick for the east. What could be more noble than a great oak or maple? Surely not the towering saguaros?

Sighing, Aimee sat on the bed. She felt restless, dreading the long night ahead—how unlike her to feel loneliness. On her night table sat a tome of Shakespeare plays that she was no longer interested in reading. She dropped backward onto the bed, letting her bare feet dangle off the edge. The whisper of an almost imperceptible breeze made her candlelight seem to dance across the ceiling. She stared at the pale light, watching as a spider crawled into it and then disappeared into the dark corner. Normally, she would have jumped up to squash it—she had long ago abandoned the female propensity for squeamishness at such things—but this time she lay unmoving, letting her thoughts drift, hoping they would distract her.

Suddenly, a quiet tapping caught her attention. Was someone really at the door at this late hour? Draping a shawl around her shoulders, she cautiously went to the kitchen, heart pounding. Sure enough, someone was knocking. Cursing herself for leaving her pearl-handled derringer in the bedroom, she looked about for something to use as a weapon.

Then, softly. "Aimee? Aimee, can you hear me?"

Her heart still pounding, though no longer with fright, Aimee opened the door. She smiled as she beheld Cory. Taking Cory's hand, Aimee pulled her inside.

"I'm so happy to see you," Aimee said.

"I wasn't sure . . . it's so late . . . maybe . . ."

"You're always welcome, no matter the time."

She grabbed a couple of shot glasses and Jim's whiskey before leading Cory to the sofa. Her hand shook ever so slightly, making her splash the whiskey as she poured. "To new friends," she said breathlessly, then downed the drink, hoping it would calm her nerves. She felt like some raw schoolgirl.

"You nervous?" Cory asked, grinning, before she too downed her drink.

Without a word, Aimee poured refills. Belatedly, she remembered she'd not eaten supper, but she drank the second whiskey anyway. She would feel the liquor's effects quickly. "Why should I feel nervous?" she asked.

Cory took the empty glass from her and placed it carefully on the table. Then she took both of Aimee's hands in hers and looked deep into her eyes. "I know you feel it too—this attraction between us."

"But we've only just met," Aimee protested automatically, though she did not withdraw her hands. At Cory's grin, Aimee smiled back. "Yes, I feel it too," she said.

"I would never force you to do anything you weren't comfortable with, but I really would love to spend the night with you."

Aimee felt her pulses quicken. "I would like that," she said, feeling reckless and the effects of the alcohol.

In answer, Cory swept the shawl off of Aimee's shoulders, then leaned over to kiss her collarbone. Aimee gasped at her touch, feeling a flush of heat she knew was not from the whiskey. Then Cory was fumbling with the buttons on Aimee's chemise.

"Wait," Aimee said, standing to lead them into the bedroom. She closed the window, then turned to face Cory. Slowly, she finished unbuttoning her chemise, liking the way Cory's gray eyes glittered with desire as she watched. Aimee let the cotton shift slide off of her shoulders and onto the floor. She untied the strings of her pantalets, letting them too fall to the floor so she stood naked and trembling in the dim candlelight, feeling like a newlywed. Only she did not remember feeling like this on her wedding night. Or any night, for that matter.

"You are so beautiful," Cory said, but she did not move toward Aimee.

Aimee held out her hand. "Come to me," she said. "Let me take away your pain, even for a little while."

With a groan, Cory pulled her close, burying her face in Aimee's hair. Then her breath was warm on Aimee's bare skin as her lips nuzzled Aimee's throat. Her hands played over the curves and valleys of Aimee's body, making Aimee arch under her touch.

"Oh," Aimee said in surprise as Cory's lips closed over an erect nipple. Cory's mouth and tongue were soft, then her teeth nipped ever so lightly. "Oh," Aimee said again, throwing her head back and thrusting her breast against Cory's face. Aimee moaned long and loud as Cory's fingers tweaked the other nipple, making it harden even more. The heat between her legs grew more intense, and she felt her wetness flow.

Cory pushed her down on the bed, laying atop of her. Aimee felt's Cory's belt buckle bite into her flesh, but she didn't mind. Cory kissed her long and hard, then trailed wet kisses down her throat, across her collarbone, and over her breasts. She sucked first one nipple and then the other into her mouth, making Aimee moan and squirm beneath her. Aimee spread her legs, feeling Cory settle between them, feeling the roughness of denim and hardness of metal buttons press against her wet heat.

She felt completely wanton, wanting Cory to take her, to ravish her, to make her feel alive with heat and sex and lust. Cory moved down Aimee's body, her mouth alternately harsh and soft across Aimee's belly and hips. Cory's hands moved up and down, over and across, fingers fluttering softly, then grabbing hold hard. And all the while, her mouth teased and her tongue licked and her teeth nipped. Aimee felt ripples of desire course through her body, making her flush with excitement. She opened her eyes to find Cory looking at her, the sight of which made Aimee draw in her breath.

"Dear Lord!" Aimee cried out as Cory's mouth hovered above her most secret place. She instinctively tensed. What was this new sensation? Aimee tried to close her legs, but Cory's body remained firm between them. Her hands clutched Aimee's hips, holding her down. Cory's tongue darted out, flicking over Aimee's sensitive spot, sending shivers of delight through her. She'd never felt this way with Jim, never. But then, he'd never been so intimate, so bold.

"Cory," Aimee said. "Cory, what are you doing?"

"Shhhh," Cory replied, "just feel it. Let me pleasure you."

The air in the closed room grew still and hot. A candle burned down, then sputtered out, making the room dark but for a pale shaft of moonlight that filtered in through the thin curtain, casting a yellowish glow over Aimee's body. She moved and moaned to Cory's ministrations, alternately clutching Cory's hair and the rumpled sheets on the bed. Cory's tongue darted in and out of Aimee's moist center, making her wetness flow like the flash flood of a desert storm.

Cory's hands never stopped moving over Aimee's body, grabbing hold of luscious hips, then moving up to play with swollen nipples. With each pinch to her nipples, Aimee arched her back and thrust her hips against Cory's mouth, gasping each time Cory's tongue went deeper inside her. She liked the feeling of something inside her, and she screamed out loud when Cory's fingers replaced her tongue, thrusting even deeper.

Then suddenly Aimee felt something she'd never felt before as Cory thrust with her fingers and sucked with her mouth. It started with a pleasurable twinge between her legs, then grew like a bubbling brook to a roiling river. She thrashed and bucked beneath Cory's mouth, calling out her name again and again.

"Oh, dear Lord!" Aimee cried out as she grabbed Cory's shoulders, feeling the leather of her vest smooth and cool beneath her fingertips. "Yes, please don't stop. Dear God, please don't stop!"

She knew not where Cory's mouth and tongue and fingers started and ended. All sensations blended into one. Just when she thought it was over, the storm-ravaged river flooded again, then yet again. And as the pleasure slowly ebbed, she feebly pushed against Cory's head. "Stop," she pleaded. "Please stop."

"Are you sure?" Cory said, the vibration of her voice tickling Aimee's center.

"Yes, oh yes."

Cory gave one last lick, then came up alongside Aimee on the bed. They were both breathing heavily. Cory sat up long enough to strip off her vest and unbutton her shirt, then lay down again, taking one of Aimee's hands into her own.

"What was that?" Aimee asked at long last.

Cory laughed. "I believe that was, as the French call it, an orgasm."

"I've never felt that way before. Ever."

Cory laughed again. The sound made Aimee smile with pleasure. "In all these years of marriage, you've never had an orgasm?"

Suddenly feeling inadequate, Aimee felt herself blush. She was glad for the darkness, for it hid her embarrassment. Was something wrong with her that she'd not had an orgasm before? No one had ever told her of such a thing. And she'd never even heard the term before. As if sensing her discomfort, Cory sat up and leaned over her. She lightly touched Aimee's cheek.

"I didn't mean to cause you any distress. There's nothing wrong with you, you know. Most men just don't know how to pleasure a woman."

"So, it's not me?"

Cory kissed her. "No, my dear, it's not you." She grinned. "But I'm glad I was your first."

Aimee pushed the damp curls off of Cory's forehead. "One day, when you're ready, I want you to tell me about the woman who taught you how to love like that." Cory stiffened, and Aimee saw the pleasure die from Cory's eyes. "I can help you, if you let me," she said, kissing Cory softly.

As Cory collapsed sobbing against her, Aimee took her into her arms, smoothing back her hair just like Miss White had done all those years ago.

CHAPTER SEVEN

When Aimee awoke the next morning, she was alone. Cory had left sometime during the night. Though disappointed, Aimee knew it was for the best. It would not do for Cory to be seen leaving. She leaned back into the pillows, suddenly feeling a bit overwhelmed by what had happened last night. She had cheated on her husband, yet was it really cheating? After all, she'd been with a woman, not another man. But would Jim see it that way? She smiled, remembering the feel of Cory's mouth, soft against her lips, and Cory's hands, gentle in their caresses. How unlike Jim. This marriage was not right for her, but what could she do?

As she got out of bed, she wondered if she would see Cory that day. She sighed, knowing it was not likely. She didn't have anything else at the store for her to do, and Cory had promised Rufus Jones she'd help him. She smiled, thinking about Cory up on a horse. How long had it been since she, Aimee, had been out riding? Although she and Jim owned two horses, he was usually the only one who rode them.

She calculated mentally—Jim had been gone six days now. That meant she had six or seven more days without him, depending on how successful his trip went. She found herself hoping he'd be delayed, but she knew that was unlikely. He didn't like to be gone more than necessary. Sighing, she forced herself out of bed. When he did return, they would have a lot to talk about. In just these few days, she'd come to realize that she was not really happy. She splashed her face with water, then cleaned her teeth with a rag dipped in alcohol. The taste made her grimace.

Not expecting to see Cory in the store this day, she took her time with breakfast, even enjoying a third cup of coffee in her sitting room. Puss followed her in, curling around her ankles and then darting out in front of her. Aimee stumbled, splashing coffee all over her clean apron.

"Darn cat," she muttered under her breath, but she didn't really mean it. She'd come to love the animal.

Sitting in the chair beside the window, she breathed deeply, leaning back against the cushion. Sipping her coffee, she remembered what had happened the night before. The mere thought of it made her cheeks grow warm. Her body had never experienced that before, never. Jim so rarely touched her other than during their quick lovemaking, and even then it wasn't with the tenderness shown by Cory. And the things Cory's mouth had done!

"Oh, Puss," she said to her cat, stroking his soft, fine fur. "I think I'm truly in love for the first time." He purred, all the while turning in circles on her lap until he settled down with a soft plop. "How silly is that?" Aimee continued.

She looked out her window. The Mule Mountains rose dark and silent against the sky. The desert stretched out before her, flat with sparse vegetation and exotic creatures that could kill a

man. Strangely, the sight made her think of back home for the
first time in years. Right about now her mother's garden would
be filled with blooming white and pink dogwoods, the last of the
bright yellow forsythia, and azaleas just coming into bloom. The
grass would be a new green, pale and soft to bare feet. She would
hear bird song from her bedroom window.

"I miss New York," she said to Puss. "How long I've been out
West now. Six long years."

She closed her eyes, letting the memory of Cory's hands and
mouth wash over her. Were her feelings merely lust?
Dissatisfaction with the physical attentions of her husband? And
what of her feelings? When was the last time she could say she
loved Jim? She was sure she had loved him once. Hadn't she?

She thought about Cory's face, the way she smiled, her hearty
laugh. She had a strong body, lean and hard, yet soft, the way a
woman should be. Cory didn't use her strength to her advantage,
the way Jim sometimes would. The idea of his hands on her body
made Aimee frown with distaste. She opened her eyes, staring
into the ever-brightening room.

"Dear Lord, what am I going to do?"

• • •

Creeping out of Aimee's apartment before the early morning
light, Cory cautiously descended the stairs. She looked carefully
up and down the street before scurrying to the other side so she
could walk back to the hotel. She knew how important it was
that no one suspect she'd stayed with Aimee the night before.
She stepped over a drunk sleeping it off, then smiled and winked
at Fanny Palmer, who she'd quickly learned was the madam at
the more respectable brothel in town—if one could call a brothel
respectable. She knew her more Puritan brethren back east
would not find it so.

She tipped her hat. "How do, Miz Palmer," she said.

"Quite well, Mr. Adamson," Fanny replied. "Might we expect a visit from you sometime, Mr. Adamson?"

Cory grinned. The girls at Mrs. Palmer's would be in for quite a surprise if she were to visit. "Don't rightly know, Miz Palmer." She tipped her hat again. "You have a nice day."

"Much obliged, Mr. Adamson."

Cory couldn't help but turn and watch Fanny walk away. She was still a very good-looking woman, trim of figure and carrying herself tall and elegantly. Cory felt her face grow hot when Fanny turned around and caught her staring. With a sheepish wave, she turned away, hearing Fanny's delighted laughter fill the morning air.

Cory hurried to her room. After a quick wash up and change of clothing, she went to Davy's room, entering without bothering to knock. He groaned and covered his face with his pillow when she rolled up the window shade.

"Late night?" she asked. "And how many times have I told you to lock your door?"

He moved the pillow away and looked at her balefully with one eye. "Your advice is not needed." He groaned again. "I have the worst hangover."

She sat in a chair by the bed. "Don't you have one of your concoctions to cure hangovers?" She shook him. "Come on, we don't want to lose our chance to make money. Rufus Jones is expecting us."

"You are merciless." He tossed the covers aside. "And where were you last night, missy? I've seen you eyeing them girls over at Miz Palmer's place."

Cory turned her eyes from Davy's nakedness. It wasn't like she'd never seen a nude male before, but she could probably count on one hand how many times that had been, and most of them had been boys. "If you must know, I was with Aimee Calhoun." At a loud clattering, she looked up to see Davy had dropped his shaving brush into the basin.

"Please tell me you didn't," he said.

"What are you getting all riled up for? Before we took off for the saloon you were tellin' me I was like a cowboy coming off the range and laughing about it."

Davy slathered foamy shaving cream on his face, neck and chest. As he took careful strokes with his razor, he said, "Stealing some kisses is one thing. Sleepin' with a married woman is another. People in these parts don't take too kindly to people like you an' me."

Cory knew he was right, but she didn't care. "I haven't been with a woman since I left Virginia." She took a deep breath. "I haven't been happy in a long time, Davy. Please don't take this away from me."

He turned from the basin and came over to hug her. "Don't mind me, Cory. You deserve all the happiness you can find." He grinned. "Maybe I'm just a bit jealous. Nice as this town is, Bisbee just don't seem to have much for a man like me."

"We're just a couple of lonely souls, aren't we?" She wiped foam off her cheek. "Come on, hurry up. The cattle won't mind if you have stubble."

"No, but I will," Davy called out as she left the room.

When they got to the Johnson ranch, Rufus Jones was waiting impatiently. He took one look at Cory's horse and ordered her to go to the stable and get another. "That ol' nag o' yorn ain't good for nuthin' but the glue factory," he said.

Cory patted Red's neck. "Don't you worry old fella. Nobody's taking you anywhere." But she went to the barn and did as she was bid. She traded Red in for a muscular quarter horse, Lucifer by name, with a wild look in his eyes.

"You and Adamson take the north pasture," Rufus was saying to Davy. "I heard tell old man Smith got fifty head taken yesterday, and his ranch borders ours up there. You two think you can patrol a hundred acres okay?" He looked a bit skeptically at Cory, no doubt thinking a "man" of her size wouldn't hold up too long.

"Not a problem," Davy said.

"We'll be fine," Cory said in her deepest voice while trying to sit taller in the saddle.

"All right then. I'll send someone to relieve you tonight at seven. That'd be a good twelve hours o' work."

Cory added up in her head. At a dollar an hour, that would be twelve dollars. She couldn't remember the last time she'd made that much money. And maybe she could take Aimee out to dinner, just the two of them.

As if reading her thoughts, Davy said as they galloped away, "Don't be plannin' on spendin' all that in one place."

After an hour's ride, they made it to their destination. They could barely make out heads of cattle scattered over the vast property. It was easy to see how rustlers could steal without being seen or caught. Davy and Cory had a daunting task before them.

"Hard to know if any cattle have been stolen if we don't know how many there are to begin with," Cory said.

"I reckon their thinking is, if they got people patrolling, maybe the thieves will think twice about it. But I'm with you, I don't think there's much you can do against determined outlaws."

"You think we should stick together?"

"Probably safer that way, but then we wouldn't cover as much ground. You okay with goin' out on your own for a bit?"

Cory patted the rifle strapped to her saddle. "I think I'm good."

She watched as Davy galloped away, then set her own steed to a gallop. Despite the fact she'd been on the road for so long, it had been months since she'd felt so free. An aimless wanderer trapped in her own nightmares, she slept fitfully at night, haunted by the images of her beloved. In this remote region, she'd found a reason to be alive again. And though she might attribute it to finally feeling useful again, she knew a certain chestnut-haired beauty was a big part of the reason.

Aimee had been so wonderful last night. Eager and shy at the same time, yet not totally naïve. She couldn't help but wonder if Aimee had had more experience with women than a simple kiss, yet she knew it was unlikely. And Aimee had told her she was not happy in her marriage.

Cory slowed her horse to a trot, trying not to let her thoughts wander too much. After all, she had a job to do. Yet the image of Aimee's naked, responsive body would not go away. "God help me," she said. She shook her head, willing Aimee away. She searched the wide open space, squinting in the sun, looking for any signs of trouble. The sun rose steadily overhead, making the sweat trickle down her neck into her bandana. She felt the chafing of the bind around her breasts, feeling it soak up her perspiration. The flies began to buzz incessantly around her horse, who twitched his tail and ears in an effort to be rid of them. Lucifer's hair darkened with sweat. Cory slowed to a walk, feeling the heat sap her energy.

"This has got to be Hell," she muttered, impatiently swatting at a pesky fly. She blinked up into the relentless sun. Taking a sip of precious water, she looked around for some kind of shade. The spiny cacti offered none. Was it only days ago that she'd been in this very condition? The sand shimmered in front of her, seemingly like water.

It occurred to her belatedly that she should have stayed with Davy. She didn't have a clue as to where she was. For all she knew, she was way beyond the north pasture. Pasture? What kind of joke was that? There was no pasture here—just miles and miles of sand covered with scrub brush. Where the heck did the cattle go?

Her horse stumbled and almost fell. Caught unawares, Cory flew over his head and landed with a painful thud. "Damnation!" she yelled, coming face to face with a scorpion, its tail held high, ready to sting. She quickly rolled away, relieved to feel nothing was broken. Standing, she saw the reason for Lucifer's stumble—a hole just big enough to catch his hoof. There was no telling what might be down there, so she led Lucifer away before kneeling to examine him for injuries.

"You're okay," she said as she ran her fingers gently up his front legs. She stood up, the movement making her sway slightly. She shaded her eyes. Was there no place to get out of this darn sun? There was no way she'd make it to one o'clock, let alone seven if she didn't find some shelter. She retrieved her hat, then got back into the saddle and set off in a canter.

With each stride of her horse, she became more and more aware of a blinding ache behind her eyes. She groaned aloud, feeling every jarring motion shoot pain through her body. Then Lucifer shied to the left and whinnied in panic. Ever more dizzy, Cory clung to his mane, but felt herself sliding forward, felt the rough hair of her horse against her cheek, then darkness.

"Cory! Cory, wake up!"

"Go 'way."

"Cory dammit, wake up."

She opened her eyes to see a hazy image kneeling beside her. "Davy? Where am I?"

He helped her sit. "I should've realized you had no experience at this," he said. "Aimee would never forgive me if I let something happen to you."

"I just needed to get out of the sun," she said groggily. Why did her head hurt so much?

"Looks like you took a tumble. Hit your head on that rock there." Davy pointed to a chunk of gold-flecked pyrite, one jagged corner bearing scarlet evidence. "That's quite a cut over your eye."

Cory raised a hand to her forehead, feeling the stickiness of blood. She vaguely remembered Lucifer being spooked by a rattler. She looked 'round, horrified to think he'd been bitten, breathing a sigh of relief when she saw him standing near Davy's horse.

"Guess I'm not much of a ranchhand," she said ruefully. "You won't tell anyone, will you? Ruin my reputation?"

Davy laughed. "Your secret's safe with me." He helped her stand. "Now, let's get you back. Between the cut and the sunburn, you look a fright. And I've got just the remedy for you."

She struggled up onto her horse. "No thanks. I think I'll stick with some old-fashioned rest and relaxation. And a call to Doc Templeton if need be."

Davy pouted as he swung up on his horse. "I'm hurt. You don't trust my remedies? And I thought we were friends."

"We are," Cory laughed, "and I want it to stay that way."

After about an hour, Cory couldn't fight her dizziness and nausea any longer. "Can we rest a bit?" she asked, just before she slid unconscious off her horse for the second time.

"It'll take us until tomorrow to get back if this keeps happening," Davy said when she came to. He helped her to her feet. "Just lay against your horse's neck. No need to ride tall in the saddle."

Groaning in pain, Cory let him push her up onto her horse. He tied a rope around her waist, securing it to her saddle. "This way," he said as he tightened the knots, "if you faint again, you won't fall off."

"I don't faint," she mumbled, but the effort made her light-headed again. Heeding his advice, she leaned forward, resting her cheek against the rough hide of her horse.

It turned out, Cory had managed to stay out only six hours, and that counted the time it took to go and come back. Rufus was understanding, though she overheard him talking to Davy. "Never did think that one could handle the job. Too small a man, but he were a friend of yorn so I thought I'd give 'em a try."

"Appreciate it," Davy said. "But you're right, he is a bit green." He leaned close to Rufus. "Might do better if he just stays in town and helps that nice Miz Calhoun."

"Yeah, least-aways till Jim gets back. But tell your friend to be careful. Jim's been known to have quite a temper. Might not appreciate another feller hangin' 'round his wife."

"Duly noted," Davy said, walking over to where Cory stood with Red. "You heard the man, Cory Adamson. Let's get you back to town for some face time with the lovely Mrs. Calhoun."

Cory smacked him on the arm, but she was smiling as she leaped up on Red and spurred his flanks, the throbbing in her head forgotten.

• • •

Aimee looked up as someone came into the store. She gasped when she saw Cory. "What happened to you?" She came over and touched the bandage on Cory's forehead, then her bare cheek. "You're burning up with sunburn!"

Cory winced at Aimee's touch, light though it was. "Fell off my horse and got knocked out." She gave a sheepish grin. "Actually fell off more than once. Good thing Davy found me, or I would've ended up some coyote's dinner."

"This is nothing to joke about," Aimee said as she went to the window sill and cut off a fleshy stem of aloe from the plant she kept there. "You can get sun poisoning." She squeezed the stem until thick, sticky juice oozed out, which she spread over Cory's face and neck.

"Davy says I should just stick around and help you out." Cory grinned. "Anything in particular you care to have me help you with, my dear?"

Aimee was sure her face was as red as Cory's, but she was saved from replying by a group of children coming into the store from after school. While she busied herself measuring out candies and wrapping them in colorful paper, she kept glancing at Cory, who watched her the whole time and grinned like she had a big secret to share. Aimee couldn't get the children out of the store fast enough.

"You've got something on your mind," Aimee said when they were alone.

"I do believe," Cory said, grabbing Aimee and pulling her down for a series of kisses, "that . . . I need . . . a woman's . . . tender care."

Aimee laughed and pushed her playfully away. "Not now, not here." She walked quickly to the door and locked it. "Let's go upstairs," she said. "You can 'help me out' with my new project."

"It would be my pleasure."

CHAPTER EIGHT

It didn't seem like so many days had passed, but by Aimee's reckoning, Jim would be home in a day or two, so that morning she took her time washing up. Without Jim home to cook breakfast for, she could afford the luxury of a more leisurely toilette. She brushed her hair, carefully counting out one hundred strokes, then put it up in an elaborate braid. She picked out her best day dress, a green one that she'd been told complemented her coloring. Looking at herself in the mirror, she tried to remember the last time Jim had told her she looked pretty. She was dressed far too nicely for the store, but she didn't care. If she was honest with herself, it was Corrine she was dressing for these days.

They'd spent the last five nights together, with Cory sneaking out well before dawn. They knew it was risky, but couldn't stop. And Aimee was closing the store early every day, which drew comments from the townsfolk, but it made no matter to her. Jim would be home soon enough, and all would return to normal. Aimee frowned at the thought.

A beribboned box on the dresser caught her eye. How long had it been since she'd worn them? she wondered. She opened the box to reveal a pair of emerald and gold earrings. They caught the early morning light, sending a flash of green across the whitewashed wall. With a smile, she put them in her ears, liking the way the gems flashed against her skin.

Grabbing a quick breakfast, she hurried down to the store.

"You look very fetching this morning."

Aimee shrieked. Her heart pounding in her chest, she turned to face Cory. "Cory! Oh my God, you scared me to death," she said. "I thought you'd gone back to the hotel."

Cory got up from the window seat. "I did, but returned about half an hour ago." She pointed to a straw broom. "Your porch is sand free. Widow Adams came by and complimented me on my early morning energy."

Aimee laughed. "I wonder sometimes if the woman ever sleeps." She glanced out the window. "I'm surprised she's not here."

Cory looked a trifle embarrassed. "I hope you don't mind, but I let her in the store early. She needed some cough syrup. Said she couldn't wait for you to open up."

"Everything she buys, she needs immediately."

"I have an idea, but I don't know if you'll do it."

"What is it?"

Cory actually blushed. "As beautiful as you look in that dress, why don't you go change into riding attire and let's take the day off. We can take a picnic lunch, spend the whole day out."

"You sure you want to? You've not fully recovered from your sunburn."

"I don't plan for us to be out in the sun all day. Besides, I'll bet you know someplace we can go."

Aimee didn't need a second invitation. "You're right, I do, and

I'd love to go out with you."

She hurried upstairs to change, putting on a dove-gray split riding skirt and matching jacket with a soutache trim and fabric-covered buttons. It had been an extravagant purchase, and this was her first time wearing it. She was rewarded for her efforts yet again as she saw Cory's eyes light up. This time it was her turn to blush at Cory's unabashed admiration.

Locking up the store, she left the CLOSED sign turned out and walked with Cory to the hostelry. The horses were already saddled up and waiting. Aimee shot Cory a look of surprise. Cory was grinning from ear to ear.

"I didn't think you'd say no," she said as she patted Red's neck, then fed him an apple. She took another from her pocket and handed it to Aimee. "I took the liberty of asking if you and Jim have a horse stabled here."

"Pretty sure of yourself, were you?" Aimee gave the apple to her horse, then let Cory help her mount. "Poor ol' Stardust here hasn't been ridden in months. Jim has a preference for Blaze when he travels."

"Not to worry, Miz Calhoun," said a young lad of indeterminate age with freckles and flaming red hair. "I ride 'em ever'day."

"You're a good boy, Joshua," Aimee said as she followed Cory.

"Lead the way," Cory said, holding back to let Aimee's horse pass.

"The Johnson ranch has a river that runs through it." Aimee gently spurred her horse. "There's a particular place Jim and I used to go when we wanted some private time." She glanced at Cory. "You won't mind goin' there, will you?"

"Not at all."

Aimee eyed her speculatively. Was Cory telling the truth?

As if reading her mind, Cory said, "Honestly, I won't mind. I'm not the jealous type."

Aimee felt a twinge of disappointment. Not the jealous type? She wanted Corrine to be jealous. Aimee frowned. Why would she even be thinking such a thing? Lord, what was going to happen when Jim returned home? What would it mean for her relationship with Cory?

Absentmindedly, she led them out of town, the silence between them deepening. It was as if Cory knew Aimee needed time alone with her thoughts. But did Aimee want to be having those thoughts? She pressed Stardust's flanks, and he set off in a gallop, Red following close behind. Before long, they came to the boundary of the Johnson ranch. Aimee led them on a seemingly random trail. Someone not familiar with the terrain would find themselves hopelessly lost, but soon the two women came upon a dry riverbed with only a meager trickle of water down the middle of it.

"I thought you said the Johnsons had a river on their property," Cory said, looking around.

Aimee laughed. "When the rains come to the mountains, this river will flow faster and deeper than you'd expect. Many an unsuspecting traveler's been caught in a flash flood, never to be seen again."

Before long, they came to a large rock formation surrounded by manzanita brush. "This is it," she said, leaping off her horse unaided. She led the animal into where the rocks formed a V shape. Cory followed with Red. At the very tip of the V, they passed through a narrow opening and found themselves in a cool, darkened space. Not exactly a cave, it was more like a big circular room. Cracks in the rocks overhead sent shafts of light penetrating the gloom. Aimee loosened the bridles of both horses, then led them to where one of the rocks had been worn away enough to form a shallow bowl. She poured water into it from her canteen, then unstrapped the blanket tied at the back of her saddle. With a flourish, she spread it on the sandy ground.

"Wow, this is quite a find," Cory said, as she unbuckled her holster and let it fall to the ground before she took a swig of water from her canteen.

Aimee removed her jacket and hat, laying them carefully on another outcropping of rock. "I don't remember exactly how Jim and I found this place, except that we were looking for shelter from a sudden storm. Afterward, we'd come here every other month or so, just for a feeling of adventure." She felt herself blushing at the memory of what they used to do here, and turned so Cory would not see. "It's probably been at least four years since the last time. I'm a bit surprised I remembered where it is."

Feeling Cory's presence behind her, she turned to find her close. Without a word, Cory leaned down and caught Aimee's mouth in a long kiss. She took hold of Aimee's narrow waist, pulling her in closer. Aimee couldn't help but moan, feeling herself melt into Cory's arms. Her heart pounding, she also felt the throbbing between her thighs. She put her arms around Cory's strong shoulders, letting her fingers twine in Cory's soft hair. Their tongues danced together as their bodies melded into one.

Stepping back, both were breathing heavily as they fumbled with the buttons on each other's shirts. Cory released the binds that held her breasts down, before stripping off her trousers. Aimee made short work of her skirt and underclothes. They both stood naked before the other, skins flushed with heat and desire, bosoms heaving with every breath. Brushing aside a momentary feeling of insecurity, Aimee reached out and cupped Cory's breasts. They felt heavy, melon-ripe in her hands. As if she'd been doing it forever, she leaned forward and took one of Cory's nipples into her mouth. Cory moaned, pushing her breast into Aimee's mouth, holding the back of Aimee's head. Aimee sucked one nipple while she played with the other, letting her fingers roll it between them.

Wordlessly, they fell together to the blanket, sweat making their bodies slippery. Aimee's hair tumbled out of its pins to fall long and full down her back. Their hands roamed over each other, finding places secret and wet. Aimee tilted her head back as Cory's mouth closed over one swollen nipple, crying out as

Cory's teeth nipped sharply. The throbbing between her legs intensified, making her take Cory's hand to put it there. She caught her breath as Cory's fingers slid wetly between her folds, then dipped inside her, making her tremble.

"Cory," she said. "Cory."

"Do you like that, my sweet?" Cory whispered, her breath hot against Aimee's neck.

"Yes, oh yes," Aimee said, pushing her hips upward so Cory's fingers went deeper. She tangled her fingers in Cory's hair, pulling roughly as Cory continued to thrust and tease her. She could feel the buildup of something sweet and good in the pit of her stomach.

Cory laughed lightly. "No yet, my sweet. Not yet." She nuzzled Aimee's ear, then bit her gently on the neck.

Aimee groaned, squirming in her arms. "Don't make me wait. Please!"

In answer, Cory withdrew her fingers, soliciting yet another groan from Aimee. She pushed Aimee flat against the blanket. "I want you to enjoy this. Slowly."

"Jim never made me feel like this. Never."

Cory smiled, leaning down to cover Aimee's mouth with her own. She played her fingers over Aimee's breasts, making the nipples harden almost painfully. Aimee's hands traveled down Cory's back, her nails leaving red streaks across tender flesh. She cupped Cory's buttocks, pulling her closer still. She could feel their hearts beat together as one. She gasped as Cory bit her neck again, harder this time. She spread her legs, feeling her own wetness sticky on her thighs.

"I want you to make me feel like you did last night," she said, feeling wanton.

Smiling, Cory teased her. "What do you mean? What do you want me to do?"

"I want . . . I want . . ." Aimee felt her face flame. "Oh God, please Cory . . . Corrine . . ."

"Tell me," Cory urged.

Aimee felt unexpected tears well up in her eyes. She was overwhelmed by her feelings for this woman, for the things she wanted done to her body. Things she'd never even known could happen. Cory's hands and fingers continued their caresses of her body, her mouth and tongue teasing wherever they touched. Aimee's body felt on fire. She took a deep breath.

"Put your mouth . . . touch me . . . down there."

Cory kissed her way down Aimee's body, stopping only long enough to suck first one nipple, then the other. Aimee squirmed impatiently, waiting for Cory's mouth and tongue to bring her to ecstasy. She grabbed hold of Cory's head, guiding her, sighing long and loud as Cory's tongue at last found her most sensitive spot. As the waves began in her body, she grasped Cory's shoulders, her nails digging deep. Cory groaned, her tongue moving faster and faster. She grabbed Aimee's thighs, holding her down as she began to buck and strain against her.

"Oh yes, please!" Aimee cried out. "Don't stop, Cory. Please don't stop!"

Her whole body shuddering with pleasure, Aimee felt the ripples start in her stomach, travel to her core, then zing down her legs and up her torso. "Oh, oh, oh!" she called out. Her back arching as her fingers clutched and unclutched Cory's shoulders, she felt one last burst between her legs before she fell back, feeling the scratchy wool of the blanket against her skin.

"Cory," she breathed.

Cory looked up at her from between Aimee's legs. Already over-warm, the sight made Aimee flush hotly. She grabbed hold of Cory's damp curls and pulled, urging her up. Cory complied, stopping to kiss and lick Aimee's sweat-dampened stomach and chest and the hollow at her throat.

"Mmm, salty," she said, making Aimee blush more.

Aimee looked deep into Cory's gray eyes. Seeing laughter and trust there, she sat up suddenly, pushing Cory back onto the blanket and straddling her. Cory looked surprised but not inclined to stop her, so Aimee leaned down to kiss Cory full on the lips while she splayed her hands over Cory's breasts to squeeze and knead them. Usually bound down flat, they felt full and lush in Aimee's hands. Cory closed her eyes, moaning ever so softly as she let Aimee caress her. Aimee licked Cory's cheek and neck, tasting salt. She teased Cory's nipples, bringing them to hard peaks.

Cory started moving beneath her, her hands grabbing hold of Aimee's arms. Her fingers pressed deeply into Aimee's flesh, but Aimee felt no pain. Still straddling Cory, Aimee moved her body downward, working her way between Cory's legs, forcing them apart. The lay together, private place to private place, bodies slick with sweat and tingling with desire.

"You . . . don't . . . have . . . to do . . . this," Cory said.

"I want to," Aimee replied, taking Cory's earlobe into her mouth and nipping with her teeth.

Cory gasped, wriggling beneath Aimee as Aimee trailed her fingernails down Cory's arms and then her sides and to her hips.

"Tell me what to do," Aimee said between kisses.

"I think you know," Cory said, her whole body trembling.

Aimee took a nipple into her mouth and sucked. "You like this?" she asked.

"Oh, yes."

Aimee bit lightly. "And this?"

"God, yes."

Aimee worked her hand down between Cory's legs. She slipped a finger into Cory's wet heat. She was slick and hot. "This?" she murmured.

Cory's breaths came out in short gasps. "Yes," she said. "Oh, yes," she said again as Aimee added another finger.

Aimee moved lower down Cory's body. "Am I doing all right?"

"You're doing . . . just fine."

Then, Aimee lay between Cory's legs. She breathed in the heady scent of a woman for the first time. "Mmm," she moaned as she tasted her, salty and sweet at the same time. Her fingers, still inside Cory, felt pulsing against them. She licked Cory, finding her swollen and tender nub.

"Anne!" Cory called out.

Anne? Aimee hesitated only momentarily, then continued licking and sucking like she'd felt Cory do to her. Cory's trembling increased. She had a hold of Aimee's hair now. Aimee withdrew her fingers from Cory's center, concentrating with her mouth and tongue. Cory grabbed Aimee's hair more tightly, making her scalp tingle with pain, but she didn't mind.

With one long sigh, Cory stiffened, then let out a long breath. Aimee felt Cory's body relax. Should she stop? She kept licking. Cory gently pulled on Aimee's hair, urging her upward.

"Come up here," Cory said. She was grinning, her eyes sparkling.

"Are you sure?"

"Yes, my dear, I'm sure. You have a wonderful mouth. I'd never guess this was your first time."

Aimee felt herself blush at the compliment. "Thank you," she said, not knowing what else to say.

Cory brushed a stray curl away from Aimee's face. "You are so beautiful."

Aimee lay down next to Cory and put her head on Cory's chest. Listening to Cory's heartbeat and the soft clank of their horses' bridles, she began to doze. She felt languid, heavy. One of the horses snorted, startling her into wakefulness. She absently circled one of Cory's nipples with a finger while she thought about the name Cory had called out. Anne.

"Who's Anne?" she asked. She felt Cory stiffen.

"Why are you asking?" Cory's voice was tense, almost angry.

Aimee sat up. "You called out her name."

Cory's face flushed. "I'm sorry."

"Tell me about her." Aimee put a soothing hand on Cory's arm. "Please."

Unprepared for the tears in Cory's eyes, Aimee felt guilty for asking. Cory said nothing. Aimee touched Cory's cheek, then started to stand, but Cory pulled her down. "No, stay. You have a right to know."

"You don't have to tell me anything. I told you before I would wait until you're ready. And I meant that."

Cory took a deep breath. Her words rushed out. "Anne was my lover. We were together five years. She had a daughter, Lisbeth." She took another breath. "She'd been widowed a year when I met them."

Aimee waited. She could see Cory's mouth quivering, even in the dim light.

"I felt protective. They had no one. Anne was at her wit's end, not knowing how much longer she could survive, a woman alone with a young daughter. I offered them a home with me."

"When did your relationship change?"

"About six months later." Cory smiled, though the pain was still stark in her eyes. "I came home to find her waiting in my bed. She was not known for shyness, my Anne."

Aimee put her hand over Cory's. "I'm glad that she made you happy."

The tears spilled from Cory's eyes. "She did. They both did. We lived outside of Richmond. People didn't seem to think it odd—two women living together. If anyone asked, we said we were sisters." She took another deep breath as the tears continued to fall. "I was out hunting. I'd been gone two days. I came home to find them dead. Murdered."

Horrified, Aimee gasped. She took Cory's hand. "I'm so sorry. Oh my God, do you know who . . . ?"

"Outlaws. Renegades. They destroyed my homestead, slaughtered all the animals. I couldn't stay."

"Of course not." Aimee felt her own eyes fill with tears. "So, that's when you came out West?"

"Yes. I've been traveling about eight months now. Aimlessly. I'd overstay in some small town here and there. Earn some money, then move on." She smiled again. "Then I ran into Davy."

Aimee smiled too. "I'm glad you did. He brought you into my life."

"Aimee . . . I don't know where I'm going or what I'm doing. I don't want to hurt you . . ."

Quelling her tears, Aimee shook her head. "I'm not expecting anything of you, Corrine. After all, we've only just met."

"And you're married."

That dash of reality made Aimee scramble to her feet. She felt her cheeks grow hot with embarrassment and confusion. How easy it was to forget that fact. And how wrong to do so. In her heart she knew she belonged with Corrine, yet that alone was not enough to justify her actions.

"It's late," Aimee said, hearing in her mind the sound of a cage door swinging shut. "We have to get back."

• • •

Cory dressed quickly, worried at the hollow tone in Aimee's voice. She glanced over at her, but could tell nothing from the expression on her face. She wanted to say something soothing, but no words came. These last few days with Aimee had been wonderful. Being with her had made Cory realize how lonely she had been, and she realized too that Anne would want her to be happy again. She wouldn't want her, Corinne, to continue to mourn. But what kind of life could she give Aimee, a woman used to respectability and stability? Still, Cory reflected, she had given Anne and Lisbeth that very thing. They had been happy, of that Cory was sure. She could give Aimee happiness too. She was a strong, hard worker. And Aimee's business sense would benefit them both, no matter what they decided to do.

Feeling more secure, she turned to Aimee. "Let me help you," she said, assisting Aimee into the saddle, before swinging up onto Red. Her fingers tingled just from the touch of Aimee's hand.

Aimee gave a wan smile, her thoughts hidden. Cory opened her mouth to speak, but decided she'd wait until Aimee was ready to talk.

Leaving their secret sanctuary, the two women somberly rode back into town. Cory glanced up at the ever-darkening sky, hoping the rapidly approaching thunderstorm wasn't a portent of things to come.

CHAPTER NINE

Aimee felt her heart leap into her throat when they finally returned to town to find Blaze stabled in her stall next to Stardust's.

"Jim's home early," she said, feeling a brush of fear.

As if sensing Aimee's unease, Cory asked, "You want me to come home with you?"

"No, oh no," Aimee said. She tossed Joshua a coin. "Take good care of Stardust."

Cory followed her outside. "Are you sure?"

Aimee took out her handkerchief and patted her cheeks. Her nerves were crackling with tension. She wished she had a few drops of laudanum to calm her, but the drug was back at the store. She briefly thought of asking Davy, but decided not to take the time. "I'll see you soon," she said, turning from Cory and hurrying up the street. Her sense of foreboding deepened when people averted their eyes as she passed.

She paused outside the store, its open door menacing rather than welcoming. She took a deep breath and put a smile on her face, then walked up the steps. "Jim," she called out as she stepped inside.

She screamed when he came out of the shadows and appeared on her left. "Where have you been?" he asked, his tone clipped.

"Just out for a ride. It's so nice to see you." She leaned forward to give him a kiss, but he backed away.

"I was surprised to come home and find the store closed. Then I hear it's been closed early quite often since I've been gone." He waved his arm in a wide arc. "And everything's been rearranged. What have you been doing?"

Aimee took off her hat and jacket, placing them carefully on the counter. "I hired some temporary help when the last order came in. I guess I didn't watch close enough while Cory stocked everything."

Jim grabbed her arms painfully. "Did you know you've been the subject of gossip in this town? Oh yes, I heard all about this Cory Adamson. How he's been hanging round here like a lost puppy. How you two have been dining at the hotel." He shook her ever so slightly. "Couldn't you at least have been more discreet?"

She wrenched free of him. "There's nothing going on between us. He's from the East, like us. We've been reminiscing, is all."

"And today?" He pointed an accusing finger at her, then swept her fancy jacket and hat off the counter. "You dress like that for an afternoon chat? Where did you go?"

"We went riding, that's all." Aimee heard her voice rise, but it was in fear, not in anger.

He slapped her then. Following the sting of his hand, she heard a ringing in her ears. She stumbled in shock. He'd never hit her before. She raised a hand to her cheek, feeling it burning hot beneath her touch. Tears welled in her eyes.

"Why did you do that?" she asked, backing away from him.

She felt the counter at her waist. She could go no farther.

"Don't lie to me," Jim said, his voice tense with anger. "The whole town knows what you've been up to. Cheating on me with some no-good drifter."

"No, no," Aimee sobbed, knowing full well she was not being entirely truthful.

"I'm going to kill him, you know."

Aimee felt a rush of fear so strong, it made her dizzy. She had done this. She had put Cory in jeopardy with her selfish actions. "Please, Jim, I know you're angry. You have every right to be, but only with me, not Cory."

For one crazy minute, she thought of an outrageous lie. She'd tell Jim she was pregnant with his child. It's what he'd always wanted. Surely he would forget his anger?

He shoved her out of the way. Her eyes squeezed shut, Aimee heard Jim's rapid footsteps across the wooden floor, heard him climb up the ladder, then take down a box of ammunition. The unmistakable sound of bullets being loaded made her open her eyes. Now was the time to run, to warn Cory, but she was paralyzed. Even as Jim came toward her, she could not move. Breathing heavily, her heart beating painfully in her chest, Aimee managed to grab his arm as he walked by her.

"Please, Jim, this is wrong. You're wrong. Cory's done nothing. I swear."

In answer, he hit her in the face with the pistol. She felt a blinding flash of pain, then nothing but darkness.

• • •

"Mrs. Calhoun?"

Someone was calling her. The voice sounded so familiar.

"Mrs. Calhoun? Aimee? It's me, Belle."

Belle?

Someone shook her. The motion made her cry out as a stab

of agony ripped through her head. She felt someone dab at her left temple.

"Please, Aimee, wake up."

Aimee opened her eyes. Belle Foster knelt beside her, dressed in scarlet silk. Behind her stood her wide-eyed children, Amos and Jezebel. "Belle, what are you doing here?" Aimee struggled to sit up. When she did, she felt blood run down her face.

"I came to see Jim." Belle helped Aimee stand, holding on tight as Aimee swayed. "I found you like this. What happened?"

"An accident." Aimee put a hand against the counter to steady herself. "Belle, you need to go to the Copper Queen right away. Jim's gone there. He's very angry. There's been a misunderstanding . . ."

"About you and that Adamson fellow? Yes, I know."

"Damn, does the whole town think I'm a harlot?" Ignoring the startled gasps from the children at her language, she winced as a sharp pain seemed to pierce her skull.

Her face pink with embarrassment, Belle said, "Amos, Jezebel, please go outside. Yell if you see Mr. Calhoun coming."

After the children left, Aimee turned to Belle. "I need you to go to the hotel and stop Jim from hurting Cory. Please. You're probably the only one who can do it."

Belle blushed and lowered her lashes. It more than convinced Aimee that Belle had strong feelings for Jim, feelings she was ever more sure were reciprocated. She recalled several afternoons when Jim had disappeared for hours. It had never mattered to Aimee, for she was quite content being left alone. But of course, it was different when a man cheated on his wife. Yet Aimee could not be bitter, for Belle Foster could very well be the answer to her prayers. Yes, Aimee had been unfaithful to her husband, but he had no right to hit her and she knew now she could no longer go on in life just being his property. She deserved better. And he deserved a woman who truly loved him.

She grabbed Belle's hands, forcing her to look up. "I'm serious, Belle. Listen, I know you love him. I don't care." She almost laughed at Belle's look of pure astonishment. "You can have him, but not if he's in jail for killing a man!"

Her words were what was needed to propel Belle into action. Belle ran out of the store and down the street, Amos and Jezebel following as fast as they could. Disregarding the searing pain behind her eyes, Aimee stumbled up the stairs to the apartment and began throwing clothes into satchels and traveling bags. She didn't know where she was going or how she would get there, but she had to be gone by the time Jim returned. *If* he returned. He could very well be under arrest for murder by now.

"Oh, God," Aimee said, terrified at the thought of Cory being dead. Or maybe it was Jim who was dead and Cory arrested? She stopped her frantic packing. What was wrong with her? She needed to get to the hotel. She shoved her half-packed bags down the stairs, almost tripping over them in her haste. She rolled them behind the building, then stopped. What about Puss? How could she leave him?

"Don't worry about a cat," she scolded herself as she took off running down the street. It was strangely empty. Oh God, was everyone at the hotel? Just as she reached the saloon, she heard the clattering of a wagon. Around the corner came Davy's brightly painted mode of transportation, behind which was tied Red. Atop the driver's seat sat Davy and a woman Aimee had never seen before. She ran up to them.

"Davy! How can you leave? Have you seen Cory? My husband's gone crazy. He's determined to kill her!"

"Is he now? Can't say I blame him, Intelligent, nice-lookin' woman like you, cheatin' on him with another man." His eyes narrowed. "Looks like he done punished you good too. That's quite a cut above your eye."

Aimee frowned. Davy didn't sound like himself. "Davy! Have you gone crazy too?" She glanced behind the wagon. "Oh my God, is she dead already? Is that why you have Red?"

He moved back enough so Aimee could get a clear view of the woman beside him. Aimee gasped as the woman pushed aside her veil. It was Cory! And though Cory appeared calm, Aimee knew her well enough to recognize the growing anger in her eyes. Davy reached out and put his hand across Cory's waist, almost as if he was holding her back.

"Why don't you join me and the missus? Seeing as how you're soon to be *persona non grata* in this town, if you aren't already, seems like a good idea, don't you think?" He jerked his thumb back toward the wagon. "And I've got that Siamese cat of yours in the back, howlin' up a storm."

"Aimee, please come," Cory said. She held out her hand. "Let me and Davy take care of you."

Still worried, Aimee said, "I don't understand . . . Jim . . ."

"Came looking for Cory Adamson, the man who'd seduced his wife. Sorry, Cory checked out soon after returning from an afternoon with you." Davy grinned. "All Jim found was Cory's friend Davy with his new wife." A man staggered out of the saloon, pausing to look at them curiously. Davy continued, loudly, "Seems I had a little too much to drink last night. Ended up at Fanny Palmer's fine establishment and came home with a wife after an early mornin' meetin' with the justice o' the peace."

With a guffaw, the drunkard practically fell down the steps, then headed in the direction of the store. At that moment, Cory pushed aside Davy's arm and jumped down from the wagon. She looked so strange to Aimee's eyes, dressed in a lady's maroon traveling skirt and jacket, her matching hat adorned with an elaborate ostrich feather. She must have seen something in Aimee's eyes, for the quiet rage in her eyes faded as she laughed and pointed at the hat. "This cost Davy a pretty penny. He expects you to wear it, for I have no intention of keeping it on one minute longer than I have to." She reached up and touched Aimee's wound. "We won't let anyone ever hurt you again."

Before Aimee could say anything, there was a commotion

outside the hotel. She could see a crowd milling around. A flash of crimson told her Belle was there. Squinting, Aimee could just make out Jim beside her. His hands appeared empty. She heard shouting, then a gunshot. The sheriff was trying to bring order back. Several men came out of the saloon and went to join the ruckus, ignoring the wagon and its occupants. The men of Bisbee didn't need much of an excuse to start a good fight, and Aimee didn't care to stay and see what happened.

"I've got my bags packed already," Aimee said, knowing for sure there was nothing left for her in this town. In that instant, she realized too that her journey out West had been just the beginning of a journey to freedom, one that she would take with Cory.

"Well, let's go then," Cory said, lifting Aimee to the seat, then hopping up there herself.

They rode the short distance to the store, knowing it wouldn't be long before Jim and Belle would be on their way there as well. Keeping an eye on the goings on at the hotel, Aimee directed Davy where to collect her belongings from behind the building while she and Cory went into the store one last time. She stood looking around her, feeling an intense sense of loss. This had been her life for five years. She ran her fingers along the edges of the counter, thinking back over the long days of hard work. She felt her eyes grow moist. As if sensing her mood, Cory laid a hand on her arm.

"I promise I'll make this up to you," she said.

"You already have," Aimee said, smiling and blinking back her tears.

Cory took her arm gently and led her out the door. "I hear there's a lot of opportunities in San Francisco," Cory said. "Davy says the town could use a good bookstore."

"I like the sound of that," Aimee said. Pausing at the top of the steps, she leaned forward to kiss Cory. At the touch of their lips, Aimee felt her heart beat faster. Just like Miss White had said all those years ago, everything had turned out fine.

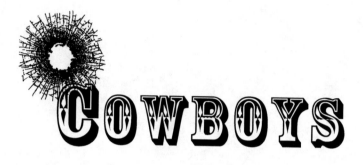

COWBOYS

&

KISSES

KARIN KALLMAKER

CHAPTER ONE

Every time the big front door opened the wind blew in dust and a cowboy.

Cherry predicted we'd have twice the customers a week from now, when the fall drive reached its peak. As it was, with only the leading edges of the herds arriving in the waning days of late summer, the rooms were turning over three and four times a night. Cowboys entered flush with their season's pay. Whiskey, a bath and an hour or two of female company was all they had on their minds.

I kept my attention on my needlework. The door opened, there was a scuff of boots and my unfashionable brown curls were overlooked again when the customer made his choice. Sooner or later I'd have to go upstairs. Cherry wasn't running a sanctuary. She'd told us all that more than once, and I had no wish to have her do the picking for me.

The next time the wind blew in a customer I stole a quick glance. Not a cowboy this time, a local. Jinny caught his eye with a decisive gesture that warned the rest of us to keep in our places. Like most locals he no doubt wanted what a missus had no time or energy to give—a sympathetic ear and a quick tumble. I'd have not minded being his choice. Jinny smiled and laughed all the way up the narrow stairs, her lively face a contrast to the faded roses in the wallpaper.

I needlessly smoothed my sewing floss and took another stitch, worrying inside that I'd missed my best guest for the night. There were locals who weren't nearly so easy to please. With the beginnings of the cattle drive in town there also were strangers whose needs were unknown and hard to anticipate. I showed ample curves as I worked under the brightest lamp, but compared to some of the other girls, I was not prime livestock. Given a choice, what customer wouldn't pick Angel over there, with her shining blond curls, air of innocence and exuberant smile? She'd been here a year and it didn't show. This cattle drive was the fourth I'd seen and, at seventeen, the years that didn't show in my face were revealed in my eyes.

Angel was a nice enough girl. She drew customers easily, had worked her way to the best room in the house and could take off for blood days even. Since talking wasn't what most guests wanted, few realized she was not just illiterate—most of the girls couldn't read or cipher—but stupid as well. Her common sense could fit in a pea. As Cherry said, she'd known turkeys smarter than Angel. No turkey ever made Cherry the money that Angel did, however, and in this place that is what counted. I had all my brains, and what did they get me? If I did not have some additional use because I knew my letters and numbers, my earnings would not be enough to pay for the room where I made my money. As it was my meals were curtailed, both from my lack of earnings, and because Cherry was certain I would grow fat the older I got. Curves were valued at bosom and hip, but not at the waist.

I raised my face when the door next opened and felt my smile freeze stiff as a winter wash basin. Otis, the colored boy who fetched water and whiskey but sometimes played the piano in the evenings, paused momentarily, then resumed his jaunty tune. All the girls found someplace else to look. Loomis—first name or last, I didn't know. Trying to call no attention to myself I slowly refocused on my needlework, listening to the exchange between him and Cherry.

"Back so soon? We're honored of course," she said as she rose to greet him.

"Can't disappoint the *ladies*," he answered.

I knew he was staring at each of us and I willed myself not to look up. Not me, I prayed. Please not me. I'd had several appointments with Loomis and didn't want to repeat any aspect of them. He was a month of bad news rolled into a single hour. He hadn't been pleased with me anyway, though like all men he got the finale he wanted. The last time his earlier displeasures had been part of what he'd wanted to tell me all about.

"We've got a fine variety tonight."

He made a show of it, examining his horseflesh before venturing to buy. "I might take myself two."

That was a relief. It would go easier for both.

"Tell me," Cherry said, her tone like sugar water, "that little girl you took in, Milla? How did she work out?"

His tone roughened with scorn. "Well, after I fed her and cleaned her up, gave her a warm place to sleep and treated her like family, she wandered off one night. Found her a few days later by following vultures. The thanks I get when she'd have starved all the sooner without me."

I caught back a noise of distress that would have attracted everyone's attention. Milla had been in the room next to mine until something had gone wrong with her. Cherry called it Prairie Madness, but it had started after she'd been sent out to a party for the first arrivals in this year's cattle drive. Entertaining a group was one way Cherry could boost a girl's earnings if she was unpopular with the house customers. Milla had been older than me, nearly twenty, and cost Cherry a doctor's fee. Needing the doctor to fix a girl's missing courses had become Cherry's constant complaint since the Comstock Law had made it impossible to acquire french letters. They were too dear for most men to afford regardless, but none of us had seen any for going on a year now. The doctor made more money off of Cherry than anyone else in town.

Just a few days after Milla's visit from the doctor, she'd been sent to entertain the first-arrived cowboys and drovers and come back to her room not the same. She wouldn't smile. Couldn't smile. You have to smile, I had warned her. Milla wasn't stupid, and I liked her. She'd been nice to me when I'd first arrived. But she wouldn't listen to me and sure enough, Cherry put her out. Milla had just folded in on herself and huddled at the back door, like a horse that knows it has no run left.

I'd tried to slip her food out the door with a tin of water at least once a day, but when Loomis noticed that she was on the street, he'd taken her with him. I'd seen him half-carry her to the wagon. The stupid girl. She could have offered herself to a farmer for the harvest work and anything else the hands might want. At least that would have meant a nook in the barn and food. There was a chance that even after the harvest was done the wife wouldn't have run Milla off if she'd proved herself useful for anything. Another girl had told me she knew of a girl who'd been taken in by a family because she knew how to butcher of all things. It was a hope at least, while staying outside Cherry's back door was no hope—if not Loomis, someone else. Men like Loomis were the end.

I blinked back tears, thinking of Milla wandering in the tall grass, no path to help in sight. I didn't want that future but every year the cattle drive seemed to make it more unavoidable. But I wouldn't go to Loomis. I'd plow fields with my bare hands before Loomis.

"Some girls haven't any sense." Cherry turned slowly to look over the room herself.

Not me, I prayed again, more fervently. *Please not me.*

"I'd not had use of her anywhere near what I spent to feed her up." Loomis made further grousing noises, as if Cherry was responsible for her cast-off property, and I knew what Cherry would do.

"Teena and Jade, you show our guest here upstairs, won't you?"

Not Angel, she was too valuable. Teena and Jade were the next prettiest girls there were and that would silence Loomis's complaints. He'd have whined further about his lost food in Milla's stomach had Cherry chosen the likes of me.

I was weak with relief. Luck was not something I counted on, though, and I knew I'd have to make an effort to earn more than an hour tonight. Milla had been silly to put herself at Loomis's mercy.

The door blew open again and I looked up, too wary to actually hope for another local man like Jinny's. This cowboy was on the small side, saddlebags and coiled whip slung over one shoulder, very dirty, but as full of bravado as the lot of them. Along with a gust of dust the air was now laden with the strong stink of horse and cow. A few of those swaggering steps inside the parlor, however, and I knew that I wanted that dark gaze to seek out mine. But like so many, it turned instead to the yellow curls and voluptuous promise that Angel offered as she leaned over the piano.

Otis didn't know Chopin from Mozart, but I could hum a little of something and he'd pick it up right away and make it a tune of his own. I sometimes wished I remembered more from the family years to add to his repertoire. Mostly he played campfire tunes and church music everyone knew, at a joyful pace that added to the sparkle of the lamplight. Just then the tune was sweet, as sweet as Angel's expression.

The new cowboy came to a stop mid-room. A glance at Cherry, who nodded permission, brought an easy nod in return. Otis stopped playing as the cowboy took two steps nearer to Angel.

With a charming half-bow, the cowboy gestured at Otis, but never stopped looking at Angel, who was smiling back an anticipatory yes. The girl hadn't a brain in her head, and likely didn't know what I—and Cherry no doubt—had figured out at the cowboy's first step.

"Please," the cowboy said to Otis, in a voice thickened by trail dust. "'If music be the food of love . . .'"

Angel simpered. Otis looked confused.

My needlework tight in my hands, I said, "'If music be the food of love, play on.'"

The cowboy swung 'round to face me.

Dark eyes studied me and I returned the favor with my own intensity as I added, "Duke Orsino, *Twelfth Night*, act one, scene one, line one."

"This girl," the cowboy said to Cherry, pointing at me. "For the night."

I took her upstairs.

CHAPTER TWO

"I'm not a man," she said as we reached my door.

"I know," I answered. Looking down the dim hallway I called to Aaron, one of Otis's kin. "Hot bath, please."

"Thank you," the cowboy said. "I haven't seen one for a month of Sundays."

"'Out, damned spot, out I say,'" I quoted. I paused to light a rush from the lamp outside my door, then led the cowboy into the room.

The small space wasn't close to the best Cherry had to offer. When I'd first arrived I'd had a better room. Young and fully developed, my value had been steady. I did not miss my former grandeur because none of the other girls envied me my tiny space. No one schemed to take anything from me; it's the reward for having so little. As I quickly lit the lamp I prided myself that my room was at least clean. The window was small but faced away from the street. On a sunny morning I could look past the rear yard and the mud of trampled earth and see where the tall grass began, then on as far as the horizon. The window was my one luxury. Otherwise, the small room was taken up mostly by the bed. My linens I changed twice a week when once was the house rule. There was enough floor space left for the tub when it got here. An old drapery covered the small alcove where I kept all that mattered to me, obscuring it from the bed. I turned the lamp flame as high as it would go, but something in the tint of the aging wallpaper seemed to drain the room of light.

From behind me the cowboy said, "Not many of your kind know the Bard."

"Not many of your kind do either," I replied, my tone not nearly so flattering as what Angel would have no doubt managed.

Her only answer was to hang her well-creased hat on the bed-post, then sling her gun belt, whip and saddlebags on the chair. The dust-choked vest fell to the ground.

"The boy can clean your clothes, if you want." I busied myself helping with buttons and ties. The stench of horse, cow and woman was powerful and I pledged a small amount of my carefully hoarded bathing oil to the cause of a more pleasant evening and sheets I'd not regret sleeping on later.

"That would be welcome."

Aaron knocked, then entered noisily with the bath, still wet from its last occupant.

"I'll be wanting enough water to fill it twice before I'm done," the cowboy told Aaron, who nodded respectfully and ducked out.

"He doesn't speak," I told her. "So, what am I to call you?"

The deep brown eyes sparkled. "Orsino?"

"Alas, I don't think I can play Olivia." She was far too pure for the life I lived.

"Then I shall be Falstaff, and you a merry wife."

I smiled, grateful she'd not used the other word that began

with *W*. Most of the guests used it affectionately, but the respectable women and the preacher used it like a knife, with little jabs. "If you want to hear yourself called Falstaff long into the night—"

"Connor," she said quickly. "Everybody calls me Connor."

"Family name?"

She shrugged. "Just a name."

There was no point in asking further. Nobody this far out on the frontier had any name but the one they told you. I continued to help remove the trappings of a cowboy. The scars of her trade were evident in the two fingers on her left hand that had mended crookedly from a break, and a burn on her right shoulder that suggested a calf had objected to the branding iron. A bump on her nose spoke of brawls, but not too many, and the washboard ribs of just enough food to support hard work.

"Where'd you stable your horse?"

"Argo's at the one with the foul-tempered owner."

"You've described both. North or south of town?"

"North."

"Ingle's got two good hands who know their horseflesh," I said, repeating what numerous guests had told many of us. "The tanner's apprentices are excellent with cleaning and fixing saddles too."

I felt her relax slightly. Cowboys and their horses—neither would rest happy if the other wasn't comfortable. I didn't know why I cared but I wanted to make sure Connor slept well. She'd bought me for the night and, given her weariness, the night would not be filled only with shivering cries. A hot bath, a soft bed and sleep would follow, after she discovered her bedmate knew enough about pleasing a woman to make that part of the evening as enjoyable as the bath—and perhaps a mite more memorable.

Once her clothes were scattered on my floor, I offered her my dressing gown. Aaron and Otis knocked shortly thereafter, lugging in large buckets of hot water. When I let them out of my room and turned back to Connor I tried my darnedest not to smile.

She frowned. "Go ahead, say it."

"I'm sorry, but your horse would likely look better in my dressing gown than you do. You look more like a woman in men's breeches than in my clothes."

"I get taken for a man often enough, but I don't care. It's not like there's any other choice of clothing that makes sense. Some fool women do their branding and riding in skirts, but not me. I can't rope a calf sitting sidesaddle in a corset."

I sprinkled bath oil into the water, then stood back as Aaron and Otis appeared again with more buckets to empty into the bath. "Most goods from Mr. Ward's catalog don't make sense for life in Long Grass, Wyoming, let alone on the Goodnight-Loving Cattle Trail."

"Where are you from originally?"

I shrugged. "Does it matter? Everybody out here is from somewhere else."

"I'm going to guess up Boston way, just the occasional word here and there. Otherwise, I'd say you were from 'round here."

"You're not wrong," I hedged.

Her expression told me she understood she wasn't quite right either. "Lots of people in a city like that. No sky, no air. No real horses."

"I'm not sure the horses would agree."

"They don't know what it is to run. A life spent pulling a cart is like living in a cage." She shook off a shudder.

I might have said something about cages and living in them. Milla had discovered the vast cage of the prairie, hadn't she? The sky went on forever, but she hadn't been able to escape.

I said none of that, because in spite of the rarity of a woman customer she was just that—a customer. Other than the specifics of my talents I would later put to use, I would treat her like any man who'd bought me for the night. Customers don't tip when they feel as if they've bought something that wasn't willingly for sale. Some of the girls believed the lie, that we were all here by choice.

A choice between living or dying was not a choice.

The new ones believed they had a choice, though, until they came up short in their earnings or needed the doctor's needle. Then their lack of options became painfully clear. Milla had once upon a time called herself lucky to make money on her back instead of as a slave to a crop or a herd of cows. She must have felt differently after the doctor, all that blood for days, then the . . . party.

"Sounds to me like you're from farther south than I am."

"Yes ma'am." She sketched a bow. "I've spent some time back and forth on the Chisholm Trail, but originally I'm from Charleston, then San Antonio."

"Why you're just a southern belle, then."

"Like none my mama ever did see." The humor of our banter was in her eyes but something else flitted over her face. She was perhaps thirty—she may well have been in the South when Sherman cut his bloody swath across it nearly a decade ago. Half the town was folks who'd run from the South and kept running until this place claimed them. White and colored alike, if you could survive you could stay. Until the preachers had shown up, no one cared how anyone managed to live. It may not be godly, but at least there had been no confusion. You presumed your neighbor had no thought but himself and you were never disappointed. If I never forgot that Cherry's first concern was money, I would survive much longer in this house than Milla had.

Aaron and Otis clattered in with the last buckets. Connor flipped them both a coin on their way out, saying, "In about twenty minutes bring another round."

The door no sooner closed than she slipped off my dressing gown and sank gratefully into the water. It turned black seconds after she curled up enough to submerge.

She wasn't tall, not even as tall as I was, and her skin was leather dark where the sun had touched it, and pale but for grime where it hadn't. Her back and hips were also marked with scars of her work—rope burns, nicks and the jagged tears of bull horns. There was no doubt that she worked a herd. The gun said she was a cowboy, not merely a drover. What amazed me was that she was small for the work. Light on horseback, I figured. Maybe that was a good trait, time to time. But even on a horse a bull would be a formidable weight to master.

With a splutter she sat up in the water. "That's a piece of heaven."

Taking my gentlest soap from next to my ewer, I positioned myself behind her. Running the bar over the breadth of her shoulders, I appreciated the muscles that corded her arms. Slowly, I soaped from neck to elbow but when I moved the bar over her stomach she took it from me and washed her front herself.

My hands were sudsy enough to rub into her hair. After a few minutes of scrubbing, she passed the bar back to me and I lathered her hair more carefully. It was short, shorter than I'd ever seen on a woman, but it didn't put me in mind of a man either. Nothing about her had me thinking about men. I felt an unusual twinge of anticipation. I did not know what she might like, but as she relaxed under my hands I knew she would not be cruel.

"What else of Shakespeare do you know?" With a sigh she slipped lower into the filthy but still warm water.

"'Shake the yoke of inauspicious stars from this world-wearied flesh,'" I quoted as I scrubbed her shoulders again.

She turned in the tub and our gazes locked, and something there in her depths stole my breath. Her voice like the memory of a smoky fire, she added, "'Eyes, look your last. Arms, take your last embrace.'"

I didn't recall the rest of Romeo's speech, except the end.

"'Thus with a kiss I die.'"

Her lips moved as if she might smile, but instead they only parted enough for her to say, "Oh, surely there won't be death in your kisses, darlin'."

The half-smile of promise, the flutter in my lashes—flirtation suddenly came to me easily. "I had quite the opposite in mind."

She leaned toward me with a now open grin, but a knock at the door brought me to my feet. "Fresh bath water."

While Connor waited again in my dressing gown, Aaron and Otis emptied the bath with their buckets, flinging the water from my window to the yard below. When the tub was empty enough they poured the remaining contents out in a single slosh, then repeated their multiple trips with fresh water. Connor stood quietly throughout, then tossed each another coin. I locked my door behind them and turned to her, my heart beating in an unusual rhythm.

She slipped off the dressing gown again and, hell fire be damned, nothing about her put me in mind of a man. Her shoulders were broad and strong, yes, but her breasts were full and tipped with roses. Some of Cherry's girls would envy their weight and shape. "Join me, darlin'?"

"The tub's not that big."

"I think if we're very close it could be a good fit."

My fingers were trembling. She wanted me bare and, of course, she could have what she wanted, but there was something in her eyes that confused me. I wasn't used to taking all my clothes off, either. She had bought me for the night, I reminded myself, not the half-hour.

She sank into the water with a deep sigh and closed her eyes. "I feel nearly human."

"You're less horse, that's for certain." I turned my back to undo my bodice, feeling unaccountably modest. You're not a lady, I told myself. You're a whore and you should be stripping for her. That's what she wants.

I turned around again, my practiced smile ready, but her eyes were still closed. I finished with my laces, skirts and chemise. Only when my hand stirred the water did she open her eyes to look at me.

"Glory be," she said softly. "You are all woman, aren't you?"

I blushed. "So are you."

"Not the same way." She shifted in the water as I stepped in.

We fit in the bath, barely, and some water slopped onto the floor. My head was on her chest as I rested on one hip between her legs. I could not ignore what pressed against me there. It had been a long time since I'd loved a woman. I'd never had one as a customer, but some of the other girls were occasionally interested in an encounter that was freely given. It was even longer since more than lust had found me in a woman's bed. More than lust had been my downfall, after all. I was here because of my youthful ardor, that I'd dare name my feelings, not merely because I'd been caught in an intimate embrace with another girl. My parents put me on a coach with a one-way ticket, inconvenient in my affections for my family's sense of place.

I could have stayed had I said I did not love that girl—I no longer remembered her name. God didn't like liars and didn't like perversion, leaving me betwixt and between. Truthful, but damned anyway.

I shifted my hip against her and felt her move in response as we steeped in the water, trading lines from Shakespeare. When fingertips ran lazily from my shoulder to the tip of my breast I watched in amazement as it hardened to her touch. It almost felt like it was happening to a girl I wasn't anymore.

Connor was my customer. I was there to please her. I turned my head to see that she too was watching my nipple.

"You don't find me strange?" Her fingers closed around the swelling point.

"No stranger than I am." Part of me wanted to hide that her touch was penetrating past all my false smiles and pretenses.

Customers were supposed to think we were whores who liked our work, but it was my falsity, the pretending, that was my shield. It allowed me not to care what happened. I sold the only thing I had and though no preacher would ever agree, it was honest trade. I didn't have to like it, though. I only had to fool the customer into thinking that I did.

But I liked this. I liked her touch, the soft tug on my nipple. I couldn't say no to her, true—she was a customer. But I still liked it, and that further confused me.

"Oh darlin'," she breathed. "Does the rest of you respond this way?"

"Sometimes."

"Then I'm a lucky woman tonight."

"I hope that you think so by the morrow."

She said the strangest thing. I did not believe, then, that I had heard her rightly. "Let me please you tonight, and I will be very lucky."

CHAPTER THREE

"Darlin'." She held out a hand, her hair still wet from the bath. Aaron and Otis had taken the tub for someone else's use and claimed Connor's filthy clothes for laundering. On their last trip they'd left behind two shots of whiskey. I'd locked the door once again and busied myself with the blankets until she'd turned from her saddlebags.

I handed her one of the shot glasses, then joined her sitting on the edge of my bed. We touched glasses, then tossed back the shots. She was smiling as we shared appreciative gasps and her gaze never left my face.

Finally, I felt a rare blush steal up my throat. "What?"

"You're lovely," she said and strange, so strange, I think she meant it.

But even stranger was that she leaned forward then and kissed me.

I couldn't help myself. I drew back with a gasp.

"I'm sorry," she said.

"No, you surprised me, that's all."

"Why? Are you really not used to a woman's touch?"

"No, no that's not it. I'm not . . ." How could I explain it without reminding her of what I was? I didn't want to remind myself even. I wanted to be here by choice, for once.

She exhaled, then one corner of her mouth lifted in a crooked smile. "I don't care what they want or don't want. I want to kiss you. It's a starting place for all the things I want to do with you."

"Yes. I'm sorry. I won't—"

My lips tingled with the light pressure of hers once again. She made a small noise and kissed me more deeply. I opened to her as I felt my body swell with desire. Her strong arms went around me, gently, and she pulled me against her to kiss me more earnestly still.

I closed my eyes and enjoyed the way she loved my mouth. Her tongue teased against mine.

It had been so long since I'd been kissed. Men had use for my mouth and knew that others had as well—kissing a whore was nearly as foul as tasting her down there. Connor's kiss grew more heated and I moaned as the needful hope rushed over me, that if she could kiss my mouth she might . . . she might . . .

"Darlin'." Connor licked my lower lip. "You're really enjoying this, aren't you?"

"Yes," I admitted. I didn't know how to tell her that I told that lie a hundred times a month, but right now I was speaking the truth. It was not flattery. Her hands were warm on my waist and her arms very strong and secure around me. "Yes, Connor, I am. I think I am going to enjoy tonight."

"That's my plan."

I brushed my fingertips over her shoulders, aware that her breasts had tightened. I wanted to feel the rosy tips against my teeth.

She forestalled my lips moving to her shoulder by pulling me onto her lap. As her fingertips ran over my body I felt like fine velvet, caressed for the pleasure of the sensation. Her hands were calloused yet moved over me with subtle, attentive touches. A fingertip grazed under my nipple, exploring the roughness of the puckered skin. Her other hand petted slowly down my still damp shoulders, pausing now and again to circle lightly until I arched. Then the pressure was more insistent and warmth spread over my entire back.

"Now where did you learn to do that?" I nuzzled her jaw. "It feels wonderful." She said nothing and after a pause I leaned back to catch a look of chagrin. "What?"

"My horse," she said. "He enjoys a rubdown."

I arched one eyebrow. "As long as you're enjoying this more I'll forgive the comparison."

With a whoop she dumped me on my back on the bed, and landed on top of me, grinning madly. "I assure you that my thoughts right now are some I've not had about my horse."

"Glad to hear it."

"Glory be," she said, and she took one of my nipples into her mouth.

She didn't bite or suck like a starved babe. At first, I couldn't think what it was she was doing to me, what purpose it had, then the pleasure of it washed over my skin. She was teasing, toying, blowing softly, rubbing the hard tip against her lips. "Now that," she murmured, "is the definition of beautiful."

With a lustful glint she concentrated her attention on my other nipple, not stopping until it too was stiff and ruby in hue.

Aroused, but still aware that she was here to take her pleasure, I reached for her breasts. I could only be honest—I did not want to touch her because I had to. Their firm fullness was alluring and ripe, like long forgotten fruit.

She raised her head to look at me in response to my touch. I softly stroked and squeezed until she moved out of my reach with a grin. I let out a long, loud groan, quite beyond stopping myself, as she touched her breast between my legs. Moving instinctively toward the contact I lifted myself as she pushed forward, and the firm pressure of our bodies, so openly desirous and mutually pleasing.

"Oh darlin'. That's right." She ground against me until the lamp shimmered behind my eyes. Abruptly she wasn't there anymore and I made myself focus only to see her looking down at her wet breast with another lustful, sensuous grin. With one finger she gathered up the slippery love from between my legs and then tasted it.

I shuddered and she gave me a knowing look, then bent over me. Bent low, kneeling between me and the footboard, curling so she could put her mouth on me. Put her tongue inside me.

I wanted to cry, to scream, but the only sound I could make was a low, welcoming moan as my hips jerked against her mouth in response. She had bought me for the night and I could do this all night, enjoy this all night. I knew before we were done I had to please her, but if she was willing to warm me up this way first, there was nothing I would not do for her quite willingly. It felt so good, so consumingly right, that I cared not if it made me a whore who liked her work.

The pleasure I felt grew intense and I wanted to cleanse my mind of so many other images. She could have required me to do this to her, before her bath. She might have called me names and used me as a stand-in for someone she couldn't strike or intimately hurt. I should not expect more than that, in spite of this pleasure, but I couldn't fight it back as she continued to lick and please me. There was no pretense in my sudden shout and the quaking of my limbs. The thump of the bed was not to entice those downstairs to imagine the pleasure they could have if they'd pay the price. I gripped her hands as tightly as I could and lost all control.

• • •

She laughed when she finally raised her head. "Well, that was better than a month of Sundays."

"Please," I said weakly. "Let me catch my breath."

"Of course darlin'." She stretched out next to me, lightly petting and stroking my shoulders and sides as if her fingers simply could not help themselves.

"You didn't have to do that," I finally said. "But I thank you."

She gave me a puzzled look. "That's why I'm here. Say the word and I'll do it again."

I stopped myself before I said, "But I'm a whore." From a nearby room came a guttural shout, followed by the crash of glass and raucous laughter, but in the circle of her arms it seemed as far away as childhood. "I would more than enjoy returning the favor."

"Not necessary right now. Later. Before we sleep." Her lips nuzzled my nipple again and a melting lassitude swept over me. "I want to enjoy you completely. That you like it so much amazes me."

"I don't . . . I mean I . . ." There was nothing I could say that would not shatter this moment.

"You didn't . . . ?"

"No, no, I did. I did like that. I *loved* that." Suddenly it was too frightening to tell her that I'd not enjoyed such pleasures in years. Even times with other girls looking for something freely given had not held such abandon.

"Good." She still looked a little doubtful. "I never wanted a man—just born different. There's something about a woman, when she makes that noise, that seems like the closest to heaven I'll ever get."

"I was born different too," I said, thankful for her gift of the words to express it.

"Really? You're not just saying?"

"I'm not just saying." Shyly I stretched up to give her a kiss, which she returned.

"So even if," she whispered in my ear as I settled my head again on the pillow. "Even if you were born different, that doesn't mean I can't touch you inside, does it? Because I want to feel you, from the inside. Feel all those wonderful places."

Surprise that she would even ask permission for anything left me momentarily startled. "Yes, of course, yes . . . I'd like that—*oh*."

One finger parted me, played in my wet curls. "I like this too," she said, her smile gone.

Her tongue slipped into my mouth as she slipped inside me. It felt as if she was opening me wide so she could look deep, learn my every secret. A twist of her fingers had me gasping against her mouth. She was slow, no rutting jabs and slams, and she touched me soft and easy, in places I'd long forgotten had such explicit, exquisite sensation to give.

Just when I thought I was going to explode or die, she moved on top of me, her hand more insistent and the exquisite wet heat of her desire on my thigh. I cried out and felt telltale spasms against her thrusting fingers, and her low moan of response was welcome in my ears. Dizzy with pleasure I slipped my hand down so I could feel all of her and she ground herself against the ridge of my palm. I wanted to drown in my release but was aware that hers was close. If I could wait, even as she did such delicious things to the inside of me, we could have something I would never forget. I desperately hoped she would not forget it either.

I clung to the edge of my sanity, relishing her rising moans and the force of her on my hand. She was deep inside me now, finding magic places, spreading ripples of lightning that flashed and burned behind my eyes.

When she reared back with a hoarse shout I could contain myself no longer. Straining with the intensity of my response to her I reached for the corded strength of her forearm and pulled her into me, bucking against her hand even as she jerked and ground down on mine.

• • •

She collapsed next to me, words a jumble, breathing hard. After a few minutes I used the fan on the table to waft enough of a gust at the lamp to put out the flame. Her arm tightened around me.

Gunfire in the night brought Connor awake with a gasp. Laughter and commotion was loud from downstairs while Otis hammered out *Old Rough and Ready* with enough force to rattle the dishes.

"It's okay," I soothed. "They'll quiet down. Go back to sleep." I'd woken several times already, enjoying the feel of her there and playing back the memories of the night over and over.

With a sleepy sigh she answered, "'I never heard so musical a discord, such sweet thunder.'"

"No Titania, no Oberon. Just cowboys," I said, with a fondness for the breed I had never felt before.

This cowboy, whose warmth I could feel against my skin, this cowboy had loved me as if my pleasure mattered, as if pleasing me was what pleased her. She knew I sold my body, was damned hundreds of times over, yet still thought I was worth pleasing. When I'd touched her it had felt as if she enjoyed not just my touch but the union of our passion. It was me, us, the fire that we shared, that moved her. I knew there would not be another night like this one, but I felt granted something I'd not felt for so many years . . . and I could not quite name it, but the feeling was so very welcome.

I thought she had dozed off until she said, "I've always had trouble sleeping under a roof."

"Shall I open the window?"

"No." Her arm tightened around me again. "Stay."

I played lazily with her hair as I snuggled closer against her warmth. The uproar below us finally subsided and I was nearly asleep when I felt her hand cup me with intent. My response shocked me. I moaned, loudly, suddenly aflame. She moved with surprising quickness, turning me over, then touching me again with her body behind mine.

I pushed back against her as she pulled us both to our knees. I was dizzy with fever and strong with desire. "Is this what you want of me?"

"Yes." She was growling in my ear. Her hand went under me to find my breasts as she pushed ever more quickly, more firmly, inside me.

"You can have it." There was nothing left of my protection. I wanted her to do this and could not hide it. "You can have anything you need of me." My voice broke. I had nothing to give her but my surrender. "Whatever you want, just take it. I don't care."

I ought to have been ashamed. I gave my body for money, and it was honest trade. I was giving her far more than that, and didn't even know if she wanted it. If I gave her something so precious for free, I no longer knew what that made me.

She was forceful, powerful, but did not hurt me. As I came closer and closer to my ecstasy she was, if anything, gentler, more subtle, as if to find the most precise place to touch me that would wring from me everything I had to give.

She found it, but it wasn't a place her fingers could reach. Something else was touched, something else inside me broke wide open.

I was a dam burst, and tears poured from me. A few minutes later she tenderly dried them, crooning to me softly.

"Darlin'," she murmured in my ear as I fell asleep, as if that was truly my name. "Darlin'."

Chapter Four

Her name was Rachel. I could remember now. The girl I'd loved desperately, who'd read poetry from her aunt's study to me and let me explore her body until one day she'd cried because I kissed her *there*, in that special place. I kissed and touched and learned and finally she touched me too. There were no girls like us in all the books I'd read, not in the poetry she adored. Still, I knew I could be the Juliet—I had been that age after all—who wakes before Romeo drinks the poison. No tragedy for us, but a comedy, wedding and all.

When my parents tore us out of bed, sending her home to a fate I never knew, I had not believed they would beat me. At first they had only threatened, but when the word *love* crossed my lips they had made good on their threat. When they said they would send me away, I hadn't believed that either.

There had been no kin waiting for me in Long Grass; it was

simply the end of the stage line. They wanted me as far away from family and name as I could get, and assured me with blind falsity that I could start over in the West. A foolish notion—life is too short for second starts.

There was no work for a young woman in Long Grass, and no merchant willing to feed and house me in return for my unpracticed needlework and entertaining stories. I had too much education to know a skill anyone would pay for, and not enough education to teach. I was not old enough to marry under territorial law, even had I been able to stomach that alternative. When I had nothing left I could afford to trade, I traded my body because I was old enough to whore. At first it seemed irrelevant, what men did to me. It never felt as if they could truly touch me, but repetition wore away that defense as a wind wears away even the most yielding tree.

My eyes closed against the intrusion of morning, I could hear the reluctant sounds of the house awakening. The treads on the stairs creaked from slow and clumsy feet. The back door clacked as much as the front as men of the town made an effort not to encounter each other on their way out of the building.

I wondered that Cherry had not yet stirred Connor out of my bed, but the somber sounding of the church bell reminded me it was Sunday. Town law said all "entertainment" commerce was illegal from sunrise to sunset on Sundays.

To me, Sunday mornings were my time of peace. I rarely entertained anyone overnight, so the few hours of respite from any demands on me I often spent at the little table hidden by the drapery.

The bed was warm and I didn't want to leave it. I quietly felt behind me for the reassuring solidity of Connor's body but when I didn't feel her right away, I opened my eyes. The gray light of morning seeped through the window, but the lamp was also lit.

Connor was not in the bed, so I sat up, letting my eyes adjust to the weak light. I only needed to turn my head once to sweep the room and there she was, in the chair, at the table, having pulled the concealing drapery aside.

"I'm sorry," she said immediately. "I was looking for the basin and when I saw you had some newspapers to read I couldn't help myself."

Her smile was winsome and it melted my annoyance until I realized what was in her hand. "Those papers are private."

"Forgive me," she said easily. "The opening line caught my eye, that's all. You've written so much."

I pulled the blankets up around my shoulders. "There isn't a lot of time to do so."

"Has anyone else ever read—"

"No."

"Oh. I was enjoying this story, very much."

"Which?"

"'The Hand of the Virgin Queen,' it says."

"I wrote that a very long time ago. Two years at least."

"Eons ago, then." Her smile was indulgent.

I wanted to say "In this place, a lifetime," but instead I matched her tone. "Eons. Books are scarce. What pocket money I have I spend on paper and ink. Paper is dear."

She rose to recover her saddlebags from the floor. "All I have is what I can carry in here. Just room enough for one book, but it's enough. But when I saw a fresh story on your table, I couldn't resist."

Drawing out a volume bowed in the middle from years of yielding to the shape of a horse, she brushed the worn leather cover lovingly before handing it to me. I took it with reverence, even as I recalled those sensitive fingers appreciating my skin with the same level of intimacy.

The title was so faded that I had to open to the title page to read it. "You're right, it's enough." The collected tragedies of Shakespeare rested in my lap. I'd have given a great deal to have had even the text of one to pore over.

"'A needy, hollow-eyed, sharp-looking wretch,'" I read from *Titus*.

"'A living-dead man,'" she finished for me.

"I don't remember much of *Macbeth*," I admitted. "I read it very long ago."

Her smile was indulgent. "He listens to witches, decides he's Napoleon and starts seeing ghosts. Sometimes I tell the story at the campfire, though truthfully most of the fellows like the hurly-burly the best."

I laughed. "That means you don't get much past the first scene."

She shrugged and her gaze went back to the page in her hand. It was a hungry look, as needful as the one she'd given me last night. I rested back into the pillow with a sigh.

"Go ahead and read," I told her softly.

"Sleep," she answered, her tone already distant.

I drifted for some time. I would surface to hear a page softly turned with a sigh of pleasure, then go under again to the memories of the night.

When I woke to find her gone, both night and morning echoed back to me in equal measures. I couldn't tell then which mattered more, the pleasure she believed I was worthy of having, or the pleasure I gave her that she clearly treasured.

By noon, Sunday church services were over. By two the church was empty but for the preacher, his wife and her sister, who taught school, and the denizens of Cherry's entertainment establishment, including me.

To get there we had to first cover our dresses with long buttoned coats, regardless of the weather. It spared us some of the more scornful glances, but more importantly the coat would protect our clothes from inadvertent or intentional mud flung our way.

The walk was short, which was a blessing because my boots were suitable for carpets and wood, not mud. Some of us put our heads down, others held them up. This was also true of many of the townsmen who scurried out of our path. I noticed Jinny's customer of last night give her a little smile, but mostly we were treated to the same curls of the lip they gave when they were done with us.

We filed into the church quietly, ready for the weekly attempt to salvage our souls. Cherry had agreed we would all attend church the last time there had been a serious attempt to clean up Long Grass. Mostly it was just talk, but Cherry always ended up tithing to the council a little more. Our turn at godliness also reduced the sin of consorting for the menfolk.

When I had finally stirred again, Connor had gone. I had not expected her to stay and yet the loss I still felt keenly. Usually I welcomed our weekly stint at prayer, surreptitiously reading from the Good Book throughout. I was up to the story of Jacob, Leah and Rachel. More than once I'd wanted to hide the book in my coat but such a theft would weigh heavily on me.

Today I could not settle to reading. I thought about the look in Connor's eyes. No customer had ever taken pleasure of me that way, through my own pleasure. The more I liked it, the more pleased she was with me. I would not hope she'd be back. I would not suffer the plague Othello pronounced for all strumpets, who beguiled many yet were beguiled by only one.

The preacher began his usual sermon on the sins of the flesh and the sanctity of holy matrimony. Now who, I wanted to ask him, would marry the likes of us? How can you preach honesty to women who have no hope of it? It was like telling someone who'd never seen water that they were sinners for not knowing how to swim.

I shut out his words and watched instead the two women who sat quietly on his left. Their dresses were similar, though the preacher's wife's was darker and better made. I'd seen neither without a bonnet but could guess they wore the same curled bun. His wife was pale of face and hair. Her features, while individually fine, did not quite come together to please the eye. Her sharp gaze, however, examined us as we listened. I believed her shrewdness matched Cherry's, and it was a compliment I'm sure the preacher's wife would not have appreciated.

To avoid being caught staring I glanced down at the Bible. After mulling over a passage for a minute, I surreptitiously studied the wife's sister. The resemblance was strong, but higher cheekbones, a more generous mouth and darker hair made her worth looking at. I'd only taken slight notice of her before—she was part of what I considered the preacher's domain and therefore of little interest. She read aloud to us, after the preacher was done, from the Bible or a collection of fables by Aesop. Her voice was like fresh cream on berries. Today as I looked at her I thought that she was someone who could play the sweet and tart of Olivia quite well.

With a start I realized the sermon was over. I'd completely missed being told I was a sinner which only underscored how little hope there was for me. The preacher and his wife left through the door to the residence and I exchanged a droll look with Jinny. After a sermon about the sins of the flesh the preacher always seemed to need to experience rapture, and quickly.

The sister rose and I realized I'd never known her name. Her drab clothing wasn't much help to settle on a nickname either. The last fable she'd read to us had been "The Frog and the Ox." She was too small for Ox, so I settled on Frog, even though it hardly suited her voice.

After a passage about David being too old and cold to be warmed by a fair maiden who ministered to him, she opened the fables to the story of "The Farmer and the Stork." Poor stork, caught among the grain-eating cranes. I thought it was a fable better suited to the menfolk who frequented Cherry's establishment rather than us. We were, after all, the cranes luring the storks to bad behavior, but the object lesson of the story was advice to the storks about the company they kept. I let myself drift to the lilt of her voice and it mingled in my mind with Connor's whispers and the soft noise of the pages she'd turned for hours this morning. Together they created a quiet harmony that made something inside me purr with happiness.

Happiness was so foreign to me that I tried not to feel it. I tried not to notice the sunlight that streamed in through the high window and the glint of motes dancing in it. With Connor I'd felt as if I could dance like that, flit and float in a swirl of light. I didn't realize I was smiling until Frog stopped reading to give me a quizzical stare.

I attempted a contrite look in reply but from her frown I guessed that I had failed. Her eyes narrowed and I realized they were a mix of green and gray. Hazel, I thought, was a better name than Frog. I smiled again and she gave me another look so I studied the Bible on my lap while she finished her story.

We were finally in the required state of grace, I suppose, because Hazel stopped reading and we all stood up. The bright sunlight outside the church left me momentarily dazzled but I recognized the voice immediately.

"Hello, Darlin'."

Cherry quickly said, "You can't be arranging for anything on Sunday."

I had to shade my eyes to clearly see Connor push back her hat as she sat astride a horse not nearly as compact as she was. "Now ma'am, I've been into the saloon and they told me all about the law. I figure we can work something out if I take Darlin' here for a ride and we get back around sunset."

My heart throbbed several times in my chest. It was unheard of, what Connor was suggesting. I daren't indicate that I wanted to go as Cherry could withhold anything she liked. I kept my gaze low, finding the hem of Hazel's dress to occupy myself. She had not yet closed the church door and was watching the exchange with interest. Money could not be mentioned in front of the preacher's kin.

"That's one of the most dang fool things I've ever heard."

Connor shrugged. "I've been called worse, ma'am."

I don't know if it was the politeness of the *ma'am* or that Connor didn't bluster or bully. Cherry said, "Fine then, but you're responsible if she's not back and able to work."

Connor tipped her hat in answer, then leaned down to extend a hand to me. I eyed the saddle uncertainly. It didn't seem like there was enough room on the horse's rump for me behind the high-backed saddle, and the sharp-edged pommel wasn't something I was thinking I wanted to be resting on for any distance.

"Come on, Darlin'. Before anyone changes their mind. You're gonna perch right here in front of me. I'm sure we'll fit." Something in her eyes made me think of the way her hands had gripped me in the night, measuring me, moving me against her.

With a lifting twirl and a shuffle of the horse's hooves to balance us, she scooted back in the saddle and planted me in front of her. I hooked one leg around the pommel, which forced me back into the circle of her arms. I didn't mind.

With a cluck and a minute movement of the reins, Connor wheeled the horse almost in place and we headed out of town at a brisk trot.

"You're crazy."

"I really have been called worse, Darlin'."

I'd not been out of the town from the day the stage had left me and my portmanteau on the dirty street. We crossed the boundary of the last building and the wide track spread out ahead of us like a faded brown ribbon uncoiled through the golden grass.

I closed my eyes for a moment, overwhelmed by a sense of freedom. The sky was vast and the horizon forever away. I wanted her to keep riding until we got there, got to the end of it all. Foolish, I thought, for me to still think second starts were possible in this life, even under a sky this huge.

"I've got a few things to eat in the saddlebags, and a flask. Thought we'd make for that tree and have a picnic in the shade."

The tree was at least a mile off. Several others stood just a bit farther off as well, indicating some kind of creek, maybe, at least in the springtime. I'd been told there was a river seven or eight miles to the south, but I'd never seen it.

Connor rubbed the horse's neck as we trotted along.

"Argo," I recalled. "Does that make you Jason?"

"I think I'd be closer to Ulysses."

I did not bring up Penelope for fear it would be too apt. "Encounters with Cyclops and Circes and such?"

"Something like that." I could feel her smile against my neck. "You are by far the most interesting and beguiling witch I've ever met."

"Alas, I am no witch or I'd spell you to be my willing consort. I'm awful warm in this coat," I added. "Not that what I've got on under it is meant for horseback, but I'd be more comfortable."

She clucked the horse to a stop and let me down. I unfastened the coat and she slung it over the saddle where it would provide some padding from the pommel.

She began to reach for my hand to help me astride again, but with an uncharacteristically sheepish look, she paused to say, "If you'd like to, you could make a fantasy come true."

"Could I now?" Did she want more of my clothes off, my underthings perhaps? I didn't fancy sweating on the leather of the saddle with my bare skin rubbing against it.

"Face me as we ride. I could kiss you."

"Oh." I only hesitated because I wanted to shout yes. She was still a customer. I was not some silly schoolgirl dealing with her first beau. I *should* find a way to spell her, to get all the money she had out of her. It would put me in Cherry's good graces for longer. "Yes, please."

The second time she lifted me I was even more impressed by her strength. I could see how she and the horse could throw a cow. She protected my back from the thrust of the pommel using my coat, and pulled my bottom into the vee between her legs. Though I was bent more than was truly comfortable, curling into her arms and putting my head on her chest was welcome indeed.

"How does this suit your fantasy?"

"Perhaps neither of us is as comfortable as I might have thought," she said honestly, "but it's every bit as heavenly."

She kissed me, then, soft and slow, as we rocked together. My shoulders tingled in the sunlight as warmth spread all the way to my toes. There was nothing I wanted in that moment, except more of her kisses. We weren't in Cherry's house. I was just Darlin' as she murmured it against my mouth. Just Darlin' and hers in an afternoon that could last a lifetime.

The buzz of lazy insects in the grass blended with the whisper of the tall stalks moving in the light breeze. The dull thud of hooves on packed dirt mixed with the jangle of saddle buckles, all combining to a kind of music I didn't know. But the food of love was her arms and her kisses. The soft sounds of our lips meeting and parting was the most precious melody of all.

The shade of the tree was welcome, and I wasn't surprised to see the grass trampled and rutted from many hooves and wagons. There were signs of water at the surface, but not recent. Connor slipped lightly to the ground and helped me down after her, then went about unsaddling Argo. It wasn't long before we were sitting in the sweet shade, heads together on the pillow of the saddle, sharing a loaf of bread, dried peaches and wrapped cheese. Argo nipped contentedly from the very tips of nearby grasses.

"This is most pleasant. I thank you." I gave her a peachy kiss on the cheek.

"I don't get many days like this myself. But it's the Lord's day.

I ought to recognize it now and again."

I propped myself up on one elbow. In the bright daylight I was aware that my dress was patched and the poplin showed the burn that had resulted from sitting too close to the fire last winter. I wriggled my toes and wasn't sure my boots would survive the coming one. "And here I was thinking you might have something more than prayer on your mind."

Her smile was slow. "Such as?"

"More earthly delights, perhaps."

She pulled at the ribbon that tied back my hair. "I have to say that I have dreamed a long time about an afternoon like this. I never met a woman who . . . would enjoy it."

Like last night, there would be no other afternoon in my life like this one. Only sky and prairie to know, only sun and shade to mind. My curls fell around my face and soon brushed my bare shoulders as she undressed me.

Her kisses burned down my throat as I knocked her hat to the ground. She made an anticipatory low noise of desire as my fingers dug into her scalp. "Yes," I said against her mouth. "Yes, I enjoy this."

I had been ready to forget her, to erase the memory of being cared for, of my pleasure being not just noticed, but needed. My body burned with flames of prairie fire, running fast and hot as she touched me in places that for once felt private.

Her need in the warm afternoon was earthier than during the night, or perhaps she was simply more certain of me.

"Like this?" She leaned her weight behind her hand, fingers finding all the silken wetness I could give her.

"Yes, Connor, like that. Please . . . oh . . ." She couldn't know that my voice was softer, deeper than I had ever heard it. My underskirts were up around my waist as I tried to pull her more deeply into me.

She stroked me, in, around, teasing, hard, more and more, then put her mouth down there too, with a noise of delight. The only thing I could give her was my pleasure. I had given it last night, but she had paid for me then. Right now she had not— that she might later did not worry me. In this moment my body was free, and mine, and I gave it to her.

She liked me naked, and I felt like Eve, naked and without shame. The Tree of the Knowledge of Good and Evil was too far away from the world of grass that hid us from anyone who might wander by on the road. The preacher talked about the Tree all the time. I did not ask him, as I had once asked years ago, how if God made all, then hadn't God made Satan and hadn't God then made the Apple, and how was frail Eve supposed to resist the temptation offered by God? Not that I thought the preacher would box my ears as the nuns back home had done, I simply didn't want to endure the resulting lecture.

I didn't feel ashamed, being naked in front of her. I perched on her saddle where it rested on the ground as we discussed Macbeth's temptations and Portia's mercy.

"I wish I was a painter. You are a proper vision like that." Connor chewed on the end of a stalk of grass as she regarded me.

"I think you make a fine image too." I liked her with her shirt off, liked her very much. Truly, I'd never seen anything like her, parts of her strong and corded like a man, and parts of her the soft swells of a woman that made my fingers curve with longing.

"My saddle will never be the same, not with such sweetness getting all over it."

I blushed madly. "I'm sorry, I can get my—"

"No, don't. I'm never going to get rid of that saddle. In fact . . ." She scooted toward me and I was aware that her nipples had tightened but what caught my attention more was the red flush that stained her chest. "Darlin', I don't think there's a fantasy you couldn't make come true for me."

Kneeling next to the saddle, she slipped a possessive arm

around me. Her body pressed between my legs as she kissed me. I arched to her, feeling owned by her in a way that had nothing to do with money.

"Would you straddle the saddle?"

"Is that how you want me?" I changed position and used the stirrup leather under my knees to protect them from the spikes in the grass.

"Please yes, Darlin'."

"I'm very . . . damp. I don't want . . . the leather, you know . . ." I wanted to do anything she asked of me, but my own desire was making me shy. "Like this?"

"Yes, as if you were riding. Scoot forward a bit and I'll settle behind you."

Her breasts were hard against my back and I moaned at the heat of our bodies. I could feel her hard nipples atop the soft crush of her breasts and the scratch of her twill trousers against my bottom was equally exciting. I leaned back into her arms, stretching so I could clasp my hands behind her neck as she explored my body, my tummy, my hips, my breasts, my neck.

"There's so much more room," I said, "without clothes in the way."

"I swear I feel drunk," she admitted. "You go right to my head. I'll never saddle Argo without thinking of you."

The idea of her never being able to forget me was deeply pleasing. It was a kind of immortality, I supposed, earned in a moment like this. Sins of the flesh, knowledge of evil—how could this pleasure I gave her, freely, be anything but good, and good for both of us? I felt closer to goodness, grace and God in her arms than I had ever before in my life.

Her persistent touch, rippling up and down my body until her hand cupped me between my legs, was stirring a definite feeling of ecstasy. The path to heaven trod by the holy was not for me, but in her arms I felt as if I could find another way. The pleasure grew as I jerked against her hand.

"Ride with me," she whispered in my ear.

"To the end of the world," I wanted to answer but instead a short, sharp cry escaped me and I shivered in the same delirious wonder that she had wrought in me last night.

I felt a ripple of laughter from her as I gasped in her arms. "That was finer than I ever thought it would be."

"You've spent a lot of time thinking about it?"

"The trail is long and dull. With little more than cows for company, I'd rather think about women."

I couldn't help the low, lazy laugh that escaped me. "With little more than men for company, I have to say the same."

She joined me in laughter, then shifted against me. "Would you like some water, Darlin'?"

"Yes, please." I watched as she went to the discarded saddlebags.

"I've another flask in here." She rifled through the large pouches and I went to help her as a coil of papers fell to the ground. "Oh, I'll get those . . ."

I already had them in my hand and knew them for what they were. I was gratified, then angry. "Were you going to give these back?"

"Yes, of course," Connor said immediately. "I hadn't finished reading and I wanted to read it all again, to savor."

"It's not that good." I handed over the sheaf with a shrug. "It just helps me escape sometimes."

"It's wonderful." She rose to her feet with the papers in one hand and the flask in the other. "I was going to ask you to read some to me, so I can hear it and think about it ever after."

I took back "The Hand of the Virgin Queen"—it was a silly, improbable story of a young girl, an unloved queen and their escape from the Garden Country where even the plants did the king's bidding. I couldn't believe she had liked it that much. It wasn't "As You Like It" or the history of some long-dead king.

I sat down on the saddle, still naked though that wasn't why I felt shy. She stretched out in the grass, watching me with an eager smile.

Most of the time, a man wants a woman for her female features, and any woman will do. Their desire is not specific. Some clearly prefer yellow or black curls, lean or fulsome curves, but the woman who possesses those traits is irrelevant. Rarely, a customer wants a specific woman because she is unique to him. The deal is struck, his property is rented. But she is still not a woman. The parts of her he does not want do not exist.

Connor looked at me as if I were real. Saw not just the pieces of my body, not just the accumulation of its shape into the form she'd named Darlin'. I was as close to being a woman with her that I could be with anyone who'd paid money to buy my time.

Her purchase didn't include my stories. It didn't include my thoughts. It certainly didn't include real laughter and real passion. I faced the question I had not been able to answer last night: if I gave myself freely what did that make me?

I turned the sheaf of papers over in my hands. That she saw me as a woman made me something more than property. Something more than a cast-off child who had found a way to stay alive. Something more than a lesson in sin to be paraded on the streets so decent people could feel holy. Having something of my own that I could freely give made me a person, and I had not felt alive for years.

"'The gardens of the king, lush with colors and heavy with perfumes, spread through the whole of the land. Oranges fell to hand at a wish, and fair flowers bloomed at every windowsill,'" I read. "'At the door to Her Majesty's bower I paused, afraid that my choice of blossom for her morning tray . . .'"

CHAPTER FIVE

I had seen the ocean in high winds, and knew the rushing terror of tall waves coming to shore, unstoppable. Prairie fire is like that, but red and crackling like guns.

At the first hint of a distant red glow on the horizon, shouts of alarm had echoed in the streets outside. When Cherry had risen that very morning, in fact, she'd said over a lean breakfast that the hot, sharp wind was fire weather. By this time in October we might have expected to see the first rains, but a spell of dry heat had culminated in these rising winds. Thunderheads swirled in the distance, promising rain, but too late to quench the flames.

From the rooftop we girls watched the glow increase until the sky was drenched red like sunset. In the streets the merchants were loading wares and family hurriedly into wagons, hoping to outrun the sweeping inferno. They would head to the river to the south of town, Cherry told us, and wait for the fire to run out of fuel. Safety was possible for anyone who could travel that distance faster than a walk. The winds were high, however, and a slow-moving wagon could be easily consumed, as could women on foot without decent boots, carrying their meager possessions on their back. If we got to the river and Long Grass went up in flames, the nearest town from there was another six miles. It was no bigger than Long Grass and we would not be welcome. Only Cherry might have money to buy some measure of shelter.

So we would take our chances in the town we knew. The fire wasn't the only danger outside. There were carrion like Loomis, and the decent folk who'd not share any scarce resource—water or space on the road, shade from the sun or shelter from the rain—with the likes of us. They would spend their money for a romp with exuberant Angel or the soft welcome of Lisbet, a sweet girl who had seen one season and sometimes sang when Otis played. But when it came to survival they would sacrifice us without a thought. Like Jesus' poor, there would always be more whores.

I did not care overmuch which of the merchants made it to safety. Had they only gathered their families and left immediately, they would have been safe. But instead they took goods with them as well, and risked being overtaken by the fire once they were on the road. Given the load some of them were tying down, their chances were better staying in town, along with the other unfortunates with no horse to carry them south.

The cage of the prairie was just as it had always been, inescapable. That I had spent time with someone who thought I was a person did not change the facts. Connor had left weeks ago with "Be seeing ya, Darlin'."

The smoke in the sky met the sun and blotted it out so quickly that Greta and Lisbet, both German girls, declared in unison, *"Gott in Himmel!"*

"It's going to take us all!" Angel wrung her hands whenever she wasn't wiping away tears of fear.

"The town hasn't burned yet," I pointed out. "We had prairie fires three years ago and the cleared space around the town is wider than before."

"I'm so *glad*," Angel said earnestly, "that you are older and know so much."

I wanted to tell her I wasn't born a few years before she was just to act as her almanac, but in the ominous light of the impending disaster, Angel looked like the near-child she was. I felt immensely older.

The red glow seemed to take on solidity and I wasn't sure I was seeing the actual flames yet, but it wouldn't be long. I thought of Connor, wondered where under that huge sky she might be. Hoped that no matter where she was that she would spend a few moments of her day reflecting on the pages I'd given her to keep. That her Darlin' was a memory she treasured. That she could not look at her saddle and not think of me. If the fire did take the town, and us with it, well, I could not help the fancy that I could rise from the fire. That if Long Grass rose again, so would I, somehow, and I would have choices in that life denied me in this one. Juliet found Romeo, just not during the play, I told myself. There could be a second start, just not in this place, in this life.

I knew how the church felt about such ideas. I was thinking about the kind of second chance that wasn't supposed to be real. The church said we all had one chance to lead the perfect life, and if that failed, we burned. Red fire was plainly crackling in the distance now, and these thoughts seemed important, though I'm sure the preacher would think my time better spent praying for deliverance or preparing myself to meet the flames of hell a little earlier than expected.

Conjured perhaps by my thoughts, an uncovered wagon rumbled onto the main street just beyond where we were perched like painted crows on the rooftop. The preacher and his kin were loaded closely together, along with what appeared to be pieces of the church altar.

His voice carried as he said, "I've done all I can to save their souls. The Lord will provide the rest!"

His words were directed at his wife's sister. I thought I saw her hazel eyes blaze with some strong emotion, but it might have been the filtered sunlight. She did say something, however, and her gaze brushed over all of us.

The preacher's reply made liberal use of "strumpets" and I wanted to shout down to him, "'Doomsday is near; die all, die merrily,'" but he had already whipped the reins to urge the horses more quickly on their way. Hazel looked back, just once, and it wasn't too far from the truth to fancy she was looking at me.

Cherry and I herded the girls across and down the long street to the schoolhouse. Some carried their clothes or trinkets. I carried a bed sheet in which all of my scribblings and clean paper were wrapped. The schoolhouse was the building nearest the center of town and farthest therefore from blowing embers and flames looking for a roof to feed on. The well was also dug deeper than most. With no one to tell us not to, we gorged ourselves on the cool water and wet our hot cheeks and necks.

The building was empty but for us, but then a few other folks came in as well, taking care to stay away from us. None, however, tried to claim we had no right to stay.

The air reeked of burnt grass and it weighed heavily on my skin. A few more townsfolk found their way inside, some panting with the effort to carry their most precious belongings. The last arrival banged the door open with a clatter.

"Jinny! Are you here?" The man at the door was in shadow for a moment, then he stepped into the light. Her favorite customer, I realized.

"I'm here, Henry. Why aren't you away safely?" Jinny stood there, trembling and ashen-faced.

"I couldn't leave you." He opened her arms and in full view of all of us, Jinny ran to him.

In spite of the heat I felt frozen inside. He held her close but with care, as if she were precious. I thought, struggling to breathe, that Henry was an unlikely Romeo, arriving before Juliet became a sheath to the fatal dagger. The word *marriage* was said. Kansas City was mentioned as a stopping point on the way to a brother's farm. They would start anew. Right in front of me, a second chance.

Fire is hot, and it is also loud. It roared like a tidal wave, hit the island of the town and poured around the edge, seeking fuel. We were all on our hands and knees, gasping in the thin air. The noise buffeted my ears like the percussion of thunder and all the while I watched Jinny and Henry, holding each other. I doubt they heard a thing.

A girl knew of a girl who'd heard of a girl that had found a place with a good family. Another girl had heard about a girl a long time ago who'd married a customer and had a second chance at respectability. Now I knew a girl who had had such luck. It would always be that way, I knew that. I would know of a girl . . . but that girl would never be me.

The fire swept around the buildings but not a roof went up in flames. The stench of charred grass was even more powerful when we ventured outside. The dusty brown ribbon of road now stretched between fields of smoldering black.

My gaze did not follow the road to the horizon with the idea that I might see a solitary figure, a knight riding to the rescue of her lady or even a cowboy returning to her favorite whore to see if she was all right. Such hopes were as lifeless as the fields.

There was a sudden flare of lightning, not far, and the almost immediate crack of thunder. Jinny walked away with Henry and never looked back. More lightning, more thunder. I was back in my room, putting my papers away under and on the table, when the rain broke.

• • •

What keeps a woman alive, beyond food and a warm blanket? A regular customer helps, and to my surprise I found one, as consistent as Thursday nights, as generous as would keep me in my little room and in Cherry's good graces. That I reminded him of his second wife's eldest daughter did not bother me, nor that he called me by her name. For two months of Thursdays so far he'd put his money in Cherry's pocket and taken me upstairs.

Through those nights, and others with less congenial company, I imagined a great adventure of two strong women escaping prairie fire with only each other for help. When this story did not occupy my mind I imagined my gentleman cowboy, the rogue of Kansas City, and all the adventures that could be had by a woman so bold and so brave.

The holiday season seemed to arrive suddenly. The newest girl, Greta, left behind by a gold-fever crazed family who'd paid her way out a year earlier to be farm help, was especially lectured by the preacher when he finally noticed a new face among the fallen. Why tell the poor girl she'd chosen iniquity when her other choice was Loomis, who would work her like a mule, use her like a whore, give her no ring, and pay her only food, and not enough of that? Cherry was no saint, but we weren't hauling a plow for her all morning and on our backs for her the rest of the day. Greta had had no money, at the time spoke nothing but German and none of the other farmers wanted help, nor their wives either—not when Greta was such a pretty thing. There were enough Germans around who welcomed their native language in bed to keep her and Lisbet quite busy. Unfortunately, she was a quick study and had picked up enough English to understand the preacher's sermons. Every week her cheeks stained with the color of shame.

Christmas Eve, in the afternoon before the rest of the town would have their service, we heard the tale of the nativity and were duly urged to repent our sins. When the conception of the Christ babe was described I glanced over at Greta. Every year since I had arrived, the Christmas story took on its own Long Grass telling. I caught her eye and wasn't sure what expression was on my face. She colored and looked away.

Greta knocked on my door after we'd all returned and readied ourselves for a festive supper. I knew what she was going to tell me—I had eyes. So did Cherry. She was such a tiny thing for a German girl that the by-product of our work was already showing. She'd only been here a few short months. I wondered if she'd gotten with child from one of the men in the family she'd worked for. Perhaps that had factored into why they'd left her behind.

"If you wait any longer the doctor won't do it," I told her. "Cherry will put you out long before you have the baby, and you'll both be lost." As if to emphasize my words the harsh wind rattled the shutters over my window.

"But I don't want doctor—woman healer?" Greta's English had improved rapidly, but she still struggled. She earned enough for Cherry not to grouse too much about the doctor's fee.

I shook my head. "There's no midwife anymore. She left about the time I got here. Doctors don't like them."

"Doctors don't know—herbs?"

"That's the right word, but the only herb you find in this town is sassafras. I'm not even sure that is an herb. You have to have a doctor. Go to Cherry now."

I shooed her out of my room, wondering why she had chosen to confide in me instead of Lisbet. With Milla gone I was the oldest girl, I suppose, and that might have something to do with it. Every once in a while a girl would ask me to write a letter for her, so most of them assumed I had some kind of special book learning.

I sat down at the little table and looked at the papers I'd been writing for days. "Cowboys and Kisses" was my current endeavor and I lost myself in it to the extent that I could. It was no surprise that the hero was a cowboy by the name of Connor, and her lady was strong and could survive without her, but life was more interesting once they traveled together. Outlaws and miscreants tasted the lead of Connor's pistol while the lady secured respect with a flick of a sinuous bullwhip.

Connor'd slept poorly the night after our glorious afternoon, fighting the bedclothes and shrugging out of my arms. In the morning she had been quiet after spending half the night reading. When I woke she'd kissed me and taken me back to bed; I'd not cared that I'd missed breakfast. I had expected her to return that night, even though I told myself it was foolish hope. I had wanted her to return. But her role in the cattle drive was over for the year. I didn't know where she might go until the spring. When she did not show up that night I thought she had needed to escape the indoors. I didn't know what drove her to want the open sky always overhead but I wished I understood. I wished I knew more about her. But she didn't return the next night, or the next week or month. It was possible I would never see her again, or not for a very long time. Ulysses took twenty years to return to Penelope.

I told myself I was no Penelope, and I already knew all that I needed. She had treated me like a person, had been kind to me, romantic even, and she had blinked back tears when I had told her she could keep story I'd read to her during our idyllic day in the tall, golden grass. The tears had been mine watching her layer each sheet between pages of her collection of Shakespearean tragedies, treating my words like equal treasure.

By the time I went downstairs to partake of our Christmas Eve feast, the night had turned bitter with wind-driven rain. The fare was ordinary, but more plentiful than usual. Greta's appetite was clearly off and from her red-rimmed eyes it was clear Cherry had given Greta an ultimatum. Angel studiously ignored Greta, though it might have just as easily been any of us. Cattle drive demands resulted in at least one girl in a family way, and townspeople and Cherry all behaved as if the conception had been immaculate, if that was how one described an event where the girl became pregnant without even the intervention of a god. We were told often enough that even god did not want us.

Though none of us expected commerce that night—it wasn't unlawful, just unlikely—Loomis appeared out of the icy night, his breath thick with whiskey and holiday plans on his mind. Cherry quickly selected Bridgette, Greta, and to my horror, me. I understood Bridgette, who'd spent half of last month in bed with stomach troubles, and Greta, who was about to cost a doctor's fee. But me? I'd done nothing that I could think of, and my earnings were decent enough. Loomis didn't care for me, either.

He had, perhaps, forgotten that, as he slung his arm around my shoulders and pronounced himself ready for a party. I smiled, you have to smile, and happily sent Aaron downstairs for a requested bottle of whiskey. The drunker he got the sooner he'd be asleep.

Loomis was no different than any other man, with himself as the sun and the world in revolution around him. The three of us were of a mind, and made sure he drank a few more shots before anyone got to the bed. Laughter and teasing gave the liquor time to work. I spent my time thinking of my hero's adventure, of what gentleman cowboy Connor would encounter in Kansas City. Small but strong, I could picture Connor's laconic smile. Loomis had been passed out on top of me for a minute before I realized it.

Greta began to leave the room, but Bridgette stayed her. "Don't go—Cherry will know he's out. We can be another whole hour. Just bounce the bed once in a while."

I squirmed out from under Loomis and made use of the basin. We were in Bridgette's room, which I liked mostly because she had kept scraps of newspaper and covered one wall with them. Though it was all old news, it was something to read.

Greta sat on the edge of the bed, as far away from the snoring

Loomis as she could get. "Doctor's coming day after tomorrow."

Bridgette settled onto her only chair. "Well, he can't come on Christmas."

"What does he do?" Greta was appealing to me, and I could only shake my head.

"I don't rightly know. I've never had it done." I glanced at Bridgette, but didn't volunteer that she could describe it. I thought harshly of her for a moment when she still said nothing, but then took note of her pallor.

I saw her swallow hard, once, then she said, "You'll feel real sick. It'll be like the worst blood you've ever had. If you don't catch a fever, you'll be fine in a few days."

"Fever?" Greta looked at me with her wide, frightened eyes. "What fever?"

What fever, indeed. Greta must have formed some attachment for me because she asked me to be the one who held her hand when the doctor arrived. He was all hurry and bluster, and spoke with a strong accent of the east that Greta couldn't translate easily. I thought this fortunate because he spoke to himself as if neither of us was there, about the filth of Greta's female parts and his preference for ministering to clean cows and horses versus women, and women of our ilk especially. He took no notice of the basin of hot water or the clean rags with which I'd carefully lined Greta's bed. He got out his instruments and I looked away, after giving her a towel to bite.

Before he was done I thought she would break my hand. Sweat stood out from her forehead and when it was finally over she cried in more than just physical pain. She cried like I felt sometimes, but nothing ever hit me hard enough to break the dam that held back my river of tears.

The doctor left without another word and I realized that someone had to clean everything up. Dispose of . . . the bloody mess.

A sharp rap at the door startled me before I could even make myself look at what was between Greta's legs on the bed. Cherry didn't try to look into the room when I opened the door.

She passed me a bottle of whiskey with a couple of shots left in it. "One for you, the rest for her. Have you wrapped it up?"

I shook my head.

"Wrap it up and I'll take it."

We shared a long look and I wondered, not for the first time, how old she was. Thirty, perhaps? I knew she gave a great deal of the money she made to one of the town's upstanding leaders and that their business arrangement included personal elements too. He could, and had, supplied persuasive men to deal with customers who damaged or stole Cherry's property. His hands were never bloody, however. How had she ended up being the one who coped with the mess? So young a body, I thought, with so old a head.

I gave Greta a strong shot of the whiskey, had one myself, then held my breath and closed my eyes to slits as I gathered up the blood-soaked rags and the gore that lay on them, rolling it all over and over until I could no longer feel what crumpled in the center, going cold. At the door I thrust it all into Cherry's arms, who turned on her heel and disappeared down the hallway toward the stairs.

I mopped at Greta's blood while she continued to cry, using the basin of now cold water the doctor had left untouched. When I realized my head was spinning I went to Greta's window for cooler air. Through the thick glass I saw Cherry with the bundle disappearing into the street. It was early yet and the streets were quiet. I had no idea where she was going—it could not be far. The church would not let her bury it. There was nothing to see from the window but the light curl of smoke from the blacksmith's forge. I had almost turned away when the smoke went from gray to a greasy, blanketing black.

My stomach heaved. Gone with no chance, no choice, to the fire. Not to have even lived, and failed. That bundle of rags and flesh was forgotten by all moments after it was consumed. An inconvenience ignored by everyone but me and she who would have been a mother, sobbing on the bed behind me.

In the street below I saw Cherry returning, arms empty. Through the thick glass her face looked like stone. I turned away, hands over my stomach as if that would somehow calm it to flinch anew at Greta's extremity of grief and pain.

If Cherry were here she would tell Greta the terse facts of our existence. Remind her that she'd have two nights to recover, then it was back to work or else. I remember thinking Milla a stupid girl for having been in Greta's position, and saw in myself the stone of Cherry's face, threatening to take me over completely.

I had a choice after all, it seemed. Not between life and death, staying or leaving, whoring or chastity. It was a choice of how to be alive. I could be Cherry and turn to stone. Or I could feel the sun on my naked body, remember the light of passion in Connor's eyes and hear the words I read aloud to her. I could not be both.

Cherry's way I would survive longer, perhaps as long as she. But I knew my pen would still and the colors that made up my imagination would fade to black, like the smoke of the smith's forge. My soul would go up in that fire and if there was only one thing I understood from all I knew of the Bible, there were no choices, no second chances, if one lived, or died, without a soul.

I gave Greta more whiskey and held her until she slept.

CHAPTER SIX

By night Greta was shivering. Her eyes were glassy, too, and she could keep no food down. I saw nothing but immovable rock in Cherry's face when she told me that she'd seen it go thus before, and the girl had still survived.

My worry vexed Cherry, that was clear, and I made an effort to earn more that night. I knew it was sensible to turn over my bed as much as I could, but it was not sensible that in between I checked on Greta, bringing her hot, sugary tea and forcing her to drink it, along with the whiskey that seemed to dull her pain.

As the frigid morning approached I felt more tired than I could ever remember. Tired of men and their needs, tired of smiling, tired even of trying to continue my story in my head. I could usually make it my reality and the real things happening to me the fiction, but every adventure was fraught with visions of prairie fire and black smoke.

Greta didn't notice when I entered her room. She was still bleeding, but not as much. I fetched fresh rags and tried to get her to drink more whiskey so she could sleep.

"No, *nein*," she insisted.

"What can I bring you then? You need to keep up your strength."

"My book." She gestured at the bureau and I made a quick search, finding in the second drawer a small leather-bound book no bigger than my palm. I flipped the pages curiously—a miniature New Testament in her native language.

"Here." I handed it to her and sighed when she clasped it to her breast. "Breakfast. You need breakfast or you won't be able to work tomorrow night."

A shudder went through her.

"You can help another girl when someone wants two. Cherry will make it clear you're not up for . . . everything." I added desperately, "It'll be all right."

She closed her eyes and the shivers increased. Her brow was clammy and I no longer seemed to exist to her.

I slept fitfully after breakfast, then stripped my bed for wash day. After my share of soaking linens in freezing water, then twisting and spreading them near the fire, I peered into Greta's room to find her blissfully asleep.

The gray clouds overhead hardly let any light through, and the frost-crusted glass took care of almost all the rest. Standing at Greta's window I saw a man of the town quickly crossing the street after leaving our door. He had just made it, and no doubt heaved a sigh of relief, as the preacher and his wife turned the corner in their wagon. They were headed out of town, I thought, wrapped tight against the cold. I was glad to see a heavy portmanteau—wherever the preacher was bound, it was for more than one day. No doubt he would return in time for Sunday services, more's the pity.

Greta made a little noise and I felt her brow only to draw my hand back from her heat. Where she'd been clammy before I found her skin dry and papery. She turned toward my touch as if it helped but her fingers moved reflexively on the little volume she still held close.

I should have slept in preparation for my evening's work, but I stayed with her. Her room seemed to grow darker by the hour, so much so that when I glanced from her window again I was surprised to find the clouds had broken up and there was sunshine with patches of clear blue sky peeking through.

Laughter and chatter in the hall increased. Angel said something about saving for new hair ribbons and I heard Bridgette bemoaning the arrival of her blood. It was supper and I should have gone down to partake. I was hungry, but didn't feel it. Jinny had escaped, I reminded myself. I watched Greta's chest struggle to rise for every breath and didn't want to acknowledge the truth: for every Jinny there were a hundred Gretas in this house. In other towns, there was a Greta, a Milla—a Darlin'.

Cherry's unmistakable rap on the door brought me out of grim, dark thoughts.

"Leave her. You can't help." Once again, Cherry stayed outside in the hall.

"I think she's dying. She shouldn't be alone."

"You can't change it. She'll survive or she won't."

Cherry was much older than I was, true, but I felt as if I'd learned something she had not. "Either way, how these hours pass matter."

"You sound like the preacher's been at you." Cherry frowned and I could see her adding up the money Greta had cost, wasn't making tonight and what it appeared I would not make tonight either.

"No preacher could understand what I mean. Or what she's going through."

Her expression softened just slightly. "That is a true thing you've said. But it don't change the fact that you need to get downstairs."

"I made extra last night, Cherry. And I promise again tomor-row night. But tonight—let me at least be here. Milla . . ."

"Stupid girl." But her gaze flicked to the bed behind me and she turned her back and walked away. No permission for me to stay, but no order for me to leave.

The house was noisy with activity when I could no longer deny that Greta was sinking, quickly. Her fever was if anything hotter and she would not swallow when I drizzled water or whiskey at her mouth. I rifled through her bureau to see if there was anything else that might give her comfort, and found only a thin chain with a locket—empty—and a cross hanging from it. I put it in her hand but I'm not sure she knew it was there.

Footsteps on the stairs were frequent—Cherry would be angry with me for not working. I couldn't ask anyone else to join me either. So I put on my long coat and risked what was left of my boots' resistance to mud and slipped out the back door. In the dark I couldn't avoid the pools of bathwater, partially iced over, and other waste that was flung from the windows in the course of a night, but I clung close to the house and made my way to the street. The wind was icy but men still roamed the night. In the dark none of them would know which woman I was, but that I had emerged near Cherry's made me a target should they decide to take advantage of my lack of escort and have some fun for free. I moved quickly, turned into the church yard and made my way around to the back door there.

There was light and so the preacher's wife's sister was still awake. I tapped quietly, then louder, and waited.

Through the door the voice I sometimes heard in a soothing dream, said, "What is your need?"

How did I explain? "I need to talk to you."

"The minister isn't here."

"It's not him I need."

The door opened a bit and I could see a narrow slice of her

face. Her expression was not welcoming. "It's late. What is it?"

"One of us—she's not well. I think she may die by morning. She's got her own Bible and a cross and I don't know what to say. But I think something might comfort her. It's important. It matters to her."

I had thought she might give me a Bible and a verse and send me away, but instead she opened the door more and I smelled bread, fresh bread.

"Come in," she said.

There was a little mat just inside the door and I stayed on it. My boots were indescribable with muck, and the kitchen, in the low lamp light, looked immaculate. My next realization was that the room was warm, blissfully so. She turned the lamp higher and I saw on the far counter a row of loaves looking golden and firm.

"I don't like to be here by myself," she explained after catching the direction of my glance. "Baking passes the time."

I nodded and aimed to be casual, even though I saw for the first time her face and hair free of the shadowing bonnet. "My grandmother used to bake. I've not learned."

Her expression was mildly surprised, as if the likes of me having a grandmother was unexpected. If my grandmother hadn't been dead I liked to think she'd have not let me be sent away. She's the one who had made me read Shakespeare, and so carefully it was all still in my mind, the only kind of treasure no one could take from me.

"Would you like a cup of tea and some bread? I need to change."

I tried not to show my surprise as I accepted her offer. She moved quickly to provide me with the repast while I surreptitiously took note of the thick hair that reached her waist and the firm line of her jaw. "Thank you. I appreciate it."

"Be at ease. I'll be back in a few minutes."

The sound of her footsteps was light overhead while I sipped from a delicate teacup the likes of which I'd not held since family years. She'd spread apricot jam on the warm bread and I could have been in my grandmother's kitchen. It was the best bread I'd had in years, even and firm, strong enough to hold the jam, but melting away at every bite.

Like Connor's impromptu picnic, it was food given in hospitality and to be worthy of the gesture was also to be treated like a person, not an outcast. When she came back I thanked her again, then added, feeling shy, "May I know your name?"

"Violet—did you not know?"

"You are always 'sister' in church. I confess, I am not always paying attention." No Frog, no Hazel, but a rich, lush, exotic flower. It matched the satiny coil of her hair that she had caught into a net whilst upstairs.

"I noticed that you read."

"Yes. Books are scarce, and the Old Testament has many good stories."

"They teach us a great deal." She slung a heavy cloak around her shoulders, covering a serviceable but plain poplin dress. "If you're ready?"

"I am. It was delicious. You make wonderful bread, as good as my grandmother's."

"Practice." Her smile allowed that she was pleased by my compliment.

We went into the night, two women moving quickly. The men that were out appeared deep in drink or looking to be. I led her what I hoped was the cleanest way to the back door and watched her take a deep breath in the wan light. She had never set foot in a place like this, that was plain. The preacher would not have thought anything could be done for Greta and would not have even bothered.

Aaron was busy boiling water. He nodded respectfully to Violet and I led her quickly upstairs, past the rooms where it was plain what was going on. She was pale but held her head up.

Greta's room smelled like blood and sickness. Violet felt her brow and gave me an alarmed look.

"Have you sent for the doctor?"

I shook my head. "He can't do anything about this kind of fever."

"How do you know?"

"It happens. She's not going to have a baby now, but she caught a fever."

Violet looked faint for a moment, like the reality of whores getting with child was as unreal as them having grandmothers.

Something in me snapped. "What did you think? That we fornicate all night and eat lotus flowers the rest of the day? Customers leave us with their seed and she's going to die."

"She could have chosen—"

"Chosen what? She was a servant with a Christian family that left her here with no money, no place to live, and nobody in this town would give her work or a place to sleep. So she came here. Just like I did. Just like we all do. Everyone wants to reform us. You church people are happy to provide heaven for our souls, but what do we do with our bodies in the meantime? All you'll tell us is what not to do. Where does our daily bread come from?"

Greta coughed and my anger broke. Violet didn't answer me and I felt badly for having yelled—though she was obviously made of sturdy stuff that could survive out here, in Violet's world sin was only theoretical. Like anyone who had not been faced with my or Greta's choices, she could not understand how they had even existed. Somehow, we brought those choices on ourselves. No doubt if she knew I was here because I said I was in love with another girl she would agree that I had only myself to blame.

"I'm sorry," I muttered.

"No," she said quickly. "No, I'm sorry. 'Judge not, lest ye be judged.' That has always been a difficult one for me. I will try to do better."

I was stunned that Violet would actually apologize to the likes of me. She quoted a sentiment I thought her brother-in-law had long forgotten. Her expression was gentle as she looked down at Greta. The cross, locket and Bible clutched in her hands were pathetically small.

"She's just a child."

"Not really—fifteen, I think."

There was a flare of anger in Violet's eyes that was not directed at me. "How old are you?"

"Nearly eighteen. And you?"

Even though my question was impertinent, she answered me. "Twenty-eight."

And unmarried, I thought. And unlikely to find a suitable husband in Long Grass. Ironic that Jinny had, when Violet was a good, respectable choice. Intelligent, strong, spirited, even.

She felt Greta's forehead again, then drew up the only chair and took her hand. I busied myself turning up the lamp and fetching fresh water for the ewer and basin. I had no means to offer anything else.

Settled on the edge of the bed opposite where Violet sat, I bathed Greta's forehead with water. Violet opened the Bible she'd brought with her and settled on a page marked with a faded red ribbon.

Her voice was soft, velvet-like, as she read quietly, "The Lord is my shepherd . . ."

I woke with my head on my arms, slumped on Greta's bed. Violet didn't have to tell me what I sensed even as I stirred.

Violet was at the door, saying quietly, "Just a little bit ago. I took the time to say one last prayer."

Cherry answered, "I'm surprised to see you here."

I looked up to see both women in the wan lamplight. In profile I was struck by their similarity, like opposing sides of the same coin. Where Cherry was hard as stone, though, Violet was soft like corn silks. One cold, one warm, but both were unmarried, strong-willed and intelligent. One merciless and one merciful, but taking two different paths to the same end: survival.

Both were on roads not available to me. I would never be Cherry, nor could I be a true believer. Try as I might I couldn't look forward and see myself as either of them. I couldn't see myself at all. All I had to cling to was a moment, naked in the sun, when all Connor had wanted of me was my words and they were mine, free to give.

"Does this happen often?"

"Hazard of the trade." Cherry's voice was diamond sharp. "It's no concern of yours."

"She was just a girl."

"That's how your men like them."

I touched Greta's cooling hand and made myself look at her face. Was that my face, my future? Or would I be vulture food, like Milla, after wandering in the cage of the tall grass?

"Very well," Violet was saying. "I'll go."

Cherry said nothing, but cleared the doorway so that Violet could exit as she swirled her cloak around her shoulders. For a moment Violet paused and looked at me. Then her gaze went pointedly to the Bible on the bed. She swept past Cherry with dignity, leaving me to pick up the book and clutch it to my heart. I couldn't help Greta anymore, and my pity for her wouldn't stop me from accepting the gift of something to read.

I rose hurriedly from the bed, sorry that Violet was leaving and worried that as soon as she was gone, I'd be helping Cherry with Greta's body. I wanted to be out of that room.

"She can't go outside by herself."

"If you're so worried," Cherry snapped, "go with her."

I paused only long enough to put the Bible on my bed and once again pull on my long coat. The night sky blazed with stars. Ahead of me, Violet's dark form was almost at a run, avoiding the calls of a cluster of what I took to be farmhands who ought to have long since headed home.

My running footsteps must have startled her, because she turned quickly with a fierce expression. "Oh, it's you. You shouldn't be out here."

"I wanted to make sure you are safe. It was a good thing you did. I wouldn't want you hurt because of it."

"Did you know her well?" Violet continued her hurried pace toward the church and I followed just as quickly after her.

"No, not at all, really. Except she was sweet and scared and her customers liked her."

"I'll bet they did."

I couldn't see her face as she said that, but her tone was heavy with irony. She opened the door to the kitchen and held it open, so I entered as well. The stove was still giving off plenty of heat and the room's warmth was like a balm. "The customers don't always like you."

The lamp flared and her intriguing face, lined with fatigue, was all I could see. "Then why do they—never mind."

"For some it's about pleasure. Others it's about companionship. Many of my customers like to talk to me. I know a little bit about a lot of things. They talk about their crop or herd or money worries and I listen. Sometimes . . ." I shrugged. "Sometimes, I seem to help. But other customers I don't know what it's about. It's not pleasure."

I knew perfectly well what it was about, but didn't want to tell her. Why darken those eyes any further?

She looked as if she knew anyway, and I wondered abruptly how a woman such as her could possibly be still unmarried. She *was* a fine catch, but she lived in Long Grass, just like I did, and seemed to have no way of escaping it either.

"Would you like some tea and bread? I'm famished." She

dropped a chunk of wood into the stove, then set the tea kettle on the hot spot.

"Thank you." I accepted not because I was hungry but because I didn't want to leave. It was only when I took the first bite of her wonderful bread, this time smeared with some kind of soft cheese, that I realized I was also famished. "You've been very kind to me."

She smiled. "I was merely trying to be Christian, but it's easy to be kind to you."

Not sure what she meant by the last bit, I focused on the first. "There's many Christians here who would not feed me, let alone allow me inside their door."

"This place makes people hard."

"Yes. Yes, it does."

"But not you."

I looked at her across the table, not sure what it was I felt. If I hadn't known better, I'd have said she was flirting with me. There's a particular cant to the head, a look in the eyes—I knew these gestures from men, and from Connor, who had been no more subtle about her desire than a man. Violet was . . . nearly . . . looking at me the same way. "It has made me hard and I don't want to be that way."

The teakettle whistled and she got up to pour the boiling water into the pot. "This isn't a place where softness lasts long."

"I've been here five years."

I watched her do the math in her head, then swallow hard. "I'm sorry."

I didn't want to tell her why I had ended up here alone. "I chose to live. Suicide's a sin, you know."

She responded to my wry tone with a matching smile. "Choosing life can't ever be wrong. It's what you do with the life."

"Maybe not so much what you do, but how you do it. I've only recently realized the only choice I really have is over how, not what."

"Somewhere you had some good schooling."

"Not enough to be the school teacher here."

"I don't mean to pry," she said slowly. "But you're pretty and smart. Why didn't you marry?"

"I wasn't fourteen. Twelve is too young to marry here. So I had to figure out how to live for two years and, well, by the time I was old enough to marry . . ." I shrugged. Her expression didn't change but I was suddenly wary of her motives. What did she want from me? "Now it's your turn to answer that question. You are also pretty and smart."

"I loved someone once. No one else has even come close."

Her response was so smooth and quick I would have thought it a lie except for the look on her face. I'd seen that look in my own mirror, thinking of that girl, Rachel. Or, more recently, thinking of Connor.

"I never asked your name," she said abruptly.

"You can call me Darlin'." I don't know why I gave her Connor's pet name for me, except she was also treating me as if I was real. Unlike Connor, she'd not even paid for my time.

Abrupt gunfire from the street startled us both. I used my sleeve to dab at the tea I'd spilled.

"I never get used to that," Violet said.

"I sleep through it, unless it goes on for a bit."

The noise outside subsided and the subsequent quiet finally felt like the latest hours of the night to me. Abruptly, I yawned.

"Well, you saw me safely here, now how do you get safely home?"

"I'll be all right," I said. "Down the street and in the door before anyone even sees me." As if to make a liar of me, more gunfire broke out and there were drunken shouts.

"You could sleep here."

It was tempting. The kitchen was warmer than my room would be. "I'd almost say yes just to have more bread in the morning. But I must go back."

"Isn't it too late to work?"

"Given the noise, no. Besides, you'll not want to be explaining why I slept here to your sister or her husband."

She shrugged, but rose with a resigned air. "I'll watch from the window. Call out if there's trouble."

"Thank you." I didn't mean just the tea and bread.

At the door she was standing close and that feeling came over me again that she wanted something more from me. It was in her eyes and the slight tremble of her mouth. Did she even know that two women could touch, could love?

"Thank you again," I said. She didn't answer, only looked at me with that question in her eyes. Softly, I asked, "Was there something you wanted?"

Her arms went around my waist; that was all that was clear to me. She gasped against my mouth and then kissed me hungrily.

Even though I wanted to respond I was passive in her arms. I was fearful she would blame me for anything that happened. I was temptation and sin and she the good Christian. The warmth of her hands on my back made me shiver and my resolve wavered. I could feel the shape of her body against mine, and I wanted to explore it. This was all freely given. There was no hint of money and no reason for restraint. I could say yes or no if I chose.

I could taste the power of that no in my mouth. It was a feeling I wanted to experience, to say no with the knowledge that she would not force me to do anything. The idea of her forcing me was ludicrous and I felt a little drunk. This was my choice—is this how some women felt all the time?

"Violet," I whispered. "Be careful what you want, what you are doing."

She let go of me with a shocked noise. "I'm sorry, I'm so sorry. So sorry."

"No, it's all right—"

"No, it's not all right. You didn't say I could kiss you. You didn't have to let me. I'm not—I'm not going to pay you."

"I know. And you're right, I didn't have to let you kiss me." She looked so lost that I abruptly felt the elder. "You don't have to let me kiss you either."

She did, though, with my hands gently cupping her face. I could not tell her what a simple conversation had meant to me, and how many hours I suspected we could talk before we broached any topic twice.

Something in our kiss changed, as if she had also reached an inescapable conclusion: we would not have another time like this. We would never be free to simply talk to each other. The gulf between church and whorehouse was an ocean men could cross, discreetly, but an uncrossable one for women.

She turned her head away.

I said, "The one you loved?"

"She was much like you."

I felt a pang. I could be a surrogate for a customer, but I didn't want to be one for her.

She looked me in the eye, and added, "And nothing like you."

My heart was fluttering in my breast and I felt that same, welcome feeling of desire that I had felt for Connor. I was free to give myself to her.

For a moment her eyes asked. Then mine said no. Not because I wanted for once in my life to be able to say no, but because common sense said we would never get another chance. Though it hardly made sense to me then, it seemed that a free gift must have the highest value placed on it.

Besides, in all the tragedies the lovers who took their only chance always ended badly. I was already well on my way to a bad ending; I saw no reason to further tempt destiny.

The look in her eyes haunted me, though, as I ran quickly across the street and into the back yard. I slipped on ice-sheeted patches but mercifully didn't fall. The kitchen was cold compared to the one I had just left and my abrupt entrance startled Otis and Aaron, who were pulling on their coats in anticipation of sunrise. Shovels rested near the door. With the ground frozen outside I knew the grave would be shallow. Come spring Greta would be settled further down, along with anyone who joined her.

I made my way up the stairs to find Angel and Lisbet standing outside Greta's open door. Lisbet seemed to be eying the room, larger than the one she currently had, with more than a little avarice.

Cherry was with Jade inside the room, wrapping Greta's nude body in a thin sheet. In a few hours it would be as if she never was, except to the worms. A worm can eat of the body of a king or a lost girl just the same.

CHAPTER SEVEN

In spite of the charred devastation left by the fire, the prairie beyond Long Grass sprouted green in the spring after the last blizzards of March had melted away. The golden grasses of summer would be as tall as ever—nature would begin again. A small flock of geese cawed overhead as we earth-bound painted birds made our way to Sunday service. The sun was welcome on the nape of my neck. It reminded me of a different day.

The preacher had lately been waging war on demon alcohol. Near as I could tell, he was providing free advertising for the distillers, as most customers were asking for a double shot these days. Perhaps it was spring making everyone itch.

It was hard not to look at Violet. After our kisses I had watched her closely every week, but had never caught her glancing my way. She could not converse with me publicly, nor was there any opportunity to talk privately. Even if I could slip out some night, cross the street unseen, what would I do? Climb to her balcony? We were both Juliets on this stage. Another stage we might find ways, but the preacher would answer any knock at the door, and I was not a sword-bearing youth free to come and go as I pleased. We could not risk speaking to each other—punishment in some form would be swift and cruel. I didn't know what form punishment would take, but I had very little to lose that would not cost me dearly. My regular customer had stopped visiting and my tallies weren't encouraging. Cherry was capable of withholding the paper and ink, of burning my stories, of putting me out of the house for calling undue attention to her business.

Even all these months later I didn't want Cherry to catch me looking at Violet, nor did I want Violet to think I wanted anything of her. To risk punishment when all there had been was a little bit of talk and a few kisses was to hope that together we could find someplace else to start over, with no money, no horse, no wagon. Even bread took flour and an oven to make. Whoring required a blanket and I did not even have that.

Romeo had loved Juliet to distraction, that love had been returned and their stars had still crossed. I had no reason to think Violet had feelings for me beyond a nostalgic recollection of the love she had lost. I had thought, of late, that I was born under crossed stars and I couldn't ask her to cross her stars with mine when, like Romeo and Juliet, there was no place for us.

I closed my eyes when she read to us, savoring the inflections, the rise and fall of her melodious voice. These were the times I most regretted my decision to leave her warm kitchen that night. She could have read about loaves, fishes or pieces of silver and I'd have not cared about the substance. I heard the echo of her sweet voice praying over Greta, and it wrapped me in the same comfort. I also heard that whispered, dangerous assurance that I was very much and nothing like the woman she had loved before.

They were foolish thoughts, irresponsible hopes. They, a worn Bible, used paper and some ink, were all I had. Every month that passed there seemed to be less of me. I'd celebrated my eighteenth birthday with a hoarded swallow or two of port, feeling already too old for most of the experiences any life could offer.

The sunlight gave me a slight headache when we ventured into the street again. I shaded my eyes and wished I hadn't agreed to plait Lisbet's hair this afternoon.

"Why there you are, Darlin'."

For a moment my heart didn't beat. The image of Jinny walking away, arm in arm with her favorite customer, was all I could see. Then my vision cleared and I looked up.

Connor blotted out the sun, moving slowly forward on Argo so as to keep me in the shade. I couldn't clearly see her face and I had no idea what my own expression might reveal.

"Come back tonight," Cherry said briskly.

"I was hoping I'd proven myself trustworthy before, and we could agree to—"

"Times have changed. You'll have to come back tonight."

What would Cherry do if I went to Connor anyway, I wondered. She'd done nothing to Jinny, but then Jinny's beau had offered a wedding ring. A husband's claim of ownership would trump any claim of Cherry's, even debt. Connor would never be able to make any claim for me and Cherry's upright citizen partner would find plenty of helpers to drag back her errant property and get rid of the thief, permanently.

"Just a short ride and a picnic."

"How do I know you still have any of your drive pay left?" Cherry continued to herd us down the street.

"You have only my word. I can't prove it here in the street. Back by sundown and I'll settle then, all legal-like."

Cherry opened her mouth to refuse, I could see it in her expression, but Connor added, "Have mercy on a tired soul. I rode half the night to get here by this afternoon."

"Oh, all right." She gave me an irritated look. "There'll be hell to pay if you're not back."

Connor twirled me up onto the saddle, but even in the midst of my joy to feel her close and the heated anticipation of her touch, I could not help but realize that no one had asked me what I wanted.

We rode, as before, to the tree in the distance. I chattered about the prairie fire and did not mention Greta. Connor was a customer, I told myself, and to a customer the only past I had was with her. Nevertheless, I could ask about hers.

"Where have you roamed since I last saw you?"

"Omaha, been down to Texas. There's some pretty canyons where the night sky almost sings. Heaven is close enough to touch when I'm sleeping under the stars. Before here I was in and out of Kansas City, mostly." Her arms tightened around me. "I usually stay a week there, but dang me if I couldn't stop thinking about you, Darlin'."

"There are many pretty women in Kansas City," I said with sober certainty, even though my heart beat a little faster at the thought that she had come back to Long Grass simply to find me.

"That there are. None like you. I couldn't find even one that liked what I wanted as much as you."

"And you looked in every woman's bed in Kansas City trying?"

She laughed. "Something like that."

"So why did you leave with your search unfinished?"

Her arms tightened around my waist. "To visit you, of course."

A visit, and that's all it was, I told myself. Wanting more had no use. Journey's end did not always lead to lovers meeting. I firmly reminded myself that after today I'd not see her again until autumn, when the cattle drive came back. That is, if she wasn't trampled in some stampede, and I didn't succumb to prairie madness. I relaxed against her, willing myself to look no further forward than the next few hours.

They were pleasant hours. Connor undressed me, slowly, feigning ignorance of various fripperies as they were unlaced. She tickled me, I giggled and we sighed into laughing kisses. When I was finally naked and spread out on the horse blanket, once again using the saddle for a pillow, her teasing faded.

"You're lovely, Darlin'," she said just before her lips closed over my nipple.

Her tongue played with it and I reveled in the shivers that prickled my skin. "I'm glad you think so."

She bit down, drawing a little cry from me, then her hands were stroking my thighs, finding my wet. Her moan of pleasure surpassed mine when she went inside me, but my vocal appreciation of her touch was loud and lusty.

She grinned at me, pushed harder and said, "I've missed the way you sing for me. The food of love . . . Like that, Darlin'. Do you like that?"

"Yes," I managed, through gritted teeth. "I do like that." She opened me as easily as a book, and I felt her writing on the pages of me something new that could not be erased. Something I could not write for myself.

I could only write what I knew, and some words were foreign to me. I had no defenses and didn't want any. The pleasure grew to a pulsing fire and even though I could not say no, I still found I could say yes and it have some meaning. Again I gave her the only thing that I could—my abandonment.

"Enjoy me," I begged her. "Have what you want. Anything you want." Moans and whispers, nothing held back. She could do anything she wanted and I would have liked it because it was what she wanted. I was a whore who liked this pleasure, the pleasure she gave me. It made me shameless, but I didn't want her to leave again. I had nothing with which to buy her love except this and until this moment I hadn't realized that I still foolishly hoped for escape. "Please don't stop. Enjoy me, please."

"Darlin'," she murmured. "Yes," she said.

With an exhausted sigh, she settled her head on the saddle next to mine. "Thank you."

I could scarcely catch my breath. I would ache tomorrow, and remember her. Men would touch me and I'd remember her, feel her for days. Was that what I had wanted, for her to mark me somehow? When I could, I assured her, "The pleasure was all mine."

"Not entirely." She traced my lips with a lazy finger and I smiled against it. While her abandonment had not equaled mine, that she had allowed herself to feel ultimate bliss still pleased me. "I like the feel of your hand against me. And your kisses are like fine brandy. I'm quite drunk on them."

"I could say the same."

"Never," she said softly, studying my face with her own dark gaze, "has any woman made me feel the way you do. What I want—it makes sense with you. It never felt like it makes sense with others. I don't know what they see when they look at me. I often fear it's a pile of coins."

"You are more than that to me," I said honestly. You could be more than that, I wanted to add, but only if you want to be, if you need to be. I carefully phrased my next question. "Have you never sought out a woman who wasn't interested in coins for her time?"

"I'm not the settling kind. I couldn't ask a woman to share my roaming or one to sit and wait for me most of the year."

But what if she wanted to wait, I could have asked. What if while she waited she wrote your stories? What if that led to the kind of devotion that became of story of its own?

She fumbled in her saddlebags, then handed me a parcel wrapped in string and oiled paper. "For you."

Gifts were rare and I could already tell it was a book. I didn't waste time on protests or social niceties. I bit the string and tumbled the book out of the paper and into my lap.

I was speechless. The volume wasn't large, but it contained all there was to care about in the world. Four plays by the Bard were promised within its covers: *Romeo and Juliet*, *A Midsummer Night's Dream*, *Macbeth* and *Twelfth Night*. A lifetime of reading, a hundred parts to consider, thousands of lines to taste and savor. Truths and laughter, tears and happy endings, I could study this one volume for the rest of my life and not know all its secrets.

"Do you like it? I hoped you would."

Mutely, I nodded.

"I don't know the comedies as well—oh, Darlin' don't cry."

She pulled me into her arms and I had no words to tell her that I understood. It was a gift to remember her by. She would give me all the world in a book, but she would not stay.

She bought me for the night, which pleased Cherry. She pleasured me, then slept with me close. I tried not to fall asleep. The sound of her breathing was so precious and I knew it so little. The moon was faintly visible through my window when I could stay awake no longer. I woke to find her gone and the book of plays on the bed as if she had been reading it as she dressed.

She did not come back that night. Cherry charged Loomis extra for splitting my lip, but I didn't feel the cut or taste the blood. I didn't hear him voice his displeasure. I didn't feel him or anything for that matter, while I tried to find a smile. There were others after Loomis, and more nights. Each one I escaped into the world of my gentleman cowboy, the one who took her lover on the long trail for adventures. Sunday mornings I scribbled frantically on all the paper I could find. For weeks the moon rose in my window and I remembered the sound of Connor's breathing.

When the moon no longer rose where I could glimpse its silver in the night I lost its cool, soothing comfort to the harsh heat of summer. I walled up foolish hope and tried to find smiles because, as I knew so well, you have to smile.

I wished my soul's hunger for more than a night's pleasure would spark a matching hunger in her, but she was tied to this world, this life, with different tethers than I. Our discourse was my body and Shakespeare. Beyond that our two stars would not survive in the same sphere.

During sweltering nights when customers were few, and those wanting me even fewer, I scribbled on paper damp with my sweat. I could make any reality I wanted with my words and dwell there any time I chose to. The customers, the heat, the thirst—they all went away when I lived in my story.

I don't know what I could have done, or not done. I don't know what I might have said, or not said. I gave all I could and took nothing that wasn't freely given. I was no thief, no cheat, no liar. I'd only spoken truth to her, only offered things that were mine. We made each other real in ways no one else had. For me, the need to feel that way was a daily gnawing ache. For her only a seasonal itch. For Violet there was even less than that. While I would give everything for a second chance in this life, neither of them seemed to have the same desire.

Throughout the lonely heat of that long summer I tried to accept that the future was just like the past—full of people who gave their all, only to fail.

• • •

Heat or not, we had to wear our coats outside, to get to church. Water was scarce this summer, with thunderstorms a-plenty and little rain to go with them. We had less water than whiskey and for the third morning in a row there'd been naught but a weak cup of tea with breakfast. My coat was deadweight on my shoulders, weighing me down for each step in the dusty, pitted journey.

There was no escaping the scorching temperatures, and I was not the only one who surreptitiously loosened her coat the moment we were in the stifling confines of the church. I dabbed my sweat-soaked sleeve to my parched lips, feeling as if I would dry up and blow away were it not for the weight of the salt and sweat that covered most of my body. On the pews we spread out and fanned our dresses to move the air.

The preacher's sermon was short and lacked fire. It was too hot to speak much of brimstone either. Violet was subdued and her voice sounded distant, as if she spoke through water.

Thinking of water only made it worse, I told myself. Made what worse, I wondered, then I realized the room was spinning. The pews swayed as if we sailed on the ocean, and I remembered home, suddenly—home and chowder, fresh pudding and apples.

If only I could have lied and said I didn't love that girl. If only I could have lied and said I loved Connor when the truth was I needed her to read my stories, to talk to me and acknowledge that I existed. I had once believed I could be the Juliet who didn't die. But a life in a comedy had eluded me. There would be no double wedding, no happy final sentiments. No audience to leave the theater exultant from my story. There would be no audience at all for my tragedy, either.

Violet was hazy. Her face rippled like the sun on tide-covered sand. I could turn her away, and I had. I'd said no to carnal intimacy so I could learn to love her, hadn't I? If only I thought she could love me, but she held the Bible close to her heart when she might have held me.

Foolish thoughts, I told myself. Violet was in a different cage than I, but a cage nonetheless. What a sad collection of souls we were: two Juliets, a Romeo who leaves town, no Puck to scatter magic, not even a common wall through which we could whisper words of love.

Lady Macbeth whispered to me, "Life is but a walking shadow."

"Are you all right?" I wasn't sure who asked.

I tried to answer, at least I think I did.

Water, cool and sweet, filled my mouth. I swallowed, shivered, and swallowed again. Upon opening my eyes I found the room steady and myself caught in the contemptuous gaze of the preacher and his wife.

"She is probably with child."

I shook my head and turned my face from their judgment to take refuge in the little shelter the pew gave me. My head rested on something soft and warm. There was a heartbeat not far from my ear. I looked up. Hazel eyes, full of something that I could not name, gazed down at me as Violet offered me another swallow of water. I drank to keep my head on her lap.

"I will take her back as soon as she can walk." Cherry, standing at the end of the pew, was looking at me with dissatisfaction. The rest of the girls seemed to have left.

"Just thirsty," I croaked.

"I think you have a fever," Violet said.

"In this heat," the preacher pronounced, "everyone has a fever. She needs to go back to where she belongs."

He was quite right. Staying here would be more costly than merely fainting. Cherry would worry that news of this would be used to impugn the health of her girls. I had made nothing for nearly a week, and been only useful as a "something extra" with which Cherry rewarded a frequent customer.

I sat up carefully and felt the strength of Violet's hand at my back. Dizziness bested me again, but only for a moment, then I gathered my strength and my wits to stand.

Violet's hand touched mine. I hoped I showed no surprise.

By the time I reached the door I had hidden in my sleeve the note she'd pressed into my grasp.

During the walk to Cherry's I imagined what that note might say. *Come away with me* or *Come to my balcony*. Common sense interjected, *Stay away* and *Don't look at me like that*.

"You'll work tonight, and you'd better make it good." Cherry took me inside via the front door. "Likely the preacher will want some kind of fee for assisting you."

"A fee for water?" I thought of Violet's easy, polite hospitality.

"For cleansing his church of your presence."

"I just needed water," I said. "I'm not having a baby. I got my blood last week. Ask Angel."

"You'll work tonight," she repeated. I plainly heard the "or else" she did not say.

Finally alone, in the privacy of my room, I took out Violet's note. The square of paper was small and worn, and closely covered on both sides. The date was January, nearly eight months ago, and I fought back tears imagining her hiding it every week, wondering when she'd be able to give it to me. The divide between pulpit and pews was as wide as the Mississippi. But had I suspected she wanted to give me a note, I might have found a way to brush against her—a jostle at the door as we left, maybe— but I hadn't known. So she had waited, with only a hope that I would someday read these words. It was with a mix of feelings that I considered I was not the only woman in the world who could live in foolish hope for the impossible. Perhaps all women did because we were born with so many roads already closed to us, even though we saw them plainly and had the strength and wit to walk them.

I cannot sleep for thinking of the wrong I did you. I have never forced my attentions on anyone and fear I did so with you because of the work you do. I had not realized that you could and would value your virtue if you had a choice. I am sorry for my actions, even though those few minutes are the best of my life for many, many years.

There was a space, and a new date of April.

For weeks now I have watched and there seems no way to have contact with you. When prayer meetings speak of a life like yours none seem to appreciate that your 'carnal freedom' is lived out in a prison. I hadn't realized that you don't leave that place but to come here, and here is the place we cannot speak. I would give much for just a few words, and to know that you forgive me.

In the last inch of the paper's reverse side were scant sentences from July.

Since coming here I have had my own thoughts as a sanctuary but you intrude. I have tried hard to have no want and I fail. I hope that I have not inflicted this hopeless longing on you. Forgive me if I have. I meant you no harm.

So I was wrong in all my imaginings. All she asked for was my forgiveness.

I don't know what opens the door to love. Is it kindness, where none was expected? Connor and Violet had both been kind. One exulted in my body and treasured my words. The other understood that I was not a whore in my heart, and therefore my opinion of her mattered to her. If I knew what love was, and if there was a hope of a second chance in this life, I could love them both, differently. I knew enough of life, however, to understand that love can die like any unwatered seed.

As Cherry insisted, work I did. I was aware of revelry around me, that the other girls seemed not to feel the heat or the thirst. Their customers laughed, left pleased. I made very little, and only because I'd become a bargain. A glimpse in the cracked mirror startled me—for a moment Milla stared back, and then Greta. I wanted to shake Angel and tell her to really look at me because if she did she would see her future in my hollow eyes. Yet, even if I could make her understand, what would it change?

Sometimes, when I couldn't escape to the story in my head, couldn't ignore the bruises and abrasions inside and out, I wanted to curse Connor for spoiling me for the life I had to lead. She treated me like a person and yet I had survived more easily without that knowledge. She had valued my pleasure, shattering the fiction that I didn't care what customers did to me.

Violet, too, had spoiled me. The simple act of breaking bread together, neither of us playing the saint nor the sinner, had reminded me that I had been raised in a kinder life. It had reminded me of my grandmother, of my family, of the life I ought to have had.

I huddled over my scribbled pages and fought with unfamiliar bitterness. Why tune me to a woman's touch, Lord, only to require I repent it? Why drive me to write, Lord, only to leave my work unread? Why give me the power to think, Lord, and put me in this life where thought is an enemy?

Two women had given me moments of truth, of light and kindness. They made my soul stronger with those gifts. But when the heat wave finally broke I discovered my shield of falsity was weakened beyond repair. Even with cool air and water I could not smile.

CHAPTER EIGHT

"Cattle will start arriving tomorrow," Cherry said at breakfast. "Some of you will have to get over your laziness."

She didn't look at me, which I found odd as I certainly deserved the warning. I'd not earned enough to pay for my board, let alone the bed I occupied that could be put to more profitable occupancy. I kept telling myself I had to hold out. Connor would be back in perhaps as little as a week. I could survive anything for a week.

My plate, when handed round to me, had scarcely an egg's worth of food on it, which made it plain Cherry's feelings about my worth. I'd scarce finished what little I had when Cherry fixed me with her gaze. "The cattle arrive tomorrow. Tomorrow night the first camp manager wants a party to welcome the drovers and cowboys. This is your chance to prove you still deserve a bed in this house."

The last bite of food turned to dust in my mouth. Angel openly smirked, but most of the others studied their plates exactly the way I'd studied mine when Cherry had said much the same words to Milla.

"This is your *last* chance," she added, as if I was as clueless as Angel.

Tomorrow night, I thought. I had no options, unless Connor arrived and agreed to take me away, somehow, to someplace I could survive, to somewhere that she could bear to stay for more than a few days. I'd live in a hovel with no roof if she'd stay, but time was running out. I'd wear sackcloth and ashes in the church, but it had no sanctuary and Violet's room would never be open to me.

I didn't want to be at the party. I didn't want to be the only girl at the party.

In my room, aware as never before of the passing of time, I went through my papers. The night trade began and I ignored it as long as I could. Page by page I put "Cowboys and Kisses" together, scratching down page numbers with the last of clotting ink.

When Cherry ordered me downstairs I found myself assigned as a free gift to this customer or that, two-for-the-price-of-one. Angel's smiles were genuine and rich. She was the picture of a whore who liked her work. I had been bitter earlier but now all I wished her was staying just as she was. To know there was more than this place in the world was a poison.

I slept little, went down to breakfast expecting nothing but tea and was not disappointed. It was washing day, but I didn't strip my bed. Instead I continued to put pages in order and to fuss about whether my writing was legible. I wasn't entirely sure how to spell *inchoate*. I discovered my cowboy rode under a full moon two weeks in a row.

It would never make sense, yet I labored. As the sun passed into late afternoon, I finally stopped and set the pages in a narrow box that I tied closed with twine. Carefully I wrote Connor's name on the outside and added, "From your story-teller."

I had just lifted my last blank sheet of good paper when Cherry called up to me that the wagon was here.

I put Connor's box and the book of plays on my bed and the Bible Violet had given me alongside it. The note for Violet was left undone.

From the back of the wagon I had two choices. Facing forward I could see the distant outline of the temporary stockyards. I'd never seen them before, but I knew they were a central ground where ownership of herds changed hands. From here the cattle would be driven to ranches for breeding or to the train yet farther east, near Miles City. Someday, a customer had told me, the train would come through Long Grass. Somehow I didn't think so. The train would pass through some other little town, which would grow up overnight. The prairie would reclaim Long Grass, along with our graves.

Had I been curious about cattle and their maintenance I might have faced forward. But I knew what waited for me at the end of this bone-jarring journey. So I faced backward and watched Long Grass slowly disappear behind the roll of the land and the tall, golden grass.

If I closed my eyes I could hear the drum of hooves, of a cowboy riding like the wind, trying to catch this wagon before it reached its destination. But when I opened my eyes the brown curl of road remained empty.

The wagon stopped at what I judged was near suppertime. There was no shade except for the long shadow of the wagon itself on the road. I made my way into the grass for the privacy to relieve myself, and returned to find the two men drinking from flasks and sharing dried meat and trail bread.

I didn't ask, but one said, "Are you hungry? Want some?"

I swallowed and nodded.

His smile wasn't cruel. It had no real emotion at all. "How you gonna pay for it?"

"I don't have any money."

He shrugged toward the grass.

"I only want some water."

The other man said quickly, "The water's mine."

"Bastard," the first said, but he turned away, the matter settled.

The grass prickled my back through my dress, and the relentless sun was a good excuse to keep my eyes closed. He didn't last long but he wasn't stingy about the water after. I drank, but inside I felt like a well drained dry.

The road was still empty when I looked again.

Not surprisingly, my nose told me we were close. There was a chance, I told myself, that Connor was already here, that Connor would see them taking me wherever it was.

For a few minutes they treated me like a princess. Men crowded around the wagon, and I was handed down with a polite bow.

"Call me Darlin'," I answered to the drive manager's question. Perhaps someone would mention that name. Connor would hear it, perhaps . . . Perhaps this wasn't actually happening.

Whiskey had been flowing freely, that was obvious. I quickly downed the generous shot I was offered. The room was obviously a bunk house, and the kitchen on one end still smelled of beef and beans for dinner. My skin told me the room was warm but I was as cold as I had been the first night at Cherry's.

The drive manager poured me a second shot, but put the glass down on the small table next to the bunk nearest the kitchen.

"Why don't you make yourself comfortable?"

This was my last chance to smile. To like my work. I couldn't go back to Cherry's with complaints. I only knew my heart was beating because it hurt so much in my chest.

I took off my coat to appreciative whistles. There wasn't a separate room for me. They weren't . . . there wasn't . . . privacy. Just a little screen, that was all. I undid my laces and took care with my dress, though I wasn't sure I would ever wear it again. I wasn't sure once I was on that bed that I would ever rise from it. I hadn't counted how many . . . I didn't want to know.

Milla had done this days after the doctor's needle. There had been others like her and I knew where some of them were buried. Only a few ever got over a party; it was as rare as a girl getting married, like Jinny. They would all have me, then the vultures or worms would have me unless I could go away some-how. Leave my body here and escape into my head as I had so many times. When it was over I had to find my way back. That was where Milla had failed.

I sat on the edge of the bed and the drive manager, who was obviously in charge and going to be first, sat down too. We touched our whiskey glasses.

"Y'all get to doing something else," he barked just before he pushed me down.

In the Garden Country the king's jealousy kept the queen under constant guard, and I brought her majesty breakfast with the finest blooms I could find. Her tray today was graced by her favorite violets. When I set the tray down she thanked me and we shared a glance. Tomorrow we escaped. I knew she still loved me when she lightly pressed a flower to her lips, then gave it to me.

It tasted of whiskey, suddenly, and I swallowed from the glass put to my lips.

"She's an easy ride—not too much liquor or she'll go to

sleep."

"Won't stop me—"

"Well, I want her awake."

The next day I scattered cherry blossoms on her tray. I'd seen them long ago, flowing down like pink rain. But I forgot that in the Garden Country the plants do the king's bidding, and the cherries betrayed us, telling the tall, golden grass all our plans. The king's soldiers approached from one side, but from the other, at the last desperate moment, I saw a knight on a gallant charger, pistol in one hand.

"How long you gonna be?"

"You'll get your chance."

I turned my head and realized I could see the bunkhouse door. The man on top of me, another new face, forced me to look back at him.

"That's right. You'll want me back for more."

Maybe the door opened and I just didn't know it. Maybe Connor's pistol would sound and I wouldn't have to help the queen escape anymore.

But even the leaves were against us and the trees too. Their betrayal hurt, because usually trees can be counted on for romance. They shade lovers during warm afternoons, when one lover shows another what it's like to be cared for, to be wanted and to matter. To be more than a pleasingly shaped bit of flesh and muscle.

I didn't care when the next or the one after turned me over. I could see the door and I could pray for it to open. Prayer . . . Violet. I wished that I had written her that note. I wanted her to know there was nothing to forgive. She had given more than any minor offense could tarnish.

If I could write that note now, I would tell her I was sorry I'd said no. The truth was very simple now, and I could study it even though my thighs burned and my breath could hardly fill my lungs. Love was all there was and love given freely was never to be spurned. No matter the consequences, there would have been a moment, in the merging of two stars, a moment that could never be spoiled or sullied. A moment of purity that I could not cling to now, because I'd not let it happen. I'd wasted love and the pain of that regret in my soul was more than anything I felt for my body.

A scuffle made me realize that there was not a body on top of me. I could breathe easier.

"I was next—"

"You wait your turn."

Would someone like Angel take men fighting over her as flattery? I was meat to the dogs. I wanted more whiskey. I wanted to get back to the queen, to helping her through her perils until we were free.

When we were free I would bring her flour. We'd live near water and she would bake bread. Didn't the world need bread? Couldn't we sell bread instead of our bodies? How could I bring the queen flour when my shoes scarcely covered my feet? I would trade Connor's book for flour and the thought of it hurt in my heart, like the pain between my legs.

Open the door, I prayed, please Connor, open this door. My gentleman cowboy, the rogue of Kansas City, bold and proud, open this door. Lost between prayer and fantasy, I could no longer focus on the real world. I had no sense of time, no sense of change. The bodies were relentless, the turns endless.

I tried to smell the violets, even the cherries. What seeped into my brain, however, was that the smell of beef and beans was gone. Now it was bacon and maple syrup.

The queen and I walked on a river, evading hands from the depths that grappled at our clothes, at our breasts, at our lips. If I fell into the maple syrup I would surely drown. The queen didn't seem able to help me as my foot first touched the muddy surface and the hands reached up to pull me under.

The sticky sweet smell was in my nose and my mouth. I

turned my eyes one last time to the bunkhouse door as if it were the hills of the Psalms, from whence cometh my strength. You made me, Lord, help me now, I prayed.

The door opened. The cowboy was small, with that confident walk that nevertheless gave her away. I heard the click of a pistol cocking, then her strong arms gathered me up, lifted me from the mud, from the syrup, from the bed.

She held me in her arms as we rode west, into the open prairie. The sun was rising and she carried me so quickly I felt like a bird skimming over the grass.

"Darlin'," she whispered in my ear. "I'm sorry. I couldn't find you. This is no life for you."

I wanted my clothes off—they were sticky and soiled. Find me a river, I wanted to tell her, so I can feel clean again. I was so cold, and that was strange, because the sun was blazing and the horse steaming. Her body behind me should have warmed me.

"I can't go where you're going, Darlin'. 'The bright day is done, and we are for the dark.'"

I hurt so much and I couldn't breathe. "You, too?"

"Someday." She urged the horse faster, but it wasn't Argo. It was gold like the grass we were galloping through. Stalks lashed at my bare feet. I needed to rise above it.

She let go of me and I soared over the grass, free of the stench of syrup and men. The prairie was forever and I would fly its breadth today, but there was one unfinished matter that drew me back to Long Grass.

She was in the window of her room, looking out at the street. Did she wonder if she'd glimpse me today? On Sunday would she ask where I was?

The Bible was open on her lap and with the glorious wings that lifted me out of the pain I fanned the pages to Luke 6:37. She frowned and flipped the pages back to the story of Ruth. Another life, I thought. Another chance and maybe that would be our story. But for now I sent the pages turning again to Luke

6:37. And ye shall be forgiven, Violet.

She read the passage, then her gaze turned to the street again as a lone tear spilled onto her thin cheek. I would look for her again, and see that cheek full and smiling. See her in a nest, not a cage, surrounded by the things she loved and one of them would be me. There was place where that life existed, or would exist.

The light grew brighter and my wings carried me above the town. Then I saw that other welcome face, standing at the door to Cherry's house. Under her arm was a box of papers and a book of plays, on her face an expression of confused loss. Penelope hadn't waited for Ulysses, after all. The loss didn't run deep, though. The open sky would call and she would move on. She would find other bodies. Wandering would long be in her blood.

All that was left to her was my words. Maybe, if we were granted a second chance, they would draw her to me again. Maybe, by then, she would long for roots in one place. We might have a future where the tragedy was already in the past and a chance for a happy ending where we told the tale to suit ourselves free of the judgment of others. Free to share words and dreams, free to make them one and the same.

"It's my turn," someone insisted.

No, I thought. It's my turn.

This is my choice, and I get to say no.

I am my own book, and the writing in that book will only be what I choose. The story of this life has turned to ash, but I am still here, still the author of myself. Perhaps the grace exists to add new pages, to begin fresh, to live a second chance.

I would begin that second chance as I had not begun this life: I would know that I could be treasured and valued even in the midst of shame and violence. In some new life I would give love freely and know how to honor and accept it when offered to me. I would find them both again, and perhaps they too would have found a way out of the cages that separated us.

The harsh land, the vast untamable expanse, had taught me strength. I soared as high and as hard as I could, until the last tether snapped and I was free.

I made myself go away, and I flew over the tall grass, a creature of the wind, caged no longer.

The Sweetheart

and the

Spitfire

Julia Watts

Interview One

If you had told me back in the Forties that people would still be interviewing me about those lousy B Western pictures I was making, I would've laughed right in your face. Hell, it's a compliment to call those pieces of junk B-grade. I don't think any of them deserved better than a C minus. And yet I do a couple of interviews a month at least, mostly with old codgers who have little fan magazines about the Westerns they loved as kids. The old guys always say the same thing when they get to talking about the movies: "They don't make 'em like that anymore."

I think *thank God for that*, but I'm too polite to say anything. These boys grew up thinking of me as the cowboy's sweetheart who'd keep the campfire burning while they went off to catch those blasted cattle rustlers. Who am I to destroy some ole man's fantasy life by opening my big mouth?

But you . . . you're not old, and you're not a man. Oh, that's right—you're the one who called the other day. I'd forgotten for a minute, but I remember now. You're the one writing that book called *Hollywood's Hidden Loves*, aren't you? And you want to know about me and Consuelo Flores.

I can't believe I've agreed to do this, but Connie breathed her last eight years ago, and I figure I won't stay behind for much longer. So I might as well set the record straight, though that word might not be the best one to choose. If for no other reason, I'd like to lay the rumor to rest that Buck Bronco and I were a couple just because we played one onscreen. Roy and Dale we were not. Even if I had liked men that way, I wouldn't have gone for Buck. He was too stuck on himself, and his breath stank of cheap cigarettes and beef jerky.

Before I get to the hidden love part for your story, I ought to tell you how I came to Hollywood. I was raised on a ranch in Oklahoma, so unlike a lot of folks in Westerns, I was actually from the West. My mother died when I was just a baby, and Daddy treated me just the same as if I'd been a boy—a boy ranchhand, at that. I learned how to rope and ride and knew everything about cattle, from branding them to helping birth calves when they got stuck. I worked hard on the ranch, and I loved it. I loved my daddy, too.

It was because of my daddy, who used to be a champion bull rider, that I got into the rodeo. They didn't let girls ride bulls, but we could trick ride and rope calves. Well, right after I turned twenty I won the championship in my division at this big rodeo in Tulsa, and the prize was one hundred dollars and a screen test with Republic Pictures. I was so green I thought that a hundred dollars was a lot of money and that Republic was a major studio!

I took the train from Tulsa to Hollywood, and I showed up at the screen test in my rodeo clothes—a white Western shirt, a white fringed vest and matching skirt with red roses on it, and a white Stetson and boots. I knew I looked as good as I could look. With my ordinary mouse-brown hair and brown eyes, I never was a raving beauty, but I was cute, with friendly features—the nice-girl type who old ladies wanted to sit next to on the bus. For my screen test I read a few lines of dialogue, sang a verse of "Home on the Range," and showed a few rope tricks. I thought nothing would come of it, but as you well know, they hired me. I was excited and grateful and stupidly sure that with my new name of Jaycee Harvey, I was going to be the next Barbara Stanwyck. That was in 1941.

When I got to the part of the story you want to hear, it was three years and God knows how many movies later. Republic ground out Westerns like McDonald's grinds out hamburgers, and just like McDonald's, all Republic products were pretty much alike. The ones I was in were the singing cowboy type. Buck always played the hero, a good-hearted sheriff or rancher. Then there was the bad guy—a train robber or cattle rustler or some other kind of outlaw—lots of times played by my dear departed friend Eli Bainbridge, who was always good for a few laughs on the set. Buck always wore a white hat while Eli wore a black one; in movies in those days, good and evil were color-coded.

As for me, I was the girl, which meant that I didn't do much of anything. Oh, I rode a horse, but with no tricks or stunts, and I always sang a number with Buck. But in terms of the story, I didn't have much to do with it unless I got kidnapped by the bad guy and had to be rescued. The rest of the movie would be filled out by one of Buck's funny sidekicks, cowboy extras, Indians usually played by white guys, and saloon girls who were just there to show their legs.

I met Connie on the set of "The Dusty Trail"—a movie that was exactly like every other movie I'd ever made. I only remember the name of it because it's the movie where I met Connie and because Eli always called it "The Crusty Snail," which I thought was funny. By this time, I was utterly bored with my film career, though I felt guilty about it. I knew there were plenty of girls who'd give their eyeteeth to do what I did. And of course, there was a war going on. Young men were getting shot, and young women were slaving away in factories, and here I was, upset because I wasn't getting to be the kind of movie star I wanted to be. Really, the war was the only reason I didn't just give up and go back to Oklahoma. I figured that if the people working so hard to protect freedom wanted some predictable, formulaic entertainment at the end of the day, the least I could do was help provide it for them.

Republic always filmed its Westerns at Broadwater's Movie Ranch, a mock-up Western town a couple of hours away from Hollywood. The ranch was a mock-up of an Old Western town, complete with a saloon, a general store, a livery stable and a dirt street where many a shoot-out was filmed. Right next to the mock-up town was a stretch of field and hills, where stage-coaches could be robbed and Indians could attack. Eli always said filming felt like a Boy Scout campout: a bunch of people flung together in the middle of nowhere, with bad food and uncomfortable sleeping conditions. The up side to this was that the cast and crew always had something to talk about. People find common ground when they can all complain about the same thing.

On the first day of shooting, Eli and I were sitting near the coffeepot, playing cards and waiting around until a scene of ours came up. For all that it's supposed to be glamorous and exciting, that's what a lot of moviemaking is: just waiting around.

But I liked waiting with Eli. He was a good twenty years older than me and had been in the movie business for almost as long as I'd been alive. His chiseled good looks made him an A-list star in the silents, where he made goo-goo eyes at some of the biggest actresses of the day. But when talkies started, his days as a romantic lead were over because his voice was higher and softer than his female costars'. He told me that after he'd been out of work a couple of years, he realized he could make his breathy, wispy voice sound menacing—a trick Vincent Price also learned—and he found a steady gig as a B-grade baddie.

So there we were, drinking our coffee and playing some card game neither of us was much good at.

"Have you heard from Charming Billy lately?" Eli asked. He lit a cigarette. His blue eyes crinkled at the corners as he took his first drag.

"I got a letter the day before yesterday," I said, looking down at my cards. "He's doing all right, trying to keep his spirits up."

"I don't guess your Billy thinks much of us fellows who are here playing cowboy with fake bullets while he's out in the Pacific dodging real ones."

"Oh, Billy wouldn't want all the actors to quit making movies and enlist," I said, sipping my coffee which, like all coffee on the set, was terrible. "He says soldiers need those pictures. They're good for morale."

"Well, I'm glad they're good for somebody's morale," Eli said. "They're sure as hell not good for mine."

"Mine neither." I was glad we were moving away from the subject of Billy and back toward the familiar territory of complaining about the quality of the film. I didn't mind talking about Billy to Buck or to the bit players I didn't know very well. But talking to Eli about Billy made me feel bad.

"Howdy, pardners!" The booming voice belonged to Buck, who used each of his gigantic, gloved paws to slap Eli and me on the back. "I tell you what, this picture's a real rip-snorter. Plenty of action, good tunes, pretty girls"—Buck tipped his white hat and grinned at me, his eyes narrowing into their trademark squint—"this might just be the best picture Republic's ever made."

"You always say that on the first day of shooting," Eli said.

"Well, what can I say, Eli?" Buck said, laughing. "I guess I'm just an optimistic kind of fellow. When I look at a cup, it's half-full. Speaking of half-full cups, how about you pour me some of that coffee over there, Jaycee, honey? A full cup, not a half one."

He was standing close to the coffeepot, and I was sitting farther away from it, but I stood and said, "Sure thing, Buck." On the set, Buck was the star, and it was everybody's job to keep the star happy. Pouring coffee for Buck offscreen felt like a rehearsal for all the coffee pouring I had to do onscreen.

When I looked up from my pouring, I saw Consuelo Flores for the first time. She was wearing the standard get-up for Latina actresses in B Westerns: black, lacey, low-cut gown; a black lace veil with a big red flower. Her skin was the color of caramel, and her lips were as red as the flower. She was beautiful, but she looked unhappy.

"Well, there's the little spitfire herself!" Buck said. "I just did a scene with Con-sue-ello here, and she is a firecracker, let me tell you!" He draped his big arm around her and squeezed her shoulder.

Consuelo slipped out of his grip like a cat escaping an over-affectionate toddler. "No touching, Buck." Unlike in the scenes I'd seen her play onscreen, her English was accentless. "My Juan gets very upset when other men touch me."

I was still holding out the steaming cup of coffee. Connie looked at it, said, "Oh, coffee? Thanks," took the cup from my hands, and flounced away.

Buck shook his head and guffawed. "What did I tell you? A firecracker! But I'll give you a piece of advice, Eli."

"What's that, Buck?" Eli's tone was sarcastic, but not so sarcastic that Buck would pick up on it.

"Stay away from the Mexican gals," Buck said, accepting a new cup of coffee from me. "They look right pretty, but those tempers—shoo-ee! I had a buddy that got himself mixed up with one of them. She saw him out one night dancing with another girl, and do you know what that hot-headed little filly did?"

"What's that?" Eli said, though I could tell he couldn't care less.

"She slashed the tires on my buddy's car! And she told him if she saw him with another girl again, it would be his throat, not his tires." Buck ran a gloved finger across his neck and clucked his tongue. "So remember, buddy." He slapped Eli on the back again. "When it comes to the señoritas, look, but don't touch. Of course, looking at Con-sue-ello there a minute ago made me just about forget that myself!"

"Thanks for the warning, Buck," Eli said, but then he looked at me with a twinkle in his eye. Eli didn't talk to me much about the details of his personal life, but he had told me, in strictest confidence, that women were never a temptation for him.

"See ya back at the ranch, pardners!" Buck said, tipping his hat as he left.

Eli shook his head. "You know, Buck's like one of those overgrown, over-friendly dogs that jumps up on you and slobbers and knocks down things wagging its tail. It annoys you, but you can't hate it because it wants you to like it so much."

"Well," I said, sitting down with my warmed-up coffee, "I don't think Consuelo Flores thinks as much of our over-friendly puppy as you do. Did you see how she took Buck's coffee right out of my hand?"

Eli laughed. "See it? I wallowed in it. A truly great moment. But not necessarily a moment that ensures Miss Flores a long future with Repugnant Pictures."

"True." While I hated myself when I poured Buck's coffee, I knew that this kind of deference protected my job.

"But to think about it from Consuelo's point of view," Eli said, "there's no need for her to bow and scrape to Buck. He's always been in the Bs, and she . . . well, she used to be taken quite seriously. She was up for an Oscar several years back. But I guess the offers started thinning out. It's a tough business anyway, but it's especially tough if you're not lily-white. Or in my case, if you're a man who's not especially manly. We've got to take our jobs where we can get 'em, even if it means clicking castanets or wearing a big black hat." He shook his head. "Of course, I threw my pride out with all the other garbage years ago. It seems like Consuelo's still got hers."

"And what about mine?" I asked, looking down into my half-empty cup.

Eli patted my knee. "Oh, kid, there's no need for you to have lost your pride. B movies are for two kinds of actors—those on their way up and those on their way down. All you have to do is look at the difference in your birthdate and mine to know which one of us is which."

I did my first scene with Connie the next day. It was in the saloon where Connie's character had supposedly been hired as the new singer. The sugary sweet little virgin I was playing had never set the toe of her boot in a saloon before but had braved it in this case because she was trying to collect money for needy orphans. And just from that much information, you can probably tell what a big stinker this picture was.

Charlie Wooley was directing. He directed all of Buck's pictures, with about as much art as a cop directing traffic.

But one thing I can say is Charlie dressed the part of the director, with a beret, an ascot, the whole bit. I think the beret was mainly a way to disguise his bald head. "All right, people!" he hollered through his megaphone. "Let's get this in the can!"

In the can was definitely the place for Charlie's films—in the can followed by a good, strong flush.

When Charlie shouted "action," I was supposed to shyly enter the empty saloon and look around with wide, frightened eyes. My daddy took me to bars to drink Cokes while he drank beer when I was just a little girl, so it was hard for me to imagine being scared of a saloon. The only way I could pull it off was to pretend the saloon was crawling with huge spiders, so that's what I did.

Connie was supposed to enter, look at me, and say the highly original line, "What's a nice girl like you doing in a place like this?" I was supposed to explain about the collection I was taking up for the orphans, and Connie was supposed to tell me she'd be willing to cough up for the orphans but only if I'd agree to sing a song with her first.

When we got to that last part, Connie blew the line, and Charlie barked, "Cut!"

"I'm sorry, Charlie," Connie said, adjusting the rose in her hair. "That line just doesn't make sense. I mean, why would I want her—a person I just met—to sing a song with me?"

Charlie sighed and took out a hanky to mop his forehead which, because of his receded hairline, took up a lot of acreage. "You . . ." he said, sounding exasperated, "want her to sing a song with you because the audience for this picture wants her to sing a song with you. If that's not a reason, I don't know what is." He tucked his hanky back into his jacket pocket. Now . . . let's do it right this time. And Consuelo, honey, thicken up that accent a little. Folks love a funny Mexican accent."

"Sí, senor," Connie said in the exaggerated nasal drawl white B actors used when playing Mexican roles.

This time, we got up to the song. Connie and I had already recorded it separately, so all we had to do was mouth the words. I moved my lips and pretended to strum a prop guitar that didn't even have any strings on it. Connie, though, moved her lips and her hips. She danced well, a slither here and a shimmy there, and all of a sudden our ridiculous song, which was some rubbish about a cactus and a tumbleweed, had sex appeal. At least it did until Connie's lips and hips stopped moving.

"Cut!" Charlie yelled. His face was turning a color which made me worry about his blood pressure. "what is it now?"

"It's her." Connie jerked her head in my direction. "Are her boots glued to the floor? Can't she move a little? I feel like I'm dancing around a statue."

I've always hated it when people talk about me like I'm not in the room. "Look," I said, "I can rope, and I can ride, and I can shoot. But if you want a dancer, call Ginger Rogers."

"I hate to admit it," Charlie said, "but you did look a little stiff up there, Jaycee. How about you just sway back and forth with your guitar a little bit?"

We shot it again, and I swayed. I felt stupid, but I swayed. The trouble was, when Connie came close and did a move where she shimmied her hips, I swayed right into her and broke the neck of my prop guitar across her backside.

"Aiiee!" she yelped. "What are you doing? Trying to give me splinters in my ass?"

Marco, the new cameraman, laughed so hard he couldn't catch his breath. "I didn't know we were shooting a slapstick comedy," he said.

"You'll think comedy when you're all on the unemployment line," Charlie muttered.

So we got back down to business. Another prop guitar was found, Connie and I mouthed the words again, and she kept her swaying hips well out of the range of my swaying guitar. It's funny to watch her and me in that scene now, though. You can tell we're mad as hell at each other.

I came to the premature conclusion that I didn't like Consuelo Flores. One night Eli and I were flopped on the cot in my trailer, drinking warm beers because a trailer with a fridge in those days was more than you could hope for.

"You know," Eli said, "Connie was sketching today between scenes. She's really quite good."

"Connie?"

"You know, Consuelo. She told me to call her Connie. She graduated from art school before she started acting. She's really quite a remarkable woman."

I took a big slug of beer. "Well," I said, "I still don't like her."

"Why not?"

"If you'd heard the way she talked about me during that scene the other day, you wouldn't like her either." I nudged him gently with my elbow. "At least you wouldn't if you're any friend of mine."

Eli laughed. "You women—you're so suspicious of each other. You know, when men meet they automatically like each other, and they keep right on liking each other unless there's a good reason to stop doing so. Women, though, the second they meet, it's like they start looking for reasons to despise each other."

"Well, with Consuelo, you don't have to look that hard," I said. But I could tell he thought I was being petty, so I decided to change the subject. "Say, why don't we take advantage of the fact you have a car and get out of here for a while? I bet we could find a roadhouse where we could get some dinner. You drive; I'll buy."

"Normally, I'd be absolutely delighted," Eli said, getting up from the cot and stretching. "But I already have a dinner engagement this evening."

"Oh," I said, "do tell."

"I would love to tell you, dear, and I trust you absolutely. But the party that I'm meeting insists on total discretion, so my lips are sealed. Except I will unseal them long enough to kiss you goodnight." He gave me a peck on the forehead and was out the door.

I felt trapped in my trailer, but I didn't really want to go out and rub shoulders with the cast and crew either. Eli was my only real friend on the set. He was the only fellow who was good for a real conversation and who didn't try to make time with me. I opened a second beer and flipped through the latest issue of *Life* magazine, only to discover that I'd read every article in it. I resorted to reading the ads, which were funny for a while. Most of them featured a pretty, aproned housewife who was absolutely driven to distraction over the dirtiness of her husband's shirt collars or the dryness of her cakes or the infrequency of her children's bowel movements. After a few more ads, though, the housewife held no more humor; instead, she made me sad. I thought, what the hell kind of a life is that?

I tossed back the rest of my beer and decided to try to be grateful. Even if I was making a bad movie in a bad location and having a bad day, my life was still much better than most women's. Compared to that fretting housewife, I had a lot of freedom. And I decided to use some of it and go for a walk.

A dozen bit-part cowboys were hanging out around the trailers, smoking cigarettes and passing around a bottle of whiskey. "Hey, Jaycee," a skinny cowboy called, holding out the bottle. "Why don't you come wrap your lips around this?"

"I don't much like putting my mouth where a dozen other people's mouths have already been—especially when some of those people are lacking in the hygiene department."

"Oh, come on over here, Jaycee," another cowboy—this one especially greasy—yelled. "What Billy don't know won't hurt him."

"Oh, but Billy has his ways of keeping up with me," I said. "And if he did know, he'd hurt you."

The boys laughed, and I walked past them. If I couldn't have Eli's company, then I wanted to be by myself out in the open—to feel the evening breeze and look up at the big sky. Riding would have suited me better than walking, but all the horses were already in the barn for the night.

As I walked away from the camp, I saw a small, bright light in the distance. When I got closer, I saw it was a small campfire. Who would be camping out here? I wondered. The movie ranch was really strict about trespassers.

As I approached the campfire, I saw it wasn't a trespasser at all. It took me a minute to recognize her with her hair down and without her black lace gown. She was wearing a loose-fitting, button-down shirt, rolled-up jeans and penny loafers. Her face was scrubbed free of all the makeup she had to wear for the movie, and her hair hung all the way down her back, sleek and shiny. She was sitting close to the fire, where a pan was heating. When she saw me, she jumped a little and put her hand to her heart. "Aie! You scared me. I thought you might be a coyote or something."

"Nope, just a B-grade cowgirl." I remembered the awful line she'd said to me in our scene together. "So what's a nice girl like you doing in a place like this?"

I was surprised when she laughed. "Oh, just getting away for a while. I didn't want to be in my trailer and didn't particularly feel like socializing. When this kind of mood hits me, I like to come out here. I build a fire, cook my dinner. I've even been known to bring my sleeping bag a time or two. I feel different out here, you know?"

She seemed so relaxed, so different from the high-strung diva I knew from the set. "You seem different than you do at work."

"I seem nice, you mean?" She was smiling—not the kind of stiff smile actors do for promotional photos, but a real smile that took up her whole face.

I thought about denying it, but finally I said, "Well, yeah."

She laughed again and patted a spot on the ground next to her. "Sit down, why don't you?" She dug around in her duffel bag, pulled out a napkin, and unwrapped it. Inside was a stack of tortillas. She set a tortilla in the pan and unfolded another napkin full of white shredded cheese. She sprinkled the cheese on the tortilla and folded it over. "I know I'm difficult on the set. But you've got to understand that being in this picture is hard for me. I pride myself on being an artist, a perfectionist. And so to be in a picture like this—where the director's only goal is to 'get it in the can'—it causes me real pain, Jaycee."

I hadn't expected her to know my name. "I understand."

"Do you? That's good. So you know how it feels to try to give the best performance you can when the people around you are content to mindlessly squeeze out another picture the same way they mindlessly squeeze out a bowel movement."

I laughed. "Yes."

"Jaycee, have you eaten dinner yet?"

"No, but after that bowel movement comment, I'm not sure I want to."

"Don't be silly. Have this quesadilla. I'll make another one for me." She tilted the pan and slid the tortilla onto a tin plate. "Let it cool for a couple of minutes, though. You don't want to burn your tongue on the cheese."

"Thank you."

"It's nothing. I'm usually much more elaborate when I cook for people, but here I don't have much to work with." She set the pan back over the fire and put another tortilla in it. "So," she said, "if I had my pick I'd go back to making artistic movies . . . or at least to the kind of movies where I don't have to dress up like a doll you'd buy in a souvenir shop in Tijuana. What about you, Jaycee? If you could make any kind of movies, what would you pick?"

"Well," I said, after I'd swallowed a mouthful of quesadilla, "I'd still make Westerns, I guess, but they'd be different. The Westerns I'd like to make would be a kind where the girls don't just pour coffee and look pretty. They'd ride and rope and shoot and do the rescuing sometimes instead of just getting rescued. And I know nobody's ever gonna make a movie like that, but if they did, I'd sure like to be in it. I know it wouldn't be great art or anything like that, but I love the idea of a little girl going to the movie theatre and seeing me onscreen playing somebody who's brave and smart and skillful and thinking, that's what I want to be." I didn't realize it as I was making my little speech, but my eyes had filled with tears. I felt embarrassed for getting so emotional. "Pretty silly, huh?" I said.

"No," Connie answered, and her dark eyes, shining in the firelight, looked like they might be on the verge of tears, too. "Not silly at all." She reached out and brushed my hair back from my face. "So," she said, "How did you learn to do all these tricks they don't let you show off in these terrible pictures?"

"From my daddy, mostly. And from some of the boys that worked on the ranch."

"You grew up on a ranch?" Connie said, sliding her own quesadilla onto a plate. "Me, too."

I had just taken a bite of my quesadilla, and a long string of melted cheese hung from my mouth. I laughed, and so did Connie. "A ranch in Mexico?"

"No, here in California. Charlie Wooley may be trying to market me as a Mexican spitfire, but I was born in California. Mami and Papi are from Mexico, and I still have family there, but I've lived in California all my life. I'm as American as you are. I'm just never going to get cast in those nice-girl parts you blancas get."

"Well, don't shed any tears over that," I said. "At least your character has some sex appeal and moxie about her. The girl I get stuck playing always has the sex appeal and moxie of a limp white hanky." I took another bite of my quesadilla. "This is delicious, by the way."

Connie shrugged. "Well, much like my performance in this movie, it's not my best work." A slow smile spread over her face. "I can offer you something really good, though."

"What's that?" There was a little flutter in my stomach, but I didn't know why.

She reached into her duffle bag and pulled out a bottle. "Let's see . . . I've got a shot glass in here, too, and a salt shaker and a lime. I travel light, but I always remember the essentials. You like tequila?"

"I've never had it. I'm usually just a 'coupla beers' kind of girl."

"You'll want to be careful, then." She used her pocket knife to carve wedges out of the lime and demonstrated how to toss back a shot, followed by a lick of salt and a suck of lime. "Your turn."

I never was one to shy away from a challenge. I positioned my salt and lime and threw back the shot, which burned its way through my gut like a ball of fire. "Damn!" I yelled. "That's some serious stuff!" My eyes were running like faucets.

Connie laughed. "Yep." She took the glass from me and did another shot, this time without the benefit of salt and lime. "You want another?"

The words I had been thinking were "better not," but the words that actually came out were "maybe just one more."

"Good. You have one more, and then I want you to show me something."

I did my shot and cussed again. I was still sucking my lime when she pulled a shiny pistol out of her duffel bag. "Show me how to shoot," she said.

"Yeah, guns and tequila—there's a safe combination."

"Come on, show me how."

I took the pistol from her hand and examined it. "Why do you have a gun if you don't know how to shoot it?"

"I'm out alone at night a lot. Even if I can't aim, I figure I could shoot well enough to scare off an attacker if I needed to . . . or out here, a snake or a coyote."

"You thought I was a coyote at first. Would you have shot at me?"

Connie smiled and looked at me longer than I was used to. "I'm glad I didn't."

My face felt hot, but at the time I thought it was the alcohol. When I stood, I felt unsteady for a second, but once I had my footing, I felt like I could do anything. "All right," I said. "I'd shoot better in daylight, but I'll give it a try. What do you want me to shoot?"

"I've got something." Connie dug in her duffel bag and produced a can of tomato soup which she set on a tree stump about ten feet in front of me.

"Lord, that's easy," I said. I raised the gun, aimed, and squeezed the trigger. I blew the can right off the stump, tomato soup gushing like blood.

"*¡Madre de dios!* That was amazing," Connie said.

"Not really. Here, let me show you how." I fetched the punctured can and set it back on the stump, then gave Connie the gun. I stood behind her, positioned my arms around her arms, and put my hands on hers over the gun. That was the first time I touched her.

I helped her aim and told her to squeeze the trigger. She did, but when the gun kicked, she jumped, and we stumbled backward, laughing. She'd missed the can by a country mile.

"I think we'd better do another shot—of tequila, that is," she said, still laughing. She got the bottle and drank straight from it this time, then handed it to me.

I drank, too. "I guess if I was a guy Juan would kill me for putting my arms around you like that, huh?"

"Juan?" She clearly had no idea who I was talking about.

"Juan, your jealous husband? You were telling Buck about him?"

She rolled her eyes and laughed. "Oh, Juan . . . yes, he was my husband, and I guess he still is since we never bothered to get a divorce. I married him when I was nineteen, and he left me when I was twenty-one. I've not seen or heard from him since, but I do like to mention I have a husband when some fella's getting a little too friendly."

I laughed so long and hard she probably thought I was crazy drunk or just downright crazy.

When I finally calmed down, she said, "And you have a boyfriend, don't you, who's off fighting in the war? His name is Billy, right? I heard one of the cowboys saying he thought you were awfully cute, but he'd never try to take a serviceman's gal."

I started laughing hard again. Once I caught my breath, I said, "Let's just say Juan and Billy have a lot in common."

"What do you mean?"

"Billy was the name of my boyfriend when I was fourteen years old which, by the way, was the last time I had a boyfriend. I just use his name to keep the cowpokes' paws off me."

Now Connie and I were both laughing so hard we gasped for breath. Once Connie settled down a little, she grabbed the shot glass, poured it full, and held it up in the air. "To Juan and Billy," she said. "Absence makes the heart grow fonder!"

I shared the toast, and that's the last I remember of the evening, except that I staggered back to my trailer and left Connie to sleep under the stars.

I can see from the look on your face that you expected more to happen between Connie and me that night. You thought we'd crawl into her sleeping bag together or kiss at the very least, right? Well, those were different times. Girls like us were more cautious back then, and for good reason. I tell you what. I'm getting too tired to talk anymore today, but if you want to hear the juicy stuff, come back for another interview the same time next week. And bring a bottle of tequila.

INTERVIEW TWO

My stuffy young doctor would shit a brick if he knew you'd brought me a bottle of tequila. The poor boy tries to keep me in line, making me walk a mile a day and eat this high fiber cereal that keeps me in the bathroom half the morning. He does let me have a glass of red wine in the evenings because it's good for my heart, but somehow I don't think Cuervo Gold would make it onto his list of heart-healthy choices. What he doesn't know won't hurt him, though, and if it hurts me, who cares? I never claimed I wanted to live forever.

I have to say you mix a mean margarita, girl. And I figure a margarita's got to be healthier than straight tequila at my age. It's less of a shock to the system. Plus, it's high in vitamin C.

Well, I see you with that expectant look on your face. I guess I'd better start talking, shouldn't I?

The next evening I spent with Connie was in her trailer,

which she had made homier than mine with pillows and candles and colorful throws. This time with the tequila there were tortilla chips with guacamole and some oranges she'd filched from the trees that grew behind the movie ranch, then sliced and sugared.

"So, Jaycee," she said—and I remember she was wearing a loose-fitting white peasant blouse that kept falling down to bare her golden shoulders—"you told me the other night that Billy What's-His-Name was the last boyfriend you ever had. Is that really true?"

"Yep," I said, dragging a chip through the guacamole. "I mean, I've been out on dates and everything, but I've never had what you'd call a steady boyfriend. I guess I just haven't met the right fella yet."

Connie poured a shot, knocked it back, then poured me one. "Maybe the right person for you isn't a fella."

I downed the shot and looked at her, confused. "What do you mean?"

She put her hand on mine. At the time I attributed the tingling sensation to the tequila. "Surely," she said, "you've read about women like Gertrude Stein and Alice B. Toklas?"

"Who?" I said. Except for Zane Grey novels, I wasn't much of a reader at the time. Connie would end up educating me in more ways than one.

She sighed. "All right, let me try it this way. Juan's and my marriage ended because of another woman. I was the one with the other woman, not Juan."

I started to remember a name I'd been called by some boys once because I knew how to rope and ride. "You mean you're a . . ."

"The word for it isn't important. What's important is . . ." She looked down at my hand, which was still beneath hers. "You remember the other day when we shot that ridiculous scene and Charlie couldn't tell me why I wanted you to sing a song with me?"

"Yes." I looked down at her hand on mine. Her nails were short but painted a shiny red. A silver ring encircled her pinkie.

"Well, since Charlie wouldn't give me any answers, I decided the reason I wanted you to sing with me was that I had fallen in love with you the second I saw you. And I wanted to sing with you, to dance with you, to make you want me, too." She laughed. "And I think part of the reason I got so upset when we were shooting that scene is that I suddenly realized that I wasn't acting. I knew that my silly cantina singer's feelings for your silly cowgirl were really my feelings for you."

By this time I had taken my hand away. "But . . . but you hadn't even talked to me before then except to say thank you for a cup of coffee."

"Sometimes you don't even have to talk. You can just look at a person and know. That's why they call it love at first sight, not love at first sound."

I stared down at my lap, not sure what to say, trying to sort out my feelings. Confused. Scared. Interested. I felt Connie's finger on my chin, tilting my face upward so I could look at her. Her eyes were hooded and dreamy with desire.

"Jaycee, I'm going to kiss you now. Is that all right?"

"All right," I whispered, though I was so afraid my belly was doing backflips.

The first time I rode a horse I was scared to get on something so big and fast and wild. I remember standing beside it, looking up at it, and thinking, there's no way. But once I swung my leg over and got both feet in the stirrups and felt the big animal move underneath me, I thought, yes, I can do this. It's the most natural thing in the world. And that's also how I felt when Connie kissed me.

I think she would have pulled away and made our first kiss a polite peck if I hadn't kissed her back so forcefully, with feelings I didn't even know I had gushing forth like a Texas oil well.

Soon we were standing, our arms wrapped tight around each other, our lips still pressed together. I reached up and pulled the pins from Connie's hair and felt it, soft and heavy, tumble into my hand. And at that moment, I knew why it was I'd never been "wild with boys," as my daddy always said. It was because boys weren't who I wanted to be wild with.

When we had to break our kiss to breathe, Connie gasped, "I want to keep going, don't you?"

"Yes," I said. Even though I wasn't sure exactly what we'd be doing if we did "keep going," I knew I was all for it.

Connie took my hand and led me the three steps to her narrow cot. "I want you to know," she said, resting her hand on my cheek, "if you were in my home, things would be different. I would have cooked you my special pozole and played you my favorite songs, and now I would be laying you down on my big, soft bed which would be strewn with rose petals for your arrival."

"That's beautiful," I said, with a catch in my voice. "But I don't have to have all those other things. You're enough."

She kissed me hard then and pushed me back on the cot. It squeaked so much we both had to laugh. When we had arranged ourselves on the cot so that neither of us was in danger of falling off, Connie said, "You've never been with a woman like this, have you?"

"I've never been with anybody like this," I said. Up until then, I was a stranger to all physical affection beyond chaste goodnight kisses.

"Well," Connie whispered into my neck, "then I'll have to be your lover and your teacher. Tell me, Jaycee, have you ever really looked at another woman's body?"

"No." I'd never even really looked at my own body, but I didn't tell this to Connie.

"Here, look at me." Connie pulled off her blouse and her skirt and was naked before me. Her breasts were full, her hips were rounded, her skin was tawny. I looked at the dark triangle between her legs, then looked away, shy. "You're beautiful," I said.

"So are you," she said. "Undress for me."

I didn't get my clothes off nearly as quickly as Connie. I was so nervous my fingers fumbled with the buttons. Also, unlike Connie, I did wear a full set of underwear, which made getting naked more time-consuming.

When all my clothes were on the floor instead of on my body, Connie looked me up and down and smiled. "Perfect," she said.

"Oh, I wouldn't say that." Next to Connie's golden curves, my figure seemed small, pale, uninteresting.

"Shh," Connie said, pressing a finger over my lips. "You're perfect." She kissed me and pushed me back on the bed, her hands and then her mouth exploring my neck, my shoulders, my breasts. Under her touch, I felt perfect.

When her mouth moved lower and she gently pushed my legs apart, I got shy again. "I feel funny . . . with you looking at me there."

"But there's nothing I'd rather look at . . . nothing I'd rather kiss."

It's no secret that when riding a horse, women sometimes feel flickers of pleasure from the motion of the animal and the pressure of the saddle. I had felt these flickers before and had taken them as hints about what people's most secret pleasures must be like. But compared to the feelings from Connie's mouth, the sensations of the saddle were next to nothing. The strokes of her tongue were soft and slow at first, then faster and more insistent, until I was bucking like a bull at the rodeo, and Connie had to clamp her hand over my mouth so nobody would hear my cries through the trailer's tin-can walls.

"Now," she purred, spooning up against me, "I'll give you a few minutes to rest. And then I'll teach you what I like."

Connie was an excellent teacher.

• • •

I'm not going to be nosy enough to ask you how many lovers you've had, but I'm going to guess that you'd need at least two hands to count them all. Am I right? I thought so. That's how it is with most people. You get in a new relationship, and it's great, but then, just like fresh fruit you buy at the grocery store, after a while it loses its sweetness and starts to stink. So you throw it out and go shopping again. That's how it was with Connie before she met me—she'd stay with one girl for a while, then get restless and move on to the next. But it wasn't like that with her and me. With me, she stayed. She was my first and only lover. Not many people are lucky enough to get it right the first time, but I was.

So things started to get a lot more interesting on the set of "The Crusty Snail." Connie and I spent every minute we could together. We ate together, took long walks together, and while we didn't actually sleep together because we feared one of us would be seen leaving the other's trailer in the morning, we paid frequent visits to each other's cots.

One day when Connie was doing a scene with Buck, I ran into Eli on my way to the break area. "Does my favorite villain have time for a cup of coffee?" I asked.

Eli draped his arm around me companionably. "With you, always. I wish it could be beer instead, but I've got another scene to shoot."

"Me, too."

Once we were settled with our cups, Eli said, "I'm sorry you've not been seeing much of me in the evenings. This new"—he looked around to make sure we were alone—"friendship of mine is proving to be rather intense. But I certainly don't mean to leave you lonely."

I looked down at my coffee for a minute. "Well, I miss you, but I've not exactly been lonely. I'm . . . I'm kind of seeing somebody."

Eli raised his dark eyebrows in surprise. "Really? Someone working on this picture?"

"Mm-hm."

"Well, I must say I'm dying of curiosity, but I'm not one to pry."

"Come here, and I'll whisper it in your ear."

As soon as I whispered her name, he yelled, "No!"

I laughed. "Yes."

He looked around again. We were still alone. "But what about Billy?" he said.

I laughed even harder. "Well, to be honest with you, Eli, that relationship was over a long time ago."

"Really?" He leaned across the table. Clearly I had his full attention. "When did you break up?"

"When I was fourteen and a half years old."

Now it was Eli's turn to laugh, which he did, long and loud. "So you're telling me Billy was just a beard?"

Once Eli had explained what a beard was, I said yes.

"Well, you're certainly full of surprises, aren't you? But as I recall, your initial feelings for Connie were the complete opposite of your present ones. But they do say love and hate are two sides of the same coin." He reached across the table and touched my hand. "Am I correct, Jaycee, that you've never played in this particular . . . uh . . . ballpark before now?"

"That's right. But it's the only park I can imagine wanting to play in."

Eli giggled and clapped his hands like a delighted little kid. "Well, I've always adored you, my dear, but I adore you even more now that I know you're one of our own." He knitted his brow, the sunshine fading from his expression. "You do know, of course, that for people like us, discretion is absolutely key?"

"Yes, of course."

"I'm sure Connie knows, too, being older and more experienced than you. But honestly, when I think about how many friends of mine in the business have never worked again just because they got a little careless once . . ." Footsteps were approaching, and Eli made his voice loud and jokey. "So then I said, 'Not in my hat, you don't!'" He laughed uproariously, and so did I.

"Look at these two good-for-nothings," a baritone voice said. "Drinking coffee and cutting up on studio time." It was Dick Babcock, the producer, whose name was an endless source of puns for Eli when he'd had a few drinks. Mr. Babcock always lurked around during the second half of shooting to make sure we were on schedule and not over budget. He was a puffy, gray-haired, bespectacled penny pincher . . . a banker type which, I suppose, is what producers are.

"Hello, Mr. Babcock," I said.

"Hi, Dick," Eli said in a way that made me have to look away to keep from giggling.

"Well, I tell you, I would've expected this sort of indolent behavior from Eli here," Mr. Babcock said, "but from you, Jaycee, I'm surprised." This was Mr. Babcock's usual form of conversation with actors—a kind of just-kidding-but-not-really banter that reminded them they'd better be doing their jobs.

"What can I say, Mr. Babcock? Eli's a bad influence on me."

"Now that," Mr. Babcock said, chuckling, "doesn't surprise me at all. Seriously, though, kids, Charlie says you're doing a terrific job. Right on schedule. Keep it up, eh?"

"Yes, sir," Eli and I both said, as though we were suddenly in the army instead of on a movie set.

"Listen," Eli whispered once Babcock was out of earshot, "on Sunday since we're not shooting, my friend and I are going to a party . . . a poolside brunch for like-minded individuals, if you catch my meaning. If I can convince my discreet-to-the-point-of-paranoia paramour that you and Connie are capable of keeping your mouths shut, would you like to join us?"

I felt like I'd just been invited to join some fabulous secret society, and, in a way, I had. "Well, I can't speak for Connie, but I'd love to."

• • •

Connie and I found out Sunday morning that Eli's secretive lover was Marco, the Italian cameraman. I never would've guessed it. Marco never seemed to pay any special attention to Eli or talk to him differently than he talked to any of the other actors. Marco was quite a catch, really. He was probably in his early thirties, with a small but muscular frame; dark, wavy, hair; and sooty-lashed liquid brown eyes. I wasn't much in the habit of noticing fellow's looks, but even I had noticed that Marco was handsome.

It was a two-hour drive to the party, but the time zipped by. Eli drove and Marco sat beside him, his hand on Eli's knee. Connie and I had the whole backseat to ourselves for cuddling and hand-holding. We talked about all kinds of silly stuff— Connie taught us dirty words in Spanish, and Marco taught us dirty words in Italian. Then Eli led us in singing songs from the big Broadway shows of the past several years. At first Marco protested that he couldn't sing at all and that he'd just listen to Eli and Connie and me. But finally, after Eli kept egging him on, Marco joined in, too, in a pleasant tenor.

When we finally pulled up to the imposing stone gate in front of the house where the party was to be held, I let fly with a bunch of the foreign cuss words I'd just learned. Even though the view of the mansion was partially blocked by the gate, I could see it was huge. And pink—the color of the frosting on a little girl's birthday cake.

A handsome young man in a blue uniform stepped out of the gatehouse and said, "Nice to see you again, Mr. Bainbridge."

"And it's always nice to see you, Christopher," Eli said. "I hope you'll be joining us at the pool later."

Christopher showed off a perfect-teethed smile and swung the gate open. Marco playfully pinched Eli's arm and said, "Flirt."

A huge stone fountain bubbled and flowed in front of the mansion. "That," Marco said, "wouldn't look out of place in Rome."

When the car got closer to the fountain, we saw that some of its streams of water were coming from the private parts of muscular male statues. "I don't guess I mind statues of boys peeing in the fountain," Connie said, "as long as the real boys here don't pee in the pool."

"I wouldn't worry," Eli said, laughing as he parked the car. "The boys here are a fastidious bunch."

Around the back of the mansion, the sparkling oblong pool was surrounded by older men and filled with young ones. The older gentlemen were dressed in summer suits with ascots and boutonnieres; the young men in the water were barely dressed at all. A tuxedoed waiter came by with a tray of champagne. Eli, Marco, Connie and I each took a glass. "Come over here, girls," Eli said. "I want to introduce you to the founder of the feast." Eli led us to a lounge chair where a willowy middle-aged man in a white double-breasted suit sat. He had the kind of pencil-thin mustache that looked hard to maintain and was smoking a cigarette in a long, gold cigarette holder.

"Todd Carstairs," Eli said, "meet my lovely co-stars Jaycee Harper and Consuelo Flores."

"I really enjoyed that Civil War picture you directed a few years back," Connie said.

"Ah, yes." Todd rolled his eyes. "I nearly tore what little hair I have out over that one. I don't know what was most maddening, the battle scenes, the horses or the leading lady." He looked at a point over our shoulders, his eyes lighting up. "Speaking of leading ladies, it looks like you two won't be the only girls at this party after all. Look who's here!"

Living in Hollywood back then and working in movies—even if they were just B movies—it wasn't unusual to see big movie stars. It was always fun to see them and find out if they were shorter or taller or prettier or homelier than they looked onscreen, but I didn't tend to get starstruck. Not until the moment I turned my head and saw Todd Carstairs' other two female party guests.

Minerva Millbank was more of a star of the stage than the screen, but I knew her by her reputation, which was colorful to say the least. A hard-drinking Southern belle, Minerva was always showing up in the pages of one magazine or another for saying or doing something outrageous. And now here she was, with her big blue eyes, cupid's bow mouth, and lion's mane of hair, looking even prettier than she did in pictures.

But it was the woman on Minerva's arm that made my mouth hang open. How many times had I sat in a movie theater hypnotized by the way the light and shadow played on her glorious cheekbones? How many times had my arms broken out in goosebumps at the sound of her husky, German-accented voice? And when she sang, especially that number where she wore the tuxedo . . . I realized I was staring at her like an idiot, and when I looked over at my beautiful Connie, I saw that she was staring, too.

" . . . Minerva Millbank and Ilsa Wulf," Todd was saying. Apparently he had been introducing us.

Ilsa's cheekbones were as stunning in real life as they were on the screen. Her cheeks, her hair, the hollow of her throat, and her collarbones, which showed thanks to her half-unbuttoned men's white shirt, seemed to have been dusted in golden glitter the way they shone in the sun.

"I'm sorry we're late, Toddie," Minerva drawled. "Ilsa and I lost track of time on accounta bein' . . . busy." She then lifted her skirt, revealing a patch of blond hair dusted in the same gold glitter that covered Ilsa's face.

Todd hooted with laughter. "Minerva, you've shown your pussy to more pansies than any other starlet in Hollywood!"

"I don't know what to do vith her," Ilsa said, a sly smile on her lips. "She's a vewy bad girl. Maybe I should shpank her."

"There are men who'd pay thousands of dollars to watch that," Eli said. "Unfortunately, none of them are at this party."

It was a magical afternoon. Sunshine and champagne and the laughter of the like-minded. The only time the laughter faded was when Connie and I were standing by the pool with Ilsa and Minerva. Todd raised his champagne glass and yelled, "A toast to those frequent party guests who are no longer with us. Rudy Banner, John Carlisle and Paula Hart . . . wherever you are, I hope there's champagne!"

We raised our glasses. I had heard of Rudy Banner and John Carlisle and had seen a picture a few years before where Paula Hart played a leggy bad girl who ruined some poor sap's life, but I hadn't seen her in anything since then. I half-whispered, "Are they dead?"

"They're dead to Hollywood," Connie said, and I heard her sadness.

"They were indiscreet," Ilsa said. "God knows what they're doing now, but they're not making movies."

"Probably waitin' tables or turnin' tricks," Minerva said.

"That's not funny," Ilsa said. Her voice was cold, hard steel.

"Oh, I'm sorry, dahlin', that was in poor taste, wasn't it?" Minerva said, squeezing Ilsa's hand. "I forgot for a minute that you knew Paula Hart."

"I knew her, too," Connie said.

The word *knew* carried all kinds of meaning the way Connie said it, and I fought back my jealousy. Whatever Paula Hart was doing now, she probably was miserable doing it. It would've been small and mean of me to think bad thoughts of her because she once *knew* Connie.

"Oh, this is getting downright depressing," Minerva said. "Somebody needs to do something outrageous and liven things up." She drained her champagne glass, then turned a series of cartwheels all the way down the length of the poolside. She still wasn't wearing any panties.

Later, as Connie and I lounged on a towel, sharing a plate of fresh berries and drinking our umpteenth glass of champagne, Ilsa appeared on the high diving board. She was wearing nothing but a snug pair of men's swim trunks. Her breasts were high, her belly taut, her shoulders broad and muscular.

"Magnificent," I breathed. I couldn't help myself.

"You want her, don't you?" Connie said. She didn't sound hurt exactly, just matter-of-fact.

"No," I said. "I love to look at her, but it's like looking at a great piece of art or something. I want to look but not touch." I reached for her hand. "You, I want to touch."

Connie smiled, lifted my hand, and kissed it. "I'll tell you a secret," she whispered. "When I went in the house to go to the bathroom a while ago, Ilsa grabbed my hand and pulled me into a bedroom. She tried to kiss me."

I watched as Ilsa executed a perfect swan dive. My heart dove, too. I knew I could never compete with someone so perfect.

"What did you do?" I asked, although I didn't think I probably wanted to know.

"I gently pushed her away and told her I was flattered, but no thanks. I told her you were my girl."

That's one of those precious moments in my life when I have felt perfect happiness. The sound of laughter, the sparkling blue water, the popping champagne bubbles on my tongue, the fat red strawberries on my plate—the pleasure around me was a reflection of the pleasure inside me because Consuelo Flores could have had the star who had been voted the world's most beautiful woman, but instead she chose me.

What happened later that evening wasn't as spooky as it first seemed. "No," Connie told me later, "it wasn't that somebody speaking Paula Hart's name at the party summoned her. Paula comes to see me every couple of months or so . . . when she's making her rounds of friends who are still willing to help her. I'd just never talked to you about her because I don't like to dwell on sad stories, you know?"

Later, those words would comfort me. At the time it happened, though, Paula seemed like a visitor from the grave.

Connie and I were in her trailer on her cot, lying with our arms and legs wrapped around each other, kissing, caressing, taking our time on the road to lovemaking and enjoying the scenery. As soon as we heard the knock on the door, we were off the cot and yanking our clothes into place. I sat down at the little card table and set a teacup in front of me. It was an empty teacup, but still, sitting at the table with a teacup looked a hell of a lot more respectable than lying on the cot with my skirt hiked up around my waist.

Connie flipped her hair away from her face and opened the door. From where I was sitting I couldn't see who she was talking to when she said, "Oh . . . it's you."

"What's left of me," a smoky female voice answered.

Our visitor was tall and leggy, wearing a black dress, a black and red headscarf, and dark sunglasses despite the late hour. When she took off the glasses and shook her long, white-blond hair free of the scarf, I recognized her immediately as the girl with the great gams who'd made a fool of the gumshoe in that picture I couldn't remember the name of. I remembered her name, though. I'd heard it spoken that very afternoon.

"Paula, this is my friend Jaycee," Connie said.

Paula smiled, but the smile showed neither humor nor kindness. "I bet you two are *real* good friends," she said. "Oh, and look! You were having a little tea party." She picked up my cup. "But it was one of those little-girl tea parties, wasn't it? The kind where everything's *pretend*." She turned the empty cup upside down. "But that's perfect for this business, huh? It's all about pretending. I always loved to pretend onscreen. It was the pretending offscreen I was no good at." She sat down on the cot, slipped out of her pumps, and folded her legs underneath her. "Say, Connie, you got anything stronger than pretend tea around here?"

"Tequila," Connie said, "though you don't care much for the taste of it, if I remember correctly."

"You remember correctly, but let's just say my present circumstances make me a lot less picky than I used to be." She held out the teacup. "Fill 'er up."

Connie poured Paula's drink, then got out glasses for herself and for me. Maybe she didn't want Paula to drink alone, but I don't think it would've mattered much to Paula one way or another. She drained the teacup as if it had been full of tea.

"So, Connie," Paula said, "I guess if this girl's in your room at eleven o'clock at night, it must be safe to talk in front of her."

"Jaycee's okay," Connie said, then gave me a little smile. "She's better than okay."

Paula rolled her eyes. "Fools . . . fools in love, the both of you. But at least you know how to be discreet, Connie, unlike some people." She lit a cigarette. When she puffed on it, her cheekbones looked as sharp as blades. She was still beautiful, but she was much, much too thin.

"Yeah, unlike some people you left me for," Connie said. Her tone was joking, but it left a bitter aftertaste.

"Believe me, I regret it every day," Paula said.

Connie smiled. "Because you miss me or because you got caught?"

Paula reached for the tequila bottle. "Both."

"Very diplomatic," Connie said, "which you'd better be, if you're going to keep drinking my tequila."

I just sat there, nervous, wondering if I should excuse myself since whatever was between them was obviously none of my business. But I felt glued to the chair.

"You," Paula said, pointing at me, "you probably think I'm

some kind of a monster, interrupting your tea party and staggering in here spitting bile. But I've not always been like this. I used to be a sweet girl, didn't I, Connie?"

"Yes," Connie said.

"But you can't stay sweet when you've got no choices." Paula gulped down some tequila. "Now, for instance, that rag *The Tinseltown Tattler* has some letters I wrote to a certain someone. She's twisted it around, see, to look like I had a crush on her, and she rejected me. But those hacks at the *Tattler* say they'll print the letters unless I give them five hundred dollars."

I couldn't stay quiet anymore. "But that's . . . that's illegal!"

"That's right, Shirley Temple," Paula said, "and so is what you and Connie were probably doing when I knocked on the door."

I wished I could argue with her, but I knew she was right.

"That's what I mean by no choices," she said. "I don't have the five hundred bucks, and I'm not gonna ask you for it, Connie, because you've already been too good to me as it is."

"So what are you gonna do?" Connie asked.

Paula knocked back the rest of her tequila. "Well, here's what I'm thinking. I'll go back East . . . not to Jersey 'cause I don't want my folks to have to live with the shame of having me there. Maybe Pittsburgh. There's lots of factory jobs for women with the war on." She ran her index fingers under her eyes. "I figure I'll cut my hair, dye it brown. Maybe nobody will recognize me."

"Oh, honey," Connie said. She sat down on the cot and draped her arm around Paula.

I wasn't jealous. I felt too sad for Paula to be jealous.

"Of course," Paula said, not even trying to hide her tears, "the kicker is that I don't have the money to get to Pittsburgh either."

"Now that," Connie said, "I can help you with."

I didn't look at the check Connie wrote, and I never asked her how much it was for. What I did do was get out my own checkbook and write out a check for a hundred dollars.

Paula hugged Connie, then hugged me, too. "Thanks, kid," she said. "You didn't have to do that. You don't even know me."

"I know we've got to take care of each other when nobody else will," I said.

That was the last we saw of Paula Hart. You've probably got a whole chapter about her in your book, about how she ended up driving her car into a tree, how nobody was ever sure if it was an accident or suicide. I think even on the night we wrote her the checks, Connie and I both knew we were throwing money at a problem that couldn't be fixed. Can you imagine having been a rich, glamorous Hollywood starlet and then trying to start over as an unknown Pittsburgh factory worker?

Once Paula had left with the checks, I put my arms around Connie. "That was hard, huh?" I said.

Her eyes were wet. "It is hard to see somebody's life ruined like that, especially when it's somebody you . . . you . . ."

"Loved?" I said. If she had loved Paula, I wanted her to be able to say it to me. I didn't care if she'd loved Paula once, as long as she loved me now.

"No, cared about," Connie said. "I cared about Paula. I love you."

That night, we held each other for a long time.

INTERVIEW THREE

Over the years, we came to call it the night that changed everything. But at the time, I was just hoping for a regular romantic evening. We were getting close to the end of the shoot, and I had invited Connie on a picnic with me at the campsite where we'd first gotten to know each other. She sat with me by the campfire, the light from the flames dancing across her beautiful face.

"So," I said, reaching into a paper grocery bag, "we're gonna have an all-American weenie roast."

"Aren't hot dogs originally from Germany?" Connie said. "Frankfurters, right?"

I laughed. "That's why we're supposed to be calling them liberty sausages nowadays. Just like dachshunds are liberty hounds and sauerkraut is liberty cabbage."

"Does that mean Ilsa Wulf is a liberty lesbian?" Connie said, laughing.

"Well, as much work as she's done selling war bonds, that's a good name for her."

Connie tilted the bag so she could peek in it. "No tequila in there, huh?"

"No, but I do have cold beer. And marshmallows for dessert."

We drank our beers and roasted our hot dogs and then our marshmallows and talked about how glad we were shooting was almost over and about the restaurants where we'd go soon for romantic dinners and about this place Connie knew where women could dance together.

After our beer and charred dinner, we doused the campfire and ended up, as I'd hoped we would, cuddled up in the sleeping bag I'd brought. It was a sleeping bag for one, so the quarters were deliciously close. We were pressed breast to breast, hip to hip, thigh to thigh. Our clothes were on, but Connie slipped one hand underneath my blouse to stroke my breasts, then another up my skirt to stroke my thighs. I know Connie only had two hands, but sometimes it felt like she had a dozen the way she moved all over me, finding all my sensitive spots. She slid her hand into my underpants and then slid her fingers into me, rocking me back and forth, back and forth, soft and steady at first, then faster, harder. I dug my fingernails into her back and came with my eyes wide open, howling at the moon.

Connie leaned into me. I wrapped my arms tight around her and floated for I don't know how long on the blissful edge of sleep.

But then a heavy weight fell on our sleeping bag.

At first I was afraid it was a coyote, but then I heard a gruff male voice bark, "Goddamn it!"

When I saw who it was, I wished it had been a coyote.

Dick Babcock must have been out for an evening stroll. And then he'd tripped over our sleeping bag in the dark.

Our clothes were on, but they were mussed, and so was our

hair and makeup. And seeing two adults in the same sleeping bag, unless they're huddling together for warmth in sub-zero temperatures, you don't have to be Einstein to figure out what they're doing.

"Never in my life have I seen such an abomination!" Mr. Babcock railed as he stood and dusted off his suit. "I've heard of such perversions, of course, but to literally trip over them on the set of my own picture! We're making family entertainment here, for God's sake. How can Republic Pictures stand for wholesome American family entertainment with perverts like you polluting our very name?" He took off his glasses and rubbed the bridge of his nose. "Charlie and I will be seeing both of you in my office tomorrow morning at eight o'clock." He turned his back on us and walked toward the set.

"Well," Connie sighed, "that's that."

I slithered out of the sleeping bag. My whole body felt heavy and achy, like I had the flu. "I'm sorry," I said, my eyes filling with tears. "I shouldn't have asked you to come out here. I shouldn't have . . ."

"Don't be silly," Connie said, standing up and walking toward the fire. "We've been out here before and nobody's ever bothered us. There was no reason to think someone would find us this time." She let out a joyless little laugh, the kind of nervous laughter that comes out when you know the worst has happened and nothing can be done about it. "I knew my career was on the way out, of course. I just didn't know it would be over so suddenly. And you . . ." She shook her head. "Your career has ended before it even really began."

The mostly dead campfire was still sending off a few sparks, and Connie tossed some dirt to extinguish it. She looked like a mourner throwing handfuls of dirt onto a coffin in a grave.

Looking back on it, Connie and I probably should have spent that night together. We didn't have anything else to lose, and that way we at least could have comforted each other. But the fear of someone else discovering us drove us back to our own separate trailers to spend a lonely night dreading the morning meeting with Dick Babcock and Charlie Wooley. I didn't even lie down on my cot that night. Sleep was impossible.

Dick used a back room in the saloon building as a makeshift office when he was on the set, and so to get to my dreaded meeting, I had to swing the saloon doors open and walk in the same way I'd done in that first scene I'd shot with Connie. Of course, in that scene I had been pretending to be terrified. This time, I wasn't pretending.

Connie was already in the office when I got there, sitting stiffly in a chair in front of Dick Babcock's desk, wearing a conservative blouse and skirt, her hair in a knot at the nape of her neck. I had seen Connie in her cantina singer costume, in jeans with her hair down, and in nothing at all. But it was unnerving to see her in such ordinary clothing. Somehow she seemed more in costume that way than she did in the get-up she wore for the picture.

"Close the door behind you, Jaycee, and sit down," Charlie said.

I did as I was told.

Charlie was chewing on a cigar, probably out of nervousness. "Well," he said, "there's no need to beat around the bush, is there? Dick told me about the little scene he stumbled on last night, and he and I are both in agreement that we can't have these kinds of . . . activities on the set of a Republic picture. As Dick says, we're a wholesome family studio producing wholesome family entertainment, and as such we have to hold our performers to a certain standard." He took the gnawed, wet cigar out of his mouth and gestured toward Dick with it. "Now, Dick and I were up almost all night discussing how to handle this problem, and we finally came to an agreement. Dick, do you want to talk about it?" He returned his cigar to his mouth, looking relieved to give Dick the floor.

Dick stood and walked to the front of his desk, only a few inches away from Connie and me. "Miss Flores," he said, as though her name was somehow distasteful, "you came to Republic on a trial basis to make this one picture with the possibility of signing a contract for more pictures with us."

"Yes, sir," Connie said. She was looking down at her lap, but somehow I knew she was seeing Paula Hart's tired, thin face.

"Well," Dick said, crossing his arms in front of him, "I think we can safely say that your trial period is over and that you were found morally unfit to continue with us as a contract player. How many more scenes does she have to shoot for this picture, Charlie?"

"Two. One we're shooting today. The other, we're shooting tomorrow."

"All right, then, Miss Flores." Dick returned to his spot behind his desk. "You may stay on the set long enough to complete your work on the picture. After your last scene tomorrow, however, you will be required to leave the set permanently. You will be paid for the work you've done, but you are permanently barred from working for Republic pictures again."

"Yes, sir," Connie said again. Part of me wanted to hear her argue with him—or to see her spit in his face. But her body language said she knew the battle was already lost.

"You may go, Miss Flores," Dick said, looking down at some papers on his desk.

Connie stood. She caught my eye for a second. I could tell she didn't want to leave me alone with these men, but really, what choice did she have? She had been stripped of her choices.

As soon as Connie left, Dick closed the door behind her and locked it. "You've had a long and lucrative career with Republic, Jaycee," Dick said. "Charlie and I had a long talk about you last night . . . and about what you've meant to this company."

"We did," Charlie said, around his spitty cigar. "And Jaycee, honey, the more we talked about it, the more obvious it became that you're the victim here. I mean, here you are on your own, with your boyfriend off fighting in the war—you're lonely. You're worried. You're scared."

"Yes," Dick said. "And there's a certain kind of person—a certain kind of woman—who might try to take advantage of your weakened state."

"Connie didn't take advantage of me," I said.

"Well, you say that now," Charlie said, "but I think you'll see things differently once you've had a chance to think more clearly. Listen, Jaycee, we're giving you something we didn't give to Consuelo: a choice."

"That's right," Dick said, trying for a smile. "Because you mean so much to us here at Republic, we're willing to forget about this debacle with Miss Flores—not a word will ever be said about it—if you're willing to agree to a few conditions that are advantageous both to you and to Republic studios."

"What kind of conditions?" I felt like I'd just been thrown from a horse—hurt and disoriented and not sure how much damage had been done.

"Well, there have been some rumors," Charlie said, "that you're not happy making our Westerns anymore . . . that when your contract's up at the end of the year, you might not sign another one." He shook his head and chuckled. "Now myself, I never understand it when you actors get on your high horses about wanting to grow and stretch and be *artists*." He punctuated the word "artists" with finger quotes. "Movies aren't about art; they're about making people happy—people who work hard and make sacrifices for this country. We know how to give these people what they want. Working at Republic, you've got a full belly and a steady paycheck, and you make millions of people happy. What could be better?"

It was a passionate speech, but I was damned if I knew what it had to do with Dick tripping over Connie and me in our sleeping bag the night before. "Sir, I'm not sure I understand . . ."

"Well, let me explain it to you in a way you will understand, Jaycee," Dick said. "I'm the producer. I'll give you the bottom line. We're willing to forget this whole mess with Miss Flores ever happened if at the end of this year when your current contract expires, you'll sign a new contract with Republic for five more years of being Buck Bronco's—and America's—sweetheart."

"Five more years?" If I signed a five-year contract, I would be thirty by the time I was free. Thirty was young in the real world, but not so young in Hollywood, where age is counted more like in dog years than in human years. A thirty-year-old actress trying to get a start in A pictures would be stampeded by eager nineteen-year-olds.

"Five more years," Dick said.

"And if I choose not to sign the contract?"

Dick looked over at Charlie, who looked back at him. "Well, you know what a gossipy town Hollywood is," Dick said. "People talk. Rumors get started. Careers get ruined every day just because of gossip."

Sometimes when you get thrown from a horse, the wind gets knocked out of you, and no matter how hard you try, you can't catch your breath. This is exactly how I felt in that small, locked office with Dick and Charlie. "I . . . I have to get some air," I said, gasping.

Dick moved to the door and unlocked it. "Well, you get some air, then, Jaycee. Get some air and do some thinking." He patted me on the shoulder as I staggered out the door. "I know you'll make the right decision."

I ran into Eli on my way back to my trailer. I was still gasping.

"What's the matter, cupcake? Are you ill?" Eli asked, his brow knitted in concern.

"Connie and I need to talk to you," I whispered. "And to Marco, too, if he's willing. And we need to talk away from the set if we can." Rationally, I knew it was probably safe to talk in one of our trailers, but I wasn't at my most rational at that moment. I felt like spies were everywhere.

"I'll pick you up at eight," Eli said.

That afternoon, I had to play a scene with Buck where I kissed him and said, "I'm the happiest girl in the world." Saying that line convincingly . . . well, let's just say it was one of the few times in a Republic picture when I felt like I was really acting.

Eli took us to a roadhouse about half an hour's drive away. The place was dark and seedy and crowded. Between the loud music and the loud drinkers, the four of us could sit at our table and talk freely to each other without anybody hearing us over the racket. Hell, we could've been talking about overthrowing the government, and nobody would've heard us.

We did take one necessary precaution since it was a straight place, though. Connie sat next to Marco, and I sat next to Eli, so we looked like two boy-girl couples. Over beers, Connie and I told everything, starting with the moment Dick fell over our sleeping bag.

"See?" Marco said. "This is why Eli and I won't so much as shake hands on the film set. That's why we're gone so many evenings. We go to this hotel several miles from the set that's run by a man who is . . . sympathetic to us."

"Well, you two are smarter than we were, I guess," Connie said.

"Oh, Marco's much smarter that way than I am," Eli said. "There've been times on the set when he's practically had to borrow a horsewhip from the prop department to keep me away from him." Eli and Marco shared a smile that, if any stranger had seen it, would've left little doubt that they were lovers.

"You know," Connie said, running a finger under her eyes. "Charlie and Dick were really doing me a favor by firing me from Republic. Otherwise, I could've gone on for years there, making terrible films, dragging my reputation through the mud, promoting stereotyped views of my people—all in a vain attempt to prove that my acting career wasn't over." A tear trickled down her cheek. "But I'm all right. I mean, this is not what I want, but I can accept that my career is over. What I couldn't accept, though, is for what you and I have to be over, Jaycee."

Under the table, I reached out and took her hand. "I don't want us to be over either." I wiped away a tear with my free hand. "I'm willing to work on a ranch shoveling cowshit, as long as I don't have to lose you."

"Oh, you kids," Eli said, his voice choked. "Now you're making me cry, too. I wish there was something I could do to make this easier."

"Well . . ." Marco said, looking at Eli. "We could let them in on our plan . . . invite them to join us, I mean."

Eli nudged me. "I told you he's smarter than I am." He looked across the table at Marco. "My God, we could, couldn't we?"

"Could what?" Connie said.

"At the end of the year, after Eli's contract with Republic is up," Marco said, "he's coming back to Italy with me."

"Really?" I asked Eli, and he smiled and nodded.

"You see, I worked in pictures in Italy for years," Marco said, "but when the political situation started getting ugly I knew I had to leave. I mean, I couldn't answer to my conscience if I was responsible for making propaganda pictures for Mussolini, and propaganda was the only available option to me. So I came to Hollywood, but I swore I'd go back. Now that things are changing there, I'm ready." His eyes shone with excitement. "And in film in Italy, anyone who has been in American film is automatically a star. Even if you've only done B-grade movies or Z-grade movies, it doesn't matter. All that matters is that you've worked in Hollywood. And girls"—he beamed at Connie and me— "these young new filmmakers in Italy are amazing. They're making films that reflect life—that say something about society, you know. And the roles for women are not like your Hollywood roles. You don't have to play either a good girl or a bad girl. There, you can play a real, complex person."

It sounded like paradise, but I couldn't believe it was a paradise where I'd be welcome. "But Marco," I said, "I can't speak Italian. And even if I could learn the language well enough to order meals in restaurants and find out where bathrooms are, I don't think I could *act* in a foreign language."

"Oh, that's what I said, too," Eli said. "But Marco told me that Italian pictures are dubbed. You do the acting, and the dialogue will be added in by Italian actors later."

I was starting to feel like even though I'd gotten knocked off my horse, I might be ready to get on again.

"What about couples like Jaycee and me and you and Eli in Italy?" Connie asked. "Is it any easier there?"

"There still must be discretion," Marco said, "but Italians are a physically affectionate people. Within reason, you can touch in public without drawing stares. There isn't that Pure—what is it you always call it, Eli?"

"Puritanical heritage," Eli said.

"Yes, there isn't the Puritanical heritage in Italy that there is in the United States," Marco said. "Also, unlike here, the public doesn't feel like it owns the movie stars' private lives."

I looked across the table at Connie and saw her smiling for the first time all day.

Well, you probably know the rest. Connie and I spent twenty years in Italy acting in the movies that film scholars call Italian neorealistic cinema. I got juicy supporting roles at a steady rate, while Connie became a bona fide star—a diva, as the Italians called her. Eli acted in Italy for a couple of years, but then drifted into directing, with Marco as his number one cameraman. If you're ever watching late-night TV and come across one of those swords-and-sandals movies with skimpily dressed, muscle-bound, badly dubbed actors, chances are Eli directed it. We all loved our work and loved each other and were happy.

But as you can see, since you're sitting in our house in West Hollywood—and yes, I still think of it as "our" house even though Connie's gone—we did end up moving back here. Our folks were getting older, and we didn't want to be so far away from them. The funny thing was, a few years after coming back to Hollywood, Connie and I landed supporting roles in a TV show called "Big Sky." It was a Western, and it ran for ten years.

This time, though, I played a widowed rancher, and I got to rope and ride and shoot with the best of them. Connie played the hotel owner whose wisdom and insight made all the other characters on the show come to her for advice. Gone were the days when I had to play the inept virginal sweetheart, and Connie had to play the spitfire with the heavy accent and heavier makeup. Gone, too, were the days when we lived in constant terror of being found out. At the end of each day, I went home with Connie, who was through playing the spitfire, but who was then and is forever my sweetheart.

ABOUT THE AUTHORS

BARBARA JOHNSON lives in a Maryland suburb with her partner of thirty-three years, Kathleen DeBold, and their four cats. She fell in love with the Arizona desert, despite scorpions in the bathtub and black widows on the porch, while living in Yuma Proving Ground and then Tombstone. These days, though, the closest to the West she gets is when she wears her white cowboy boots, fringed, of course.

KARIN KALLMAKER was never a fan of westerns, *Bonanza* or rodeos. When she was still a bitty baby femme, however, Barbara Stanwyck rode across the horizon in "The Big Valley." The commanding voice, the undaunted attitude, the leather, the riding crop—everything a girl could want in an icon. Karin's discovery that she was descended from Lady Godiva was a bonus. It may be a good thing she is deathly afraid of horses. Otherwise, there's no telling what she might be inspired to do.

Karin is the Goldie and Lammy Award–winning author of more than twenty romance and fantasy-science fiction novels. Short stories have appeared in anthologies from Alyson, Bold Strokes, Circlet and Haworth. Her writing career began with the venerable Naiad Press and continues with Bella Books. She and her partner are the mothers of two and live in the San Francisco Bay Area.

THERESE SZYMANSKI is an award-winning playwright. She's also been short-listed for a couple of Lammys, Goldies and a Spectrum, as well as having made the Publishing Triangle's list of Notable Lesbian Books with the first anthology she edited.

She's edited five anthologies for Bella After Dark (BAD), written seven books in the Lammy-finalist Brett Higgins Motor City Thrillers series, one book in her new Shawn Donnelly mystery series, and had a few dozen short works published in a wide variety of books from Naiad Press, Bella Books, Alyson Books, Bold Strokes Books, Haworth Press, Suspect Thoughts Press and a number of others.

Reese really isn't into westerns much at all, which is why she had so much spoofing fun with this one. She does, however, wear a mean hat, cool cowboy boots and some rather large belt buckles.

You can e-mail Reese at tsszymanski@worldnet.att.net.

JULIA WATTS isn't a cowgirl, but being from Kentucky, she does have a fondness for horses and whiskey. Her novels include *The Kind of Girl I Am*, *Women's Studies* and the Lambda Literary Award–winning *Finding H.F.*